PASSION D'AMOUR

PASSION D'AMOUR

Anne-Marie Villefranche

Carroll & Graf Publishers, Inc.
New York

Copyright © 1982 by Jane Purcell
All rights reserved

First Carroll & Graf edition September 1994

Carroll & Graf Publishers, Inc.
260 Fifth Avenue
New York, NY 10001

ISBN 0-7867-0171-4

Manufactured in the United States of America

PASSION D'AMOUR

PLAISIR D'AMOUR

BACKGROUND TO AN IMPROPER BOOK

The sexual escapades of close friends and relatives may seem an ususual theme for a young woman of good family and careful upbringing to write about. Some brief account is therefore due to the reader of these episodes.

They were written by Anne-Marie Villefranche, who was born in Paris in 1899, the fifth child and second daughter of well-to-do parents. After the conventional education for girls in the early years of this century, she was married by family arrangement at the age of eighteen to a young man five years her senior. He enjoyed the resounding name of Alexandre St. Amand Mont-Royal and at that time held the rank of captain in the French army. Not long after the wedding, and only a month or so before the Armistice which ended the Great War in 1918, he was killed in action. Anne-Marie was by then pregnant.

Mont-Royal left his widow well provided for, but she did not set up her own home after her son was born. For the next ten years she lived alternately with her parents in Paris and her late husband's parents at their estate near Châtillon-Cotigny. The world of her childhood had been swept away by the war and attitudes were changing fast in the 1920s. As an independent and attractive woman, Anne-Marie was equally welcome in town and country, not least for her natural gift for friendship.

She surprised and pleased her family in 1928 by announcing that she intended to marry again. Her choice had fallen on Richard Warwick, an Englishman attached to the British Embassy in Paris. After the marriage he resigned from the diplomatic service and never aspired to work again.

The Warwicks lived in England for about half of each year, in London for the season and at their country home in Berkshire at other times. Until 1939 and the outbreak of the Second World War they made long and frequent visits to France to stay with Anne-Marie's family in Paris and her

1

parents-in-law in the country. There were also long visits to several European capitals to stay with friends from Warwick's days in the diplomatic service. Anne-Marie had two more children, Natalie and Gervase. Natalie was my mother.

Anne-Marie died in 1980, two years after her husband. Among her many affectionate bequests to her family and friends there was for me a gold bracelet she had been given on her twelfth birthday, a sum of money and an old-fashioned cabin trunk, securely locked. Her solicitor handed me the key in an envelope on which my name was written in Grandmère's distinctive hand. Enclosed with the key there was a letter in which she wrote that as I alone of her English grandchildren could speak French correctly, it was to me that she bequeathed her 'little memoirs'.

A week or two elapsed before I had time to begin reading the bundles of papers contained in the trunk. Astonishment is too weak a word to describe the emotion I experienced. The ink had faded, the paper was brittle and yellowed, but the handwriting was unmistakable. Anne-Marie had set down in narrative form some of the more scandalous episodes in the lives of those close to her. From the form I judged that her account was based on what had been confided to her in strict secrecy and what she had been able to piece together from her knowledge of those concerned. Never before had I come across such open descriptions of relations between men and women – and this from the pen of my elegant Grandmère! What compounded my surprise was that I had met some of the people she wrote about during visits to Paris as a child. At some point I reached the conclusion that in deference to Anne-Marie I must attempt to translate at least some of these adventures of a by-gone age.

For all its felicities of expression the French language is slippery to take hold of. Often it lacks the hard-edged concepts of English. Even the best of translations can leave the English reader wondering how Proust or Gide or Colette achieved such a reputation in their own country. To understand that one must read them in their native language.

2

I have been compelled to take many liberties with Anne-Marie's words to make her tales acceptably idiomatic in English. My method has been to look for the nearest modern equivalent with the appropriate emotional content, bearing in mind the theme of these tales.

Since the 1920s Paris has changed greatly, especially in the last thirty years. Old landmarks have disappeared completely, streets have changed their names, districts have come up or gone down in the world. As the city has changed, so it is to be presumed that attitudes to sexuality have changed also, though of that I have no direct knowledge. Except as an occasional passing mention, Anne-Marie does not figure in her stories, but it is possible to deduce that her own stance was one of tolerance and amusement at the antics she describes. She has a sharp eye for the ridiculous, a truly Parisian characteristic.

There are no dates on Anne-Marie's papers, but the manner in which they were tied in bundles indicates proximity in time and, from evidence within them, it is possible to date them approximately. The small selection offered here is from the period from 1925 to 1928, the year of her second marriage, as nearly as I can be certain. The Villefranche family are given the name of Brissard and all the other names were changed by Anne-Marie. No one will be in any doubt as to why she did this after reading her 'little memoirs'.

Jane Purcell,

London 1982

3

JEANNE TAKES A LOVER

Christophe sat alone in the darkness of the Verney's drawing-room. Only a chink of light from the street-lamps of the avenue Kléber showed through the not quite fully drawn curtains. Midnight was past, the guests had gone and the household asleep, but she would come to him, he was sure of it.

Hours before at dinner she had been wearing a jade-green evening frock that descended only a little below her knees and was cut straight across the top to reveal the division of her breasts. Her slender bare arms were so inviting that Christophe had longed to lean towards her and kiss them from wrist to arm-pit. What a commotion that would have caused among the guests, not to mention her husband!

Guy Verney was a most boring man, Christophe thought. Rich of course, but self-opinionated and dull. He talked of little but business and politics and neither topic was of the least interest to Christophe. But Jeanne Verney – that was another matter entirely. She was nearly twenty years younger than her husband, charming, lively – altogether the most attractive woman Christophe had ever had the fortune to meet. The tiny gestures of her hands as she emphasised her words were as delicate as the fine skin of her half-displayed breasts.

The soup plates were hardly cleared away by a black-clad servant and fresh plates set, before Christophe's eager male part was alert and ready, utterly enslaved by Jeanne's presence. She read his emotion in his eyes as they conversed and, hidden by the table, her small hand fluttered for a moment in his lap and was withdrawn as she turned to speak to Christophe's mother.

The other guests at the table were of Jeanne's family, not of Verney's. There was Jeanne's mother, Madame Brissard, seated on Verney's right, a lady at once delicate and formidable. Jeanne's eldest brother Maurice was there with

4

his wife Marie-Thérèse, a woman of about Jeanne's age. And because Jeanne's father had not been able to attend, the numbers were completed by Jeanne's youngest brother Gerard, who had escorted his mother.

Five of the Brissard clan, Christophe thought when he was introduced before dinner, and only three of the Verneys – if indeed mother and I can even be reckoned as Verneys with so tenuous a connection. Why has our charming hostess arranged it so? During the course of the evening he reached the conclusion that the purpose was to exert silent pressure on Guy Verney to ensure that he conformed to the superior family expectations of the Brissards in his dealings with Christophe and his mother.

Marie-Thérèse, seated on the other side of Christophe from Jeanne, was a marvellously beautiful woman. She had dark and luminous eyes in a delicately pale face and wore bright red lip-rouge. Her frock was magnificent and was quite obviously from the hand of one of the master couturiers of Paris. It seemed so simple – a jet-black creation which left her arms bare and had a deep square-cut décolletage – yet the effect was stunning. The diamond choker around her long neck must surely have cost more money that Christophe could imagine earning in a lifetime. Yet nevertheless, he found her intense and sombre beauty less enticing than Jeanne's vivacity.

Gerard, across the table from Christophe, was at university and so of the same age as himself. Young as he was, he was an interesting conversationalist and he appeared to be completely aware of the nuances in the table talk which Christophe found impossible to interpret. Was he perhaps a little too aware, Christophe wondered, for at the instant that Jeanne's hand had touched his lap, Gerard's right eyelid moved briefly in something remarkably like a wink.

A little later, while Verney was discoursing on the criminal inadequacies of the government, the hand returned slyly to Christophe's lap. This time it stayed longer, nervous fingers tracing the outline of his upright flesh through the fabric of his trousers. The excitement of what was being done to him was so keen that he felt in a few more seconds he would

5

flood his underpants. For an instant he considered reaching down to restrain her caress but the sensation was too delicious. The very danger of discovery fired his imagination and his nerves as much as the secret stroking. If she made it happen – so be it! Verney would surely kick him out of the house but it would be well worth it.

Just in time, as if she had accurately gauged his emotional temperature, Jeanne took her hand away. Red of face, his mind reeling, Christophe emptied his glass of wine and fought to calm himself.

Yes, she would come to him that night, he was certain. Not to the room they had put him in, inconveniently adjacent to his insomniac mother's room. After dinner, when they were sipping black coffee and fine cognac in the drawing-room, Jeanne had conveyed her intention to him with a quick turn of her wrist and a look that explained more than words could. For a moment, as Verney pointed out to his guests the merits and value of a painting hanging on the wall, Jeanne's legs moved in a way that pulled her short skirt high enough to expose a green satin garter holding her rolled stockings just above the knee. Christophe was sitting beside her on a settee and was compelled to cross his legs to disguise his arousal as the frock slid decently back into place.

Here he was then, still in his formal evening clothes, stiff wing collar and bow tie, waiting for her in the dark and silent drawing-room. The door opened and closed so quietly that he might have thought that he had imagined it but for the rustle of loose clothes as she moved into the room.

'Over here,' he whispered, 'on the chaise-longue.'

In a moment she was seated beside him and in his arms. She kissed him again and again, strange little nibbling kisses, while his exploring hands opened her frilled négligé and encountered the exquisite warmth of her flesh through a thin shantung silk nightdress. He sighed in sheer joy as he cupped a soft breast in each hand.

'I can't stay,' she whispered, 'It's too dangerous.'

But for all her protestation her hand was in his lap, unbuttoning him. She found his staunch part and fondled it nervously.

6

'Is your husband fast asleep?' Christophe asked and her head nodded against his cheek, the perfume in her hair intoxicating him.

'He drinks so much,' she said, her fingers playing slowly now on his straining part. 'Oh, how enormous!'

Christophe reached down to slip his hand under the hem of her nightdress and stroke tenderly up her thighs until he touched the short and crinkly hair where they met. He opened soft lips with a finger-tip and heard her little gasp. Her juices were running and it was as if he had pushed a finger into a ripe apricot.

Naturally, Jeanne did not inform him that less than half an hour before there had been enacted on the marital bed the regular nightly scene in which she was a reluctant participant. No sooner was she between the sheets than her husband, whether drunk or sober, rolled her briskly on her back and hoisted her nightdress to her navel. With none of the preliminaries which lovers delight in, Verney climbed onto his wife and penetrated her with one fast lunge. He was finished at once, that being how he was by nature afflicted.

To Verney it was not an affliction, it was normal. That was how it had been for him since the first time he went with a woman at eighteen – one hard push and immediate results. For poor Verney the entire romantic comedy of love-making, from the overture to the final curtain never lasted more than seconds. Even so it satisfied his needs and he was still a regular performer in his middle forties. After the event he rolled off his wife with a contented sigh and fell asleep immediately.

At twenty-six and after six years of marriage to Verney and having borne two children, Jeanne regarded her husband as little more than an insensitive rapist.

'Take care that you don't get me too aroused,' she murmured to Christophe as his fingers teased lovingly within her secret place.

'But why not? You've got me so excited that I'm ready to go off like a squib.'

'So soon? I have only held you for a moment,' she said in

7

dismay, thinking of her husband's abbreviated performances.

'You have been arousing me for hours, even before the moment you touched me under the table. Each time you smiled at me, each time I looked at your face and arms and legs, I was impelled a little further along that marvellous path which leads to the ultimate pleasure. In truth, I have been making love to you in my mind for at least four hours. I am astonished by my own power of restraint. I cannot believe that I did not seize you in front of everyone and lay you down on your own settee and lay bare the beauties of your body.'

'Then put it in!' Jeanne whispered, her excitement apparent in her hasty words.

Christophe knelt on the floor between her spread legs and admired the pale gleam of her naked thighs as she pulled her nightdress up to her waist. He kissed them delicately, high up near her patch of crinkly fur. He kissed her warm belly and probed her navel with the tip of his tongue. But Jeanne was suddenly impatient and pulled him towards her. She guided his hot-headed part into position and an easy push sank it deep within her.

'Oh yes!' she moaned, 'do it to me, Christophe.'

Now that he had attained this rapturous position after all the teasing at dinner and afterwards and half an hour alone in the dark waiting for her, Christophe was in no mood to hurry matters along and so put an early end to the long-anticipated pleasure, no matter what he had said to her about his readiness. His strokes were long and slow between her thighs, his hands fondled and kneaded her breasts. Jeanne's breathing was loud and ragged.

'You are taking me too far,' she exclaimed, 'you mustn't . . .'

Even as she spoke she took his head between her hands and pulled his mouth to hers and dissolved in a silent, quaking release. The rhythmic spasms of the velvet glove of flesh that embraced his penis did for Christophe. He gasped into her wide open mouth and fountained his ecstasy into her, his loins jerking convulsively and his heart pounding.

8

When he was finished and still again Jeanne stroked his hair.

'That was naughty of you,' she said, 'you made me go too far.'

'To the point you wished to reach,' he answered, not sure what she meant. 'Was it good?'

'Overwhelming ... it made me afraid.'

'I don't understand,' and he kissed her neck.

'Perhaps I will explain to you sometime. Now I must go back to bed in case Guy wakes up and wonders where I am.'

'So soon? Let me kiss your breasts before you go.'

She pushed him gently away from her and the gleam of white skin vanished from his sight as she pulled her nightdress down and fastened her négligé. She stood up and Christophe, still on his knees, put his arms about her hips and pressed his cheek to her warm belly.

'When can we be together again?' he asked urgently.

'I will try to arrange something. Until then you must be very discreet. Let me go now.'

He heard the rustle of silk as she crossed the dark room, the careful opening and closing of the door. He sat on the chaise-longue, his trousers still undone, speaking wordlessly to his limp part as he tucked it away.

'Dear friend, you and I have had a most marvellous experience this evening. I regret that it was all too brief. If only Jeanne had stayed a little longer you would have been ready for another close embrace in a quarter of an hour. But I give you my word, at our next encounter with her you shall have permission to express your admiration for the lady until you run out of compliments to pay her. For now, be grateful for what you have enjoyed and be pleased not to disturb me again tonight. I intend to go to bed and sleep, to be ready for whatever delights tomorrow may bring in this enchanted city.'

As all the world knows, logic and reality do not always coincide in true life. Towards morning Christophe dreamed of Jeanne. They were at the dinner-table, her hand in his lap. He was unable to contain himself and eased the narrow straps of her frock off her shoulders and pulled it down to her waist to expose her pretty breasts. Verney continued to talk to Christophe's mother in his boring way as if nothing out of the ordinary were taking place in his dining-room. Christophe bent forwards to kiss Jeanne's nipples in turn.

'Be careful, you will take me too far,' he warned, using the words she had said to him.

'I hope so,' she answered, both hands manipulating him through his clothes.

Christophe sighed, a soft breast in each hand, his thumbs circling their proud nipples.

'It is enormous, did you know that?' she asked, then turned to Christophe's mother to say, 'Madame Larousse, do you realise how enormous it is?'

Christophe spurted furiously, his trapped part jolting in his trousers. While the spasms of delight were shaking his body he looked Guy Verney full in the face and shouted:

'Do you see? Your beautiful wife has made me do it in my underwear – what do you think of that?'

He woke up, his legs still trembling and a feeling of warm wetness on his belly inside his pyjamas. Daylight was showing at the curtained windows and he was lying on his back in bed.

'She has ensnared me,' he thought as his body relaxed pleasurably. 'Even in my sleep she makes me do it. I must have her again. Not just once in a hurry but again and again and again.'

At breakfast his mother said,

'I heard you cry out about six o'clock. Were you dreaming?'

'Yes, I believe that I was. I hope that I didn't wake you.'

'No, I wasn't asleep. I hardly closed my eyes all night. Was it a nightmare?'

'I wouldn't call it that,' he said and looked up from his café au lait to catch Jeanne's eyes on him, shining with secret amusement.

Christophe's father and Guy Verney had been cousins, though Verney was much the senior. He was assuredly the one who made money. He started with a factory in Paris to make mass-produced shoes and during the War he had prospered on contracts for army boots, to the point where he had acquired two other factories, one at Nantes and another at Clermont-Ferrand. Christophe's father, along with a million other Frenchmen, died defending his country against the Germans. At Verdun in 1916, the muddy boots he was wearing when a shell blasted him and half a dozen of his men into eternity were quite probably made in one of his cousin's factories.

Christophe, an only child, was intelligent and well-mannered but he had not done well enough at school to derive any benefit from enrolling at the University of Lyon, the city where he and his widowed mother lived. He was now twenty-one and his prospects in life were doubtful. His mother had brought him to Paris to visit their rich relatives to see if Verney could be persuaded to take him under his wing. All understood the reason for the visit but nothing was discussed on the evening of their arrival – the evening of Christophe's nocturnal rendezvous with Jeanne in the drawing-room. It was at lunch the next day that Verney showed that he knew where his family duty lay.

'Your dear father died a hero,' he declared to Christophe, 'he made the supreme sacrifice in laying down his life to defend France against the filthy Boche. I was not permitted because of other national requirements to enlist in the army, but believe me, nothing would have given me greater pleasure than to fight alongside your father, grappling hand-to-hand with the murderous invaders of our country. But I never shirked my duty. I did my part as best I could, though it meant slaving night and day, to ensure that our brave soldiers in the trenches had the essential supplies they required to throw back the Boche. Now I am equally ready to play my part again by stretching out the hand of friendship to the orphaned son of my dead cousin. You shall enter my business as if you were my own son. If you work diligently and well, who shall say that one day you may not be as successful as I am.'

'Embrace your uncle,' said Christophe's mother, dabbing at her eyes with a tiny handkerchief. 'Thank him for his generosity.'

11

Christophe and Verney rose from their chairs and embraced each other awkwardly.

'I am more grateful for this kindness than you can imagine, uncle Guy,' said Christophe.

To himself he thought that he owed this chance not to Verney's sense of family duty but to the fortunate that he had pleased Jeanne in the dark and she had brought the pressure of the Brissards to bear on her husband. Presumably they had money invested in Verney's enterprise.

When his mother had enjoyed a few days shopping in Paris Christophe escorted her home to Lyon, packed his belongings and took the train alone back to Paris to start his new life. Jeanne herself helped him to find a tiny apartment close to the Luxembourg Gardens, in the rue Vavin. For all his fine-sounding words, it was only a clerk's position Verney had given him and the salary was not generous. Together Christophe and Jeanne inspected several apartments to let, bearing in mind his constrained income. At the one in the rue Vavin the concierge seemed more sympathetic than elsewhere. She was a plump woman, dressed in the usual faded black.

'Fourth floor,' she said as she handed Christophe the key and shrewdly eyed Jeanne's expensively fashionable clothes, 'I cleaned it only yesterday, so everything is in order. Excuse me if I do not go up with you, but I am sure that you can manage without me. I'll be here when you come down. Take all the time you want, monsieur, choosing a place to live is a serious affair.'

The apartment was no more than two small rooms, totally empty, though the windows had been washed and the wooden floor was swept clean. Christophe led Jeanne into the inner room, put his arms about her and kissed her repeatedly.

'Not here,' she exlaimed, making not the least effort to stop him.

Christophe took her hands in his to peel off her thin black gloves and kiss the tip of each finger.

'But if this is to be my new home,' he said, 'I must be certain that it is suitable for its most important purpose.'

12

'Which is?'

'To entertain you.'

'Suppose the concierge comes in?'

'She is too lazy to climb the stairs more than once a day to clean the rooms. And besides, there was a certain gleam in her eye when she saw how beautiful you are and how devoted I am. She is a woman of discretion – she will not interrupt.'

By then he had undone Jeanne's outdoor coat and had both hands up her skirt to caress her bare thighs above her garters.

'But there is nothing here,' she said, 'no bed, no chaise-longue, not even a chair.'

'We brought all that we need with us,' he assured her.

His hands were inside the wide and loose legs of her chemise-culotte, one stroking the taut cheeks of her bottom, the other fondling the fleecy mound between her thighs. Jeanne's objections ceased the moment he pressed a finger-tip tenderly into her and she reached for his buttons. Christophe eased her backwards until she was against the wall, where she stood with legs apart while he teased her to wetness. She kissed his mouth with her little nibbling kisses, her hand massaging his stiff part.

'So strong!' she said, 'how I love it! I'm dying to feel it inside me.'

Christophe bent his knees and pushed slowly upwards, steering into her clinging depths. His hands gripped her bottom to hold her close to him as he began his slow movements.

'That morning you dreamed in my house,' she murmured in his ear, 'do you remember? Was it of me?'

'It certainly was!'

'Was it nice? Tell me about it while you make love to me.'

'We were at dinner,' he breathed through the waves of erotic sensation coursing through him, 'I pulled down your green frock to kiss your breasts. Then I held them in my hands.'

'Oh Christophe ... it feels so good ...'

'You caressed me with your hand through my trousers.'

'In your dream?'

13

'Yes ... you took me all the way ... I woke up to find my pyjamas flooded.'

'In your dream? To dream of me excited you so much?'

'Yes! And more than once since then!'

'Christophe! Do it now!'

A few fast strokes and his legs shook as he delivered his gift.

'I adore you,' he gasped, 'I adore you, Jeanne ...'

When he withdrew she dried herself carefully between the legs with lace-edged handkerchief, rearranged her clothes and took out a silver compact to attend to her make-up.

'Your face is smeared with lip-stick,' she said, smiling at him, 'you must wash it off before we go down.'

'Do you love me, Jeanne?'

'Love you? But of course. Your little companion stands up so boldly when we are together that I am flattered. How could I not love you, when you are so eager to love me? But listen to me – you must be very discreet, Christophe. Do you understand? I am a married woman with children and I wish to remain so.'

'Even though your husband does not love you as I do?'

'That has nothing to do with it. Now, this apartment – does it suit you?'

'After what we have just done here I think it is the best apartment in the whole of Paris. I shall take it.'

'Good, then we will go and talk to the concierge.'

'Will you visit me here often, Jeanne?'

'As often as I can, on the understanding that you are always ready to entertain me as you did five minutes ago.'

'Against the wall?' he asked, smiling, and she laughed.

'I shall furnish the apartment for you so that the next time I am here we can do it more comfortably.'

In effect, Christophe's job with Verney proved to be a sinecure. He found himself to be one of five clerks under the supervision of Henri Dufour, to whom he was presented as a nephew of Verney starting on the ground floor to learn the business. Dufour was in his late fifties and had been in Verney's employ for a dozen years. He assumed that Christophe might be set over him one day in the not too

14

remote future and that made it necessary to cultivate the young man's friendship. He and Christophe reached a satisfactory understanding. Whenever Verney was absent, a frequent occurrence, Christophe was permitted to leave at midday on the pretence that Dufour had sent him out on important business. The other clerks, all much older than Christophe, shrugged their shoulders and kept their mouths shut. They too foresaw a time when the nephew's goodwill might be necessary to their continued employment.

With a good many afternoons free, Christophe was able to receive Jeanne in the rue Vavin. The choice of apartment had been a good one. She could easily find a taxi outside her home, cross the Seine by the Pont de l'Alma and on past the Hotel des Invalides to be with him in twenty minutes or so. True to her word, she furnished his apartment for him very comfortably.

Naturally, Christophe guessed that he was by no means her first lover since her marriage to Verney, but it was not a topic to ask about. After they had been lovers for some weeks he began to understand her a little. Six years of her husband's disastrous attentions in bed had left her unsatisfied and unfulfilled, but there was more than just that. Verney used her body as he would use a handkerchief to sneeze in and she resented it bitterly. Her resentment had created in her a need to be in control of a man's sexuality, to use it in a manner which pleased her, not to be a victim of it. Christophe went along with her desires gladly. Jeanne would lie naked on his bed and have him caress her endlessly – her elegant breasts, her soft belly and thighs – on a voyage of exploration to discover how far she could be aroused before she was unable to prevent herself from pulling him on top of her to finish her off. They played this game together countless times, to her great satisfaction, though occasionally in her endeavour to go further than before she misjudged the level of her own excitement and reached a trembling and gasping climax before he could penetrate her.

'Score one for you that time,' she would say, as if keeping points, and Christophe would pretend to make a mark on the wall with a licked finger.

15

Often too she would make Christophe lie on his back, his arms by his sides, while she teased him from head to foot with her fingers and little nibbling kisses, making his jutting stamen rear and throb. This was her secret game of power. The memory of years of frustration and resentment at Verney's mishandling of her were wiped out by her ability to make Christophe shake in frenzy by her lingering caresses – a frenzy entirely under her control.

Christophe loved all of her games of love-making. He would do whatever she wished, for as long as she wished. And why not? For the reward was always there. No matter how long she teased him, however long she kept him hovering on the brink of ecstasy, eventually she would invite him to pierce the wet fleece between her legs and give vent to the wild desire she had aroused. Not just once, of course, but several times in the course of a long afternoon, with bouts of play between. Only when his staunch 'friend' drooped limply in final exhaustion did they regard their love-making at an end for that day.

When Jeanne had dressed and departed, Christophe would return to bed alone. His pillows and sheets retained the subtle fragrance of the perfume she used, and also the natural perfume of her warm body. He lay there naked, dazed by the memory of so much pleasure, until he drifted off into contented sleep. Towards eight in the evening he would wake, refreshed and happy, wash and dress and stroll out to one or other of the little restaurants he favoured on the Boulevard St Michel, to enjoy a hearty dinner and a bottle of wine. Such days were ecstatic peaks in his life, treasured and savoured in recollection.

For Christophe this was a marvellous and halcyon time in his life. And with good reason! Here he was, a young man translated from a provincial city and the restraints imposed on him by living at home with his mother – suddenly at large in Paris! He felt that he had passed from adolescence to manhood at a stroke. He was independent, he had his own apartment and a position that paid a salary for next to no work. And best of all, he had the intimate friendship of an elegant woman with whom to explore to the full his urgent

16

sexuality. In all this a dream had come true which he had been incapable even of dreaming back home in Lyon.

He improved his acquaintance with Jeanne's youngest brother Gerard, being wise enough to recognise in him a valuable guide to the limitless possibilities and pleasures of Paris. Intellectually Christophe was no match for Gerard, but that was of no importance to either of them. Each found the other to be an amusing companion, though in the case of Gerard there was a touch of unspoken irony in the friendship. Gerard, who knew everything about everybody, was well aware of the relations between his sister and Christophe. Obviously the country cousin had become necessary to Jeanne's happiness. And since Gerard loved his sister and cordially disliked her boorish husband, it was almost an act of family duty to steer her young man along sensible paths and to assist in putting a little polish on his provincialism.

One of their outings together was to see Josephine Baker soon after her dazzling debut at the Folies Bergère. The first appearance of this ravishing young American negress was in the chorus-line of a revue at the Théâtre des Champs Elysées the previous year. And in the manner of these things, her nineteen year-old charm caught the eye of someone of importance and very soon she was the star of her own spectacular show. Both Christophe and Gerard were enchanted by the vivacity and appeal of Mademoiselle Baker's lithe and café au lait coloured body as she pranced on stage, naked but for a tiny silver cache-sexe and a tall head-dress of ostrich plumes.

Later that evening they discussed her over a drink.

'She is ravishing, this black mademoiselle,' Christophe declared.

'Exquisite,' Gerard agreed.

'Those long and elegant legs!'

'Those pointed little breasts,' said Gerard, speaking more frankly.

'Ah, yes!'

'And that delightful wiggling rump – you noticed that, I have no doubt.'

17

'It would excite even a blind man ... Gerard, tell me, you seem to have done everything – have you ever been with a black girl?'

'Once or twice.'

'Is it different from being with a French girl?'

'Not in any essential. At first I was aware of the contrast between her skin and mine and that gave a certain piquancy to our love-making. But as matters progressed that ceased to engage my attention. The second or third time I went with her, I was totally unaware of it.'

'Who was she?'

Once Christophe learned that the girl was from Madagascar and was available at a private house in the rue St Denis, nothing would satisfy him but that Gerard should take him there at once. The house was a fairly expensive one, Gerard warned him, not the sort of place where working-men made a quick stop on Saturday nights.

Mademoiselle Angelique, for so she called herself, was not immediately available when they arrived. They sat in the parlour and chatted to two or three disengaged girls while they waited and Gerard, his manners impeccable, ordered a bottle of over-priced champagne.

'Is she beautiful?' Christophe asked Gerard.

'Not so much beautiful as striking. She has a good body.'

Mademoiselle Angelique proved to be a mulatto woman of twenty-two or twenty-three with a mop of black crinkly hair and circular gold ear-rings almost large enough to brush her shoulders as she walked into the parlour. Her only garment was a crocus-yellow chemise which clung to her body in a manner to accentuate the abundance of her bosom and the breadth of her hips. She greeted Gerard with an amiable smile and accepted a glass of the house's inferior vintage. As she sat and talked with the two young men her short chemise rode up to show off her sturdy brown thighs and when she laughed her breasts swung under the thin material.

Now that he had gone this far Christophe felt that he was in honour bound to continue. Otherwise, who could say, in Gerard's eyes he might appear to lack courage – or worse,

18

lack virility. So continue he did, though it meant borrowing money from his friend and in due course he found himself on Angelique's bed, fondling her balloons of breasts and attempting to persuade himself that this was the most exotic of experiences. The encounter proved to be of short duration. Angelique urged him on with words and hands until he mounted her, at which her busy loins quickly relieved him of his burden.

Back in his own bed he dreamed vividly of Jeanne that night. She was there with him, giving full rein to all her exquisite sensuality. Her slender hands roamed expertly over his body, her little white teeth nibbled at him. Yet when they were at last joined, for all his excitement he was unable to find release, though his stiff penis ached from the effort. To no avail! Jeanne's eyes stared at him in accusation and he could find no words to speak.

He awoke with an erection and a feeling of guilt. Gerard's way is not for me, he said to himself, I am too entrapped by Jeanne to make love to another woman, white, black or yellow.

They were lovers for nearly a year before he asked her the question that had been in his mind since the first day he met her. It was during a pause on their love-making one afternoon.

'You remember the first time we were together, in the dark,' he said, 'when everyone was asleep and we met in your drawing-room.'

'Shall I ever forget it!'

'You told me then that I had taken you too far. What did you mean?'

Jeanne explained to him at some length. Not an ordinary explanation in words only but an extended and practical demonstration which required the use of her lips and hands on him. At one point the explanation required the rub of her dark hair across his chest and belly and, at anothers, the warmth of her satin-skinned thighs clasping his waist. These were only two of the truly astonishing variety of pleasurable sensations a woman's body can cause a man to experience which she employed as illustrations of what she was telling him.

19

'I have told you about my husband's three-second catastrophes,' she said, her finger-nails lightly scoring the insides of his thighs, 'I was a virgin when I married him and so I never knew what it meant to be aroused until I met someone else, after my first child was born.'

'Ah, who was this someone else?'

'That is no affair of yours. Be content to know that before you arrived in Paris I never knew anyone who could make me feel as much as you do. Why else am I here with you now?'

'Because you love me.'

'I love you for what you can do to me.'

'You are a sensualist,' Christophe sighed as her teeth worried at his nipples gently.

'Then be grateful for it,' she answered, 'as I am grateful to you for teaching me that about myself.'

'Did I?'

'My husband has never aroused me in the slightest – how could he? And after I met someone who showed me that things could be done differently it was hard for me to respond as a woman should. After all, Guy had rendered me almost frigid. I was not accustomed to the fierce pleasures of the body. But the man I met was intelligent and patient. After a time I enjoyed being touched, and soon I learned to enjoy being penetrated. But I was afraid to let my feelings go too far because I did not truly understand myself, even then. I wanted to stay in control of myself all the time, even with a lover moving inside me. For me the pleasure lay in making his pleasure possible. Can you understand that?'

'Men and women are so different in this regard,' said Christophe.

'For a long time I believed that myself. Now I know that I was wrong and that you are wrong.'

'Perhaps,' said Christophe doubtfully.

'That first time with you, on the chaise-longue in the dark – you cannot know what was in my mind. I wanted a new lover, yes, and I chose you because you seemed ideal in many ways. I teased you a little at dinner to make my intention clear to you. Then, on the chaise-longue, I wanted the touch

20

of your hands on my body. I wanted the feel of you inside me, hard and strong, for I had been taught by a gentle lover to enjoy that. But that was all that I wanted. I thought that you would satisfy yourself and then I would return to bed and fall asleep as my half-excitement slowly subsided.'

'But more than that happened. I begin to see what your words meant.'

'An astonishing thing happened – astonishing for me, that is. With you I was carried further than I expected. I lost control of myself. I drowned in sensation and reached a sudden climax. That had hardly ever happened to me before, even with ... and when it had, it always left me shaken and fearful.'

'But you enjoyed it that night, didn't you?'

'If only you could have guessed how much I enjoyed it that time! But I was confused by the intensity of my own emotions and I left you quickly to hide what I was feeling. I lay beside my insensible husband for hours thinking about what you had made me experience. I caressed myself to bring back the memory of it more clearly. My confusion vanished and with it my old fears. I was free. I knew that I enjoyed what you had made me experience. More than enjoyed – adored! I wanted more of it.'

'That was the night I dreamed of you for the first time,' Christophe murmured as Jeanne's wet tongue probed his navel and then criss-crossed his belly.

'You were dreaming of me and this naughty friend of yours was standing up stiff and discharging while I was awake and thinking of you and touching myself under my nightdress where you had pleasured me. Our bodies were apart but in some manner we were still joined together.'

'Inseparably and forever,' said Christophe, his voice almost a croak under the emotional impact of her ministrations.

'The day we looked at apartments for you – I knew without the least doubt that you would make love to me in one of them. If you hadn't tried, I would have initiated it myself. There was no escaping it for either of us that day, even if I had to strip naked in front of you. And it was here in this apartment, leaning against the wall! I welcomed the pleasure like an old friend that time, when you entered me and made me lose my senses!

'How often we have done it since on this bed!' he sighed.

Jeanne pushed his legs apart as far as they would go and her fingers made fluttering movements in his exposed groins.

'Not often enough,' she answered him, 'I am like you now – I want that pleasure over and over again until I collapse in complete exhaustion, utterly satisfied. I love you because you can do that to me.'

'Then we *are* alike, Jeanne. I can never have enough of you. When you leave me I rest awhile and go out to eat and then I want you again as soon as I get back here.'

'Good, good. That is how I am when I go home after these hours with you. At night I lie in bed and recall every kiss and every touch. When I am with you I want it to last forever so that there will be more to remember when I am at home.'

'Yes!' Christophe breathed, his body twitching in little spasms of delight under her hands. 'Oh, I will pay you back for this – I will play with you until you beg me in tears to finish you off. And then I shall lick the tears from your face and continue the torment until you scream for mercy. You will see.'

'But not yet,' she said, 'this is the best part of it, the long approach towards the eventual ecstatic moments. I love to find out each time how it can be prolonged to the very limit of endurance before those last insane moments when the whole body seems to explode.'

Christophe felt her little nibbling kisses mount his swollen stem from base to tip. That was more than he could stand. His essence jetted out and his writhing almost rolled him off the bed.

'You understand me now, I think,' said Jeanne, when his passion had subsided.

Christophe embraced her and then used a corner of the bed-sheet to wipe the traces of his tumultuous release from her pretty face.

'I begin to understand you a little,' he said, 'I have never known anyone like you.'

'Nor I you, if it comes to that. You are a superb plaything, Christophe. Now it is my turn. You must show me what you can do to me. Take me right up to the edge, step by step, and keep me there for longer than ever before. You know so well how to excite me. And by then your dear friend will be hard again and ready for service when I can bear no more. Then with all of him in, we will explode together like an anarchist's bomb.'

'You are adorable,' said Christophe.

He kissed her little breasts as she turned to lie on her back. Her use of the word plaything had made no impression on his young mind whatsoever.

MAURICE ON BOARD SHIP

Once the liner had cleared the Channel and was heading out west across the Atlantic, it began to roll steadily. Not a disconcerting roll, and not enough to make any but the faintest-hearted queasy, but sufficient to remind the passengers that they were afloat on an ocean that possessed formidable power. Maurice was walking with careful steps in the centre of the corridor on which his state-room was located, on his way to the bar for an aperitif before lunch. A door swung open as he passed it and, in mid-step, he caught a glimpse of a naked girl.

More exactly, he saw a naked girl reflected in a long mirror on the wall. Before he could even slow his pace, the door closed sharply and he heard the lock click. He strolled on, his thoughts racing. The glimpse had been most fleeting, but the impression had been deep. The girl's hair was blonde, short and parted in the middle. Her body was slender, her breasts small and set high, her haunches narrow. The tuft of hair at the join of her thighs was as blonde as the hair on her head, or nearly so. She had been a pleasing sight, almost an Impressionist painting in the lack of detail.

Had she seen Maurice in her looking-glass when he saw her? She was brushing her hair, he believed, from the position of her arms. That posed a question. Did young ladies of good family, even in these modern times, stand naked in front of their mirrors to brush their hair? It was a question he could not answer. Maurice Brissard had grown up with two sisters younger than himself, Jeanne and Octavie. If in the privacy of their rooms in the family home they had dressed their hair while in the nude, he was unaware of it. For curiosity's sake he decided to ask one or other of them about it when he returned to Paris.

Maurice's beautiful wife, Marie-Thérèse had brushed her hair naked when they were on honeymoon and for at least the first year of their marriage, he recalled. That was seven

24

years and two children ago. Nowadays she wore expensively flimsy négligés at her toilet table. Of course, when he took her a glass of chilled champagne in her bath before they went out for the evening, then she was naked under the scented bubbles. That was different, however.

Maurice sat at the bar of the *Ile de France* with a glass of cold dry vermouth and thought about the girl. The bar depressed him – it was so long that five people at least could have lain end to end along it, if so bizarre a proceeding had occurred to anyone. Evidently it had been constructed to attract American travellers, not civilised Frenchmen.

The girl – had she seen him? If so, she had not reacted in embarrassment. On the other hand, the door had been closed quickly, and if the ship's roll had caused it to open, it had most certainly not closed it, for the roll was a slow one. There was something else – was it no more than a trick of the mirrored perspective that as her hand moved from her head, her finger-tips appeared to touch the blonde fur between her thighs. The movement of the hand was not to hide anything, for it only touched in passing. In so doing, it drew attention to the part which girls usually kept covered.

A mystery, thought Maurice, and a contradiction. The door had opened at the exact second he passed it. A coincidence, no more? Maybe.

For that matter, who was she? Her state-room was not far from his. He had not noticed her in the ship's public rooms. But they were only a day out of Le Havre, and with four hundred or so first class passengers on board, that was unremarkable. Except that Maurice had an eye for a pretty woman. Could she be travelling alone? Could she have stayed in her state-room all this time?

The mystery was partly resolved for him later that day. He returned from a stroll round the deck to dress for dinner and found an envelope waiting for him on a silver salver. Inside was a single sheet of the ship's note-paper on which was written *10.30*. Maurice rang for the steward.

'This note – who gave it to you to put here, Henri?'

'A young lady, sir.'

'What is her name?'

'I regret that I cannot tell you.'

'Naturally, she asked you to be discreet, is that it?'

The steward said nothing. Maurice was pleased – the man was well-trained.

'In these matters it is necessary for everyone to be discreet. Tell me one thing. Henri what does she look like?'

'A very pretty young lady, sir.'

'With blonde hair?'

Henri nodded briefly.

'Thank you. You can lay out my evening clothes while I bath.'

A rendez-vous with an attractive stranger! Sea-voyages were supposed to foster intimate liaisons, but this was beyond anything Maurice had expected. He splashed around in his bath, singing lustily:

'*Auprès de ma blonde, qu'il fait bon dormir . . .*

The excellence of the dinner did little to restrain his gathering impatience. He enjoyed the pâté de foie gras, the potage Marie-Stuart, the petites barquettes Sévigné, the saumon de Loire à la Daumont, the filet de Charolais and all the rest of the chef's magnificent offering – seven courses of it – and the superb wines that accompanied the course, above all the Chambertin with the filet. But even as he chatted to his table companions, he was looking around the dining-room to see if he could find the anonymous sender of the note.

There was no more questioning in his mind, of course. She had seen him in her mirror. She wanted to make his closer acquaintance, not in public but in private. It followed in his reasoning that her intentions were of a very private nature and that their acquaintance would be close indeed. It also followed that, if she found it necessary to make the arrangement in secret, she was not travelling alone. A husband, a lover, a father? Whichever it might be, the element of danger fired Maurice's imagination.

'Why do you keep looking round?' the woman next to him at table asked, 'have you lost someone?'

Maurice smiled at her briefly. She too had short blonde hair and was slender. There the resemblance ended. She was certainly forty, perhaps nearer fifty, who could say? Her figure was the result of persistent dieting, which gave her face a slightly gaunt look under the elaborate make-up.

'This is my first crossing, Madame. I was admiring the style of the dining-room.'

'Really? I find it vulgar, this modern style of pale wood and coloured marble. I much prefer to sail on the *France*, but my husband insists that it is old-fashioned now.'

As she talked she moved her head a lot. Her pendant diamond ear-rings, as long as a man's thumb, flashed about and gave off little gleams of light.

'How does that ship differ from this one, Madame?'

'It is decorated in the style of Louis Quatorze, which I adore. The *France* is a veritable royal palace afloat, whereas this could be a modern tourist hotel.'

'You have crossed the Atlantic often?' Maurice asked.

She proceeded to tell him at some length. Her husband, Georges de Margeville, across the table, was a most important man in the world of coffee-broking and with him she regularly visited the United States and South America. Maurice listened, not that he was interested in Madame de Margeville's views, but because he too was on a business journey and it was useful to make the acquaintance of other people involved in commerce.

After dinner a five-piece band played for dancing in the ship's ball-room. Some of the men travelling alone slipped away to play cards elsewhere, a risky pastime on an ocean liner where professional gamblers travelled to make their living. Maurice accompanied the de Margevilles to the ball-room, to pass the time until his rendez-vous. He found himself dancing an elaborate tango with Madame de Margeville. Her lilac evening dress was entirely backless to the waist and his choice was between putting his hand on her bare shoulder-blade or on her thinly-covered backside. He chose the shoulder-blade.

She danced well, though she had some cutting opinions about the decor of the ball-room, which clearly was far too modern for her taste.

'But consider,' said Maurice, 'your hair is cut fashionably

27

short and your dress is audacious. To me it looks as if it came from the hand of Paquin, though I am no expert in these matters. Admit it, Madame de Margeville, you are a modern woman in every way.'

'I see that your wife has educated you to some extent about dressmakers. You may call me Germaine.'

Her thighs brushed quickly over his as they executed a deft turn.

'Do not misunderstand me, Maurice,' she said, 'I abhor the jazzy ways which the Americans have exported to Europe since the War, particularly the lack of good manners and style in the very young. But I am not antiquated, as you may discover.'

Again her thighs brushed his and this time her belly touched him. The gesture signalled a subtle and unmistakable invitation.

'Personally I do not find the frankness of young people disagreeable,' said Maurice, thinking of his invitation to visit an unknown young lady.

'They understand so little, the young,' said Germaine. 'They are shallow and without knowledge of life. Maturity brings rich rewards to the discerning person, don't you think?'

'Without doubt.'

As soon as he decently could, he escorted her to the table where Georges de Margeville and a middle-aged couple had settled themselves.

'Sit down,' Germaine ordered him, 'you must have a glass of champagne with us, mustn't he, Georges?'

Maurice sat and chatted to Germaine's husband, while her elegantly shod foot pressed his under the table. At the right moment he excused himself, saying that he had arranged to join a baccarat game.

'We shall meet tomorrow,' said Germaine, 'it's just come into my mind that Jeanne Verney is your sister. It's some time since I saw her. How is she?'

'Very well indeed.'

'Good – you must tell me all about her. At eleven tomorrow morning in the Grand Salon?'

Precisely at ten-thirty Maurice tapped lightly on the door which had afforded him so tantalising a glimpse earlier that day.

'Who's there?' a girl's voice asked.

'I received your note. May I come in?'

'Don't let anyone see you. Come in and close the door quickly.'

He did so, to find himself standing in total darkness.

'Lock it,' said the voice quietly. 'Don't put the light on. I'm over here on the bed.'

Maurice moved cautiously, half-expecting to bruise himself against furniture. A hand found his out-stretched hand and pulled him gently down to sit on the side of a bed.

'Why are we in darkness?' he asked, 'you are very beautiful, I know.'

'Because I prefer it so. You may leave if you wish.'

Not a gleam of light came from the curtained port-holes, but even in the darkness Maurice was intensely aware of her presence. He could smell her flower-like perfume and sense the warmth of her body so close to him. He reached towards her and touched a bare shoulder. She slid into his arms and he kissed her face and mouth while his hands stroked her naked back.

'Tell me your name,' she whispered, between kisses.

'You know it, or you could not have sent me the note.'

'I know only your family name and your initials. That is all the passenger list gives.'

'Then I am Maurice. What is your name?'

'Michelle. How old are you, Maurice?'

Her sides were warm and smooth under his questing hands.

'Thirty-five. And you?'

'Twenty. Are you an important person, Maurice Brissard? Do you dine at the captain's table?'

'Were you in the dining-room tonight? I looked everywhere for you.'

'I pretended to be sea-sick so that I could wait for you here.'

'Then you must be hungry.'

'No, I ordered dinner here after my parents had left.'

29

'Ah!'

'Yes, you must be gone before they return. Why don't you take off your clothes?'

They lay naked together on the bed. Michelle's hot readiness awoke in Maurice an intensity of passion he had not experienced since the first months of his marriage. As he was unable to see her, he explored every part of her body slowly with his lips and fingers, beginning with her smooth young face and scented hair.

Around her neck was a thin chain supporting a metal object which his sense of touch told him was a crucifix. Gold, no doubt, he thought.

'Are you religious?' he asked in some surprise.

'But of course. Aren't you?'

'Not very. I go to Mass at Easter.'

'Even so, you would scarcely like to tell your confessor that you had committed a sin of the flesh with an irreligious woman, would you? That would be to make matters worse. Think of the penance he'd give you!'

'For the pleasure of being with you now no penance would be too heavy.'

'But you can assure him that you sinned with a good Catholic.'

Maurice was not really listening to her words. The taste of her small breasts and the touch of her soft belly inspired him. Michelle sighed and shuddered in delight as he examined her every part, as a connoisseur would inspect a rare *objet d'art*.

'Oh yes, yes,' she murmured when he caressed the tender flesh between her thighs and her hips lifted off the bed in a quick climax of gratification.

'You'll know me the next time you see me,' she said, 'now it is my turn.'

She coaxed him onto his back and felt him all over with inquisitive fingers, as if learning by heart the planes and curves of his body. Her touch tuned him to a pitch of desire that fascinated him. She was kneeling between his legs, his swollen stem clasped in her hand and her wet tongue flicking at its tip when he cried out 'Stop, stop!'

Her fingers clamped the base of his shaft tightly to prevent

30

the incipient crisis.

'All right now?' she whispered in the dark. 'Can I let go?'

Maurice took her by the arms and pulled her down beside him. She was ready for him, comfortably settled on her back with her knees up and her legs splayed. Maurice slipped into her and savoured the feel of her belly under his and her breasts cushioning his chest. Her arms were about his neck.

'Ever so slowly now,' she murmured close to his ear, 'I want it to last for ages.'

Maurice wanted the same. The sheer physical joy of their encounter was something to be spun out to the uttermost. He moved extremely slowly, a short and easy probing that set up long and delicate waves of sensation in both their bodies.

'I'll be there again in a minute,' she breathed, 'don't go any faster though – I want you to last a long time.'

A dozen more slow thrusts and her loins pushed up hard against him and she exclaimed 'Ah, ah, ah ...'

Maurice played her love game for as long as he could hold out. Twice more she attained her ecstatic goal under his steady rhythm and then he could no longer contain himself. His movements became fast and hard, he plunged furiously and erupted into her straining body in long spasms of rapture.

'That was very good, Maurice,' she said, stroking his face tenderly.

'You are superb,' he said.

'Now you must leave before my parents come back. They'll be sure to look in to see if I am feeling any better.'

'And are you?'

'Thanks to you I am feeling very well indeed.'

Maurice groped around on the floor for his clothes. As he dressed awkwardly in the dark he asked, 'When can we meet again, Michelle? Tomorrow?'

'Perhaps. There are problems with my parents. I may have to be sea-sick again.'

'That's not necessary. If you can get away from them you can come to my state-room anytime during the day. No one will disturb us there, I promise.'

'I will let you know.'

He kissed her unseen face once more and departed, easing round the door warily to make sure that there was no one in the corridor to observe his going.

The next morning, after informing the steward where he would be in case of messages, he joined Germaine de Margeville in the Grand Salon at eleven.

'How was your luck last night?' she asked, 'did the cards run for you?'

'The game was enjoyable and my luck was excellent,' he said, smiling.

'I am pleased for you. Now you must tell me about your sister Jeanne. Has she any more children since I saw her last?'

'When was that?'

'It must be nearly two years. Georges and I travel abroad so much that it is hard to keep up with old friends. I think I wrote to her from Rio sometime last summer, but I write to so many people.'

Before Maurice could say another word, Germaine was waving busily to someone who had just entered the salon.

'There's Marguerite Varans. Do you know her?'

'Varans? No, I don't think so.'

Madame Varans paused at their table and Maurice stood up. She was a woman of Germaine de Margeville's age and so not interesting to him. She was very smartly dressed in dark blue and her hair had been set in horizontal waves, much like the surface of the ocean. Germaine kissed her warmly on both cheeks.

'My dear, this is Maurice Brissard. Maurice – Marguerite Varans and her daughter Antoinette.'

Maurice kissed their hands politely. The daughter, one hand on her mother's arm, was about twenty, he thought, not plain but not pretty. She was wearing a modishly tubular frock which totally disguised her figure. Her eyes startled him. They were dull brown, blank and unseeing.

'I saw you at dinner yesterday evening,' Germaine said to the girl, 'your green frock was very chic. But where was your sister?'

'She had a touch of sea-sickness and didn't want to eat.'

A tiny smile at the corners of her mouth alerted Maurice.

32

He noticed for the first time that Antoinette wore a small gold cross on a chain round her neck. There was something here that made him feel uneasy. The girl he had been with after dinner mentioned parents but said nothing about a sister. Had there been two beds? Because of the darkness he had not been able to tell. Something odd was going on, of that he was certain.

The Varans, mother and daughter, moved on.

'Poor Marguerite,' said Germaine, 'such a tragedy for her. The other daughter is as pretty as you could wish, though not very clever. Antoinette is the more intelligent one and she has been blind since she was a small child.'

'A tragedy for a mother,' Maurice agreed, digesting the information, 'The other daughter, what is her name?'

'Michelle. If you hadn't gone off to your boring card game so soon after dinner you would have seen her.'

'Her sister said that she was sea-sick.'

'Evidently she recovered because I saw her dancing in the ball-room with one of the ship's officers not a quarter of an hour after you went.'

Even more odd, Maurice thought. Perhaps it had been another Michelle he had been to bed with.

'What does she look like?' he asked, trying to sound casual.

'How inquisitive about her you are! She's blonde, with a porcelain complexion and a good figure. But she's too young for you, my dear Maurice,' and Germaine tapped him roguishly on the back of the hand. 'Really, she's only a girl. She can't be more than twenty-one or twenty-two. A man of your experience does not waste his time with goslings.'

'Please do not misunderstand me,' said Maurice hurriedly, 'I am most happily married to an extremely beautiful woman. I pay no attention to young girls.'

'There's no need to excuse yourself to me, I assure you. I know all about happily married men and their little diversions. It is in their nature to let their eyes wander elsewhere.'

Her voice sank confidentially.

'You will find it hard to believe, but Georges was amusing

33

himself with a Creole girl from Martinique before he and I had been married a year. Can you imagine it! When I discovered the truth I was heart-broken, being only a young girl myself and innocent of the ways of the world. Naturally I said nothing but my eyes were opened and after that I made certain that Georges was not the only one to have amusements.'

Maurice hardly knew what to say to such confidences. He found Germaine an unsympathetic person and knowing that there was a reason for it did not change his feelings. He left her as soon as he could and went for a walk on deck while he attempted to make sense of what he had learned about the Varans girls.

The girl he had seen in the mirror had been Michelle. She was the bait. But the girl whose appetite he had assuaged was not her, for she was by then in the ball-room. So it had been Antoinette, calling herself Michelle. She must have left the dining-room immediately after dinner and been escorted back to her bed to prepare for him.

'I have been duped,' Maurice said aloud as he paced the deck, 'the pretty sister lured me for the blind one. But the blind one is the clever one.'

The affair could not be allowed to rest there. Maurice's pride had been hurt. He went below to compose a note for the steward to deliver to her. After careful thought he wrote, 'I have found out your trick. Please visit me at 3 this afternoon to explain your motives. It would be most unfortunate if your parents became aware of how you and your sister change places.'

He did not sign the note, nor did he address the envelope. He rang for the steward and handed it to him.

'Henri, please see that this is in the hands of the blonde young lady before lunch. Discreetly, of course.'

'Of course, sir.'

'The blonde young lady, not her sister, you understand.'

'Perfectly.'

Even so, she kept him waiting. It was twenty past three when he heard a light tap on his door and opened it to admit her. She looked extremely attractive in a red and yellow

34

striped silk blouse and a white skirt.

'Please sit down,' he began quite formally, 'there are things I wish to say to you.'

Michelle's manner was unconcerned. She took a chair and crossed her knees.

'I am not at all sure that I have anything to say to you,' she replied, 'your note was beastly.'

'All the same, you are here.'

She shrugged slightly.

'What was the reason for the charade?' Maurice asked. 'Tell me that, please.'

'Surely it must be obvious. My sister has certain problems in arranging her pleasures, so I help her. That's all there is to it.'

'You entice men for her, that I understand. Who selects them – you?'

'Who else?'

'Antoinette trusts your choice completely, of course.'

'Of course.'

'There is much more to this than you are prepared to reveal,' said Maurice, 'but I am not disposed to enquire into it further.'

'Good, then I will leave you.'

'Not so fast. You owe me something.'

'Owe you what?'

'Let us consider the facts for a moment. You arrange for me to see you naked in order to arouse my interest. You invite me to your bed. You sent the invitation, not I, yes? Then when I reach your bed, someone else is in it who calls herself Michelle but who is not. As I see it, you promised me yourself and your promise is as yet unfulfilled.'

'What nonsense!'

'Say what you like, there is a debt outstanding. A debt of honour. I would like it to be paid.'

'You can't be serious!'

'But I am.'

'Really, a joke is a joke but this has gone too far,' she said angrily and stood up to go.

'A word before you leave,' said Maurice, determined to

extract his revenge from the girl who had made a fool of him, 'there is a friend of your mother's on board this ship, Madame de Margeville.'

'That gossiping old hag! What of her?'

'She already has her suspicions. She has a keen nose, that one. If I let drop one word to her by accident, be sure that it will reach your mother's ear. That would not be the end of the world for you, but how would it affect Antoinette?'

'You pig!' Michelle stormed at him. 'You know that she depends on the rest of us.'

'So I am a pig. And you are a procuress, if we wish to be exact. We should be able to understand each other.'

'It is only a game Antoinette and I play – can't you see that? Where's the harm in it? You enjoyed yourself with her, didn't you?'

'Oh yes, I do not deny that. But this game of yours is not so innocent as you would have me believe. It is a game which inflates the egos of the Varans sisters at the expense of other people. Who thought of this game originally, you or Antoinette?'

'Mind your own business.'

'My impression is that your *poor blind sister* is possessed of more subtlety and imagination than you are. But that is not my business, as you remind me. I will come to the point of what is my business – will you take your clothes off now or will you leave?'

'I am leaving.'

Maurice stepped to the door and opened it wide for her.

'I shall be sitting next to Madame de Margeville at dinner this evening,' he said casually.

Michelle stopped to look at his face and eyes, attempting to read whether he was bluffing or not. His expression was implacable.

'Oh, very well then,' she said petulantly. 'Close the damned door and let's get it over with.'

'A wise decision. Now, if you will undress yourself, dear Michelle, we may proceed to settle our differences.'

She glared at him as if wishing him dead and at the bottom of the ocean, then turned her back to him while she removed

36

blouse and skirt.

'Don't think that you are going to enjoy this,' she flung at him over her bare shoulder.

'But I shall. Whether you do is a matter for you. The rest of your clothes, please.'

'This is rape, nothing less,' she insisted, making no move to disrobe further.

'If you prefer to see it in that light. To me it is an affair of honour. Please continue undressing.'

'Damn you to hell!' she swore and took off her lace-edged lingerie to afford him a view of her smooth young back and tight buttocks.

'You may keep your stockings on,' said Maurice magnanimously. 'Turn to face me, if you please.'

She turned abruptly, holding one arm across her small breasts to conceal them and her other hand flat over the join of her thighs.

'It was very different when you showed yourself to me in the mirror,' said Maurice, enjoying the view, such as it was, 'that was when you wanted something from me. Nothing was too much to further your plan then. The whole of your body was freely offered to me.'

'Get on with it, rapist!'

'Certainly. Perhaps you will be so good as to kneel on the carpet with your head and arms on that chair!

'Like dogs!' she exclaimed aghast. 'No, it is too much!'

'Very well, you may dress and leave. I am not keeping you here by force.'

'You are blackmailing me!'

'Correct.'

Her pretty face was distorted by the impact of strong emotions – hatred, anger, dismay – so that it became tight and ugly. Then her expression became sullen and she knelt by the chair, lying over it to expose her bottom to him.

'Enchanting,' said Maurice, removing his jacket and trousers.

He positioned himself behind her, his knees between hers to spread her thighs and allow him access.

She was no virgin, of course, but she was certainly not

37

sexually aroused and she would do everything she could to resist him and so spoil his revenge. Guessing that in advance, Maurice had prepared for the eventuality by obtaining from the liner's pharmacy a small jar of vaseline. It was while he was liberally anointing his stiff projection that Michelle, face hidden in her arms, sneered at him, 'Why this delay, pig? Do you intend to keep me in this ridiculous position the whole afternoon? What sort of rapist are you – have you lost your nerve?'

'Patience, my dear Michelle. My resolve is firm, I can assure you. This rare moment is not to be rushed.'

She gasped in shock as his thumbs touched the blonde-flossed lips between her thighs and pulled them apart. She gasped again as he split her soft peach with his slippery part and pushed in.

'No, no, no, I don't want to!' she protested shrilly.

'Dear girl, what we want and what we get in this life are not always the same,' said Maurice, pushing deeper, 'but for me, at this instant, they are!'

Once mounted securely, he rode her fast, the sweet savour of revenge exciting him as much as the bodily act itself. His hands were clenched on her buttocks, holding her fast to receive his strokes.

'No, no, no,' she cried again, 'finish, finish ... not that ... not that ...'

There was a different note in her voice, a note of horror and self-loathing as Maurice's firm thrusting awoke sensations in her which she did not want to experience in such circumstances. Her fingers were entwined in her own blonde hair, tugging at it in desperation.

'Not that, not that!' she repeated, her voice very shrill.

Maurice's well-greased thumb touched the small puckered orifice between her buttocks, lingered for a moment and drove in to the knuckle. Michelle moaned, whether in pleasure or in disgust he neither knew nor cared as the well-spring of delight flowed within him and he fountained his satisfaction into her shuddering body. She tried to pull away from him the instant she felt what was happening, but Maurice gripped her fast until he had completed his act of vengeance to the full.

When he released her and moved away, she scrambled up and dressed very quickly, her face red. Maurice sat in one of the armchairs, wearing only shirt and socks, content with what had been done.

'We're quits now,' he said, but she would not speak to him and slammed out of the door.

He looked for her in the dining-room that evening, but neither she nor her sister were there. He saw the two of them the next morning, sitting on deck in long chairs, with their mother and a man he took to be the father. They were wrapped in warm plaid blankets and sipping bouillon served from a trolley by a deck steward. He smiled to himself as he strolled past the family group and made no gesture of recognition.

After lunch he was in his state-room writing a letter to his wife Marie-Thérèse, telling her of the splendours of the *Ile de France* and mentioning that he had met a friend of Jeanne's on board, but certainly not mentioning the Varans family, when there was a tap at his door, exactly as the day before. Greatly surprised, he got up and opened it, to find Germaine de Margeville standing there in a pale pink towelling robe and a matching scarf wrapped round her head. As he stared in astonishment, she slipped in past him.

'I have been exercising in the swimming-pool,' she informed him.

'It's kind of you to call,' said Maurice, recovering his poise. 'Please sit down. May I offer you something?'

'Nothing, thank you. I can't stay long as I have an appointment with the hairdresser. I came as a friend to have a word with you in private, Maurice.'

'About what?'

Germaine opened her robe to display a tight-fitting swimsuit with a design of large pink flowers. She crossed her legs and Maurice noticed that her bare thighs were lean and taut, for all her years.

'A word to the wise,' she said, 'your interest has been caught by the Varans girls. No need to deny it – there are very few secrets on board a ship, especially to those of us who

39

cross the Atlantic often and know the way of things.'

'Forgive me, Madame, but even if what you say were true, I do not see how my interests can concern you.'

'Call me Germaine. Your interests concern me because I regard you as a dear friend. There are certain rumours – no more than whispers – about the Varans girls. I will not repeat them, but I have heard these whispers for some time now, at least a year. Why should any of this concern me, you ask? After all, who sleeps with whom is a question of personal choice, not of public morality. But you should understand that those two, the pretty one and the blind one, hunt together.'

'Can this be true?' Maurice said, worried about how much Germaine knew.

'I know it is true. They procure men for each other, one with her looks and the other with her appearance of helplessness. I could mention the names of two or three men of my acquaintance who have fallen into their little trap and been made to look foolish.'

'Very young men, surely.'

'Those girls are not interested in young men of their own age. They prey on mature men – men in your position. Be warned in good time, my dear friend, have nothing to do with them or you will live to regret it.'

'What you tell me is truly astonishing,' said Maurice.

It was in his mind that Germaine surely knew about him and the two girls. He did not put it past her to bribe stewards and other servants to obtain information. What did she want in return for her silence?

Germaine stood up as if to depart, her errand accomplished. Instead, she shrugged herself out of her pink robe and slipped the straps of her flowery swim-suit off her shoulders.

'A wet costume is so unpleasant,' she explained, 'do you mind if I take it off, Maurice?'

Whether he minded or not, she pulled the damp material down to her waist, hooked her thumbs into it and pushed it over her hips. Taken aback, Maurice sat pinned to his chair and observed her body emerge from the garment. Her breasts were very small and the years had caused them to droop hardly at all, though the pointing nipples had darkened in colour. Her belly was flat, her flanks lean. She had the body of a woman who exercised regularly and dieted constantly. The patch of hair at the fork of her legs was so small and even that Maurice guessed that she kept it trimmed.

'Forgive my inattentiveness,' he said, getting to his feet, 'I'll get you a towel.'

From the bath-room he brought one of the ship's huge fluffy towels and, with perfect aplomb, wrapped her in it completely.

'That's better,' she said. 'Have you ever noticed that it is always one's bottom which feels cold after swimming? Would you mind rubbing it dry for me?'

'I'd never noticed that,' he said, reaching round her with both arms to rub her small buttocks briskly through the towel.

He was not, he told himself, in the least interested in Germaine de Margeville's body, so openly offered to him. Yet the feel of her flesh through the towel shook his resolve. Before he could recover, she twisted in his arms and he found himself rubbing her lower belly.

'Lower,' she said, her hand pushing his down so that he was massaging her fleshy mound.

'That feels very good,' she sighed, her pink-scarfed head leaning back against his shoulder.

'Germaine, this is ...' but she interrupted his protest.

'Hush! I know what you are thinking, Maurice. The unexpectedness of this moment has bewildered you. But, you see, I have never been one for pretence. I follow the dictates of my heart without question.'

Her hands were behind her back, touching his thighs and then groping upwards.

'Ah, your bewilderment has not made you discourteous,' she said in satisfaction. 'Everything is as it should be.'

Maurice was casting about in his mind for a way of escaping her attentions without arousing her hostility. That might be very dangerous. Through his sister she could easily make the acquaintance of his wife. The smallest word about the Varans girls might well poison his loving relations with Marie-Thérèse. Reluctantly he concluded that the simplest course would be to give her the satisfaction she sought and preserve the appearances of friendship.

He led her into the bedroom quickly, threw back the pale blue coverlet and lay down with her. Her mouth was tight to his, open and sucking. Her eager fingers tore at the buttons of his trousers. Maurice enclosed her small breasts in his hands, his plan to do it quickly and be rid of her.

As to that, he need not have worried. The instant his full-grown staff was in her hands, she exclaimed, 'Let me do it!'

Then she was on top of him, her fingers busily effecting the conjunction she sought.

'Oh, that's heavenly!' she said.

She rode him strenuously, so much so that Maurice felt that he was being ravaged almost.

However bizarre his emotions in the turmoil of these extraordinary proceedings, nature took its course. As if of their own volition Maurice's hands clasped his rider by her lunging hips. Much sooner than he would have thought possible, he experienced the familiar burst of delight in his loins and the mattress bounced under him as he discharged violently upwards into his panting companion. Germaine's response was extravagant – her arms jerked straight, palms flat on the bed, lifting her upper body off him and pressing her belly hard to his, her pink-wrapped head rocked rapidly backwards and forwards and she yelped loudly.

Her rhapsody lasted longer than his. He lay below her, getting his breath back, observing the flip-flop of her small breasts as her head snapped to and fro and trying to distinguish words in her prolonged outcry.

He remained where he was after she climbed off him and went into the bath-room, flat on his back on the bed, seeking to cope with his disordered emotions. This woman he had met casually on the ship had forced herself on him to the point of raping him, for all practical purposes. It was not merely incredible – for a man like him the event was ludicrous in the extreme. He shook his head in disbelief and

42

glanced down at his exposed part, now limp and discarded.

Germaine came out the bath-room wearing her pink towelling robe.

'I am late for the hairdresser,' she announced. 'Au revoir, Maurice – perhaps we can slip away together for half an hour this evening after dinner.'

She bent over him to plant a tender kiss on his cheek and then departed.

'I swear to god that woman is a sorceress!' Maurice said out loud.

On the last day he was up on deck to watch the approach to New York and catch his first sight of the famous Statue of Liberty and the tall buildings of Manhattan. The tugs were in attendance to guide the great liner to its berth. A hand touched his arm and he became aware of Germaine standing beside him at the railing.

'I have enjoyed this voyage,' she said, smiling at him.

'It has been full of surprises,' he answered.

'We have shared moments of rapture, you and I, Maurice, in your state-room and on the boat-deck last night in the moon-light. How exquisite that was under the dark velvet sky, your dear hands on my bottom as I pressed you against a davit and drew you up into ecstasy with me. I am not a silly passive girl in these matters, as you have observed. My heart tells me to participate fully and I obey its promptings.'

'I have never known a woman to put such energy into the act of love,' said Maurice, 'or to achieve the pinnacle of joy so quickly.'

'Often and brief, that has always been my way. The same is true of eating, have you noticed? Long and heavy meals dull the appetite and are most unhealthy. Light meals at frequent intervals are much better for the metabolism. I am the proof – my figure is that of a young girl.'

'Proof indeed,' said Maurice, 'I congratulate you.'

'If only this voyage could last a few more days! I could teach you my ways and you would benefit enormously.'

Politeness required that Maurice took her gloved hand to kiss it lightly.

'When my husband's business in New York is concluded

he is going on to Brazil. But I shall be back alone in Paris by the end of next month. I shall await your call, dear Maurice.'

He bowed as she departed to make her preparations for disembarking.

Maurice's voyage back to France three weeks later was less eventful than the journey out, neither the Varans family nor Germaine being on board. To his surprise he found that his steward, the same Henri who had served him on the outward journey, treated him with dog-like devotion. Towards the end of the trip, with Le Havre less than a day away, he learned by chance the explanation from another passenger, a man who had crossed the Atlantic many times. It seemed that the pleasant custom of the first-class cabin stewards was to arrange a betting-pool among themselves, each putting in the same sum of money when the ship sailed. At the end of the voyage, the pool was shared out in proportion to successful claims. A claimant was one whose charges had slept with other passengers on board during the trip. In general, Maurice was told, twenty or thirty stewards shared the winnings among them, with one score each. Sometimes a passenger succeeded with two others, giving his steward a full half of the pool.

Maurice's score of three different women on the way to America had scooped the pool out-right for Henri. The rascally Corsican expected Maurice to repeat his performance and win the pool for him on the way home, but in this Maurice disappointed him sadly.

GERARD'S EXPLORATION OF POETRY

Not long after he had entered upon his studies at the
Sorbonne Gerard became greatly impressed by Surrealism.
This new form of anarchy in the arts was hatched in Paris
after the demise of Dadaism, a type of chaos perpetrated
upon civilised Europe by the humourless Swiss during the
War, when attentions were engaged elsewhere. The high
point of Gerard's student days was the publication of a so-
called poem by him in a hotch-potch review read only by
those whose brains had been addled by too much exposure
to the ravings of the self-styled poet Andre Breton and his
friends. Naturally, this triumph called for a suitable
celebration by Gerard and his companions.

Of course, after the War no one of intellectual pretention
went any more for cheap meals and drinks to Montmartre.
Business interests took over the area once associated with
painters of repute and turned it into a play-ground for
American tourists in search of 'local colour' or '*la vie
parisienne*' – by which they understood public spectacles of
lightly-clad young women and an over-abundance of
whores. Serious writers and painters migrated to the Left
Bank and congregated in the cafes of Montparnasse. It was
here that one could find from midmorning onwards, and
most especially in the evenings, the vast army of daubers and
scribblers who made Paris their home. Many of them were of
uncertain talent, it must be understood, but some few of
them have produced work which may survive.

Gerard's celebration of his artistic victory began in La
Rotonde, buying drinks for his circle of friends – perhaps
half a dozen young men of his own age and two or three girls
of doubtful origin who had been brought along. The party
grew larger as others drifted in and attached themselves to
the festivities. Towards midnight the whole group moved on
to an apartment in a small and ill-lit street somewhere
behind the Montparnasse railway station. Gerard was fairly

drunk by then. He had no certain idea of where he was and he had never before seen the young woman who had fallen asleep with her head in his lap.

A gramophone was blaring out American jazz and two or three couples were attempting to dance. The rest of the revellers were sitting about in earnest discussion of the meaning of meaning and similar important topics of interest to followers of Surrealism. Gerard, slumped in a corner with a happy smile on his face, took no more part in the proceedings. His evening had been a success in his estimation. He was content to doze off where he was until such time as he felt strong enough to stand up and get himself home.

The girl in his lap opened her eyes and announced that she was going to be sick. Gerard assisted himself to his feet by one hand against the wall and pulled the girl upright, or as upright as possible for one in her condition of malaise. They supported each other across the room, weaving in and out of the dancers, and out on to the dark landing. Good as her word, the girl was instantly sick over the banisters into the unlit stair-well.

'Good God,' said Gerard, 'I hope no one was below.'

'I feel awful,' said the girl, 'can you help me home?'

'Is it far?'

'Not very.'

They lurched down three flights of stairs, Gerard hanging on to the hand-rail and the girl hanging on to him. Outside it had begun to drizzle in the deserted street.

'Which way?'

She gestured vaguely and almost fell over.

'Where do you live?' he tried again.

After some moments of consideration she said 'Rue Varet.'

'Where's that?'

'Near the Vaugirard cemetery.'

'I don't know where that is. Let's walk as far as the railway station. We can find a taxi there.'

'Taxi! You're throwing your money about, aren't you?'

'Would you rather walk in the rain?'

The driver naturally over-charged him for the ride but

46

Gerard was in no mood to argue, as normally he would. He paid with one hand while supporting the sagging girl with the other.

'Is this it?' he asked. 'Which floor?'

'Top floor. The attics.'

'Give me your key.'

He propped her against the wall, stopped and let her collapse forward over his shoulder, then gripped her by the thighs, her head and arms trailing down his back. He was like a man attempting Mont Blanc on roller-skates as he tackled the seemingly endless stairs. By the time he reached the top landing and set his burden on the floor, where she subsided in a heap, he thought that he was about to die from the exertion. Eventually his breath returned, and with it some glimmer of purpose. There were two doors on the landing. He tried the nearest and heard a woman's voice scream '*Who's that?*'

'Sorry, wrong door,' he mumbled, turning to the other one.

'Get away from here you no-good drunk or I'll get the police to you,' the voice raved, 'I never want to see you again in my life, you rotten thieving pimp! You touch that door once more and I'll smash a bottle over your head!'

What sort of neighbourhood is this? Gerard wondered – she threatens to assault a perfect stranger doing her no harm whatsoever. The thought annoyed him. He turned back to the first door and eased the weight on his shoulder by resting the unknown girl's backside against the door.

'Madame,' he said firmly, or as firmly as his slightly slurred speech permitted at that point, 'I greatly resent the offensive tone of your remarks.'

Something smashed against the inside of the door, as if perhaps a plate had been thrown at it.

'Clear out, you scum!' the voice shouted.

'I can see that to argue with you is without purpose,' Gerard answered with all the dignity he could muster. 'Very well, I shall leave you to wreck the remainder of your domestic utensils in your own good time. I bid you goodnight.'

'Get away from that door or I swear I'll come out there and pitch you over the railings!'

Muttering to himself, Gerard carried the unconscious girl into the other room. In the darkness something hard-edged struck him on the knees and made him fall forward. He found himself face-down on a bed, much out of breath. After a moment or two's consideration he rolled the girl off his back and lay beside her to regain his strength for the journey home. He knew where he wanted to go, he did not know exactly where he was, except that it was in the vicinity of a cemetery. The means of getting from an unknown location to a known one were obscure to him. The matter required thinking out. But in a few minutes, while he was wrestling with the problem, Gerard passed out peacefully as a result of the combined effects of his celebration and his exertions.

It was the grey light of dawn falling through a skylight set in the sloping roof that awoke him. He found himself lying fully clothed on a low bed, listening to the light patter of rain on the glass. By his side was a sleeping girl. Only after prolonged effort did he recall how he had arrived in that position. He was pleased with himself. He considered that he had become part of the true artistic tradition, at last. He had got drunk in the company of fellow intellectuals, picked up a girl and gone with her to her room in ... wherever it was. He was unclear about that bit, but the smallness and lack of comfort of the room suggested that it was not in one of the better parts of Paris.

What a subject for a poem, he reflected! Or was it? In effect, he thought, it was more a poem in the tradition of Baudelaire than Breton. Never mind that, he could combine the two traditions into something so original that everyone would be amazed, he was sure of it.

There remained one thing to complete the experience before he could approach the task in the true artistic mood, and that was to sample the girl he had picked up. He sat up on the lumpy bed to inspect her. She was sleeping on her back, snoring lightly and looking very rumpled. Her bobbed hair was a mess and her apricot coloured frock was up round her thighs. Both stockings were badly laddered.

Her legs were thin, he noted, and her bosom fuller than was considered modish. Under her smeared make-up her face was round and her nose a little too broad. He guessed her to be about his own age, twenty, or not much more.

Not a great beauty, he told himself, but none the worse for that. It would be a mark of insincerity to look for a young lady of fashion in such a place. She is what she is and I am what I am. We are a man and woman together. Well then!

Emboldened by his line of thought, he stroked her exposed thigh tenderly.

She woke up and stared at him blearily.

'Who the hell are you?' she asked.

'My name's Gerard. I brought you home last night.'

'I can't remember a damned thing. Stop doing that!'

Her manner of speech was coarser than he was accustomed to hear, but it was part of her, he told himself.

'Tell me your name,' he said.

'Sophie. Where was I last night?'

'I'm not very sure where either of us were, but we drank a lot.'

'What's the time?'

'Early, I think. Does it matter?'

'What day is it?'

'Thursday. Why?'

'No reason. Why did you wake me up pawing my legs?'

'To talk to you.'

She climbed off the bed to make coffee, grumbling to herself under her breath. While the water was boiling she turned her back to him to strip off her bedraggled frock and stockings and enswathe herself in a thin wrapper of faded turquoise with a Chinese motif on the back.

'My God, I look a wreck,' she sighed, standing before an unframed mirror on the wall.

Gerard took off his wrinkled jacket, his tie and shoes and made himself as comfortable as possible on the bed as Sophie poured cold water into a wash-basin and removed the debris of her make-up from her face.

'Were you born in Paris?' he asked.

'No, in Bourges.'

49

'I've never been there.'

'It's a dead-and-alive hole. I couldn't stand it, so I left home. How about you?'

'My family has always lived here. I'm studying at the Sorbonne.'

Sophie poured coffee into two unmatched cups and gave him one. The brew was thin, black and bitter, but welcome after the night before.

'Drink that and clear off,' she said, 'I want to get back to bed.'

'Suppose we drink our coffee and both go back to bed,' he suggested.

'You've got a bed of your own to go to somewhere.'

'That's not the point, is it?'

'What do you mean?'

'I simply mean that I want to be in bed here with you, Sophie. I want to love you.'

'What the hell do you think I am?' she flared at him. 'A quick poke for anybody who fancies it? You think I'm a whore, is that it?'

'Good God, no!' he said, trying to calm her. 'You are an attractive and intelligent girl I met at a friend's apartment. It's only natural that I should be drawn to you.'

'You're all the same, you men,' she said bitterly. 'You want to grope a girl and stick it up her. Not with me you don't. I used to fall for that but I've learned better since.'

'Well said,' Gerard agreed, 'men like that are despicable. They have no respect for women, none at all.'

'What makes you so different?'

'I am a poet, a man of sensitivity ...'

He had said the wrong thing.

'Don't talk to me about poets! Dirty little scribblers who've never done a day's work in their life and never mean to. The last specimen I met who called himself a poet had lice!'

'Mademoiselle Sophie,' said Gerard, speaking very formally. 'I offer my apologies for presuming on your time and hospitality. If you will allow me a moment to dress, I shall remove myself from your apartment.'

50

'Apartment – this tatty little room? You're a comic, not a poet.'

Gerard donned his shoes and went to the mirror to put on his tie. He shook his jacket, hoping to remove some of the creases from sleeping in it. He was extremely polite.

'A thousand pardons, but do you have a clothes-brush I might use to make myself presentable before going out into the street?'

'Clothes-brush! Where do you think you are, the Ritz hotel? Wait a minute, let me see what I can do.'

She brushed at him with her hands to remove some of the bits sticking to his suit from her bed.

'That's a nice jacket,' she said, 'where did you buy it? One of the big stores, I bet.'

'It was made for me.'

'You're not hard up then, even if you are a student. Look, I'm sorry I shouted at you.'

'It is of no consequence.'

'You've a nice way of speaking. Do they teach you that at the Sorbonne?'

'No, at home.'

'Your home's a lot better than mine was, by the sound of it. Sit down a minute – how about a drop more coffee?'

'That would be very kind of you.'

'You're not really a poet,' Sophie said over her shoulder as she busied herself with the coffee cups. 'You're only playing at it while you're a student, not like the riff-raff you meet in cafes. What are you going to be when you finish studying?'

'A poet,' he said firmly.

'Yes, but seriously, what are you going to do for a living?'

'My father will arrange for me to join him in his business.'

'Be a pen-pusher? Is that what you want?'

'Not that sort of job,' he said quickly.

'I expect you mean the well-paid bit at the top,' she said, handing him half a cup of coffee. 'Do you think I'm attractive or were you just saying that, Gerard?'

'I never say things unless I mean them.'

'You weren't just after a quick bang?'

'I told you, I respect women. To me they are persons to be

51

cherished and adored.'

'Is that so? How do you go about this cherishing of yours?'

'Take your clothes off, Sophie. Show me your beautiful body and I will worship it and make you feel like a goddess.'

'Careful, you're beginning to sound like a poet.'

'Not all poets are animals, I assure you.'

'The ones I've met weren't much better.'

'There is only one way for you to find out, I suggest.'

'I strip off and you jump on me – is that it?'

'That's not it at all, I promise you. Trust me – you can always tell me to stop if you don't like what I'm doing.'

'I've heard that one before.'

'This time it is true.'

'I must be out of my mind to even listen to you,' she said.

All the same, she opened her old wrap and let it fall to the bare floor, pulled her slip over her head and stood naked for him. Gerard stayed where he was, sitting on the bed, while he studied her. She had a long neck set on square shoulders that were as wide as her hips. Young as she was, her breasts had lost their tautness and were a trifle slack. But it was the well-developed mound between her legs that fascinated him. Under a wispy patch of thin hair the lips were permanently parted by the overfull inner lips pushing through.

'Well, you've seen the lot now,' she said, 'say something.'

'You are a unique human being, Sophie. What I see is you, unlike any other person in the world. You are not a female thing to be used for a few moments of pleasure but a living and breathing person to be understood and loved.'

'That's nice. I hope you mean it.'

Gerard slipped off his jacket and tie and knelt in front of the standing girl to kiss her belly and then the secret place between her thighs. He used his tongue on it until she was sighing, her hands on his head to hold his face close against her. A few more moments and a long shudder ran through her body from loins to head and her finger-nails dug into Gerard's scalp.

'You must understand that you are an individual, Sophie, not a possession of another.'

52

'That's right,' she agreed enthusiastically, 'do it to me again.'

He laid her on the rumpled bed and sucked at her nipples, first lightly and then more strongly, his hands massaging her quaking belly. This time it took rather longer before the shudder manifested itself and her eyes rolled upwards. Before she had time to recover, Gerard moved his attentions further down, stroking with two fingers inside her hot place.

'You'll kill me off,' she murmured, 'don't stop.'

'Your body is made for love, Sophie.'

'I can never get enough – how did you know that?'

His fingers brought her to another speedy release.

'What an advantage you have over a man,' he said, 'I am almost jealous.'

'I've never found any advantage in it,' she said as he fondled a warm breast in each hand, rolling and squeezing them rhythmically until her eyes rolled upwards again.

'You really know how to handle me, Gerard. Get your clothes off and let's see what you've got.'

When he stood naked by the bed, she said, 'That's not a bad pecker. Lie down and let me have a feel.'

She handled him briskly, then took most of it into her mouth and used her tongue on it. He was compelled to pull away, fearing that she might deplete his resources too soon. To keep her busy, he rolled her onto her back and applied his fingers once more between her thighs.

'I'm going to ...' she moaned, 'ah ...'

He played with her for a long time, as a man plays a big fish on his line, slowing her down gradually, until she lay limp, her face and body shiny with sweat.

'I'm about finished,' she said. 'Stick it up me for God's sake.'

Gerard lay on her and went in to the hilt with a single push, the way being well-prepared.

'Now, Sophie, have I treated you like a proper human being?'

'You've killed me off,' she whispered, 'and it's marvellous. Do what you like to me.'

He took her at her word. He had become very excited in

53

the process of making her reach the point of ecstatic release so many times and so he had not long to go. Even so, she shuddered and moaned twice more before he reached the moment himself in a flurry of convulsive movement that drove him in so deeply that his pubic bones were thumping on hers.

Sophie fell asleep quite quickly after he dismounted. He dressed quietly and left to find a cab to take him home for a bath and breakfast. It was still only half past eight in the morning. After that he had important work to do, composing his new poem. Phrases were beginning to form in his mind.

He had no intention of seeing her again, of course. The experience was complete. Then one afternoon he was sitting alone at a table in La Rotonde, skimming through, over a cup of coffee, a book he was supposed to have read for his studies, when Sophie came in with a man he did not know. The moment she saw him she disengaged herself from her companion, who took the desertion casually, and sat down at Gerard's table to greet him like an old friend. He ordered coffee for her and they talked. Her manner was so welcoming that memories stirred in him and almost to his surprise he found himself taking her back to her room.

Their love-making took the same course as before. At the beginning he was somewhat detached, almost of the opinion that he was doing her a favour. Her enthusiasm kindled his in due course, so that the affair ended in great satisfaction to both of them. They were lying beside each other, resting after their exertions, when there was a tap on the door and a woman's voice asked, 'Can I come in now?'

To Gerard's astonishment, Sophie called out 'Come in' and he tried to conceal his naked body under the sheet as the door opened and a woman walked into the small room.

'This is my friend Adèle,' said Sophie, 'she has the room next to mine.'

'Enchanted, Mademoiselle,' said Gerard awkwardly, his middle scarcely covered by a corner of the sheet. This must be the person who had reviled him in the dark.

Adèle sat down on the foot of the bed and looked at him.

'You must be Gerard,' she said. 'It's nice to meet you at last.'

Like Sophie, Adèle was in her early twenties. She wore her short black hair in a fringe over her forehead and she was dressed only in a pink wrap-around dressing-gown that terminated at her bare knees. It was loosely tied round her waist, allowing the top to spread open and reveal much of her extensive bosom.

'I heard you through the wall,' she said to Sophie, 'you were really enjoying yourself. I got so worked up listening to you that I had to give myself a quick rub.'

Sophie lay on her back above the sheets, hands under her head and ankles crossed, naked and at peace with the world.

'Gerard's marvellous,' she said, smiling contentedly, 'he's about finished me off.'

'You're lucky. I've got nobody but that stupid Jacques and he's not up to much.'

'Have you been friends for long?' Gerard asked, unused to this sort of open conversation between women, 'you and Sophie, I mean.'

'Since she moved in here about two years ago,' Adèle answered, 'we're such good friends that we share everything.'

'Everything?'

'That's right. Why do you think I came in here?'

'I cannot imagine.'

'To see if Sophie would lend you to me now she's had you.'

'Mademoiselle Adèle, I am not a hat or a pair of stockings to be casually lent by one woman to another!'

'Don't take it badly. She went on about you so much the time you were here before that I had to see what you are like. She said she's never had anyone like you.'

'Is this true, Sophie?'

'Adèle and I always talk about men. I told her you're good in bed.'

'Should I be flattered?' Gerard asked doubtfully.

'Why not? How often does a woman you don't know stroll in and ask you to make love to her? You're not conceited are you?'

'Certainly not.'

'So what's all the fuss about? If you'd met her in a café and got talking and fancied her, you'd have wanted to get her into bed. What's the difference if she walks in here and says she fancies you? It comes to the same thing.'

'I can see I'm not wanted here, so I'll go,' said Adèle.

'Stay where you are,' said Sophie. 'Show him what you've got.'

Adèle, still seated on the bed, slipped off her loose pink wrapper to display large and heavy breasts and a broad belly.

'Good enough for you?' she asked.

'Forgive my lapse of manners,' said Gerard, 'it was caused by surprise, I assure you, nothing more. As Sophie said, for me it is an unusual occurrence for a good-looking young woman to make so frank an approach. I respect you for it, now that I am recovered from my initial surprise.'

'Doesn't he speak beautifully?' Sophie asked.

'If you will permit me ...' and Gerard sat up on the rumpled bed to imprint delicate kisses on Adèle's breasts.

'That's nice,' she said, 'I like your ways.'

She flicked away the corner of sheet from his middle and eyed his parts.

'Satisfactory?' he asked.

'It's how you use it that counts. I wouldn't mind giving it a try.'

'Then it will give me great pleasure to oblige you, if Sophie is agreeable. Shall we go to your room?'

'No, stay here and do it,' said Sophie, 'I want to watch. Besides, I expect I'll need it again myself before long.'

'Greedy cow!' said Adèle good-naturedly. 'Are you sure she hasn't worn you out already, Gerard?'

'I assure you that I am perfectly capable. The evidence is clearly presented to you.'

Adèle took hold of his risen penis and fondled it for a while.

'Seems all right,' was her verdict.

'Then perhaps you would care to lie down?'

They arranged themselves on the narrow bed, Adèle in the

middle. Novel though the situation was to Gerard, he felt instinctively that it held the possibility of yet more poetry in it, this time rather more *Dada* than Baudelaire.

Adèle's amatory style proved different from that of Sophie. She was slower to arouse, requiring extensive use of his lips and fingers on her breasts and thighs. He came to know the feel of her skin, the varying textures of it in the crook of her elbows, on her pillowy breasts, in the folds of her groins. He mapped her body, locating a mole on her left side where the crease of the breast started and another on her back, just above the swell of her buttock. He compared the soft dark hair in her armpits with the equally dark yet stiffer hair between her legs. He learned the regularity of her intense breathing when his fingers explored the slippery interior of her sexual channel.

When at last he was mounted, it was strange to see Sophie's face, eyes bright with curiosity, on the pillow next to Adèle's face. The act itself was prolonged to suit Adèle, who was not to be hurried like Sophie. Whenever he became impetuous she flung her legs over his and said 'Slow down!' and he restrained his movements to accomodate her. Her climax, once arrived at, was silent and deep. Her hot body quaked under him and her nails scored his back. Gerard released his brakes and rammed home in delight, ecstasy flashing through him like a bolt of lightning.

He enjoyed the favours of the two friends for about a month and then one evening after dinner at home he was summoned unexpectedly to a private talk with his father. It began ominously.

'Sit down, Gerard. I have to inform you of a serious matter that has been brought to my attention,' said Aristide Brissard, glaring at his youngest son.

'Indeed?'

'The evening before last you were observed in the Hotel Claridge by an acquaintance of mine. You were accompanied by two women of a certain type.'

'That is not true, Papa.'

'You deny it?'

'I was there, certainly, but the young women with me were

57

friends, not prostitutes, as you implied.'

Aristide's thick eyebrows bristled.

'You have strange friends.'

'None of my friends are police spies at least.'

'Do not be insolent, Gerard, it is I who am talking to you. What were you doing there with these *friends?*'

'In brief, I was saying goodbye to them.'

'Would not a cheap bar have been more appropriate than an expensive hotel?'

'You must understand that they are both very poor,' said Gerard. 'A touch of luxury as a parting gift seemed to me to be very appropriate in the circumstances. They were delighted and thoroughly enjoyed the entire stay.'

'Stay? They stayed in the hotel? An expensive hotel in the Champs Elysées?'

'Why yes. I reserved a suite for the night. What would you? They found it most agreeable. Can you believe that neither of them had ever seen a proper bathroom before?'

'Let me understand you – you took them there so that they could have a bath?' Aristide exclaimed incredulously.

'That was only the beginning. We got into the bath together with a bottle or two of champagne and it was most amusing. After that we went to bed, of course.'

'You went to bed with both of them?'

'They are very good friends, those two,' said Gerard, surprised by his father's reaction.

'Listen to me. We shall speak to each other not as father and son but as one man to another. You are not a child, Gerard, you are grown up and have the normal instincts of a man. That I accept – even applaud. But you must understand that episodes such as you have described with women of that sort are out of the question.'

'But why is that?' Gerard asked curiously. 'After all, I am still a student. It is almost expected of me to engage in antics which might be unbecoming in someone older and perhaps married.'

'I do not dispute that. Students have certain privileges. If you had found your way into the bed of a married woman and the fact became known, everyone would smile behind

58

their hand and no more would be said. But you must be aware that the type of women with whom you are indulging yourself are in all probability careless in the matter of precautions against undesirable conception. Do I make myself clear? Suppose for a moment that you had impregnated both of your friends during your frolics in the Hotel Claridge. What then?'

'Good God!' Gerard exclaimed, aghast, 'I never thought of that.'

'Then think of it now. What would you do in such circumstances?'

'It would be necessary to recompense them for the inconvenience. That could be expensive.'

'Let us be precise. It would be necessary for *me* to recompense them on your behalf, isn't that so?'

'What can I say, Papa? I have been thoughtless and imprudent.'

'Then you will end this bizarre double affaire at once?'

'As to that, it is ended already. I told you truthfully that the night at the hotel was a goodbye present to Sophie and Adèle.'

'Good. Should you receive any unwelcome communications from either of them in the next month or so, refer the matter to me. Do not attempt to deal with it yourself. Is that understood?'

'Absolutely.'

'Now, for the future – it will be better if you pay your respects to another type of woman. Do you follow me?'

'Most certainly. Do you have anyone in mind?'

'It is not for me to procure for you! You are a young man of initiative and enterprise. Paris is full of pretty women. Need I say more?'

'But I would be grateful for a word of guidance from you on this subject. Having displeased you once over the matter of Sophie and Adèle, it would be unthinkable to annoy you again.'

Aristide beamed at his son.

'Your care for my feelings is admirable. Well then, let me think ... how do you regard Madame Lombard? You have made her acquaintance at your sister Jeanne's receptions. She is an attractive woman and her husband pays little attention to her, his affections being engaged elsewhere.'

'She is somewhat too old for my taste,' said Gerard, 'she is well over thirty. And apart from that disadvantage, she wears corsets to disguise the sag of her belly and backside.'

'I am sure that she does no such thing!'

'I can assure you that she does, Papa. I have assisted her in removing them on two separate occasions.'

Aristide pulled at his bushy moustache and gave his son a hard look.

'Your initiative has evidently taken you further than I imagined,' he said. 'Very well, if poor Madame Lombard is disqualified on the grounds of age and corsets, have you considered Madame Cottard as a companion? She can't be more than twenty-five. And her figure is as slim as a boy's.'

'But you can't be serious! Charles would be extremely angry with me if I forgot myself sufficiently to make overtures towards Madame Cottard.'

'Your brother Charles? Do you mean to say that he and she …'

'For a long time. At least a year. I thought that everyone knew that.'

'This modern generation!' Aristide grumbled, 'I do not understand any of my own children. They are strangers to me. It must be that I am getting old.'

'Not in the least! After all, we only do what you did at our age. And if vague rumours are to be believed about your regular visits to a certain lady who lives not far from the Bois de Boulogne …'

'Be silent! Do not speak of matters which do not concern you and which you are unable to understand. Where did you hear these vile rumours?'

'From one of my brothers, Papa, but I shall not tell you which one. Your private affairs are safe, believe me.'

'How can that be so if I am the subject of malicious gossip by my own children?'

'Not malicious, Papa. The matter was mentioned most discreetly and with admiration and respect.'

'Admiration, eh? Is that true?'

'I give you my word.'

'And respect?'

'Great respect. Your sons are proud of you.'

'In that case we will let the matter drop. I shall be obliged if you will not mention it to anyone else. Now, as to your concerns, if your preference is for young women of your own age, what do you think of the daughter of my friend and colleague Saint-Rochat?'

'Eugénie? Yes, she is very pretty.'

'She is more than pretty, she is enchanting. What more could a man ask? She has blonde hair, a good figure and a vivacious manner. If I were thirty years younger I should be most interested in her.'

'What you say is true,' said Gerard, wrinkling his forehead, 'unfortunately there is a problem. For all her charms, Eugénie is not responsive.'

'You mean that you have already invited her to go out with you and she has declined, is that it? Isn't it a question of persuasion, if you like her?'

'No, we have been around together quite a few times to restaurants and concerts.'

'Then what do you mean by saying that she is not responsive?'

'I mean simply that in bed she lies limp and inactive and that this is unrewarding to a person of spirit, as you can well imagine. Afterwards she often weeps a little.'

Aristide's face flushed dark red.

'What! Are you informing me that you have debauched my old friend's daughter?'

'You told me that we were conversing as adults,' Gerard reminded his father in alarm, 'would you prefer me not to be truthful with you?'

'No,' said Aristide, controlling himself. 'But little Eugénie – she is only nineteen years old!'

'Yes, but even so *debauch* is a strong word, Papa.'

'Then which word would you have me use?'

Gerard shrugged.

'I was not her first lover,' he said, 'there were two before me that I know of.'

'Enough,' said his father, 'I wish to hear no more about the girl. Nor about your amorous escapades. It is ridiculous for me to even consider offering advice to so experienced a person as you obviously are. Listen to me well – there are two things I require from you. The first is attention to your studies. The second is discretion. Is that agreed?'

'But of course,' said Gerard, smiling at his father in filial devotion.

ARMAND GOES VISITING

For his first visit to the home of Madame de Michoux Armand dressed with even greater care than usual, to make the best impression on her. He had met her by chance the day before, drinking an aperitif with Jeanne Verney on the terrace of the Café de la Paix. He guessed that they had been window-shopping in the Place Vendôme and the rue de la Paix. He was instantly attracted to Jeanne's smartly-dressed friend and this must have been obvious in his face for Jeanne had a knowing look in her eyes as she introduced him to Gabrielle de Michoux.

Armand and Jeanne had been friends for a long time. Indeed, they were lovers for nearly two years and though that was past, they still liked each other. Armand was certain that he had been her first lover after her marriage, for she had been as inexpert as a virgin at their first intimate encounter. All that had changed for the better, naturally, under his guidance. Their affaire terminated when she found herself pregnant – by her husband she said, though of that there was no proof.

Knowing something of the ways of women, Armand concluded after his departure from the café terrace that Madame de Michoux would be fully informed by Jeanne of his skill as a lover, his physical abilities and his entertainment value in bed.

For the occasion of his visit he wore his newest attire – a double-breasted suit in silver grey, the jacket cut by a master tailor's hand to fit closely to his body. With this went a polka dotted bow-tie and a pink carnation in his button-hole – the ensemble topped by an expensive grey homburg hat. When he took stock of himself in a long mirror before leaving home, he was pleased by his appearance. He felt that he looked stylish and yet with a hint of reserve. This seemed to him important in that Gabrielle de Michoux was evidently a most modern young woman, yet the touch of old-fashioned values might well be appreciated by a woman who had undergone tragedy so early in life. She was a war widow, as were so many young French women.

After his careful planning, imagine his surprise when the maid who answered the door told him that Madame was not at home.

'But that's impossible. She invited me to call this afternoon.'

'I am sorry, Monsieur. Madame must have mistaken the day. Who shall I say called?'

'I shall leave a note for her.'

'Certainly. Please come in.'

Beyond the door was a parquet-floored hall with a side-table against one wall. Armand put his beautiful grey hat on the table while he wrote carefully on the back of one of his calling-cards: *I am extremely sorry that I missed you. I shall give myself the pleasure of telephoning you tomorrow before noon.*

He handed the card to the maid who glanced at it and said, 'I am desolated that you have been disappointed, Monsieur Budin.'

The words were conventional enough, it was the way she said them that gave them another significance to one sensitive to shades of meaning. Armand looked at her carefully for the first time. He saw a fresh-faced woman in her late twenties, her personality concealed behind the discreet uniform. But a closer inspection revealed that the frilly cap did not entirely hide her glossy hair, nor did the plain black frock and trim apron wholly disguise the prominence of her bosom. She was aware of his scrutiny, as women always are, and when he looked back to her face she was smiling at him in a manner which might have been interpreted as distinctly inviting by a man who knew about such things, as Armand did.

'What is your name?' he enquired, stroking his pencil-line moustache with one finger-tip.

'Claudine.'

'As you say, it is most vexing, Claudine, to find Madame not at home. It is disappointing in the extreme. More than that, it is frustrating.'

'There's nothing worse than to see a gentleman's intentions frustrated by a simple error,' she said with sympathy in her voice. 'Unfortunately, Madame said that she would not return until late tonight. I hardly know what to suggest.'

The way in which her breasts rolled under her clothes as she took a short step towards Armand implied that she knew perfectly well what to suggest, if it were her place to do so.

'Your visit to Madame was to be a special one, was it?' She asked with warm interest.

'Why yes, I was looking forward to the pleasure of her company for an hour or so while we discussed certain matters together.'

'If only there were some way I could think of to assist you.'

'Perhaps there is though,' said Armand, touching his moustache again.

'What do you mean, Monsieur Budin?' She asked, her eyes downcast in simulated innocence. 'You are kind to say so, but my conversation is surely a poor consolation for that of Madame.'

'You must not disparage yourself, Claudine. Your conversation is most enjoyable, I find. In fact, I would describe it as stimulating.'

'Evidently,' she replied, glancing briefly at the growing bulge in his trouser-leg. 'Is there anything more I can do to be of service to you?'

Armand could hardly believe his good fortune. The moment was one to seize.

'I believe there is,' he said, taking a step towards her in turn, 'unless I am interrupting you in important household duties.'

'Not in the least. Everything is in order and I am at liberty until Madame returns late tonight.'

'Do you know, I am enchanted by the neatness of your clothes, Claudine. If you will permit me ...'

He unfastened the top corners of her starched apron from the upper slopes of her bosom. The frock beneath was closed by a row of buttons from neck to waist.

'I thought so,' he said lightly, 'buttons on women's clothes have always fascinated me. They invite such immediate speculation. They cause the fingers to itch to undo them.'

'Really? I would never have thought of that.'

He undid the buttons slowly from the top, counting them aloud until he reached the last one, not far above her waist.

'Buttons or not, it is difficult to see how my clothes can possibly be of interest to you,' she said, her eyes shining.

'The interest lies in what they conceal, as I am sure you know well.'

'And what do they conceal?'

Armand's hand was inside her frock, down her chemise, fondling a soft breast.

'Your prim black clothes conceal a delicious pair of attractions, Claudine.'

'Concealed these attractions may be but they seem to have a remarkable effect on you,' and she slid her hand slowly up and down the tell-tale bulge in his trousers to prove her point.

'Not remarkable in the sense of unusual,' he said, 'but remarkable in the sense of noteworthy, if I may clarify matters for you.'

'Thank you for putting me right on that,' she said, grinning at him.

For some time they remained as they were, each gently exploring the other's advantages, almost like a pair of lovers in an eighteenth century painting. Under Armand's hand her breasts were delightful to the touch, playthings of quality and worth. Under her hand his masculine distinction was at full stretch and glowing with pleasurable sensation.

'There is something else you can do to be of service to me Claudine,' he murmured at last.

'Willingly. What is it?'

'If you would turn around and lean on the hall table ...'

She turned her back to him and put her hands flat on the marble top of the small console table, her feet well apart. Armand pulled up her skirt at the back and tucked it into the bow of her apron strings.

'Excellent. I am most obliged, Claudine. Bend forward a

little if you please.'

He slipped her white cotton knickers down her legs as she leaned over to put her forearms on the table top and stuck out her rump towards him. It was a rump to make a man's heart beat faster, round, plump, smooth-skinned.

'Is that all you require?' Claudine asked with a chuckle in her voice.

'Not quite all,' Armand answered, a little breathlessly, as well he might be at the charming spectacle presented to him for his delectation.

He ran his hands over the twin melons of flesh and squeezed them.

'Then there is something more that you want?' She persisted.

'As you will see, Claudine.'

He unbuttoned his tight jacket and his trousers, released his pent-up stem and inserted it between her thighs.

'Ah yes, there is more,' she exclaimed as he pushed slowly.

Then as he took her by the hips and sank in deep, she said, 'Much more than I expected!'

'But not more than you are willing to accept?' He asked.

'Why no – I am completely at your service, Monsieur Budin.'

Armand held her fast as he rocked to and fro in great content. To the devil with Madame de Michoux, he was thinking as pleasurable sensations permeated his body – what more could she have offered me than I am obtaining from her maid? There is an old and wise saying to the effect that all cats are grey in the dark.

He would have continued his slow ride indefinitely, enjoying matters as they were, but he reckoned without the effect he was having on Claudine. She was a young woman of strong instincts and natural response and before long she began to jerk her bottom against him in her eagerness, driving him deeper. And as the tide of passion rose in her, she jerked faster and harder. As was only to be expected, under this vigorous treatment Armand's self-control quickly disappeared and his crisis of delight arrived all too soon. As he flamed into ecstasy he clung on to Claudine's bucking hips like a rider to a runaway horse. For her part she continued to beat away at him after he had finished, until she reached the point she would be at, which she announced by squealing loudly.

After she had quietened down Armand slid away from her and tucked his now quiescent part into his trousers. Claudine arranged her clothes decently and turned to face him, her cheeks still flushed.

'I hope that your visit was not a complete disappointment after all,' she said.

'It has been quite delightful. You have been most obliging and I am truly grateful.'

He pressed a bank-note into her hand.

'It would please me if you bought yourself some pretty underwear, Claudine. The attractions concealed by your clothes should be cosseted in silk.'

'It is good of you to say so, especially as you have had only the briefest glimpse of those attractions you seem to admire so much.'

Armand considered the proposition.

'True enough – the confines of this entrance hall put definite restrictions on a really extensive inspection of the charms hidden by your clothes,' he said. 'When did you say you expected Madame to return?'

'Not until late this evening.'

'Then perhaps we have time to improve our acquaintance in more comfortable surroundings.'

'Plenty of time. Would you care to see my room?' she asked.

'Nothing would give me greater pleasure.'

Claudine's room was small but very well-kept. It contained a narrow wooden bed as its main item of furniture and an old-fashioned wardrobe. While Armand watched, Claudine stripped off her clothes and lay down on the bed. The tufts of hair under her arms, he observed as she put her hands behind her head and smiled at him, exactly matched in colour the fleece between her legs.

'The bed is not very wide,' she said, 'but so much the better.'

'Yes,' Armand agreed as he started to undress, 'we shall be

compelled to lie very close together. So long as it is strong enough to bear the weight of two people ...'

'Have no anxiety on that score,' she answered with a grin, 'I can guarantee it.'

'I am sure that it has been thoroughly tested, Claudine, so far as its weight-bearing capacity is concerned. What about its ability to withstand really vigorous movement?'

'As to that, we shall see,' she answered as he lay down beside her and took her in his arms.

Gabrielle de Michoux telephoned him the next morning to apologise for her absence. She gave an account of a friend calling unexpectedly with a new car and insisting that she went for a drive in it.

'What sort of car?' Armand enquired, 'anything special?'

'Ah, such a machine! It was a sports car from Hispano-Suiza, shaped like a bullet and with coachwork of the most elegant tulipwood.'

'Fast, I have no doubt.'

'Of an incredible velocity. To ride in it was like being in an airplane.'

'Did you go far?'

'All the way to Deauville,' she said, 'it was quite insane. Deauville out of season – can you imagine!'

I have a serious rival for her affections, Armand thought as she prattled on, doubtless she passed the night with him at Deauville or perhaps in some small hotel on the return journey. I doubt that she has been home more than an hour or so. Yet why should that surprise me? So very charming a woman must necessarily have a number of admirers and one lover for sure. It may be that I have to dislodge this person, whoever he may be. Now I understand why she was not there for our meeting yesterday after she had asked me round – this type with the expensive vehicle has priority over me. That must be changed, and quickly. And yet my afternoon at her home was by no means wasted, even though she was risking her neck in some ridiculously fast car. To be truthful, Claudine had unexpected qualities in ways of entertaining men.

Gabrielle invited him to call on her the next day at about three, promising that this time there would be no diversions and that she really would be at home. He was pleased that she had suggested the following day and not that very afternoon. He was fully able to fulfil a man's obligations, of course, but there was a possibility that after his enthusiastic romp with Claudine he might be not quite at his best so soon. Tomorrow he would be at his peak again. Even so, his pleasure at the thought was tinged with a faint trace of jealousy at the realisation that Gabrielle also wanted a day off to recover from whatever had taken place between her and her insane motorist.

At the appointed time a smiling Claudine greeted him at the door.

'Madame is expecting you. This way, please.'

'Have you been on your little shopping expedition yet, Claudine?'

'Not yet. My day off is tomorrow.'

The decor of the drawing-room was stunningly modern, causing Armand to revise his preconceived view of the lady he was calling on. Like an exotic jewel in an intricate setting, Gabrielle lay face-down, her chin supported on one hand, amongst a dozen silver cushions on a vast semi-circular divan. Her slender body was encased in black silk lounging pyjamas. She turned languidly on to her side and extended a bare arm towards him so that he could kiss her hand and he saw a coiled silver snake embroidered on the front of her pyjama tunic.

'My dear friend,' she greeted him, 'I hope that you have forgiven me. Sit here,' and she patted the cushions by her head.

They talked for a while, behaving much like fencers sizing each other up with a pass or two of the foils before the real bout was joined. Each of them knew quite well what was going to happen. They had met to examine each other's possibilities for entertainment. Perhaps the meeting would prove to be no more than a casual exploration which neither would wish to continue. Perhaps it would prove otherwise. Armand at that time was without a regular companion and so for his part he had hopes that he would find Gabrielle on closer acquaintance to be sufficiently enchanting to make him wish to persevere with a longer affaire – though a non-committal one, naturally. He knew what he was looking for – a woman with a sophisticated style in love-making and the wit to be a stimulating companion in public. Gabrielle might meet that specification. At the same time he could guess what she was looking for – the same as he was and something more. He had the impression from Jeanne Verney, to whom he had talked on the telephone since their meeting at the Café de la Paix, that Gabrielle lived somewhat beyond her income and in consequence appreciated a man whose means could command the standards she enjoyed.

In a sense she had him at a slight disadvantage at this first private meeting. He was quite certain that she had questioned Jeanne about him in detail – his way with women, his intimate preferences. These were matters which Jeanne understood from her own experience with him when they were lovers. About Gabrielle's tastes in love-making he was totally uninformed. Nevertheless, his natural confidence assured him that the advantage must lie with him as a man. And so, since providence has endowed women with more natural advantages than men, there were surprises in store for Armand.

Gabrielle's elbows were on the cushions and her face in her hands. She had a heart-shaped face framed in short auburn hair. Her eyes were blue-green, her mouth red and mobile. Taking a hint from her expression, Armand put his hands on her shoulders and bent to kiss her lips. Through the silk of her black pyjama tunic his finger-tips encountered warm flesh that set his heart beating.

When he released her she rolled slowly on to her back, her head in his lap, her blue-green eyes staring up at him with a distant expression. She blinked as his hands cupped her small breasts through the black silk.

'Ah, now it begins,' she said in a tone of quiet reproach.

'Why, what do you mean, Gabrielle? You said that very sadly. Is something wrong?'

'Sad? That is not an appropriate word for what I feel. You

71

do not understand.'

'What is it that I am to understand?' he asked, rolling her nipples under the soft silk.

'This dreadful affair of physical passion – we are never free of it!'

'I hope not,' said Armand, 'but why do you call it dreadful? It has never been that in my experience – quite the contrary. I have always regarded it as a most civilised pleasure.'

'Civilised? This banal affair of touching and holding? This animality of skin rubbing against skin? And for what final result? For a moment or two of senseless convulsion, no more than that. It is not possible for anyone to describe that as civilised.'

She spoke most discouragingly, but she made no attempt to remove Armand's caressing hands from her breasts. Indeed, at the conclusion of her tirade her head turned in his lap so that her cheek was pressed to his thigh. It was then that Armand began to understand that she played to an unfamiliar set of rules of her own. He found the idea intriguing.

'Surely, men and women are the products of civilisation,' he said, slipping off his jacket. 'And civilisation is the product of men and women. This is indisputable.'

The words meant nothing at all but it was necessary to give her something to respond to so that she could continue her game and perhaps give him an opportunity to deduce what the rules were. He rearranged his legs imperceptibly in such a way that Gabrielle's cheek was pressed against the growing firmness inside his trousers. She trembled and said:

'What can be more deplorable than this abuse of the body and the mind?'

'Abuse is a strange word, Gabrielle for something so natural. You must justify it if I am to accept it.'

He eased her pyjama tunic up from her waist to reveal her breasts. They were extremely well shaped and small, as fashion demanded. His fingers played gently over her nipples, awakening them.

'One must consider the full potentiality of men and

women,' she said tremulously. 'The nobility of which we are capable, the extraordinary greatness of the human spirit – and then, if one contemplates the unspeakable waste of frittering all this away in the mindlessness of sex ...'

Her words trailed away in little sighs of pleasure at what he was doing to her.

Armand wrenched off his shoes and lay beside her on the divan so that he could kiss her face and hair while he stroked her breasts.

'You have no answer to that,' she murmured.

'But of course I have. You overlook so much in your judgment. Consider the finest writers and artists and composers of today – and of centuries past – can you deny that they returned again and again without fail to the spring of delight in their own nature in order to inspire their work? Tell me of one who was truly celibate.'

There might well have been many, he thought, but it is to be hoped that she will not know of them.

'You are wrong, wrong,' she sighed as he kissed her nipples. 'If there is any truth at all in what you suggest, then they allowed themselves to be diverted occasionally from their true greatness by the brute instincts of the body. If only they could have controlled themselves better, if they could have remained for the whole of their lives undefiled, how much greater they would have been.'

An interesting thought was running through Armand's mind – the comparison between maid and mistress. Claudine had pressed her services on him without stint, Gabrielle seemed intent on withholding hers. Claudine had commenced by offering him a well-rounded bottom. What had her mistress to offer in that department?

He sat up and rolled her unresistingly on to her face on the silver cushions. Her black silk pyjama trousers came down easily. so too did the flimsy garment of crêpe-de-Chine beneath them.

The categorisation of women's bottoms had always been a subject of interested study to Armand. There was, he believed, a corellation between shape and size and the owner's character. Claudine's had been full and wide, two

73

bouncy melons of pliable flesh. When he pleasured her from behind, standing up in the entrance hall, she had swung its abundance against him so heavily that he had been swiftly beaten into final gratification. On her narrow bed later on, he had climbed aboard her and put his hands under her to grasp those globes firmly.

Another and most fascinating type was that of the woman whose thighs were slender and did not press together on their inner surfaces, so leaving the furry mound fully exposed, whether viewed from front, rear or beneath. Jeanne Verney came within that category and Armand's theory was that a bottom shaped to reveal all was the sign of a natural sensualist. There were indications that this was true of Jeanne, in spite of her lack of experience. No doubt some other fortunate man was by now reaping where Armand had sown.

A bottom that jutted sharply outward, though completely unfashionable and no doubt an embarrassment to the woman who dressed in style was, nevertheless, an object of pleasure to Armand. Once released from whatever means of confinement were used to supress its natural joie de vivre, the cheeks fitted well into a man's hands and afforded much innocent enjoyment.

Gabrielle's rump was lean and taut, narrow in width and impertinent. A bottom of distinction and refinement, he thought, indicative of those self-same qualities in its owner. He grasped the cheeks in his hands and squeezed hard, enchanted by what he had uncovered. Gabrielle gave a little cry, but whether of protest or pleasure it was impossible to judge. He bit both cheeks gently.

'Ah, such depravity,' Gabrielle exclaimed, 'this is intolerable.'

Armand kissed where he had bitten.

'The heart is a truer guide for the soul and the intellect,' he said, 'the heart has its reasons that the mind does not understand.'

'Never,' she retorted as his hand probed delicately between her thighs to seek the natural portal for his next intended move, 'never – you are distorting the words of a famous thinker for your own purposes and that is infamous.'

'I am interpreting his words in the light of human experience,' he answered, stripping off her lower garments completely to allow himself easy access. He caressed the insides of her thighs until they moved apart of their own accord.

Gabrielle's face was buried in the silver cushions and her voice was muffled when she retaliated.

'Debauchery can always excuse itself.'

'Of debauchery I know nothing,' said Armand, lowering his trousers. 'But of the loving relations between men and women I can speak from my own experience and in all sincerity.'

'Words, empty words!'

'We need not content ourselves with mere words. A practical demonstration of what I mean may well convince you of the truth.'

He raised her with one hand to push a cushion under her belly and so lift her enticing rump. For some moments he explored and caressed its curves while Gabrielle hid her face deeper in the cushions. Armand lay over her back, reached between her legs and effected an uncomplicated entrance. His hands slid up under her body to take hold of her breasts.

'This shocking molestation ...' she moaned, 'it is insufferable ...'

Her small bottom was moving against him in time with his own movements, even as she complained. Armand went to work briskly, his imagination stirred by her pretence of reluctance. His curiosity was aroused as to what her reaction would be at the critical moment towards which he was impelling her by his firm strokes. He wondered if either her indignation or her vocabulary would prove adequate to the final outrage.

'No, no, no,' she was gasping to the rhythm of their combined movements.

'Yes!' Armand exclaimed as the turbulence of his released desire surged extravagantly through him and into her.

Gabrielle screamed, her clenched hands beating the cushions, her body convulsing under him. At the peak of emotion she had run out of words.

Later, when they were lying side by side on the divan, her face against his chest, he pursued the matter further.

'My dear Gabrielle, I hope that you were convinced by my little demonstration.'

'You deceive yourself, my poor friend,' she answered. 'All that you have convinced me of is the truth of what I said to you earlier.'

'You said so many things, my dear. Which one in particular?'

'That the grandeur of the human spirit is squandered in the sort of unbridled display of degradation to which you have submitted me. Your behaviour to me has been entirely reprehensible.'

'Not in the least. My actions have been in accordance with the promptings of my heart. How can that be reprehensible? Do you deny the value of the generous human emotions?'

'You confuse yourself with words, Armand, and you try to confuse me. But I am able to see through your deception. I fear that you are blind to the truth.'

'In what way?'

'You advanced as examples the great writers and painters even while you were in the preliminary stages of abusing my body. You spoke of the masterpieces they have created and your hands were violating the privacy of my intimate parts. Where was the sincerity in what you said? After all, masterpieces have their origin in the soul and in the mind, not elsewhere.'

'And in the heart, you must agree.'

'Very well, in the heart too.'

Her hand had found its way inside his shirt and a finger was rubbing his left nipple.

'Here is your heart, Armand,' she said, 'I feel it beating under my hand.'

She raised her head to kiss his forehead.

'And here is the seat of your mind,' she said.

'Then what follows from that?'

Her hand was gone from his chest. It burrowed inside his still unfastened trousers and took hold of his limp part.

'You mistake one thing for another,' she answered, kissing his eyelids. 'Tell me now, is this your heart that I have in my hand or is it your mind?'

'Neither.'

'Exactly. You cannot answer me without exposing the falsity of your argument. Your shameless actions towards me were inspired neither by your mind nor by your heart. What you did was prompted by *this* disgraceful organ. Isn't that so?'

The manner in which she was fondling it caused it to lengthen and grow hard in her palm. The development was entirely acceptable to Armand, who felt that he was beginning to perceive the rules by which Gabrielle played her little game.

'I cannot agree with what you say, Gabrielle. It is obvious to me that the confusion, if there is any, is on your part. You are mistaking ends and means. When I tell you that you are a charming and adorable woman, it is my tongue that speaks the words, though the sentiment comes from my heart and is formulated by my mind.'

Her hand was moving up and down his fully-extended part with dexterity that indicated long practice. Her words were at odds with her actions.

'That sounds like mere sophism, Armand.'

'Quite the contrary, it is self-evident. My tongue expressed the compliment but it was not my tongue's compliment. In exactly the same way, as you cannot fail to agree, the part of me which you described as disgraceful is but another organ of expression. The compliment is the same, though delivered in a different way.'

He eased her on to her back and removed her black pyjama tunic so that she lay utterly naked on the silver cushions. His hand was between her legs, stroking the delicate inlet that had welcomed him before.

'But this is atrocious,' she said as he probed gently for her hidden bud,' is this degeneracy to have no end?'

'When you accept the force of my argument,' said Armand, watching tiny shudders of pleasure running along the skin of her belly and thighs.

77

Her eyes were closed, her face calm, but the rest of her was not. Her fingernails were digging into the cushions. Her legs were trembling. Her breasts rose and fell to her agitated breathing.

This time, Armand promised himself, this time I shall see your face at the final moment – I will not let you conceal it from me in the cushions, my lustful prude. At last I have the measure of you.'

He was between her thighs, his sturdy extension comfortably pouched where he desired it to be.

'I cannot believe that this bestiality is occurring,' Gabrielle murmured.

Armand's movements were impetuous but he required longer this time to attain the peak to which he was climbing. Gabrielle writhed under him the whole time, her eyes closed firmly. Her body shook more and more furiously in the throes of passion, whatever may have been passing through her mind. Never for a moment did her hands leave the cushions and reach for Armand to hold him close, even though her loins were jerking with his to force a profound penetration.

At the moment of his discharge Armand saw her eyes open wide and bulge a little as she again uttered her climactic cry – a sound like the tearing of silk. Her body arched off the cushions to thrust frantically against him at that moment and she was carrying the weight of his body on her shoulder-blades and feet.

When she fell back limply, her eyes closed again, Armand grinned and said, 'But you are adorable, Gabrielle.'

After that day both of them wished to continue the friendship. Armand's reasons were clear to him, or so he thought. Gabrielle's reasons seemed to be more complicated – she said that she felt it to be her duty to persuade him of his errors, of the impossible attitude he had towards women – quite a dozen reasons she advanced, making them all sound convincing, though they were no more than an extension of the way in which she played the game of love.

The first occasion on which Armand was permitted to

pass a whole night with her was a memorable one. She wished to be taken to the Opera and professed herself delighted with a performance of La Traviata, though Armand privately felt it to be no more than passable in both singing and staging. Perhaps, he thought, Gabrielle intended some message for him personally in Verdi's account of a fashionable, kept woman dying of turberculosis and ill-starred love for a young man of independent means. Was she hinting that she loved him – the idea seemed both fantastic and unnecessarily romantic. On the other hand, who could be sure what went on in the mind of a woman – especially this one?

There were quite a few people they both knew at the performance. They waved from their box and chatted in the intermissions, introducing each other to their own acquaintances.

'They will all gossip about us,' Gabrielle said to him, 'I have been warned that you are a man of a certain reputation. My friends will think the worst of me now that we have been seen in public together.'

'Not at all,' Armand reassured her, trying not to smile. 'No one who knows you could believe you capable of the smallest lowering of your high moral standards.'

After the Opera Armand took her to a different type of entertainment at *Le Boeuf sur le Toit* on the rue Boissy d'Anglas. As ever at that time of the evening, the place was crowded with diners and dancing couples. Gabrielle surveyed those present coldly and summed them up as degenerates, a harsh judgment in Armand's estimation. Nevertheless, they stayed for an hour or two and had an excellent meal and enjoyed themselves, for in spite of her strictures, Gabrielle evidently liked to be seen in such places. And indeed, she was greeted by several acquaintances, men and women.

Eventually the time arrived when he had her alone in her bedroom – and such a bedroom! The walls were decorated with angular geometric patterns in vividly clashing colours, except where a vast hexagonal mirror covered most of the space behind the low and wide bed. The sheets were of peach-coloured silk, the pillows large and square and edged with lace the width of a man's palm. Armand was naked and in the bed while Gabrielle made her preparations, the only light in the room from a milky-white globe held high by a kneeling silver nude on the bedside table.

Gabrielle made her appearance in a close-fitting and semi-transparent black nightdress cut low over her breasts. She knelt beside him on the bed, her arms raised high in the pose of the lamp-holder. Armand ran his hands down her sides.

'You always wear black next to your beautiful body,' he said, 'whatever the colour of your frock, beneath it I invariably find black underwear. And now a nightdress of the same sombre shade? Do you do this to provide a wonderful contrast with your skin?'

'Certainly not. I wear black underwear and nightwear as a kind of mourning. The world cannot see it, but I know.'

'Mourning? For your husband?'

'Not for him. I hardly knew him. The purpose is to remind me perpetually of the shamefulness of surrender to the vile caprices of the body.'

She lowered her slender arms to put her hands on his bare shoulders.

'But how can so beautiful a body have the least shame in anything it desires?' Armand enquired, his eyes on her pointed nipples pressing against the thin silk.

'I shall never make you understand,' she said, 'you are lost in corruption.'

He slipped the nightdress off her shoulders and let it slide down to her waist. Before he could touch her she cupped her small breasts in her hands.

'Observe,' she said, her eyes on his face, 'you stare at these unimportant female appendages and your eyes burn. I cannot count how many times you have professed to admire them or how often your hands have strayed towards them.'

'Nor I,' Armand said with enthusiasm.

'Yet consider, my poor friend, what is it that you are admiring at such moments? Flesh, nothing more. How trivial a pleasure for a man of your accomplishments, do you not agree? Look well and judge for yourself. There is nothing here of any significance. These nipples you take delight in kissing – what are they but mere pink buttons set on protruberences of flesh? How can you regard such things as worthy of your attention?'

'But how elegant they are, those little breasts of yours,' said Armand, watching her flick her nipples with her thumbnails in apparent contempt.

'I fear that you are beyond remedy, Armand, you are too far gone to respond to the voice of reason. What will become of you? Why, even while I plead with you to recognise the truth and turn away from your errors, you disgrace yourself.'

'In what way?'

For answer she peeled away the bed-cover to expose his naked body.

'By permitting your body to become aroused. Look at this!'

She took hold of his upright part between thumb and forefinger and swayed it from side to side.

'How banal!' she said, 'the merest glimpse of a woman's body and *this* rises like a signal.'

'A compliment to your charms which cannot be mistaken in its intent, surely.'

'Must you always think of the worthless pleasures of the body, Armand? Reflect for a moment on how fleeting they are, how commonplace. Shall I ever convince you or am I talking in vain?'

'I am considering your words most carefully, I assure you, my dear. Continue, if you please, for I am not yet won over to your way of thinking.'

'Continue indeed! Where would be the point of that? You are so far lost to decency and commonsense that with another half dozen passes of my hand you will defile me with an emission. That is the simple truth of it – confess it now.'

'Not just yet, though there is some small element of truth in what you say about my present condition. One must not exaggerate, however. I fear that you are somewhat given to overstating matters.'

Her hand remained where it was, massaging him slowly, to his great delectation.

81

'Why are these trivial sensations of the body so important to you, Armand? Can you tell me truthfully?'

'Easily. It is human nature,' he sighed.

'Human nature does not need to be so, I assure you,' she said, curving her back gracefully to bring her face close to his engorged part.

'How shamefully it has grown at the mere sight of my naked breasts!'

'And the delicate touch of your hand,' Armand added.

'One could almost believe that it had a will of its own, yet this need not be so. You could control it if you wished, make it obey your will. Oh, if this delinquent part could learn to become modest, I would kiss it in chaste salutation.'

'Perhaps the kiss of innocence would rebuke it,' Armand murmured.

Her warm lips were pressed to the tip.

'No, I am deceiving myself with good intentions,' she said, 'this part of you is wholly depraved. There can be no response from it to the cool urgings of chastity.'

Armand sat up to take hold of her night-dress and strip it over her head.

'There is a detestable impropriety in allowing another to see one naked,' she exclaimed.

Her free hand flew to the patch of dark fur between her thighs as if to conceal it from his view.

'There is no impropriety in the freedom of love,' Armand countered, 'in that freedom all is permitted, without shame or guilt.'

He pulled her over him until she knelt above his loins and his boisterous member was positioned at the join of her legs.

'But what are you doing? What can you be thinking of!'

Without replying Armand took her by her narrow hips and urged her body downwards to impale her on himself until he had achieved a snug fit.

'Incredible!' Gabrielle gasped, 'you cannot seriously expect me to take an active part in your vicious practices? Surely it is enough for you to have desecrated my body in the past? There can never be any repetition of that, never!'

Her hips were moving slowly backwards and forwards,

sending tiny ripples of gratification speeding through Armand's lower parts.

'Armand, Armand – am I to debase myself? Is that what you believe me capable of?'

'You are capable of deep and lasting love, of that I am convinced.'

'How can you imagine for a single moment that I would be your partner in so shameful an act as you are proposing!'

Back and forth, back and forth, her movements a little faster now.

'My dear Gabrielle, do you not feel the harmony of this joining together? To me the virtuousness of it appears wholly admirable. Truthfully, I can think of no more certain way of demonstrating the strength of the regard I have for you at this moment. You cannot be unaware of this strength.'

Her movements continued to gain in force and speed. Her hands were at her breasts as if to hide them modestly from him.

'Strength you call it!' she gasped, 'I am well aware of your unrelenting hardness towards my most cherished beliefs ... your brutal invasion of my sacred privacy ... your ravening desire to pollute my poor body ... I am more aware of all this than you imagine ...'

'Hardness is only firmness of purpose,' Armand gasped in his turn. 'What you most cherish, that is what I too admire and seek to know better ...'

'Hypocrite!' she exclaimed wildly as her hips rocked to and fro in total abandon, 'despoiler, tempter ...'

Before she had time to complete her sentiment in words, the vehemence of her own movements carried her beyond the threshold of endurance. She uttered her thin cry as her body convulsed. Her fingers clenched on her breasts, forcing the nipples to full stretch.

Below her, overwhelmed by her transports, Armand erupted in streams of rapture.

The debates on moral questions between the two of them continued over several months. Armand admired Gabrielle's unflinching principles and the facility she had to express them in words right up to the instant when words were wiped out by the turbulence of climactic sensation. She was like no other woman he had ever known. At no time did she express any admiration for him. Quite the reverse – she chided him constantly on his pleasure-seeking attitude to life and his immersion in sensuality. She strove mightily to reform him, even in the throes of passion, sparing no effort to make him see her point of view. Armand resisted her arguments with all his strength and this compelled her to try all the more – at times to the point where they were both completely exhausted from the force of their discussions.

The affair was amusing, interesting, piquant, yet there was a question in Armand's mind which would not go away, however he tried to suppress it. In the end he determined to resolve it for once and for all, though it meant resorting to subterfuge to do so.

Visiting her so regularly, it was not difficult for him to obtain a key to Gabrielle's apartment by lavishly bribing the concierge. The incident which decided him to take this step was a half-overheard conversation on the telephone in which Gabrielle invited her caller to visit her at eight the next evening.

'Who was that?' he asked when she put the telephone down.

'An old friend, Louise Tissot.'

'But have you forgotten that we are going to the Daudiers' party tomorrow evening?'

'Heavens – it completely slipped my mind. I must phone Louise back and apologise.'

'Go on then.'

'I'll do it later. She said that she was about to go out.'

There was not the least doubt in Armand's mind that she was prevaricating. The Daudiers' party would be a magnificent affair – Gabrielle had already bought a new evening frock for it. There was no question that she would have forgotten the date. So what was this nonsense of inviting someone to come and see her at a time she knew she would not be at home?

At six the next evening Armand telephoned Gabrielle, making his voice sound hoarse, to tell her that he had a most annoying cold and dare not go to the party. With a thousand apologies he suggested that she should go without him. He would telephone again tomorrow and see whether the party was as good as they expected. And so on – the usual little lies that men and women tell each other on occasions when they are planning something they wish to keep secret.

At a quarter to eight Armand used his acquired key to let himself silently into Gabrielle's apartment. He heard Claudine the maid singing to herself in the kitchen as he moved on stockinged feet into Gabrielle's bedroom and sat down to wait. He felt nervous and more than a little foolish, but his intention was clear and his resolve firm.

After a while he heard the door-bell ring and Claudine on her way to answer it. He stood at the bedroom door, open just a fraction, to hear what was going on, but he could not make out any words. Claudine was in conversation with a man in the entrance-hall, that was all he could be sure about. The conversation proved to be a lengthy one.

He heard footsteps in the hall, then the sound of a door opening and closing. His heart was pounding in his chest and he felt himself to be near to the answer to the question that had troubled him for so long. Without a sound he went slowly along the passage until he stood outside the door to the maid's room. With his ear pressed against the wood he could just catch the murmur of words inside, but too indistinctly to ascertain what the topic of conversation might be. He experienced acute embarrassment as he lowered himself to his knees to peep through the keyhole – an undignified position for a man of his quality – yet a necessary one if he wished to solve the riddle.

Through the keyhole he had a restricted view of the foot of the bed on which he had once tumbled Claudine. A man of about thirty-five wearing evening clothes sat on the side of the bed with his legs stretched out. Claudine, in profile to Armand, knelt between the man's legs in her trim black frock and apron, her fingers busy with his buttons. She released his distended part from its place of concealment. A tinge of envy

85

coloured Armand's troubled emotions as he viewed the impressive size of what the maid held.

She said something to her companion which Armand missed. Evidently it was of a complimentary nature, for the man smiled proudly and nodded as Claudine's fingers curled around his magisterial staff and rubbed it in a lively manner.

'What am I doing here?' Armand asked himself wordlessly, 'it is shameful to play the voyeur in this way. The casual affaires of a maidservant are not my business.'

Even so, he was held spellbound by the scene being played out on the other side of the door. Claudine used her other hand to scoop the man's bulbs into plain view. To Armand's excited imagination it seemed that the unknown's equipment had increased further in size, if that were humanly possible, under Claudine's ministrations. As for her, she gave every appearance of enjoying what she was at, for there was a pleasant smile on her face. When she bent her head and took a good half of the engorged penis into her mouth, Armand suppressed a gulp. His own equipment was uncomfortably constricted inside his clothes and the discomfort he was suffering grew more urgent at the sight of Claudine applying her tongue and lips to her partner.

Armand had never in his life observed others engaged in the most intimate of acts. Up in Pigalle there were back-street places of entertainment where for a price one could, in company with ten or twenty other customers watch a man, very usually a black man, penetrate and service two or three women in quick succession, or so Armand had been informed by friends who had witnessed such performances. The women were then at the immediate disposal of the paying customers, hot and wet from the embraces of the male performer. But Armand had no inclination for entertainment of that type, being fastidious enough to regard it as degrading.

Yet here he was, observing something very similar through a bedroom door keyhole! By this time he had become aroused to the point where nothing could have dragged him away from the scene, for his earlier feelings of shame and guilt had been erased by a more vivid emotion.

He directed his gaze from the maid's busy mouth to the man's face in raging curiosity. How did a man look in the grip of passion? How women looked he knew well from personal experience – was it different of the same? In fact, the man was breathing quickly through his mouth, his eyes were narrowed and his expression registered little at all.

'But how can he stand that?' Armand wondered, noting the avidity of Claudine's attack.

His question was soon answered. The man seized Claudine by the shoulders and jerked her onto the bed beside him. Instantly he was on her, the two of them half on the bed and half off it, his hands fumbling to pull her skirt up and her plain white knickers down. He was moaning loudly enough for Armand to hear him through the door.

Her visitor's impetuousness took Claudine by surprise. She wriggled her bottom on the bed as she endeavoured to help him get her underwear down her legs. There was a sharp rip of material tearing in the grip of four hands.

Armand lost sight of their faces as the man pressed Claudine down. The keyhole afforded him a view only of their middles, sideways on. The man's expensively trousered bottom heaved up and down frenziedly for some moments, then his activity ceased as abruptly as it had begun.

He was off Claudine and standing upright again, hastily buttoning himself up. Claudine sat up on the bed, her face back in Armand's line of sight. Her expression was one of surprise and disappointment, he thought, not that of a woman assuaged. She stood up, letting her torn underwear slip down her legs before pulling her skirt down and smoothing her creased apron.

The man said something to her in a low voice and took money from his pocket to give to her. Armand eased himself slowly upright and crept away from the door, this time into Gabrielle's drawing-room. He left the door ajar and heard Claudine in the hall wishing the visitor a polite goodbye. The door closed, there were footsteps, another door closed. She was back in her room and the moment had arrived for Armand to press his investigation.

He knocked lightly on her door and went in without

waiting. Claudine was on her bed, propped up by pillows. Her skirt was up round her waist, her knees up and apart and her hand gliding rapidly between her thighs, half-hiding the thick black hair there. She stared at Armand in amazement.

'But ... how did you get in?' she stammered, her knees clapping together.

'I'll explain later,' said Armand, smiling at her, 'but for now ...' and he sat on the side of the bed and pressed her knees apart to put his hand to the warm spot where hers had rested a moment ago.

Her surprise and fear vanished at once and she returned his smile as he sent shivers of pleasure through her by his touch in so sensitive a nook.

'But why are you here?' she purred.

'To talk to you, Claudine.'

'To *talk* to me?'

'Yes, there are certain matters on which I would like a little information.'

'I am entirely at your disposal.'

'So I see,' he said, smiling again. 'What a pleasing thought that is.'

'Pleasing to both of us,' she sighed as what he was doing to her began to take very positive effect.

'These enquiries of mine are of a most delicate nature, Claudine. To rush through them would be impossible. First we must establish an appropriate mood.'

Her hand was on Armand's thigh, stroking gently upwards, the warmth of her palm striking through the material of his trousers.

'You have established the right mood already,' she said, 'I'm ready for you now.'

'Almost ready. A few more moments and the mood will be perfect.'

'A few more moments and it will be too late!' she exclaimed.

'Then we must proceed at once.'

Armand removed his jacket quickly, opened his trousers and lay full-length on Claudine, but did no more.

'Come on!' she pleaded, 'I'm dying!'

'You shall have all that you want,' he soothed her. 'First promise me one thing.'

'Anything!'

'Promise that you will answer my questions truthfully afterwards.'

'Yes, yes, anything you like!'

'Swear it.'

'I swear!'

Armand slid forward and found the entrance another had prepared for him. Prepared all too well, for in Claudine's ardent state the penetration was of itself sufficient to pull the trigger of her passion. She writhed beneath him, whimpering and moaning.

The scene he had witnessed through the keyhole had raised Armand's emotional temperature to an extraordinary level. Claudine's spasms sent the mercury racing up his thermometer in an irresistible silver thread and he too gasped and convulsed in sudden joy.

'My God, I needed that,' said Claudine when they had recovered.

'So I judged when I came into your room.'

She chuckled, not in the least embarrassed.

'So how did you get in?'

'Later. You must keep your promise and answer me truthfully now.'

'What is it you want to know?'

'Start with your visitor – who was he?'

'His name is Henri Chenet. Why do you want to know that?'

'A friend of yours?'

'Of course not! He is a friend of Madame's. He came to call on her but she is out and so he took advantage of me.'

'As I did the first time I came here and Madame was out?'

'Exactly.'

'Claudine, your answer to my question raises more questions. I would like you to tell me the entire story.'

Claudine at that moment was well-disposed towards Armand because of the way in which he had dealt with her emergency. She was not so well-disposed towards the man who had been the cause of the emergency. She made Armand give his word that he would never repeat anything she told him and, that done, she spoke freely. Armand in the next few minutes learned the truth of the old saying that eavesdroppers often hear things they would rather not hear.

Madame de Michoux was so fastidious in all her ways, Claudine related, that whenever she made the acquaintance of a man who gave indications that he would be pleased and honoured to become her lover she made private enquiries to ascertain whether he was acceptable before giving any sign of her own inclinations. There were enquiries to be made of mutual friends and acquaintances as to the suitability of his background and of his financial status. These researches were supplemented by an investigation of his amatory style and for this Madame de Michoux made use of the abilities of her maid. The routine was well-established – the unsuspecting candidate for Madame's favours was invited to her home, only to find her out and Claudine there to conduct the secret investigation.

Armand listened in amusement and dismay.

'So when I came here that first time it was simply a test – is that what you are telling me?'

'An enjoyable test, surely,' she said pertly. 'After all, I am neither old nor ugly and I have some experience of gentlemen's tastes in these matters.'

'Evidently I passed the test.'

'You passed with full honours. Your manners were so charming and your handling of the situation so expert that I could do no less than recommend you highly to Madame.'

'And is she equally pleased?'

'She is very attached to you. She admires your style and the way in which you conduct yourself with her. She has told me so more than once.'

'Then why are you trying out this Chenet person for her?' Armand demanded. 'Why am I to be replaced now, tell me that.'

'Listen – do you really want to ask all these questions? Why not leave things as they are? I would not like to see you distress yourself.'

'I want to know,' Armand insisted.

90

He reached for his jacket to spread out all the bank-notes he had with him on the bed beside her.

'The question is not one of money,' she said.

'What then?'

'It is a question of loyalty.'

'Well said. That is a quality I admire, Claudine. I respect your scruples. But now that you have gone this far, why not continue? After all, we are old friends, you and I. This money is not in any way a bribe to deflect your loyalty but a simple token of my esteem for you.'

'Very well, I accept it on those terms. I have a soft spot in my heart for you.'

'And not only in your heart, Claudine.'

'Ah, as to that ...' and she touched herself between the legs and smiled at him.

'Later, by all means,' said Armand, 'I shall be honoured to make full use of your soft spot. But first, tell me more. Chenet, for instance?'

'You must understand that Monsieur Chenet is rich.'

'That I guessed. I am not exactly poor myself.'

'Naturally, Madame does not know any poor people. But Monsieur Chenet is more susceptible than most of her admirers. He has already told Madame that he loves her and has given her some slight hint that he would be prepared to marry her.'

'The devil he has!'

'So far she has given him only the slightest encouragement, you understand, but he is very persistent.'

'No encouragement? She invited him here.'

'Only when she knew that she would be out.'

'All the same ...'

'Look – Madame knows that it is most unlikely that you will ask her to marry you, though you will take care of her.'

'To be truthful the thought of marriage had never crossed my mind.'

'She understands that. But at the same time it is only natural that she should give some thought to her own future. Monsieur Chenet was a possible husband, or so she believed, though that is now out of the question.'

91

'Why do you say that?'

'He is awkward in certain ways. Madame could not possibly tolerate the clumsiness to which he subjected me. No, you may rest assured that he will never be invited here again.'

'And that is all the consolation you can offer me?'

'The consolation of my body,' Claudine suggested.

'That of course. But my heart is broken.'

Claudine looked at him frankly.

'We must be practical,' she said, 'you are the ruler of Madame's heart. In the months you have known her you have established yourself as the standard by which other men must be judged. Nothing less can be considered, for Madame is an extremely special person.'

'Extremely,' Armand agreed wryly.

MARIE-THÉRÈSE AND THE RED FOX

The true pleasure of shopping is not to need anything. Setting out with an objective in mind, to buy a pair of shoes for example, that is to give oneself the bother of making comparisons, matching colours and styles, considering prices and reaching a decision. Such errands are more like work than pleasure. On the other hand, needing nothing, one looks into shop windows, goes inside to examine this and that, open to the delicious impulse to buy anything which attracts the eye and would be a delight to wear – that is the art of shopping at its most civilised.

By lunchtime Marie-Thérèse and her friend Adrienne Dumoutier had looked at a thousand things, stockings, underwear, scarves, hats, shoes, handbags, and bought nothing. Their outing was a complete success, to be crowned by a light lunch in a restaurant they both liked.

They were a striking pair, these two. They drew admiring glances from men wherever they went, instant attention from shop assistants and devoted service from waiters. They were the same age, in the full bloom of their late twenties. Adrienne wore that day a new-style knitted jumper-blouse to her hips over a pleated skirt that just covered her rounded knees when she walked and displayed them when she sat down. Her ensemble was in shades of woodland green, matched by a little cloche hat pulled down over her dark red hair. Marie-Thérèse was slightly more conservative in her taste, as evidenced by her cream silk frock under a matching three-quarter length coat trimmed at the neck with black fur.

After lunch they took a taxi to Adrienne's home. They sat together on the big sofa in the drawing-room, talking busily, until Adrienne put an arm round her friend to hug her.

'Do you know,' she said, 'when we met this morning and I saw how beautifully dressed you were, for some strange reason I thought of how awful we both looked when we met for the very first time. Do you remember?'

'That ghastly boarding-school at Vincennes! Blue serge uniforms and thick black stockings – what a way to make young girls dress! As much as I love my dear mother, I think I shall never completely forgive her for sending me there.'

Adrienne cuddled her affectionately.

'But if she hadn't, we might never have met.'

'True. At least the school did one thing for us, it made us friends. Though it did everything possible to discourage friendship. You haven't forgotten that we were forbidden to be in groups of less than four when we were allowed out in the grounds.'

'Instant punishment if two girls were caught talking together outside the classroom. That was one rule we discovered how to break without being found out.'

'Dear Adrienne! We learned so much, you and I, although the holy sisters tried hard not to let us. Those poor sad unfulfilled creatures! At the time I hated them but looking back now I have come to pity them.'

Adrienne's hand caressed Marie-Thérèse's slender neck.

'I don't feel in the least sorry for them,' she said, 'they were grisly old hags determined to make our lives miserable. They failed with you and me, but they made a lot of young girls very unhappy. You haven't forgotten Elise Moncourt, I hope.'

'Little Elise ... you are right. The regime crippled her emotions for life. She was so pretty then – but now! I told you about how I ran into her some time ago and discovered that she had been married off to a surly brute who treats her with open contempt. She has become thin and pale, her cheeks lined and her figure sagging and ruined from being forced to have five children. I almost wept for her.'

'What a tragedy! I intended to call on her, but thinking about what you told me, it seemed too depressing,' said Adrienne, her finger-tips sliding sensuously over the fine skin of Marie-Thérèse's décolletage.

'Ah, those busy fingers of yours! You know very well that I can never resist them.'

'I should hope not! After all the pleasure these fingers of mine have given you since we were at school together they

94

have become dear friends of your beautiful body.'

'I could say the same,' Marie-Thérèse replied, kissing her friend's cheek warmly.

'Naturally. Remember our first time – in the dormitory after lights-out?'

'Of course I do. Our tender interludes were the only good part of our existence then. That horrid dormitory, as big as a warehouse, divided by curtains into cubicles, with a lay-sister sleeping in each corner.'

'They never slept, those gorgons. They lay awake in the dark right through the night, listening for a whisper or a rustle so that they could pounce.'

'They never caught us. You were the bold one, Adrienne – you slipped under the curtain between our cubicles and into my bed so silently that not even the biggest ears could detect anything.'

'The hours we lay kissing and caressing each other!'

'The first time or two, yes. When you thought I was ready for more than that, your caresses became insistent one night and you took me all the way. It was like entering paradise. I would have cried out in joy, except that you had a hand over my mouth.'

'And the other between your legs,' said Adrienne, smiling at the memory.

'Are the servants out?'

'Naturally.'

'Then I shall take my frock off.'

'Let me help you.'

Under her dress Marie-Thérèse was wearing cream-coloured cami-knickers edged with golden-brown lace. Adrienne stood close, her arms around her, hugging their bodies together.

'I expect you to return the compliment,' said Marie-Thérèse.

At once Adrienne pulled her long jumper-blouse over her head, dropped her skirt and stood revealed in a lime green georgette slip. This too she removed and took her place beside Marie-Thérèse on the sofa again wearing only loose silk knickers and a very tight brassiere. She tucked her knees

95

under her and turned towards Marie-Thérèse.

'Let me kiss those delicious playthings of yours,' she said, easing the narrow straps off Marie-Thérèse's shoulders to expose her little breasts.

'Only if you let me stroke yours too. Turn round so that I can unhook your brassiere. It looks very uncomfortable.'

'I am not as fortunate as you are,' Adrienne complained, twisting her body to present the fastening to Marie-Thérèse. 'You've had two children and your breasts are still as pretty as when you were a girl. I've had one child and mine are big and obtrusive. Is it fair that I have to keep them swaddled up tight to be able to wear fashionable clothes?'

'Adrienne dear, yours were always big. When we first touched each other, mine were only the size of little apples and yours were already as full as a grown woman's. You know that's true.'

'Monstrous things,' said Adrienne, putting her hands beneath her breasts to lift them up, the gesture emphasising their fullness, 'it is not chic to have all this flesh sticking out in front.'

'I love them even if you don't Marie-Thérèse soothed her.

She put her lips to Adrienne's nipples, one after the other. When they stood firm, she devoted her entire attention to the one nearest her, flicking it with the tip of her tongue until Adrienne was sighing heavily.

'To think that it was I who taught you everything you know,' Adrienne murmured.

'Not everything. You awoke me to the delights of love, that I agree.'

'Who else has shown you anything you didn't learn from me at school or since?'

'My husband, of course,' Marie-Thérèse answered, both hands kneading Adrienne's breasts.

'I don't believe a word of it. I know that I've learned nothing from mine in the years we've been married. Men! The only experience a man can give you is the sensation of his penis inside you. We have given each other that many times with our fingers.'

'We have discussed this before and we never seem to agree.

However similar the physical sensations may be, love-making with a man is different emotionally.'

'For me sensations are more important than emotions,' said Adrienne.

She pushed Marie-Thérèse gently back against the sofa and put her hands on her small round breasts to roll the nipples under her thumbs.

'Little devils,' she said, 'all hard and greedy.'

When Marie-Thérèse was well-embarked on the magic voyage Adrienne undid the buttons of the cami-knickers between her legs and pulled the thin silk up to uncover her. Her hand stroked between parted thighs, evoking little gasps of satisfaction from her friend.

'Do you know what I'm going to do to you, Marie-Thérèse?'

'Tell me!'

'Something which will amaze you. Close your eyes and enjoy it.'

'But I don't understand,' Marie-Thérèse murmured, pretending to be a child again, 'why are you touching me between the legs?'

'You'll find out in a minute.'

'But we have to keep our bodies covered up all the time, even when we're washing. It's a sin to let anyone see your body – Sister Hortense said so. Its a sin to look at your own body, don't you know that?'

'What does Sister Hortense know about anything? Does it feel nice when I touch you there?'

'Very nice. Oh, Adrienne, what are you doing to me?'

'That's my finger going ever such a little way inside.'

'But you mustn't!'

'Don't you like it?'

'Adrienne!'

'I'm touching your little button. Does it give you a lovely sensation?'

'It makes me feel so strange ...'

'Strange but lovely.'

'Don't stop – it really is lovely.'

Adrienne had one leg folded under her on the sofa and the

other lay over Marie-Thérèse's thigh, pulling her legs wider apart while her dexterous fingers dealt out shudders of pleasure. Marie-Thérèse pressed her face between her friend's warm breasts.

'Now do you understand why I am doing it to you?' Adrienne asked.

'Yes, I understand ... it feels so good.'

'And it gets better.'

'How?'

'Like this.'

Adrienne's hand turned under, two joined fingers slid into Marie-Thérèse's soft burrow and the ball of her thumb rolled over the passionate bud.

'Adrienne ... that's incredible! More!'

'As much as you like.'

Marie-Thérèse's small white teeth worried at Adrienne's breast, her exhalations now loud and exclamatory as she neared her zenith.

'Something is going to happen to me!'

'Of course it is, darling, you may rely on it.'

'I'm going to faint ...'

Adrienne's thumb and fingers thrust with loving precision at their tender targets.

'Now,' she commanded, 'you are trembling like a leaf. It is now!'

Marie-Thérèse's back arched in spasms of delight. Adrienne's relentless manipulations prolonged the pleasure to its extreme and with a long moan Marie-Thérèse collapsed against her.

'I adore doing that to you,' said Adrienne, 'your response is so exciting. I watch your face change expression at the supreme moment and feel your body shaking against mine. There is no delight on earth to equal this.'

'Except,' said Marie-Thérèse, 'to experience those same delights in your own body. Bare yourself, my dear friend, for your time has come.'

'Has it then? Do you suppose for one moment that you can make me feel half of what I make you feel? Absurd!'

Marie-Thérèse's hand was up the wide leg of her friend's

only garment, stroking her fur and belly.

'You intend to play your old game with me, do you?' she asked, 'you still think that because it was you who crept into my bed the first time and not I into yours – and you only dared do that because I'd hinted to you all day that a visit would be welcome – you think that you are the dominant partner in our love-making. That's what *I* call absurd.'

'I have always been the one to initiate our encounters,' Adrienne retorted, 'I am always the one to caress you first.'

'Only because I want it to happen that way. Accept the fact – it is I who initiate everything, not you. You make the first move only because I wish it so. How smooth your skin is to the touch!'

'You are distorting the truth,' Adrienne murmured as knowing fingers moved slowly in her soft groins.

'I am ready for my treat, Adrienne, and you are keeping me waiting with this ridiculous argument. Unless you remove these transparent frillies at once I shall lose all patience with you. I suppose you know that they are so thin that the dark shadow of your hair shows right through them? Is that how you attract your husband at night – standing before him in these?'

Without answering, Adrienne hooked her thumbs in the sides of her underwear and her legs waved briefly in the air as she slipped off her final flimsy garment.

'There – is that what you want?' she said at last, spreading her legs.

Marie-Thérèse, naked but for her stockings, knelt before the sofa, a hand on each of Adrienne's creamy-white thighs to push them further apart.

'At last!' she said, 'you always delay this moment because you know that I enjoy it. You deliberately keep me waiting for it.'

Years and years of the application of henna had made the hair on Adrienne's head dark-red. Between her legs the pelt was her natural ginger, vividly bright against her pale skin.

'The little fox is out of its hiding-place at last,' said Marie-Thérèse, combing the wiry hair with her fingers.

'Do you honestly and truthfully like it, Marie-Thérèse?'

'You should know by now. How many times have I told you that the colour is fascinating?'

'How can I be sure you mean it?'

'How often have I stroked it and told you that I admire it?'

'Hundreds of times.'

'Hundreds and hundreds of times,' Marie-Thérèse corrected her, her fingers probing delicately.

'I shall last about five seconds if you go on like that,' Adrienne sighed.

'We'll see about that,' and Marie-Thérèse nipped the soft flesh carefully with her nails, causing the other woman to utter a brief shriek.

'Five seconds indeed! I intend to annihilate you with sensation to punish you for daring to say that you are the leader of our games.'

'But I am. I always have been ... oh my God, you're opening me up like a book!'

'A book I have read so many times that I know it off by heart. Who is the leader now?'

'I am.'

'Such arrogance. You will regret it.'

'I regret nothing.'

Marie-Thérèse lowered her dark head to touch her hot tongue to the pink surfaces she had revealed.

'You are kissing my little fox in homage. That proves it.'

Marie-Thérèse concentrated her efforts on the tiny swollen nub she had laid bare.

'What are you doing to me!'

'Teaching you a lesson,' said Marie-Thérèse, leaving off her caresses for a moment.

'Do it again, please, dear Marie-Thérèse ...'

'Ah, now you begin to suffer. I shall start and stop as I choose. We will settle once and for all which of us gives the other the greater pleasure. Beg me.'

'I implore you, don't leave me like this!'

Marie-Thérèse resumed her devotions and Adrienne's naked bottom squirmed about on the sofa. When there was another lull, she wrapped her legs about Marie-Thérèse's slender body below the breasts to clamp her tight and urge her to continue her ministrations.

'You're killing me ...' she groaned after a while, 'no one could endure this ... don't stop ...'

Marie-Thérèse had no intention of stopping again. The two women understood each other's reactions completely from their years of intimacy, each knew the other's body and its capabilities as well as her own.

'I'm dying!' Adrienne gulped abruptly.

A few more staccato flicks of the tongue within her ginger-furred lips and she moaned inarticulately in the throes of her rapturous crisis.

When it was over Marie-Thérèse got back onto the sofa and they lay cuddled in each other's arms, enjoying the closeness of the embrace. Marie-Thérèse broke the silence by laughing.

'What is it? What is so funny?'

'I suddenly thought of Monsieur Huchette at school.'

'Why him?'

'Well, we were compelled to make our weekly confession to him. I wonder what he would have said if either of us had ever confessed what we did together.'

'Good thing we didn't. He was a nasty old pervert,' said Adrienne.

'We can't be sure about that.'

'Yes we can. That look in his eyes every time I knelt on the prie-dieu by him to recite my ridiculous confession. One word – the merest hint – of anything at all and his hand would have been up my skirt. And yours too, for that matter.'

'He was a strange man,' Marie-Thérèse agreed. 'He certainly did stare. Not that he could discern even the outline of my tiny bosom under the blue serge.'

'His eyes never left mine, blue serge or not.'

'Yours was far more prominent.'

'You surely haven't forgotten what Arlette Desormes told us about him – how he exposed himself to her during confession?'

'I think she made that up for the sake of effect.'

'No, it was too detailed and real. She was only thirteen –

how could she have known about such things – it is not possible.'

'She was from the country. Children there have more opportunity to learn about matters than city children like us. They see the animals, I suppose – bulls with cows and stallions with mares.'

'Farm-hands with milkmaids?' Adrienne giggled. 'Anyway, you believed her at the time. We all did.'

'Perhaps we didn't know any better.'

'If you remember, Arlette told us that she was on her knees on the rickety old prie-dieu by his chair, confessing to the nonsense we used to make up to keep him quiet. She raised her eyes and there he sat with his apparatus out of his trousers, standing straight up in the air. She said that it was big and angry-looking and that he had a strange look on his face.'

'If he'd worn a cassock he could have played with it and no one would have been any the wiser,' said Marie-Thérèse. 'I never understood the need for the hypocrisy of the teacher-nuns pretending to be lay-sisters and Huchette wearing ordinary clothes.'

'Religion by stealth to circumvent the law,' said Adrienne, shrugging her naked shoulders and making her breasts wobble, 'Arlette was a pretty girl. I nearly went to her bed instead of yours.'

'What a monstrous lie! You had no choice in the matter. I drew you to me because I wanted you. Arlette looked like a doll with her blonde hair and pale face, but she was stupid. I wonder if she was telling the truth – she wasn't clever enough to make that story up by herself.'

'I'm certain it happened. He told her to lower her eyes and continue with her confession, but she watched him out of the corner of her eye and saw him stroking his penis up and down.'

'But seriously – would he have dared in front of her?' Marie-Thérèse asked.

'Who can say what a celibate will do when nature proves too powerful for him? You know what the old rhyme says.'

'What old rhyme?'

'Once is enough for a sick man to do,
A healthy man usually makes it two,
A hot-blooded lover will go up to three,
Four or five for a monk on a spree.'

'That's very good,' said Marie-Thérèse, giggling. 'Who told you that?'

'I can't even remember. But it proves my point, I think. Huchette was capable of anything, including ravishing little girls if he could have got away with it.'

'We must be grateful that his passions were confined to staring at us.'

'But they weren't. Evidently Arlette told her mother what had happened when she went home for the holidays.'

'Why?'

'Because she never came back to school and we didn't see her again.'

'But then her mother would have made a complaint against Huchette. But he was still there hearing our confessions right up to the day we left school. If Arlette's mother had complained they'd have got rid of him.'

'Not necessarily. The complaint would have gone to the headmistress. She was a friend of Huchette. She covered up for him,' Adrienne insisted.

Marie-Thérèse laughed.

'That awful woman in her full-length black! She was Mother Superior in all except name.'

'Five feet tall and with a body of a wrestler,' Adrienne said. 'Do you remember the stories we used to make up about her and Monsieur Huchette?'

'The stories about how she and he did it together – we had a lot of fun inventing them, didn't we?'

'Monsieur taking the balance from the school-room and using it to weigh her enormous breasts one after the other and deciding that one was several kilos heavier than the other!' said Adrienne.

'And the one about how she jumped on him in the wash-room and wrestled him to the floor and raped him.'

'If any of our tales were even approximately true, no wonder he fancied little girls as a change.'

103

'But in reality,' said Marie-Thérèse, 'she was far too religious to let a man catch a glimpse of her ankle even, let alone anything more interesting.'

'What was interesting about her ankles? She had legs like oak trees and wore thick black stockings. And as for *more* interesting – do you suppose that there was anything alluring about what she had between her thighs? Perhaps a blind man, if he were drunk enough, might have risked it, but no one else would.'

'She would have died before allowing a man to touch her, Adrienne, you know that.'

'That was what she wanted everyone to believe. But we all have the same desires.'

'That may be, but she was determined to save her body for God.'

'Poor God! I know that the priests tell us that he took the sins of the world upon himself, but surely he didn't deserve that body being thrust upon him.'

'Adrienne, you are being blasphemous, to say the least of it.'

'Am I? I've just thought of something – suppose it had been you and not Arlette who had the benefit of viewing Huchette's penis?'

'What shall I suppose?'

'What would you have done? Obeyed him meekly, like her, and sneaked a look?'

'How can I possibly tell?'

'You were not as innocent as Arlette, of course,' said Adrienne.

'Thanks to you and your busy fingers.'

'You regret it?'

'Not for one moment. You and I will still be lovers long after our husbands have started to chase younger women.'

Adrienne kissed her friend's face warmly.

'Speaking of which,' she said, 'I'm certain that mine has already found a little friend. Not that it matters to me, of course. How about Maurice?'

'He is still very attentive to me. No doubt he is an opportunist like all men and takes advantage of any pretty woman who lets him see that she is willing. After all, he travels on business quite a lot and who can say what happens then? But there is no one of any lasting interest to him yet, I am sure. Who do you suppose that Edmond has found?'

'No one that matters – just some silly young creature to make him feel like a hot-blooded lover again.'

'Doing it three times – was it three?'

'You are evading my question, Marie-Thérèse. What would you have done if you had looked up from your confession and seen Monsieur Huchette's device sticking up in the air?'

'If only he had been a more sympathetic person,' she answered with a smile, 'I might even have held it for him. I'd never seen a grown man's penis then. And one standing up – it could have been more interesting.'

'You're only saying that to tease me! You would have done no such thing.'

'Are you so sure? You had taught me the pleasure in handling another between the legs.'

'What a sight that would have been,' and Adrienne laughed aloud. 'You on your knees in your serge uniform playing with that long-faced man! He'd have loved it, no doubt about that. He would have given you a double blessing that day.'

'Of course. He might even have sprinkled me with holy water if I'd held it long enough for him.'

'Holy *water?*'

'Some sort of holy fluid, to be sure.'

Adrienne's lips found one of Marie-Thérèse's nipples and sucked it gently.

'You were a wicked child,' she murmured.

'I learned it from you, my dear.'

'So you admit it at last?'

'You taught me all that you knew inside a week. Less than that, three or four days at the most. After that I surpassed you and since then you have been learning the delights of love-making from me. Oh, that feels very good.'

'And if you wish me to continue making you feel good you must confess that I am the leader of our games.'

105

'Never.'

'Dear Marie-Thérèse – very soon you will be so excited that you will say anything I want you to say. My hand is between your thighs. You are on the verge of surrendering yourself to me, body and soul. So admit that I am the leader.'

'You may touch me anywhere you choose – you are only doing what I wish you to do.'

'You wish me to do *this* to you?'

'Yes ... that's exactly what I want you to do. How did you guess?'

'Little liar! That's three of my fingers in you now. How does that feel?'

'Divine – just what I wanted ...'

'When you are lying here shaking with passion, as you will in a few moments, you will admit to the truth. You always have in the past and you will again. Ah, you are trembling deliciously – I am waiting to hear your confession of submission.'

'There is something you forget,' Marie-Thérèse sighed, stroking her own tight nipples as passion grew.

'What am I forgetting?'

'Afterwards – when you have pleasured me to the limit – I shall have your little red fox at my mercy.'

'And what of that?'

'I intend to tease it until you ask my forgiveness.'

'Is that what you think? For the moment I have you helpless and in my power, Marie-Thérèse. I too can be cruel in love-making if I wish. I shall not let you escape into quick release this time – no, I am going to make you endure quite unedurable sensations. You will laugh and weep at the same time. Your eyes will pop out of their sockets. Your nipples will swell like ripe grapes. Do you hear me?'

'Yes!'

'Good, because there is more. Already that flat belly of yours is beginning to swell as if there were a balloon inside it. Do you feel what I am doing to you? I shall make you become so wet that your thighs will glisten all the way down to your knees.'

'Adrienne!'

'Pleasure to the point of pain – that is what you are beginning to experience. Your legs are wide apart – soon you will stretch them so wide that your bones will creak and you will open yourself so wide that my whole hand will be inside you. Are you you ready for that?'

'Do it!' Marie-Thérèse cried aloud, 'Do it!'

GERMAINE'S KEEP-FIT ROUTINE

At forty-six years of age Germaine de Margeville had the
figure of an athletic young girl. Each morning when she
arose, she removed her night-dress and stood naked before a
full-length mirror on her bedrom wall to survey her body
minutely from the front and sides and rear. Her back, was it
still straight and springy? The belly, that tell-tale of middle-
age, was it still flat and taut? She put her hands under her
small breasts to check that there was no sag. The bottom – no
accumulation of fat to make it prominent? The thighs – were
they as slender and muscular as yesterday?

Her figure had not always been so good. Twenty-five years
before, when her family arranged her marriage to Georges de
Margeville, Germaine was plump of face, round of belly and
fleshy-thighed in the fashion of the early years of the century.
At that time she wore long stays under her elaborate clothes
to nip in her waist and to accentuate her bosom and bottom.
That was what men liked then – the hour-glass figure. After
ten years of being the pampered wife of a rich man, endless
dinner parties and lunches, too much rich food, too much
wine, the birth of her son – by her thirtieth birthday she had
become, one could say, chubby. If she had continued in that
way of life, then by forty she would have become quite
distinctly flabby.

The War changed that. Or more accurately, a man she met
during the War changed matters for her. She was enjoying
little liaisons by that time, to enliven an otherwise dull
marriage. At a ball to raise funds for the Red Cross
Germaine was introduced to Major Paul Jonquy, a non-
combatant officer who played some ill-defined part in the
conduct of the War Department in Paris. She and he became
lovers in a casual way and he proved to be a seminal influence
in her life.

Jonquy was fanatical about his health. He was up at dawn
every morning, in summer and winter, to go riding in the

Bois de Boulogne, rain, shine, sleet or snow. He exercised with iron weights, he swam in the Seine, he fenced, he shot, he hunted, he rowed boats. He never smoked and drank only moderately with his meals.

Opposites attract, they say. In time Germaine formed so strong an attachment to this uncomfortable man that she modelled herself on him. He was flattered by her admiration and delighted to prescribe for her a regime of diet and exercise. Whenever his official duties allowed, he personally supervised her exercise. After only twelve months, Jonquy had pared Germaine down to a sensible weight, improved her posture and strengthened her muscles beyond belief.

After the War ended and the fashion in clothes changed to lighter and simpler attire, Germaine had the perfect figure for it. She could wear anything without brassiere or corset and look admirable. Long after Jonquy faded out of her life she continued to exercise and diet and was in consequence the healthiest person she knew.

She also assumed the Major's eccentric attitude towards sexuality. For him it was a necessary part of his daily regime for fitness. He went with women because he believed it to be essential to his health.

Up until she met him, Germaine had viewed love-making much as all the women she knew viewed it. With her husband it was a marital duty for the purpose of giving him children; with other men it was a pleasurable recreation for its own sake. She learned from Jonquy that it was a requirement for a healthy mind in a healthy body. Pleasurable, certainly, but that was not the point of it at all.

The routine morning inspection of her body in the looking-glass completed, Germaine started on her exercises. Her husband was undisturbed by this as he slept in a bedroom of his own and had shown no sexual interest in her for a number of years. His needs were taken care of by an attractive young woman he maintained secretly in a small apartment in Neuilly. Only he believed this arrangement to be a secret, for Germaine knew about it and found it sensible. Georges was ten years older than she was, he was overweight and short of breath from good-living – in short, he was unconvincing in bed. The little friend in Neuilly had to work hard for her keep, in Germaine's estimation.

The morning exercises began with the legs. Feet together, rise up on the toes, arms outstretched, bend the knees outwards and sink down slowly until her bottom touched her heels. Hold the position to a count of five, then slowly straighten the legs and rise up again. And this twenty-five times repeated! All the time Germaine studied her naked body in the mirror, watching the movements of the muscles of her thighs and belly. Then came the back exercises, bending forward with straight legs to put her palms flat on the floor between her feet. Twenty-five times! There followed the exercises for the arms ... and so on. Germaine's ordinary morning routine would have sent the average person reeling back to bed in a state of near-exhaustion. For her it was nothing. When the exercises were completed, she went into her bathroom to wash off the healthy perspiration from her glowing skin.

Her sexual exercises were no less important and this part of her daily routine was planned carefully in advance. Since the Major's time she had learned sadly that no one man could be relied on to provide the daily exercise necessary to her. Once a day was the standard, though she found herself more comfortable with twice. If circumstances were favourable, even three times were acceptable, but beyond that would have been mere excess. She had therefore her regulars to be used in rotation and, most of the time, a lover in tow who could be called upon to raise the daily frequency to twice, though he was not to know that.

One regular was her masseur, who visited her home on Tuesday and Thursday mornings each week. He was impossibly tall and broad-shouldered, as Swedes often are, with an expressionless face under a short thatch of straw-coloured hair. His appointed time was eleven in the morning, after Georges had left.

'Good day, Madame,' he said in awkward French when the maid ushered him into Germaine's bedroom. 'How are you, please?'

'Very well, Olof.'

Germaine removed her peignoir and lay face down on the bed naked.

'Good, good,' he said, pulling at his finger-joints to loosen them up before he spread a little scented oil on her back.

Olof's hands were as big as shovels and his entire talent was concentrated in them. He began with the back of Germaine's neck, easing the muscles and tendons to dispel any tension. Then he worked his way down her spine slowly and his fingers seemed to unhinge each vertebra gently from the others, to produce a sensation of incredible relaxation. By the time he reached the furrow between her buttocks, Germaine was drowsy with well-being. His strong fingers palpated her delicious cheeks to unclench any residual muscular tension in them before sliding down the backs of her thighs to smooth the tendons, and then to her calves, to unknot them expertly. Gemaine was half-asleep from his ministrations.

The Swede let her lie undisturbed for a time while he stood back to flex his fingers and shrug his shoulder-thews loose.

'Please turn over, Madame. I do your front now, yes?'

Germaine rolled over slowly, her eyes closed, and he set to work again. Olof's treatment was in two distinct parts. He massaged the back to relieve bodily and mental tension. That achieved, he treated the front of the body in such a way as to produce extreme erotic arousal. His skill in both parts of the treatment made him much sought-after and well-paid by ladies of Germaine's age. He poured some of the sweet-smelling oil in the space between her breasts and his giant yet gentle hands caressed it into the skin of her shoulders and chest, building up anticipation. At the correct moment, he massaged her breasts in a slow circular motion, his palms grazing her nipples. Her relaxed breathing became faster and more pronounced.

Olof understood his clients and took his time. Not until Germaine's nipples were so sensitive that his touch was almost painful did his hands move down below her rib-cage. His fingers sank into the flesh of her belly, stirring her internal organs excitingly. By then she was sighing loudly. He continued on downwards when he judged her condition

111

was right and his fingers were massaging her mound of love through its neatly-clipped fur. Germaine's legs moved apart automatically to give him access to her groins and the insides of her thighs.

Oiled finger-tips stroked firmly up the soft flesh of her inner thighs from knees to mound and this, a dozen times repeated, brought her knees up off the bed and her heels close to her bottom, making herself totally and immodestly open to the masseur's attentions. Soon his huge thumbs were delicately inside, softly stroking those parts which women delight to have stroked.

For many of Olof's clients, these were the final moments as his deft thumbs brought the climax of delight upon them. Not so with Germaine. Her legs lifted right off the bed and she slewed round on her back towards him, her ankles crossed behind his neck and locked there. Without haste or emotion, Olof unbuttoned and put his ever-ready part in the receptacle that awaited it and wrapped his brawny arms about her legs. Germaine was so far gone as a result of his massage that a few thrusts brought her to the boil. She shook, moaned and boiled over. Olof kept at it for a while until she was finished, then pulled away and carefully laid her down on the bed again. He packed away his masseur's equipment and waited politely.

'Thank you, Olof. You are the best masseur in Paris.'

His fee was ready for him on the bedside table, in plain sight the whole time just in case he needed any inspiration. He pocketed the money and said, 'Thank you, Madame. I come again Thursday, yes?'

More than once Germaine had considered taking him away with her for a few days. A small country hotel somewhere, well out of Paris, where there would be no risk of being seen by anyone she knew. What blissful days she would enjoy! She would have him massage her after breakfast, then take a stroll in the countryside. More massage after a light lunch, then a short sleep. Later on, a carefully chosen dinner and another massage before bed-time. She was utterly sure that three or four days of that treatment would do wonders for her health.

112

She was convinced that Olof's staying power would be equal to the task. The touch of his hands on her body was so effective that it required the minimum effort by him to complete the treatment. Not in all the time she had made use of his services had he permitted his resources to be depleted. No doubt he had trained himself in self-control so as to be able to render his professional aid to a number of clients each day. If Germaine had him to herself for a few days, the strain would be on his arms and shoulder muscles rather than on a more easily exhausted part of him. The idea of going away with him was attractive in the extreme, the problem was to fit the idyll into her very busy social life.

Twice a week, on Mondays and Fridays, Germaine took lessons from Gaston Doucet in his fencing academy. Her interest in this sport was another legacy from the gallant Major Jonquy. Again there was a double purpose – the exercise was unsurpassable for keeping her lithe and fit and, secondly, the fencing-master was an obliging man.

Her usual route to Doucet's academy was a little more roundabout than it might have been but it was planned to give her a magnificent view, across the Pont d'Iéna, of her favourite Paris landmark, the Eiffel Tower. The sight of that great and audacious metal edifice inevitably thrilled her. It stood so boldly erect, so handsomely proportioned. It was so essentially masculine in its skyward thrust!

In a dressing-room set aside specially for her in Doucet's academy Germaine undressed to her underwear and put on the white skirt and jacket that were obligatory. The skirt was of material thick enough to prevent a point passing through to scratch her; the jacket, buttoned down the side under her left arm, was of canvas. Two rings of twisted rope were set between the canvas and the lining to fit over her small breasts and protect them against hits. She pulled on gauntlet gloves reinforced on the backs and wrists to deflect a point and, suitably shod, her mask under her arm and foil in hand, she went to greet her teacher.

Doucet had been a military man himself until he was invalided out in 1917. Happily he had made a complete recovery from his wounds. He retained his military-style moustache and peremptory manner of addressing others, Germaine excepted. He treated her with considerable respect since the enhanced fees he charged for her lessons were a useful part of his income.

They approached each other across the floor and Doucet bowed.

'Good day, Madame de Margeville.'

'Good day, Captain Doucet.'

They put on their wire-meshed masks and saluted each other, foil upright and hand holding it level with the lips. They turned their bodies sideways to present their right side to each other, right arms out straight until their foil-points just touched, to put them at the right distance from each other.

'On guard, Madame,' said Doucet and both went into the fighting stance, body upright and well-balanced on knees bent and ready to act as springs, left arms held high and to the rear as a counter-balance.

The blades crossed, feinted, slipped under and around each other, each of the pair feeling for an opening for a fast lunge. Germaine attacked, her blade was blocked, she parried the counter-thrust and the bout was on in earnest. The blades clicked and rang against each other, their feet stamped and shuffled as they advanced and fell back. All the time Doucet delivered a fast commentary on Germaine's movements and style, praising, criticising, advising, instructing. His blade danced before him, always in the exact position to parry a lunge, always flicking out towards her. He drove her back, allowed her to rally, retreated himself as she came on, then halted her advance effortlessly. Germaine knew that she was a good fencer, but Doucet was a master. Only at the very end of the lesson was she able to slip under his blade and score a hit on his chest.

'Touché, Madame!' he said at once.

Since that was what happened towards the end of every lesson, she knew that he planned it that way in order to encourage her.

They removed their masks and saluted each other again with the foils. Germaine's face was flushed red from her exertions, Doucet's was not.

'That was exhilarating,' she said.

'You are a good pupil, Madame.'

Doucet accompanied her back to the reserved dressing-room on the pretext of assisting her with the buttons down the side of her tunic. There were rules for this part of the game as elaborate and formal as those for the fencing bout, and both understood perfectly. There were good reasons for these rules.

In social status Doucet stood higher than Olof Ekstrom the masseur. The Swede ranked only marginally higher than a servant. He performed a service and was paid for it in cash. Doucet was an ex-officer who taught an ancient and noble skill, for which he received a fee. Germaine addressed the masseur as Olof, as she would use a servant's first name, while he addressed her formally. Doucet also addressed her formally and she did the same to indicate that she held him in a certain esteem.

In the dressing-room, when the door was locked against possible disturbance, Germaine stood with her arms extended while Doucet with all courtesy undid her fencing-jacket and helped her out of it. Under the thick canvas her body was bathed in perspiration.

'Allow me,' he said as he unfastened her skirt and let it fall to her feet.

He went down on one knee to help her off with her shoes and roll down her stockings.

'That's better,' she said, standing now in only her *crêpe-de-Chine* slip. 'How hot one becomes inside those clothes!'

'You would find it refreshing to be sponged down,' he suggested.

'What a very good idea.'

All this was in their unspoken rules. A large bowl of lukewarm water was invariably to hand. Doucet spread a towel on the floor while Germaine discarded her lingerie. She stood naked on the towel, proud to display her athletic body, and held her arms up while Doucet sponged her down carefully. He worked expertly and conscientiously at his task, under her arms, between her breasts, under her chin, in

115

the small of her back, across her belly and, at last, between her thighs.

While he was attending to this pleasant duty he complimented her on her figure and condition. Naturally, Doucet spoke with the authority of a man who understood physical fitness and valued it highly, since he practised it himself as part of his chosen profession. Germaine prized his opinion of her body very greatly.

At length he wrapped her in another large towel to dry her off.

'I hope that the lesson has not overtired you,' he said with his customary solicitude, 'you are trembling slightly.'

There were good reasons for that, as one can well understand, and they had nothing to do with being tired at all.

'You are quite right,' Germaine replied, following her part, 'my legs are a little fatigued. I would like to rest them for a few moments before dressing.'

'Allow me to offer you a chair.'

'Thank you – but it looks most uncomfortable.'

'I'm afraid you are right. The wooden seat is hard. I must get a cushion for it before your next visit.'

'As you have promised before.'

'So I have – my memory is not as good as it was. I shall make a note in writing of it.'

'No need for that. Why don't you sit down first.'

'Of course – I shall be honoured to be your cushion while you rest.'

Doucet sat on the chair, his back straight and his knees together, still wearing his white fencing outfit. With a smile, Germaine straddled him and sat on his lap, facing him, to rest her legs.

'Are you quite comfortable?' he enquired.

'Yes, thank you. I doubt if you are though, in that tunic. Perhaps I can assist you.'

The fencing master's tunic did not terminate at the waist but had a traingular flap which passed between his legs and fastened at the back, a precaution in the event that an unskilful pupil slipped past his guard and scored a hit on a

116

part of his body too sensitive to be treated in that way. Germaine reached behind him to unfasten it and he took the opportunity to kiss her breasts gallantly. His hands were on her bare thighs, stroking them as if he were soothing a horse.

Germaine freed the flap and pulled it from between his legs and turned it up to give herself access to the buttons of his breeches.

'Why, what is this?' she asked, 'a concealed weapon?'

'You have discovered my secret,' he said.

'But is it sportsmanlike to have another weapon concealed like this?'

She was clasping it fondly as she asked the question.

'Perhaps you will remember that there is a particular style of fencing I have offered to teach you more than once. The style of our ancestors – sword and dagger together.'

'Personally I prefer the two separately – first the sword and then the dagger.'

'On guard, Madame!' Doucet exclaimed as her hand rubbed him briskly.

'Well said – though a little late, since I observe that you are on guard already. This blade of yours has a distinguished appearance. Can it be Italian or Spanish – from Toledo, perhaps?'

'It is of pure French origin, I can assure you and far superior to any imported weapon.

'Excellent,' said Germaine.

She raised herself to aim the blade and then sank down again to sink it into her warm flesh.

'I am a patriot, as you are aware,' Doucet commented.

'If only there were more Frenchmen as patriotic as you, prepared to give their all at a moment's notice when the call to arms is sounded,' Germaine sighed, 'but I fear that we live in degenerate times.'

Doucet held her by the hips as she rocked quickly backwards and forwards on his lap.

'Times have changed,' he said, a glaze of perspiration appearing on his forehead as his emotions grew stronger.

'The War drained away so much that was best in France,' Germaine said jerkily. 'But some gallantry has survived and you are a true patriot. I respect you greatly for it.'

Doucet's piercing brown eyes softened and became unfocused. Germaine's hands were on his shoulders, her fingers digging into the thick white jacket as her rocking became more demanding. Then – as nature took its appointed course – he shook beneath her and lunged upwards half a dozen times.

Germaine's head went back sharply, her mouth opened and she uttered a series of staccato cries as she achieved her her health-imparting pinnacle.

'That was most exhilarating,' she announced, using the same words as she had of her fencing lesson, 'you are a first-class instructor.'

She climbed off him and attended to herself with sponge and wash-bowl. By the time she turned back to him, Doucet was on his feet and properly dressed.

'If you will excuse me,' and he bowed to her, 'I have another pupil due now.'

Germaine did not pay him in cash, naturally. The account for his lessons was presented monthly by post and was included in her normal household expenses.

In addition to the masseur and the fencing master Germaine had a number of other men available to serve her needs. Not that she was a promiscuous woman or an immoral one – she would have viewed any such suggestion as outrageous and insulting. It was simply that to maintain herself in peak condition a certain activity was a daily necessity. Therefore, as a woman of sense, she made suitable arrangements.

Twice a month she visited her physician for a general check-up. Dr Massanet received her in style, for she was an important and influential patient. After they had exchanged courtesies and he had satisfied himself about the general state of her health, he invited her to disrobe. Whether it was necessary or not – who can judge between doctor and patient? – Germaine stripped herself completely naked.

Massanet put his stethoscope to her chest to listen to the strong and regular beat of her heart. He recorded her weight, looked into her eyes and ears, palpated her liver and felt her breasts deeply and conscientiously for any untoward developments. There never were, of course. Germaine was as strong as a horse. When he had concluded the general check-up, the good doctor proceeded to his gynaecological examination – for Germaine always insisted upon that and he had good reasons of his own to humour her, both financial and personal.

Germaine lay on his couch with her knees drawn up and splayed while Massanet inspected her intimate parts very thoroughly. The regular exercise these parts received kept them in excellent condition, to be sure, and the doctor normally made complimentary remarks which pleased her. The preliminary part of the examination was by sight and by touch in the standard manner, although Massanet prolonged the inspection by touch far beyond that deemed necessary by any other physician in Paris. Only when Germaine was in a condition of intense anticipation did he move on the the next part of the examination.

This final and most important phase departed from normal medical practice. To sight and touch all was in good working order but, and this was of paramount importance in Massanet's approach, a test for internal sensitivity was surely necessary. Germaine was in total agreement with him on this aspect of the matter.

The test required him to mount her, his trousers round his knees, and probe deeply with that part of him ordained by a beneficent providence for insertion into the female organs of pleasure. He probed very thoroughly, for he was a conscientious man with the interests of his women patients uppermost in his mind at all times. He took rather longer over it than Germaine found strictly necessary for her own satisfaction, but she recognised that he was a deligent and trustworthy man. Clearly it was in the interests of her continuing good health that he should be as thorough as he chose. She left Dr Massanet with a sense of warm satisfaction after each visit.

Yet another regular call she made on certain days was to a boutique in the rue de la Paix, where high fashion shoes were sold. The manager invariably attended to her himself in a

119

private fitting-room. His name was Roger and he was a well-built man in his early thirties. He understood Germaine's requirements perfectly, as a good businessman should if his intention is to succeed in commerce. Germaine did not buy shoes on every visit, to be sure – not even she required a new pair of shoes every week. A dozen pairs a year sufficed her and she willingly paid a special price for them because of the special attention she received. Even more important to the boutique manager was that she made a point of telling her friends where she obtained her shoes and recommending his wares to them. This made her a valuable client, for the influence she had.

'I have these classical elegant evening shoes,'Roger would begin when she was seated comfortably in private, 'golden kid-skin with just a touch of subtle decoration. They would suit you admirably, I am sure. Let me slip them on for you to judge.'

He went down on one knee before her to remove her walking shoes and ease her feet into his latest creation. And after trying two or three pairs of shoes on her, he took one of her feet between his hands and massaged it.

'Such refined and well-shaped feet you have,' he said, 'it is a pleasure to see such feet.'

'As you know, I exercise daily,' said Germaine, 'particularly rising up and down on my toes to strengthen the arches.'

'To very good effect. And naturally the exercise keeps your calves so graceful.'

'My fencing lessons are good for the calves too.'

By then Roger's hands would be massaging her calves gently so as not to ruin her fine silk stockings. Germaine would hitch her skirt a little higher to encourage him and in due course he would rhapsodize over her symmetrical thighs as his hands stroked the smooth flesh between stocking-top and underwear.

'What a privilege to be able to dress so fashionable a lady as yourself. I deal only with footwear, of course, but if I had the honour of designing clothes for you – what felicities of underwear I would create for so lithe a body!'

120

Germaine required very little caressing along her thighs before they separated themselves to allow him to slip his hands up the loose legs of her knickers and explore her most secret region. And little of that was necessary before she was quite ready for him. Roger performed his task well, thumping away energetically until her little cries announced that she had undergone her health-giving crisis. That her vocalisation of her pleasure was audible out in the shop to the raven-haired young woman assistant troubled her not in the least. She suspected that the girl was Roger's mistress and in some way that added to her satisfaction.

An interesting person in Germaine's scheme of things was her confessor. She was a staunch upholder of tradition and religion equally, holding them to be the corner-stones of civilisation. Remove them and one could expect nothing more than the excesses of the Bolshevik revolution in Russia. As part of her continuous regime of physical and spiritual health it was natural that she should make confession of her peccadilloes once a week and receive absolution, in order to keep the slate clean. In earlier years she went to church to make her confession, but after she had realised Father David's usefulness for another purpose besides the forgiveness of sins, she arranged for him to come to her home each week to hear her confession in private.

The good priest was no longer a young man and although the spirit was willing, the flesh was weakening. Germaine found herself increasingly called upon to bring matters to a satisfactory conclusion. Not that she minded in the least. It was, after all, a form of exercise and to work at it seemed appropriate enough. Sadly, as time went on, she became aware that her confessor was succumbing to an embarrassing flexibility when she most desired firmness of purpose. Mindful of her generous donations to his good causes in the parish, Father David eventually suggested that his assistant should in future hear her confession and to this she readily agreed.

Father Pierre presented himself at her home the next week. Germaine appreciated his breadth of shoulder and healthy complexion. They retired to her boudoir, where an upright chair was set for him and a cushion beside it on which she could kneel. As befitted the occasion, Germaine wore a plain grey frock for the visit of the priest – plain but elegant.

Father Pierre seated himself, an impressive figure in his black cassock. Germaine knelt at his side and began the words she had been taught as a child.

'Bless me, Father, for I have sinned.'

There followed a recital of the events of her week. Bodily connection with the masseur, twice; with the fencing-master, twice; with two men friends of hers – twice with one and three times with the other ... and so on. At the conclusion of her catalogue of her sins of the flesh Father Pierre checked on sins of pride, of hatred, of uncharitableness, of anger, of laziness, of gluttony – nil for that – and the other acts stigmatised as sinful by Church and Holy Writ. When he was sure that he had unearthed everything relevant, he said, 'This is the first time I have heard your confession, my child. Father David has advised me on the matter but I am not sure whether to pronounce absolution now or later. Which was his way?'

'Later,' Germaine answered, 'otherwise you will have to repeat it to include one more item.'

'Quite so. Later on would appear to be more economical of time and effort.'

He rose and turned his chair so that it faced her as she knelt.

'Put your arms on the seat and your head on your arms,' he instructed her.

She obeyed at once, pleased that he was strong enough to undertake the affair without assistance from her. The attitude he proposed was appropriate and satisfactory, it being unthinkable that she should observe her confessor's face at a moment when he was involved in a forbidden action, or he hers. With Father David, when the initiative necessarily was from her, this problem had been overcome by sitting on his lap with her back to him and bouncing vigorously up and down until her objective was reached.

Father Pierre moved round her and turned her skirt up her

back to reveal her bare bottom, for it was her custom to remove her underwear in advance of the priest's arrival in order to facilitate matters.

'A fine sight!' he exclaimed cheerfully, kneeling behind her.

She felt his hands on the cheeks of her rump, smoothing and squeezing.

'A sight which you see all too rarely in your calling,' she said, her spirits rising at his vivacious manner.

'Such sights are forbidden to us lest we are led into temptation and then into sin,' he answered, his hand stroking and stimulating her between her legs.

'Ah ... I have never really understood why so pleasantly health-giving an activity should be regarded as sinful,' she murmured, warming to her confessor.

'Do not question the wisdom of the Church, my child,' he replied, his voice a trifle shaky with rising emotion, 'give thanks that forgiveness is readily available for all your indulgences of the flesh.'

'Yes,' she breathed, hearing the rustle of his cassock as he hitched it up round his waist.

Something warm and blunt grazed her thigh, making her sigh in anticipation. The touch was fleeting but the impression it made on her mind was one of solidity and weightiness. There it was again, that tantalising touch, this time at the threshold of paradise. Germaine breathed out slowly, letting her finely-tuned muscles relax to permit a deep and satisfying penetration, preparing herself for the blessing that was to be bestowed upon her by Father Pierre.

And then – oh horror – the joyfully-awaited guest slipped away from the grand portal made ready for him and forced his way in through the back door!

'No!' Germaine exclaimed angrily, 'that's not what I want! Stop it at once!'

Father Pierre had her firmly by the hips and was rattling along at a frantic pace, muttering to himself the while. To no avail Germaine tried to pull away from his clutches and in her struggle she knocked the chair over. She was on the verge of calling for help – but to whom could she call? To have her maid find her in this humiliating position was utterly impossible. Even while the thought passed through her mind it was too late. The subterranean forces at work within the priest were released and at full spate the geyser spouted with the ungovernable might of nature long repressed.

The moment she was free Germaine sprang to her feet to denounce the culprit in outrage and order him out of her sight forever. But rage rendered her speechless for a time and he, the offender, his cassock decently lowered again, calmly righted the overturned chair and sat down on it.

'Kneel, my child,' he said, indicating the cushion on the floor, 'there is another sin you must confess before I can grant you absolution.'

Germaine stared at him in stupefaction, clutching her outraged behind.

'Have you taken leave of your senses?' she shrilled when her voice returned.

'Kneel, my child,' he repeated, smiling at her in an encouraging manner.

'How dare you do such a thing!'

'You are angry. That is another sin for which you require absolution. But far more serious than that, you have taken part in an unnatural act.'

CHARLES AND JACQUELINE

The four Brissard brothers were handsome men, inheriting their build and features from their father. The eldest of them, Maurice, so closely resembled his father that he could have been taken for a younger version of him, even to his manner of speech. Michel, the second son, was cast in the same mould, though his colouring was somewhat fairer, and so too was the youngest, Gerard, in spite of his efforts to be different. The third of them, Charles, combined his father's stylish masculinity with much of the grace of his mother and by general agreement he was the best-looking of the four. Like Maurice and Michel he had his father's business acumen and was entrusted with the conduct of important affairs by the head of the family.

Business journeys abroad were no new thing to him and caused him no inconvenience. At railway stations porters slouched immediately towards him to earn a few francs by taking his luggage and trotting behind him with it. On this particular occasion a sleeping-car attendant in elegant uniform escorted Charles to his private compartment, waited for the porter to be tipped, took charge of Charles's ticket and went into his courteous routine of getting him settled for the long journey. He demonstrated the bell-push that would summon him at any hour of the night or day, explained the heating-controls, the window-blinds, the door-bolt and the other numerous comforts provided by the *Compagnie Internationale des Wagons-Lits et des Grands Express européens*.

'Shall I reserve a table for you in the dining-car, sir? Dinner service will commence shortly after we leave the station.'

'Yes, please.'

'If I may have your passport I will take care of matters when we cross the various frontiers so that you are not disturbed.'

'Excellent.'

'You are travelling alone, sir?'

Charles nodded.'

'Shall I bring breakfast in the morning to your compartment?'

'Just *café au lait* at eight and then I will go to the dining-car for something to eat.'

'Very good, sir. If you require anything after dinner – cognac, cigarettes, cigars – ring for me and I will get it for you.'

Charles had told the attendant that he was travelling alone. He believed that he was travelling alone. Events proved him wrong. The dining-car was full and he shared a table with a pretty young woman whose age he guessed to be about twenty-six or seven. They introduced themselves at the beginning of the meal and talked. Her name was Jacqueline Le Prêtre, he learned, and she was married but travelling without her husband. Her manner was vivacious and her conversation amusing, not quite disguising an inner anxiety and sadness which Charles recognised early on. He plied her with an excellent burgundy through the meal and their acquaintance blossomed. After dinner they sat on at their table, enjoying a fine cognac, conversation flowing very freely between them. It was with regret that Charles eventually paid the bill for both of them when the dining-car attendants, having cleared every other table, indicated in the politest possible way that they would be pleased to finish their work for the night.

He escorted Madame Le Prêtre to her compartment, which was in the next coach to his own. She gave him her hand and before he had time to kiss it and wish her goodnight she told him that she was not in the least sleepy and would lie awake for hours. In the circumstances, perhaps he would care, if he was not too tired, to continue their conversation? Perhaps another tiny glass of cognac?

They entered her compartment and she appeared to be surprised to find that during her absence at dinner the attendant had made up the bed. She feared that there was nowhere to sit, but Charles reassured her by saying that he did not in the least mind sitting on the bed. One of the small inconveniences of travel, he declared, with all the experience of a much-travelled man. They decided not to order anything further to drink from the attendant in order to prevent any possible misunderstanding arising in his mind.

'Prudence is never out of place,' said Charles, kissing her hand as they sat side by side on the bed, 'servants invariably tend to think the worst.'

'They do,' Jacqueline agreed, 'I was compelled to dismiss a maid who completely misunderstood a certain scene she saw by chance and reported to my husband on his return to Paris. I was furious.'

'Is your husband away from home much?'

'He is away more than he is at home. His work takes him all over France.'

'You must become very lonely at times,' said Charles, stroking her knee gently.

Jacqueline wore an attractive frock, lilac in colour, scooped deeply at the neck and with a belt of the same material low round her hips and tied in front. Her silver-grey stockings complemented the colour of the frock delicately. She was a small-bodied woman with a heart-shaped face, a wide mouth and large eyes. Her black hair, cut in a bang, added to her appealing urchin appearance.

Her hand rested on his hand, neither stopping him from stroking her silk-covered knee where her frock had ridden up nor encouraging him to continue.

'I feel that I can trust you,' she said, 'in the short time we have known each other I have come to regard you as a reliable friend.'

'I am honoured by your trust,' said Charles.

'I feel that I can tell you my secret.'

'Of course you can.'

'You must have asked yourself why I am travelling alone on this train. The reason is simple – I am running away from my husband.'

Charles hand stayed still at that while he wondered briefly whether he might be involving himself in an affair which could develop unnecessary complications later on.

127

'You are leaving France to get away from him? Where are you going – to Italy?'

'To Istanbul, to be with my lover.'

'I see,' said Charles thoughtfully.

'I shall live with him there and my husband will never know where I am.'

'Your lover lives in Istanbul?'

'He is a Turk, it is his home.'

'Where did you meet him?'

'In Paris. He was there for three months. In his own country he is a Prince.'

'In esteem, if not in fact,' Charles suggested.

'Why do you say that?'

'Only a year or two ago Turkey became a Republic when President Kemal was elected by the National Assembly.'

'Such matters are of no importance, I assure you.'

'To me they are. My father has had business connections with Turkey for many years and since nothing of significance happens in that country without official permission, we are greatly interested in who the officials are from whom we must seek permission. Certain sums of money change hands, you understand, in these arrangements, and it would be unwise to bestow such benefits on people who lack the power to open the right doors and stamp the correct pieces of paper.'

'I know nothing of business matters. Mehmet was in Paris, we met and fell in love. For me that is enough. My husband does not love me and so I am going to Mehmet.'

'Naturally. Does he know that you are on your way? Do either of them know that you have left Paris for Istanbul?'

'My husband will not be home for another week. Then he will find the note I left for him telling him that I have gone forever.'

'And Mehmet?'

'Not yet. I had no address to send a telegram to.'

'But how will you find him?'

'He explained to me that he lives in a palace at Scutari. There cannot be so many palaces that I cannot find the right one.'

128

'Do you know where Scutari is?'

'A part of the city.'

'Yes, it is a residential area on the Asiatic side of the Bosphorus. You cross to it by the ferry.'

'Thank you, Charles, that is most useful to know. I see that you have visited Istanbul before.'

'Twice.'

'I knew you were my friend. You will help me find Mehmet.'

'If that is what you want.'

Her hand moved away from his hand and she kissed his cheek warmly. Emboldened, Charles hand moved tantalisingly upwards from her knee, under her frock, to touch the warm flesh of her thigh. For him this was a stupendous moment in love-making, the delicious caress between gartered stocking-top and his eventual goal. That a woman permitted this caress was more than a half-promise that he could proceed further. Yet she was not fully committed and even now could brush his hand away and rebuff him. His hand lingered while he savoured to the full the tremulous delights of this marvellous moment.

Jacqueline kissed him urgently to spur him on. His hand completed its short journey inside the loose leg of her knickers and he gasped in surprise. Where he had expected to find crinkly short hair, his fingers touched only tender flesh.

'Is this a curious new fashion?' he asked.

'No, it is a very old fashion, though not in France. Can you not guess?'

'Of course – your Turkish lover prefers you this way, smooth-shaven.'

'Not shaven, plucked, hair by hair.'

'What pain you must have endured for the sake of love!'

'For the sake of love no pain is too great to be endured. I did it gladly for him. How do you like the Turkish style?'

'For me it is so unusual that I hardly know what to say.'

The folds of flesh under his fingers were warm and soft to the touch.

'Nice?' she asked.

'Jacqueline, I must confess to you that I have never before touched a woman denuded in this Oriental style ... yes, it is very agreeable to the touch. I must see for myself!'

She slipped off the bed to pull the lilac frock over her head and stood revealed in cami-knickers of the same colour. In an instant the flimsy garment was discarded and she hurled herself back into his arms, sprawling over him and kissing his mouth repeatedly.

'You are adorable,' said Charles when she ceased at last. 'Now, let me see this unfamiliar treasure of yours.'

Jacqueline rolled onto her side, her back to the partition and her left knee up to open her thighs to his gaze.

'Take my stockings off,' she suggested, 'it would be a pity to ladder them – they go so well with that frock.'

Charles obligingly pulled her garters below her knees and eased the delicate stockings from her legs. All the while his eyes were held by the fascination of the plump and hairless mound between her thighs, so inviting, so tender, so vulnerable-seeming. The moment he had got rid of the stockings he put his head between her parted thighs to kiss those tempting lips. Jacqueline's fingers twined into his curly black hair and pulled his face up so that she could look into his eyes as she spoke.

'Charles, before you go any further there is something I must warn you about.'

'What is that?'

'If you once get me really started – and you're going the right way about it – I won't be able to stop myself. I warn you, it takes a lot to satisfy me and I shall wear you out before you succeed.'

Charles male pride was involved at once.

'As to that,' he said, 'I must tell you that I too am not satisfied in the usual quarter of an hour. You need have no anxiety on my behalf, dear Jacqueline. Look to yourself and take care that I do not exhaust you.'

'Then we understood each other. Take off your clothes and we shall enjoy a night to remember.'

She lay in the same position while Charles undressed, her charms fully displayed for him, one hand slowly smoothing the inside of her thigh as if it pleased her by its touch and texture. Then Charles was back beside her, his lips pressed to her plump mound.

She reacted very quickly to his stimulus. In moments she was panting and shaking from head to toe, her head jerking from side to side. Charles caressed her with his tongue, excited by the novelty of what she was offering to him. He was flattered by her ready response and wondered how it would be when he brought into play the part of him created for the delight of women. After a while the thought came into his mind that she was taking a long time to reach her peak for one experiencing such keen pleasure. Still, she said that it took a lot to satisfy her.

She seized him by the ears and pulled his head away from her body.

'Wait,' she gasped, 'let me rest for a little.'

'But you were almost at the critical point,' said Charles, smiling at her, 'was it too soon for you?'

'Almost at it? But I've passed it three or four times already.'

Charles concealed his surprise.

'Really? How many times can you attain it?' he asked in great interest.

'I don't know. No one has ever finished me off completely, not even Mehmet.'

'But you must be able to guess.'

'How can I say? It keeps on getting better all the time, the longer I go on. I lose count after thirty times or so.'

Charles revised his plan of campaign hastily. When she had told him that she was not easily satisfied he had taken it to mean that she expected him to make love to her two or three times that night. That posed no problems for him, he knew, and if she was still interested after the third time, he could go to a fourth, though he preferred not to push himself to the final effort if it could be avoided. Now all that was as nothing! She was talking casually about her thirtieth time as if it were the most natural thing in the world – and even that was not enough, it appeared. Charles changed his opinion of the Turk. If he had been able to keep Jacqueline content in

131

bed, he must be a man of remarkable strength and endurance.

'Thirty times,' he said, 'what truly amazing love-making. Not every day, of course.'

'Naturally every day,' she answered, 'sometimes twice a day.'

'But how do you find time to eat and drink and go shopping and meet your friends and all the other affairs of life?'

'I don't understand you, Charles. After all, love-making doesn't take all that long. At least, not for me, An hour after lunch and an hour at bed-time is enough for anyone, surely?'

'Certainly,' he agreed.

'I've been told by women friends that sometimes they've spent a whole day and a night in bed with their lovers,' she said, 'but I think they were exaggerating. I mean, how could they stand it physically? After an hour I'm so fatigued that I fall asleep for at least thirty minutes, sometimes even longer. Once I slept for nearly two hours afterwards!'

'That must have been a very special occasion,' said Charles, his heart sinking at these revelations.

'Yes, it was the first time I was with Mehmet. He crushed me utterly with his embraces and I fell in love with him forever.'

'A most significant day in your life.'

'The most important day of my whole life, of course. I'm rested now, Charles, let's do it again.'

Charles arranged her comfortably on her back on the narrow bunk, slid on top of her and made his entrance. For so small a woman she was fully developed in the essential parts and he encountered no difficulties. Indeed, her internal muscles seemed to be drawing him deeper than he imagined possible, having regard to her anatomy.

'That feels heavenly,' she sighed, 'oh, Charles, lie still for a minute and let me enjoy it.'

He did as she asked, happy to conserve his powers for when they were most required. But if he was in control, she was not. Her own body betrayed her and hurried her towards its goal. The glove of soft flesh that held Charles began of its own accord to pulse rhythmically in a long rippling massage of his embedded firmness. Within moments Jacqueline was writhing and panting once more, adrift in her private world of ecstasy. Charles lay motionless, astonished and thrilled by this extraordinary woman. He did nothing, content to let the turmoil of Jacqueline's belly carry his excitement higher and higher until sudden and rapturous convulsions drained his energies from him.

The jolting within her broke the spell in which Jacqueline was enmeshed and she too subsided slowly.

'You are marvellous, Charles,' she said, her face shiny with perspiration, 'oh, if I had met you in Paris before I fell in love with Mehmet we could have made each other so happy!'

Charles lay beside her and gently wiped the perspiration from her face and between her tiny breasts with a corner of the bed-sheet.

'You are an astonishing person, Jacqueline. Perhaps we could have had some delightful hours together. But like you I am married.'

'Where are we now, do you know?'

'In Switzerland. Does it matter? We stopped for the frontier while you and I were delighting each other.'

'Did we? I never noticed.'

'Why should you? A frontier is as nothing compared with what we were feeling.'

'How true that is. You said that I was married. I have left my husband and I no longer regard myself as married. And you, my dear friend, does your wife make you happy?'

'I cannot discuss my marriage in these circumstances,' said Charles.

'Then she doesn't. I guessed that before I asked you. Why do you stay with her?'

'We have a child. Besides, she has given me no reason for complaint, none whatsoever.'

Jacqueline shrugged her naked shoulders prettily.

'All that you are saying is that she is a good wife as the world regards these things. You do not love her and she does not make you happy.'

'Enough,' said Charles firmly, 'that is my affair, not yours.'

'Forgive me, I did not mean to offend you. I am glad that we met on this journey, however short a time we have together. I like you very much.'

'I like you, Jacqueline. Now tell me, how many times did it happen to you just now while we were passing from France to Switzerland?'

'Oh, the vanity of men,' she said, laughing a little, 'you wish to achieve the honour of being my best lover – isn't it so?'

'You must understand that men take an inordinate pride in these affairs.'

'Well, it was at least a dozen times, probably more. After the third or fourth time the ecstasy rises and falls in waves. It breaks over me as if I were lying on the sea-shore and white-capped waves are crashing over me. The breath is driven from my body and I go dizzy with the violence of it.'

'That's a vivid description, the waves. You must have thought about it.'

'No, what is there to think about in love-making? Everything is sensation and pleasure. It belongs to the body, not the mind. Thought has no place in it.'

'Yes and no,' said Charles.

'What does that mean?'

'Let me try to explain,' and Charles raised himself on one elbow to look down at her. 'Take your body first. You are small but beautifully formed. Your little breasts are perfectly round, your waist is narrow and your bottom is deliciously shaped of two cheeks in pleasing proportion to your figure. Your thighs are shapely and between them lies the most charming plaything I have ever encountered.'

'Flatterer!'

'I speak no more than the truth. In short, Jacqueline, your body is a perfect machine for love-making.'

'I agree with everything you say.'

'But there is another part of you which cannot be left out of consideration.'

'Which part is that?'

134

'The part inside here,' he said, taking her head between his hands and kissing her brow.

'How can that affect matters?'

'It does, because you are not only a body. You are a whole person. Inside this pretty head there is a part of you which is confused about life and confused about your own emotions.'

'That's true,' she sighed.

'Your body is not confused – that I have seen for myself. It knows its own needs and how to satisfy them, simply and directly. But your mind tells you that you must be with one particular man. Your body does not say that. And here you are on a train, abandoning home, husband, friends, even France itself, to live with a particular man in a curious emotional bondage. Will it bring you happiness? Will it bring you love?'

'Cruel, cruel,' she said and wept a little.

Charles put his arms about her to comfort her tears. Her mouth found his and her little hands slid down his naked sides to his thighs and stroked them impatiently.

'What you said was hurtful, Charles. Help me forget your words, please.'

'How could I resist so enchanting a plea?'

He slid beneath her so that he was on his back on the bunk and could pull her face-down over the top of him. Her body pressed warmly against his, the smooth secret place between her open legs rubbing gently against him to stiffen his resolve.

'Let me have it,' she whispered, her tears dried on her hot face.

Her hand groped lightly between their bodies, arranging matters to her satisfaction.

'That's so good!' she exclaimed, her arms round his neck.

Charles relaxed, breathing easily and waiting for her reflexes to take charge. The wait was not long before her internal stroking and massaging asserted itself, without any movement from her loins or from his. In moments she was panting and shuddering in her long drawn-out pleasure and for Charles there was nothing to do but lie beneath her and wait for the time when his body responded climactically to

135

hers. Because of the shortness of the interval between the bouts and his deliberate submissiveness when he was at other times most active, he was able to hold out for a long time, allowing himself to be drawn slowly up the lower slopes to the peak Jacqueline was revelling upon, then gradually he mounted the upper slopes until at last the summit was in plain view. Jacqueline's convulsions were stronger than ever, her entire body shaking in the grip of unimaginable pleasure. The muscles of her belly were clenching and unclenching almost brutally on his trapped part as she dragged him willy-nilly to the very peak and with a loud cry he jabbed quickly upwards into her and found release.

After that they fell asleep in each other's arms. She woke him up by shaking him hard.

'Charles – what is that noise? I'm frightened!'

'What noise?'

'Outside the train – that roaring noise – what is it?'

He listened for a moment.

'Ah, we must be passing through the Simplon tunnel, that's why the noise of the train is different. There is nothing to be alarmed about.'

'But it's been going on for so long.'

'The tunnel is twenty kilometres long. We are passing under the Alps. When we come out at the far end we shall be in Italy.'

'Are you sure?'

'Yes, I have been this way before. Be calm.'

'Where do we go from Italy?'

'We traverse the whole of northern Italy from Milan to Venice and Trieste and then cross the frontier into Serbia. But that will take a long time.'

'We are still very far from Turkey?'

'Yes. Are you so impatient to be there?'

To his surprise she began to weep again. Charles held her in one arm and wiped her face gently with his hand.

'Tell me what is troubling you,' he suggested.

'I can't – it is too awful.'

'Of course you can. What are friends for if not to share troubles?'

'You would not understand.'

'Something to do with your Turkish lover?' Charles hazarded.

'Yes,' she answered in a small voice, sounding extremely miserable.

'Then tell me and I promise that I shall understand and help you to the best of my ability.'

At that she plucked up courage, dried her tears and started to tell him.

'The last day but one before Mehmet left Paris to go home,' she said, 'I went to his hotel in the afternoon. We had planned to be together that evening and night but I couldn't wait that long and went soon after lunch.'

'Where was this?'

'He had a suite at the Ritz Hotel. After all, he is very rich. I had been there several times before and a chamber-maid recognised me and unlocked the door for me to go in. Mehmet was not in the salon but I could hear his voice in one of the bedrooms. He was not speaking as if he was in conversation – he was speaking in the way he did to me during our intimate moments – a gentle lover's voice. I guessed that he had another woman with him and I was furious. I would kill her, scratch her eyes out, tear all her hair from her head – but some tiny voice inside me told me to make certain first.'

'A terrible moment for you,' said Charles soothingly.

'An incredible moment, believe me. I was with Mehmet the night before and he loved me until he was too exhausted to love me any more and wanted to sleep. And here – imagine it – only a few hours later and he was loving another!'

'What did you do?'

'The bedroom door was not fully closed. So I peeped round it without a sound. And there he was, sitting cross-legged on the bed in his green-striped dressing-gown. Ah, he looked so handsome that my heart turned to water.'

'But?'

'Leaning against him, clasped in one arm, was a boy. A boy of thirteen or fourteen, no more, totally naked. I was utterly dumbstruck by the sight. I stood there unable to move a muscle.'

'Good God! Had there been no hint of this prediliction before then?'

'None that I had ever noticed. But I was so in love with him – I still am – that he could do no wrong in my eyes. What fools we women are when we love a man!'

'When you recovered from the shock of this scene, what did you do?'

'When I recovered? That took some time. I stood there wanting to scream or to faint or to run away, all at the same time, and I could do nothing. Mehmet was fondling the boy between the legs and murmuring words of affection to him – the very same words he murmured to me when we were together.'

'My poor Jacqueline, what a hideous ordeal for you. I am lost for words.'

'As I was then! It was like a dreadful nightmare from which I could not rouse myself. Mehmet kissed the boy's eyelids as tenderly as he kissed mine, then his cheeks, then his mouth – a long kiss of love and desire. And all this time his hand was playing with the boy – you know where – coaxing him until *pfft* and Mehmet kissed him passionately.'

She began to cry again as she remembered what she had witnessed. Charles held her close and waited for her tears to stop.

'Even then it wasn't over,' she said finally, her voice very forlorn, 'Mehmet laughed and took off his dressing-gown. His sabre stood so proudly between his thighs that in spite of everything I had seen I wanted to go up to the bed and kneel to kiss it in homage. But that was not to be. Mehmet rolled the boy over face-down on the bed. It was if a knife had been thrust into my heart when I saw what he was going to do. I screamed – my voice had returned to me – and I ran into the room screaming and screaming.'

She was trembling in Charles arms. He stroked her hair to calm her.

'He was so angry with me,' she said. 'He gave the boy money and told him to go away and then he shouted at me. Can you believe that?'

'He was hiding his guilt, I suppose.'

'No, it wasn't that at all. He was angry with me because I didn't understand his ways. To him it is completely natural to take his pleasure with whomever he chooses, it seems—women or boys. He saw no difference. To me this was crushing emotionally. I tried to understand what he was telling me. I said to myself that he was of a people with customs unlike our own. But I couldn't accept it and he became angrier with me until I wanted to die.'

Charles kept his thoughts to himself out of pity for Jacqueline, but she spoke them for him.

'Naturally, he will not change,' she said. 'In Istanbul I shall have to share his love with others.'

'With boys.'

'And no doubt with other women too,' she said bleakly.

'Yet you are still determined to go to him?'

'I love him.'

Her confession seemed to relieve her mind and very soon she fell asleep again.

When Charles next awoke the train was at a standstill and he could hear voices and bustling noises, luggage trolleys and the cries of peddlers. They were at Milan station and it was early morning. He dressed and bent over to kiss Jacqueline lightly. Her eyes opened at once.

'Where are we?' she asked, 'in Turkey already?'

'No, no, we've reached Milan. I must go to shave and change my clothes. I will meet you in the dining-car for breakfast at nine. *Au revoir.*'

On his return to his own compartment in the next coach he found the attendant in the act of knocking on his door, a tray balanced on one hand at shoulder level.

'Your coffee, sir,' he said.

'Good, bring it in.'

The attendant's quick glance took in the perfectly-made bed and unused pyjamas laid out on it. He set the tray down and poured coffee for Charles without a word.

'One spoon of sugar,' said Charles, stripping off his jacket and shirt.

The attendant held his dressing-gown for him to slip into.

139

'When you go to the dining-car, sir, shall I make up the compartment for day-time, or would you prefer the bed to be left in case you desire to sleep.'

'You are most considerate. Make the compartment up for day use.'

'As you wish, sir.'

Shaved and washed, wearing a clean shirt and another tie, Charles met Jacqueline for breakfast and they talked on for an hour before moving to his compartment to allow the dining-car attendants to prepare for lunch. She told him about her marriage to a man who spent more of his time away from home than with her. From the hints she allowed to escape he formed the impression that she had been conducting brief and unsatisfactory affairs with different men since the first year of her marriage, largely from loneliness. She told him more about her Turk and how she loved him. This, thought Charles, was mostly illusion. She had a warm and affectionate nature and had responded rather too enthusiastically· to someone who had shown an interest in her. But the interest, he thought, was wholly in her body and its remarkable capabilities, not in Jacqueline as a real person.

They went for lunch after the train left Venice and was running along the side of the Mestre lagoon, the autumn sun glinting faintly on dull grey water. One of Prime Minister Mussolini's elite had boarded at Venice and was enjoying a fine lunch, carefully waited upon by the attentive dining-car attendants. He was a tall man, resplendent in uniform and riding-breeches, cross-belted and with a holstered pistol. Jacqueline stared at him admiringly for some moments before remembering with whom she was lunching.

They were back in his compartment when the train stopped at Trieste and moved on again.

'Soon we shall cross the frontier into Servo-Croatia,' said Charles, 'from there on we shall make slow time.'

'Why do you say that?'

'It is a country created only half a dozen years ago at the end of the War, mainly from bits and pieces of the Austrian Empire. It is a patchwork kingdom and in my view

140

Alexander will not sit on his throne for long.'

'Poor man – why do you think that about him?' .

'The Balkans, in a word. The people are Slavs but they come in assorted types, Serbs, Croats, Montenegroans and the rest of them. They never agree with each other and the only manner in which they settle their differences is by the knife and the gun. The institutions of democracy are unknown to them and always will be.'

'But why should that make the train run slow?'

'Because while the kingdom is new, the tracks are old. The line was built by the Austrians in your grandfather's day. And after we pass Belgrade it will become even slower.'

Jacqueline was cuddling up to him, her hand resting delicately in his lap.

'Last night was not too much for you?' he enquired, smiling.

'For me? It was absolute heaven. Every night should be like that.'

'As you say.'

'This is about the time of day that I feel the need to be loved. Don't you?'

'I rarely have the opportunity. In general I am occupied at this time of day and cannot get away from business. Occasionally I slip away for an afternoon, but all too seldom.'

'Ah, then you have a special friend in Paris. I thought so. Is she beautiful?'

'Enchanting, like you,' said Charles diplomatically.

'I am so pleased that we met on this journey. We have the entire afternoon before us and a private place where we can do whatever we choose. Isn't that convenient, Charles?'

'It could hardly be better arranged if we had planned it together.'

He leaned forward to bolt the door securely before taking Jacqueline his arms to kiss her. He knew from the night before that she derived only limited pleasure from being kissed or from having her breasts fondled. For her these were mere preliminaries to be hurried through in order to attain the true pleasure. Nevertheless, Charles took as long as suited him over kissing her mouth and face, her neck and ears. He slid a hand down the low-cut front of her frock to handle her small breasts and tease her nipples. Only when her fingers pulled impatiently at his trouser buttons did he advance further.

She trembled in anticipation when his hand touched her knee and began a slow journey under her skirt to stroke her smooth thighs above her stockings. Her sighs grew deeper when at last he reached her secret place. Her sighing became gasping and then hard panting when his probing fingers eased her over the brink of ecstasy.

After a long time he allowed her to rest and she kissed him in gratitude, her face flushed a pretty pink from her exertions. The rest was a short one – she made as if to lie down along the seat for him. Charles pulled her onto his lap, facing him, her skirt up to her waist. A small adjustment of buttons and underclothes and his train entered her tunnel.

This, thought Charles, was the best way to accomodate her. The position put at her disposal the advantage he had to offer and set off almost at once her tremors of renewed rapture while requiring no effort from him. The consideration was an important one, since her unique temperament necessitated a firmness beyond the capacity of most men, particularly if vital energy was expended in busy movement. As he had arranged matters, Jacqueline's truly astounding body performed of itself all that was required for their mutual pleasure.

Long after another woman would have fainted from the sustained peak of sensation, Jacqueline gasped out '*I love you, Charles!*'

And he, at the critical moment of his own experience, murmured '*I adore you, Jacqueline*' as the train whistled loudly and ground to a standstill at the frontier.

So their journey continued, eating, love-making, sleeping. By the time they reached Zagreb they were fortified by a sumptuous dinner and back in Jacqueline's compartment, naked on the bunk. She lay on top of him, shaking to the rattle of the train and her own inner delight, as if she would never stop. At Belgrade the next morning after breakfast

142

they strolled along the platform, chatting about the unfamiliar sights and enjoying each other's company as if they had known each other for years. Between Belgrade and Sofia in Bulgaria they made another memorable journey together in Charles' compartment, she naked across his knees. After dinner that evening they retired to Jacqueline's compartment and played their nocturnal games, fell asleep and were awakened very early in the morning by the formalities outside the train as they crossed the frontier into Turkey.

As the train puffed into Istanbul not long after midday Charles breathed a secret sigh of relief. Jacqueline was a remarkable woman, the most remarkable he had ever known. With her he had experienced a journey that he would remember with pleasure and pride for the duration of his life. But ... her devotion to the sexual needs of her body and her diligence in satisfying them was, he had to admit to himself, a little overwhelming. He felt that he had come to understand why her husband's work, whatever it might be, required extensive travel away from Paris. The poor fellow evidently needed to recuperate and regain his energies away from home in between visits to his charming wife.

The sleeping-car attendant pocketed the tip Charles gave him.

'Thank you, sir. I have not had much opportunity to be of service to you on the journey.'

In fact, apart from unmaking an untouched bed each morning and changing the towels, he had been called upon to do nothing at all.

'The luck of the draw,' said Charles. 'If you had been in charge of a different compartment you would have had twice the work.'

Amid the noise and bustle of Sirkedji Station Charles kissed Jacqueline goodbye, wished her luck and saw her safely into an ancient taxi to go and find her Turk.

'I shall be at the Pera-Palace Hotel for some days,' he told her. 'If you have any difficulties, you can find me there. Remember always that you are a Frenchwoman and do not allow yourself to be imposed upon by others.'

143

His business affairs in Istanbul took a week and he heard nothing from her. Travelling back to Paris alone, he felt a sense of loss. He lay awake in the dark on his gently rocking bunk, listening to the clicking of the train wheels on the lines and wished that she were with him.

Eyes closed, he tried to recall how her warm little breasts had felt in his hands and the silkiness of her inner thighs against his mouth. But how fleeting are the memories of love, how impossible to recapture once they are gone. *Plaisir d'amour ne dure qu'un moment*, he thought sadly.

In his mind's eye he could see Jacqueline, small, dark-haired, vivacious, her pointed little chin and her wide smile. Yet their moments of intimacy were now only a recollection of generalised pleasure, not the exquisite touch of his fingertips on the smoothly depilated treasure between her legs.

Fled too, except as a tremulous fantasy, was the sensation of her long ecstasy pulsating about his upright stem, drawing him into the same rhapsody of the flesh. Ah, what a woman she was!

Charles threw back the sheet and blanket to let his lonely appurtenance rear up in balked desire from his pyjamas. He clasped it in both hands and squeezed rhythmically in an attempt to reproduce the joyous sensations which Jacqueline had bestowed upon him so bountifully.

What a tragic waste, he thought momentarily, that so much feminine charm and ability for love should be thrown away on a dismal foreigner not capable of truly appreciating it! An imbecile who, with such a woman at his disposal, chose to abuse boys! Poor Jacqueline – what would become of her?

He pictured in his mind her small hot body pressing down on him as it had on the outward journey – her gasps and squirmings of delight. Slowly, slowly, his sense of loss retreated before the assault of overbearing passion.

'Jacqueline, I adore you,' he whispered into the darkness and the stiff penis he was massaging throbbed and poured its hot tears into his hands.

THE DIVERSIONS OF MONIQUE CHABROL

By virtue of the trees planted along both pavements, the street might almost be called an avenue. The buildings were well-designed and substantial, with shops at street level and half a dozen floors of family apartments above. The Auteil district of Paris had long held something of a reputation as a home of writers and artists – not the types who went hungry in unheated attics, but the prosperous sort who could sell their work for good prices, eat regularly and dress well.

In truth, Madame Chabrol did not much fit in with Alain's idea of how an artist should look, but then, who could say? She was about forty or a little less, a trifle plump, comfortable in her ways, almost motherly at times. She paid the usual rate for models. To a sixteen-year-old boy with his way to make in the world, that was what mattered most.

'Time for a rest, Alain,' she said, 'sit over there and we'll have some coffee.'

'Thank you, Madame,' said Alain, stretching his arms and back.

He had been standing for what seemed an eternity in a most awkward position which, she had assured him, was the classical Greek javelin-thrower pose. In fact, she had shown him a picture in a book – a statue lacking a nose, a left hand and both feet, to indicate how he should stand. As a result, his arms ached and his back was stiff. His muscles loosened by stretching, he reached for his clothes.

'No, don't dress yet,' said Madame Chabrol, 'I want to continue after you've rested. And besides, it is useful to watch the play of your leg muscles as you move.'

The studio was one large room of her apartment. The side nearest the big window was cleared except for the artist's equipment – an easel with a half-finished canvas, a table littered with paints and brushes, a prop or two. The other side of the room was furnished for Monique's comfort when she gave herself a rest from her work. There were chairs, a sofa, small tables, all grouped on a large and colourful rug. On one of the tables was a tray on which stood a pot of coffee kept permanently hot by a small spirit-lamp.

A large oil painting hung on the wall above the sofa. It showed two women side by side, half-turned towards each other. They were shown only to the waist and were both naked. One of them held delicately between forefinger and thumb the nearest nipple of the other woman.

'That picture, Madame, did you paint it?'

'Yes, do you like it?'

'I do not understand it. They are both very pretty, of course.'

'I painted it as a joke. The original is in the Louvre if you wish to see it. It was painted well over three hundred years ago and is of the School of Fontainebleau.'

'This is a copy of the original?'

'In a way. The ladies in the original were the Duchesse de Villars and Gabrielle d'Estrées. I copied it exactly, except that I substituted the faces of a relation of mine and a friend of hers. Now do you understand?'

'Which is related to you?' Alain asked, glancing from the elegant beauty of the women pictured and Madame Chabrol's comfortable body.

'The dark-haired one on the left. She is Madame Brissard and we are related by marriage. The ginger-haired woman is her friend Madame Dumoutier.'

Alain sat down where she had indicated, abandoning the puzzle of why two ladies should be painted as a copy of an old picture. He had learned enough about artists in his twelve months of posing for them not to concern himself with their motives. And least of all with their jokes. Evidently it amused Madame Chabrol.

The chair on which he was seated had a tapestry bottom and back and felt odd against his bare backside and shoulder-blades. Madame Chabrol poured black coffee from the heated silver pot and handed it to him. Instead of sitting down herself with another cup, she fetched a big sketch-pad and a handful of pencils from her work-table and disconcerted Alain by sitting on the floor in front of him, her

146

legs crossed beneath her and the pad on her ample lap.

'This gives me a completely different angle,' she explained, 'a whole new viewpoint. A little practice at sketching is always useful.'

She scratched away with pencil on paper while Alain sipped the strong and sweet coffee. He found that sitting as he was was different from posing. Suddenly he was a person again, not a model. The move from one side of the room to the other had changed the balance between him and Madame Chabrol. He was aware for the first time of her round breasts under her loose blouse. Her big nipples were faintly visible against the thin material in a way that was no longer arty-casual but distinctly feminine. The cross-legged position in which she was sitting put her bare knees and thighs plainly in sight under her stretched-out skirt.

Inevitably at this point Alain's own sexuality intruded into his thoughts as he looked at her and saw a woman instead of a female artist. The hitherto docile part between his legs started to lengthen. Being only sixteen he was embarrassed and also afraid that Madame Chabrol might be offended if she noticed.

Monique had already noticed.

'That's good,' she said casually, 'I rarely have an opportunity to draw a man in that condition. Put the cup down and lean back with your hands on the chair-arms. That's it. Move your legs apart a little.'

'But Madame ...'

'Let us have no stupid modesty, Alain. I want to draw you, that's all.'

Alain sat awkwardly as she drew, her eyes switching between her pad and his upright part.

'Very good,' she said, as if to herself, 'a slight tapering from the base upwards to the top and a gentle curve inwards towards the body along the whole length ... an oval head. And those veins! Open your legs wider, Alain, I need to see everything.'

He was half-lying in the chair, thighs parted and legs stretched out towards her, astonished by the turn of events. He looked down the length of his own body to where his stem reared up from a nest of crinkly brown hair and was suffused by a certain pride that she should want to draw it. But then, artists were creatures of whim, as he well knew. Nearly all the pictures he had seen by male artists were of naked women, many with their legs parted as if waiting for a lover. Well then, who was to say that a man ready for a woman was not equally attractive as a subject to a woman artist?

'Marvellous,' Monique said, 'how long can you stay like that?'

She had torn her first sketch from the pad and was working swiftly at a new one, hitching herself a little sideways to improve her line of sight.

'I can't say, Madame.'

'But you must know.'

'I cannot control it, really. Sometimes it will remain like that for a long time and sometimes it will go down as quickly as it arose. It all depends.'

'On what?'

'Whether I am with someone ... or if something special is in my mind.'

'Whatever you do, don't let it go soft until I have finished my work. Think of something which arouses you.'

'What shall I think of?'

'How do I know? A naked woman, I suppose.'

'I don't think I can.'

'Wait, I have an idea.'

She dropped her pad and pencil to open her peasant-style blouse and tug it out of her skirt waistband. Her breasts rolled as she leaned forward to retrieve her implements.

'There you are. Keep your eyes on those. That should excite you enough to keep you standing up.'

Alain stared at her meaty breasts and tried to imagine the feel of them in his hands. Their fullness caused them to hang loose and slightly low, but for all that they were desirable big bulbs of warm flesh. It would be marvellous to get hold of them, he thought. He soon began to speculate about the rest of her body, the areas covered by her skirt. Her belly was broad, that was obvious, and well-padded – a good place to

148

lie on. Her thighs, from what he could see of them up her skirt, were strong. There would be a curtain of dark hair between them, he guessed, concealing her final secret.

'But it's twitching about,' Monique complained, busy with her sketch. 'Can't you make it stand still? The head is beautifully swollen and looks ready to burst – a superb subject, but difficult to draw while it trembles like that.'

'I can't help it.' Alain murmured, 'you wanted me to be excited and I am.'

'Heavens, one would think that it had a life and will of its own. Does it always jump about when it's erect?'

'Yes,' he breathed, in sweet torment.

'The little eye is open – but how fascinating! And the top is glistening wet. How can I possibly achieve that effect in pencil? Chalk would have served better, if I'd thought of it in time. Can you stay like that while I start all over again, do you think?'

'Please ...' Alain sighed, 'I can't stand any more.'

'But it's bigger and harder than ever.'

'I can't help myself now.'

'Ah, I understand what you mean.'

His eyes were unfocused but he heard the rustle of her skirt as she came to kneel beside him. Her hand grasped his trembling penis and he groped blindly for the breasts hanging so close to him. She jolted him up and down abruptly and pumped him dry in a silvery flood of racking pleasure.

'Don't move,' she said, 'not a muscle. Stay exactly like that with your eyes closed.'

He lay loose-limbed in the chair, legs sprawled inelegantly. Monique scribbled furiously on her pad to capture this moment of total male relaxation.

'That's the best I can do for now,' she announced at last. 'This has been an interesting artistic experience. I am extremely grateful to you for making it possible and I shall pay you twice the fee we agreed.'

'Thank you, Madame. Can I see your drawing?'

'Of course you can. Clean yourself up and get dressed while I add a touch of shading here and there.'

149

Her sketches were far more skilled than he expected. There was a naturalism in them which was lacking from her classical Greek studies of young athletes, not that Alain thought of it in those terms. To him it was simply more real.

Her first attempt showed him from knees to navel, the second covered the same area but with more assurance. His penis was so strong and firmly drawn that he stared in admiration.

'Was that really how I looked to you?'

'Yes, dominating and full of angry pride. A superb subject. I am astonished that I have overlooked the possibilities of this for so long.'

'You have never drawn a man like that before?'

'Many times, especially when I was younger, but not with the understanding I have now.'

'What do you mean, Madame?'

'Previously I saw the penis as a part of a man's body, erect for a certain purpose. An appendage, no more than that. With you just now I saw this column of hard flesh as a total expression of your personality at that moment. Do you understand what I mean?'

Alain shrugged. Artists usually had strange ideas which no one else could understand. It was of no importance. He was pleased about the extra money.

Monique was most pleased with her final picture, but Alain was not. It showed the whole of him, his head turned half to the left, eyes closed, face calm, his limp penis lolling against his belly. His lack of enthusiasm for the sketch arose from a sense of vulnerability it awoke in him, but he was not able to express his feelings clearly in words.

'What was in your mind when you were sprawled there so relaxed, do you remember?' she asked, busily tucking her blouse into her skirt.

'What was I thinking? Nothing much. I was just resting.'

'Well, perhaps it is too much to ask you to analyse yourself at your age,' she said. 'Let us be glad that you have a handsomely developed body. The rest may come in time.'

That night Alain told his girl-friend about Madame Chabrol. Suzanne was also sixteen and they had been infatuated with each other for nearly six months. She was very slim, with spiky little breasts and a waist which Alain could almost span with his two hands. They enjoyed each other's company whenever opportunity served, even though the limit of their exploration was mutual caressing to the natural peak of sensation. Alain desired to go further, Suzanne's prudence dictated otherwise.

'I don't believe you,' she said, 'you're making it up to tease me.'

'But it's true, every word.'

'Then she fancied you, this so-called artist woman. Are you sure you didn't do it to her? No lies now!'

'That's the strangest thing. She didn't want me at all. She didn't want me to touch her. She was simply interested in what she called a new artistic experience.'

'Artistic experience my backside! If she did that to you, then she must fancy you. Maybe she thought you were too young to give her what she wanted. Has she asked you to go there again?'

'On Thursday.'

'For the same money?'

'I suppose so. I didn't ask.'

Alain and Suzanne were still at school and money was important to them. Their only opportunities to be together were when either his or her parents were out for the evening. Alain had it in mind to rent a cheap room somewhere so that they would have a place to go for their pleasures. For that they needed more money than their parents gave them to spend.

On his next visit to her studio Monique Chabrol wasted no time on having him pose for Greek athletic studies. She got him to assist her to move the sofa across her work-room so that it was under the window and, within minutes of entering the apartment, Alain was sprawled naked on it. Monique sat herself on a padded low stool close to him, equipped with a stack of rough-textured drawing-paper and a flat wooden box of coloured chalks. He was unaroused, but this seemed not to bother her in the least as she began a trial sketch, her drawing-board across her knees.

151

She observed his body closely.

'Put your hands behind your head,' she suggested, 'elbows well up.'

'Like this?'

'That's it. The pose lifts your chest and tightens your belly muscles.'

'There is something I wish to tell you, Madame.'

'What?' she asked absently, busy with her chalks.

'I told my girl-friend about the last time I was here to pose for you.'

'Did you? What did she say?'

'She believes that you fancy me because of what you did.'

'That's understandable – I imagine that she was jealous. She's quite wrong, of course. You may tell her that I have no sexual inclinations towards you. Is she pretty?'

'She's marvellous.'

'That's a big word for a young lady. Can you describe her for me? In detail, I mean, so that I can see her in my mind's eye. Is she tall, short, fat, thin, dark, fair? Tell me.'

Alain closed his eyes to visualise Suzanne as he had seen her last. Monique Chabrol discarded her first sketch and put another big sheet of paper on her board. She was only half-listening as Lucien tried inexpertly to convey his recollection of Suzanne's face and form, her spiky little breasts, her tight round belly-button and the smoothness of her thighs. He lacked the command of words to match her physical attractions, however he tried. Not that his verbal description was of any particular importance – the attempt in itself was sufficient to bring him up pulsatingly erect and Monique worked fast to put what she saw on paper.

'She sounds lovely, your friend,' she said when he ran out of words. 'Don't stop now. I can imagine from what you have said how she looks. But tell me what it is like to feel her body all over with your hands.'

He tried, but he had no comparisons or metaphors to convey the sensations of fondling Suzanne's breasts or of licking her tiny pink nipples. Even less so the moment of parting the soft folds of skin between her legs and exploring with his fingers inside her warm and slippery opening.

'When you put it inside her, Alain, what does that feel like?'

Time had stopped for Alain as he lay in a pink haze of sensuality, as if in a warm bath, images unfolding in his mind under the stimulus of Monique Chabrol's words. He had never yet been permitted to put *it* inside Suzanne, but he could amost feel the velvety cling of flesh around his upright part. Monique drew furiously to record in pastel shades the outward manifestations of his inward delight. She wanted to reproduce on her sheets of paper the flush of his skin and the nervous tension of his thighs. And above all, the most fascinating object, the upward straining and engorged penis. To this end she kept him trembling on the brink of spontaneous emission by her suggestive questioning, until his breath was rasping painfully and his body was wrenched by muscular tremors.

With a supressed sigh, she put aside her drawing-board at last to sit beside him on the sofa. With a few hard flicks of her hand she unleashed a torrent that spattered him from throat to navel. Alain cried out at the sudden discharge of almost unendurable tension, his arms and legs flailing.

His collapse was complete. Monique went back to her stool and took up her board again. She smiled to see that some of the pink and red chalk had transferred itself from her fingers to his now diminishing penis in bright smudges.

He was utterly at her disposal, his arms hanging limply at his sides, legs turned a little sideways, spent penis at rest. She was able to take all the time she wished to draw what she saw, infusing her picture of a drowsy young man with an almost maternal tenderness. When her final drawing was completed, she was very pleased with it. She thought that it was one of the best things she had ever done. To anyone seeing the picture without knowledge of the sexual preliminaries that had preceded this moment, it was a masterly study of a naked youth asleep on a sofa. She knew that she would have not the least difficulty in selling it for a good price when it went on show in the small gallery with which she conducted her business.

'Wake up, Alain,' she said, touching his shoulder, 'we've finished for today. You are an excellent model.'

Suzanne, having a brisk nature, did not let matters rest as they were. She made her way after school to Madame Chabrol's apartment, sure in her mind that she had to deal with an older rival for Alain's affections. The building impressed her, as it had impressed Alain, but the woman who opened the apartment door did not. To sixteen year old Suzanne, Monique Chabrol appeared overweight, her bosom exaggerated and her hips too broad. For a woman who evidently had money, her dress was far from fashionable. And if that were not enough, she was without stockings and barefoot.

'I am a friend of Alain and I must speak to you, Madame,' Suzanne announced firmly.

'How nice of you to call! Please come in, Suzanne. I recognised you at once from his description.'

'He has talked to you about me?' Suzanne exclaimed as she followed Madame Chabrol through the hall and into the work-room.

'Why, yes. He began by saying that you were marvellous, but eventually he managed to give me a clearer impression – tall, very slim, light brown hair. I knew you at once. Would you like some coffee?'

'No, thank you. I came to see for myself what you are like.'

'Am I to take it that you do not like him to pose for me?' Monique asked in surprise. 'He has a superbly athletic body for so young a man. He is a good model.'

'It's not just a question of drawing him. Lots of artists do that because he is good-looking,' Suzanne answered tartly. 'No, it's what else you do to him that I object to.'

Monique Chabrol was well able to deal with Suzanne. Before long she had her sitting on the sofa with a cup of coffee, discussing Alain unemotionally. After a little time she went over to the studio side of the room to get the chalk drawing of him in repose.

'But that's very good!' said Suzanne, 'that's exactly how he looks when he dozes off. You are a real artist, Madame.'

'I'm pleased with that drawing myself. I hope that I have convinced you that my interest in your young man is entirely artistic.'

154

'Well ... what about what you did to him? Was that entirely artistic?'

'Suzanne, let us be frank with each other, woman to woman. It is my experience that young men sometimes allow themselves to become excited when they pose nude for female artists. This is in their nature, of course, we understand that. Having no clothes on, their sexual parts exposed and a woman present, their thoughts turn to something else besides art. They begin to imagine things, and once their imagination is fired, they are unable to control themselves. Poor Alain got himself into such a state while he was posing for me that I thought he might explode, like a balloon blown up too much. There was no way I could continue to work while he was like that. Nor did it seem possible to tell him to put his clothes on and go home, such was his state of desperation. And so, to render him more pacific, I touched him twice and he went off pop. Then, with all that out of the way and his mind calm, I was able to proceed with my work – which you have just admired.'

'Are you telling me the truth – was that all there was to it?'

'I am a practical person, as I believe you are. It was no more than an incident, a few moments in a couple of hours of work, that's all.'

'Do you treat all your models like that?'

'It is not often necessary. But if it becomes so, I am no prude. I have drawn and painted too many male bodies for there to be any mystery for me in their structure. With women models this does not happen, of course. Have you ever thought of posing? You have an interesting face and a good body.'

'Me? I couldn't possibly stand naked to be stared at!'

But for all that, it took Monique Chabrol less than five minutes and the promise of a fee to talk Suzanne out of her clothes.

'How do you want me to stand?'

Monique looked her up and down in thought, then moved one of her low padded stools over near the window.

'Sit on that, sideways to the light. Let me see ... yes, put your stockings on again. And the garters. The contrast is

155

good. Now, cross your ankles and let your knees move apart a little. Do you have a comb?'

'Not with me.'

'I'll get you one. Your hair is so pretty that we must draw attention to it.'

Very soon Monique was working with her chalks. Suzanne sat straight-backed, combing her light brown hair. The raising of her arms pulled her little breasts tightly upwards and gave prominence to her baby nipples.

'The light is good today,' Monique observed. 'There is a soft gleam along the inside of your right thigh, from stocking-top to groin. Head a bit further back. Left elbow a fraction higher. Are you comfortable enough?'

'Not very, but it doesn't matter. Can I ask you something or will it disturb your work?'

'Ask, by all means.'

'Your husband – does he live here?'

'To be truthful, there never was a Monsieur Chabrol in my life. I invented him years ago when I first came to live in Paris and saw how much easier things are for a woman if people think that there is a man in the background somewhere.'

'Where did you come from then?'

'Nowhere you have ever heard of. A tiny place in the country called St Aubin du Maine.'

'So this apartment and everything, it's all yours?'

'All mine.'

'May I ask you something else?'

'Anything you like, so long as you keep still.'

'Please don't be offended, Madame, but do you have much experience of men?'

'Experience of men in bed, I suppose you mean. Of course I have. I started when I was not much older than you are now. Young men of my own age, eighteen, nineteen. You must understand that things were different twenty years ago. Girls of good family were carefully chaperoned then. Since the war, much has changed in this regard. But back then ... at first it was only stolen kisses when no one was watching. But matters progressed, as they always do. I well remember the first time my breasts were touched by a young man. You cannot imagine how exciting that was for me, even through the layers of clothes we then wore. I was ready to do everything with him right then at that moment. Of course, it was out of the question that I or my sisters should be left alone long enough for anything of interest to be done. Yet all the same, we learned how to manage affairs better, through small intrigues and covering for each other. What shall I tell you? The day came when I had an entire hour with a young man. Ah, the clothes we wore when I was a young woman! Ankle-length dresses with tight sleeves, layers of petticoats, laced corsets, knee-length drawers – it took my admirer a quarter of an hour to unwrap me from all those clothes before he could lay me on the bed and commence. There's your portrait finished – do you like it?'

Suzanne took the picture and studied it carefully.

'Am I really so pretty?' she asked.

The open-kneed pose and the stockings on her otherwise bare body gave the picture a distinct eroticism which Suzanne was unable to define, but which pleased her greatly.

'Naturally, or else I would not have asked you to pose for me.'

'You work very fast, madame.'

'For this, yes. I would like to paint you in oils and for that you must come here and sit for me several times. That will be a real portrait, not a sketch.'

'I'd like that. But you have not finished telling me about your lovers.'

'How can I make you understand at your age that it was the complications of love which made me decide never to marry. But that is what happened. You must realise that the average man is a sentimentalist, whatever veneer of cynicism or sophistication he wears to impress his friends. A man has his pleasure of you and gives you pleasure in return and that is how it should be. But soon, if the pleasure is particularly keen or your personality attracts him, he begins to talk about eternal love. He wants to move in with you to live – or wants you to move in with him. Or he wants to spend four or five evenings and nights every week with you. Some of them begin to talk about marriage even and children. What a

157

nuisance men become when they roll off your body and start to talk! I have no time or taste for the inevitable compromises of living with a man, husband or lover. My work is far more important to me than that.'

'You live like a nun?'

'Heavens no! There are half a dozen good friends I enjoy sleeping with when I have time. But the invitation is always mine, not theirs.'

'And that is enough for you?'

Monique laughed.

'I am not religious,' she said, 'but in some ways I do live like a nun. Stay there and I will show you one of my secrets.'

From a cabinet with long and flat drawers she took out a folder of unmounted pictures and opened it across Suzanne's bare thighs. The girl stared in amazement at the top drawing. It displayed a woman's genital zone, life-size. Between parted thighs a fleshy mound and thick dark hair were drawn in exact detail in black pencil.

'That's me,' said Monique proudly, 'I make use of the long mirror you see standing in the corner there. I bring it over here to the light and sit up close to it on this stool.'

She turned the drawing over to reveal the next one. A faint pink blush made its appearance on Suzanne's cheeks. The subject was the same, this time in colour, the smooth white flesh of the thighs expertly done. A hand lay partly over the dark-fleeced mound. The middle finger was between the pouting pink lips, thrust in to the second knuckle.

'The picture shows a right hand,' Monique explained casually, 'and that is correct since I am right-handed and therefore use my right hand to pleasure myself. But as I also draw with my right hand, that is really my left hand you see, reversed.'

'Left hand, right hand – you are confusing me,' said Suzanne.

'It is of no importance. The result is all that matters.'

In the next picture there were two hands. The fingers of one held the wetly glistening folds of flesh apart to display a dark pink interior, in which the thumb and forefinger of the other hand rolled Madame Chabrol's small bud of delight between them.

'But how could you draw at all with both hands occupied like that?' asked Suzanne, the question of artistic technique suppressing her surprise at the subject itself.

'A good question. It required several stages, reversing the hands in the mirror one after the other. But technique is of little concern. In the course of producing these exquisite representations of myself I thrill myself to ecstasy again and again. This one now – do you see that tiny figure in pencil in the bottom corner? Eight. That records the number of times I achieved the peak of pleasure while I was drawing that picture. It required two whole days.'

'Pictures like these can never be sold,' said Suzanne.

'I do them for my own pleasure, but I often sell them. Does that surprise you? There are connoisseurs who will pay very highly for such work, here in France and abroad in Germany. And from publishers there is a constant demand for book illustrations. I sold a water-colour only last week to a collector and quite recently I was commissioned to produce a complete set of black and white drawings for a private edition of some of the unpublished poems of Guillaume Apollinaire.'

She thought it unnecessary to mention that only the day before she had sold for a very reasonable sum the sketch of Alain in a condition of arousal.

'It is enough for you, is it, to be your own lover?' Suzanne asked.

'You are missing the point. I have found a way to combine art and physical pleasure in a way that is wholly satisfactory, artistically and physically. There was a note of disapproval in your voice when you asked that question. Tell me honestly, before you met Alain, did you never pleasure yourself?'

'Children's games,' said Suzanne, blushing again.

'Perhaps. But tell me something else. There is no need to retreat into false shame with me now that you have seen these pictures. Do you not still enjoy this children's game, as you call it? I am certain that you do. When you are in bed at night, your hands stroke those pointed little breasts of yours

159

and you tickle your nipples until they awake. Can you deny it? You sigh at those delicious sensations which are so simply produced. You pull up your night-dress – am I not right – and touch yourself between the legs. You slip a finger inside, just like this picture, and you rub gently. Tremors of joy run through you. You rub faster, the excitement grows and grows until you sigh and shake, gripped tight in ecstasy as if in a lover's arms. Is that not so?'

Suzanne made no reply. Her head was bowed, eyes on the picture on her lap.

'Where is the shame in such pleasures?' Monique asked softly. 'Is this not the natural way to please and pacify yourself?'

'I suppose so ... I cannot deny it ... but somehow it is not enough.'

'Not for you, perhaps. You make your pleasure depend on another person's willingness to oblige you and his skill in doing so. Some men are very unskilled, I can assure you. They push half a dozen times and finish, leaving you unsatisfied. Then what?'

'But you say nothing about love, Madame, only pleasure.'

'To a person like myself love is an inconvenience. It demands compromises and adjustments. That is not my way. When I contemplate my body, desire stirs in me. I will not wait for a husband to come home or a lover to arrive. I enjoy my desire at once – and as often as I choose. I am never left partly satisfied by the inability of a man to perform more than once or twice. Even when I invite a man friend to visit me I am so impatient for pleasure that I do it to myself two or three times before he gets here. My friends are constantly surprised that I am so hot for them that I rush them straight from the door to the bed, without even a drink first. Of course, they do not realise that I have already lit the fuse and am prepared for the explosion.'

For Monique it was no great effort to bring the girl round to her way of seeing things. She persuaded her to pose again, still naked on the stool, but this time without the comb and with one hand between her spread thighs, her eyes downcast to admire her own body.

'Now that is quite charming,' said Monique, starting to work carefully with her coloured chalks. 'Are you comfortable?'

'Yes, thank you,' Suzanne replied, her cheeks faintly pink.

'The pose is very natural. There is nothing forced or awkward about the lines of your limbs and body. That's what we are after. Have you ever seen the celebrated portrait of Madame Olympe by Edouard Manet?'

'Never.'

'It was painted about sixty years ago. She lies naked on a bed, propped up on one elbow. Her other hand rests lovingly on the treasure between her legs.'

'Treasure?'

'The part of you that you are touching now – do you not regard it as a jewel of great worth? It is my belief that Manet copied the pose from a painting by Titian which is in the Uffizi Gallery at Florence. Titian's model lies propped on the same elbow, her other hand caressing herself lightly between the legs.'

'Famous artists really paint such pictures for public display?'

'But of course. Now, just trace one finger-tip along those pretty lips between your thighs – yes, very lightly through the hair. Good, very good – once more. What an interesting shade of brown the hair is between your legs – there is a touch of blonde in it. Not the easiest of shades to put on paper. You are not embarrassed when I talk about your body, are you? The true artist observes exactly without emotional involvement, as I have endeavoured to explain to you.'

'No, I'm not embarrassed now. You have taught me to admire myself in a way unknown to me before.'

'Then I have achieved something. Now, slip one finger just a little inside to improve the picture.'

'But ...'

'You said that you were not embarrassed. You do it when you are alone – why not now?'

So matters progressed, Monique maintaining a flow of encouraging words to gain Suzanne's confidence. Eventually she reached the point of persuading the girl to play with herself in earnest and any lingering shyness was quickly dispersed by the sensations she began to experience.

'Slowly now, or you will outpace the artist's ability to record so entrancing a scene.'

'As slowly as you like,' Suzanne murmured.

'That's better. Those exquisite thrills are to be savoured, not rushed through as if one were running a race. The arrival is never in doubt – it is the journey towards it which provides nine-tenths of the pleasure, isn't that so? Ah, how shall I ever capture the delicate shade of pink revealed between those young lips? And the gleam of light on skin as soft as silk? Where is the pigment to record what the eye observes?'

Suzanne's legs were trembling as she approached her point of departure.

'Gently, gently, said Monique. 'Give me time to fix these fleeting moments!'

'Too late!' Suzanne gasped, 'I can't hold back any longer!'

'Then let it happen.'

'Oh!' Suzanne wailed, her head thrown back and her fingers working at top speed. The position thrust her pointed little breasts forward.

'Delightful,' Monique pronounced.

Suzanne slowly bent over forward until her arms were resting across her thighs and the top of her head was showing to Monique.

'Did you enjoy that, my dear?' Monique enquired casually, still working at her drawing.

'Yes. Was that what you wanted to see?'

'Not particularly the final moments, for they put an end to my work temporarily. But before that, yes, you were enchanting as a subject. Naturally, those final moments arrive. After all, it took me eight times before I completed that picture of myself you saw. The peaks one reaches in this sort of work are the rewards along the way for the effort itself. That is how I regard them. Do you understand what I mean by this?'

'I think so,' said Suzanne, raising her head to look at Monique again. 'You must find it tiring to be an artist.'

'Never tiring, my dear. Satisfying. When I have done all that I can for one day, my body and mind are fully in repose. How many can say that truthfully?'

'You are a strange person, Madame. Your ideas are so different. You have made me think today things that would never have entered my mind. And because of you I have done things which would have made me die of shame only yesterday.'

'There is no place for shame in art or in life itself, Suzanne. Shame is a crippling fear which prevents us from expressing our deepest wishes. Dress yourself now and we will have some coffee and talk further.'

The topic of their conversation was an oil painting of Suzanne.

'You will have to pose many times, you understand, for the technique is so much slower, the colours more difficult to manipulate. The peaks you will reach will delay the work, because even if you were able to continue afterwards, the expression of your face and the tone of your skin would subtly change – believe me, I understand these matters.'

'I am sure you do, after seeing your own pictures.'

'Will you do it?'

'Yes, Madame, if we can agree on a proper fee for the sittings.'

Monique smiled. Once it came down to a question of money, there were no further problems. Just as Alain would allow for a fee her voyeuristic pleasures, so would Suzanne. The arrangement was a most satisfactory one.

After Suzanne had gone, Monique carried the cheval-glass from the corner where it usually stood and set it before her armchair, tilted exactly to give the view she desired. She removed her skirt and opened her blouse before sitting down, thighs well apart, to admire the reflection of herself. The long string of jade beads she wore around her neck looped down between her unmodishly full breasts, the green stones glowing against her white skin. She plucked lightly at her nipples until they stiffened, then wet her fingers with her tongue and teased the red-brown nubs expertly. As she

163

played, she stared lovingly at the broad sweep of her belly in the looking-glass and her navel set in it like a small eye.

She lowered her eyes to enjoy the reflected image of her strong thighs and the patch of dark hair between them. Each time that she exposed it to herself she was pleased that it grew not in a solid triangle, as on most women, but in a broad vertical strip that left her groins clean and bare. Why this should delight her she did not know, except that perhaps it was somewhat unusual, but delight her visually it did.

'The artist's eye,' she had told herself on many occasions, 'seeking out what can be set down on canvas or paper to create an impression on the viewer. And without doubt I am my own best viewer and my own best patron because I alone know the love that has gone into the creation of my pictures – the intensity of the love between artist and subject, when the subject is my own body.'

Her fingers were at the strip of dark hair, closely watched in the mirror. Very nearly black, she thought, but it contained a lingering shade of dark brown. The texture was crisp, not only to her finger-tips but visibly in the mirror. At one stage in her artistic career she had shaved the hair off completely and for a while had been fascinated by the young girl look of a smooth mound. Then she tired of it and wanted her dark strip back again, believing that it was more interesting that way.

The fingers, as if impelled by a desire of their own, separated the lips a little and moved away to allow her to see the effect.

'There is so much pleasure in this small slit,' she said aloud, for the wonder of it struck her every time. 'So many tunes can be played on this musical instrument, from the gentle piping of a single flute right up to the thunderous crescendo of a full orchestra. I have composed serenades, concertos and whole symphonies here with eight fingers and two thumbs.'

Her fingers pulled the lips wider to expose the pink and moist interior and then the bud which would flower into crimson passion.

'She has aroused me, that little girl, with her game.'

Monique said to her reflection in the looking-glass. 'See how it stands firm already, before I even touch it. I will not deny it the pleasure it demands of me.'

She shivered at the delicious sensation of a finger-tip kissing it lightly, then sighed as two fingers stroked it rhythmically.

'You are very impatient today,' she panted, watching the image of herself. 'Very well then, since you have served my pleasure so many times, this time I will serve your greed.'

Eyes half-closed, she observed her fingers moving in a blur of action. Her thighs split wide, her loose breasts shook and then she saw her loins pushing upwards at her fingers as her climax came in waves of delirious sensation.

GUY VERNEY'S BUSINESS TRIP

It was on one of his frequent visits to his factory at Nantes that Guy Verney met his match. He became acquainted with a woman who owned an important shop in the city and was a valued customer of his company. The requirements of business seemed in this instance to mix well with the promptings of pleasure and Guy took her to dinner one-evening.

They enjoyed each other's company, for Guy was charming to women when his mind was not occupied with business or politics. He was still a good-looking man, in his mid-forties, a little heavy perhaps from over-indulgence, dark-haired, expensively dressed and accustomed to commanding the best of food, wine and service in restaurants. Yvette Begard was a few years younger, a woman of experience, one who knew her own mind and arranged her own life. Guy learned that she had been married to an officer of the local police force, though they were now separated, and had two sons at university.

In all, the meal was a success and Guy was invited into Yvette's home when he escorted her there afterwards. They talked more, over another glass of good cognac, and the invitation was extended to Yvette's bed-room. Guy accepted with alacrity, being away from home and the marital services of his wife.

Physically, Yvette Begard was a big woman compared with Jeanne Verney. She permitted Guy to undress her, between kisses, to reveal large breasts and broad hips, much to Guy's delight. He preferred these somewhat obvious feminine characteristics to his own wife's fashionably small breasts and boyish hips. His tastes in these matters had been formed in his adolescence, the years before the War, when women dressed to accentuate the curve of hip and bosom, and if nature had been ungenerous in this respect, then padding made up for it.

Yvette, warm and naked, sat on his lap. Guy weighed one of her soft breasts in his hand and spoke of it appreciatively.

'Don't you think that I'm a trifle overweight?' she asked.

'Not in the least, my dear.'

'But my hips!'

'Magnificent,' said Guy, squeezing her fleshy backside.

Yvette removed his tie and collar and opened his shirt.

'Ah, how masculine I find this thick fur on your chest,' she sighed. 'So virile!'

'Not as thick as the fur down here, eh?' said Guy, running a hand down her rounded belly.

The affair progressed pleasantly between them, right up to the moment when Yvette lay on her back and spread herself for him. Guy's performance was as brief as always and although he found nothing in the least amiss, for Yvette it was totally unrewarding. When she established that there was to be no second opportunity that night, her dissatisfaction was only thinly disguised. Guy was packed off to his hotel well before midnight.

On his next visit to Nantes, two weeks later, there was a message waiting for him, requesting him to telephone Madame Begard. She received his call with every indication of pleasure, talked of business for a while and accepted his invitation to dinner that night.

The comedy was played as before, with one small difference. Guy drank even more than usual at dinner, imperceptibly urged by Yvette. Back at her house, his glass was filled more than once with golden-yellow cognac before they ascended to the bed-room. Guy was accustomed to heavy drinking, but his head was spinning slightly by the time he and Yvette were disrobed and together in the broad bed. His condition accentuated his natural shortcoming – he plunged into Yvette without even the pretence of a caress, fired his shot instantly, rolled over and was profoundly asleep before she had time to respond in any way at all.

Some time later he was awakened by a sharp pain in the region of his private parts. In the confusion of half-sleep he tried to put his hands to the afflicted area, only to discover that his arms would not move from their unnatural stretched-out position. Again the sharp pain tore at him, making him shout. He struggled to sit up and fell back defeated. The room was very dark and he was alone in bed, disoriented from the effects of the strong liquor still active in him.

Rolling his head to the left and then to the right revealed the reason why his arms would not obey him. A stout wooden board had been slipped under his shoulders while he was asleep and his wrists were fastened to its extremities by leather straps. He was attempting to solve this mystery when a renewal of the pain between his legs caused him to look down. A cord was noosed about his male equipment. Two utterly undistinguishable figures stood at the foot of the bed, one of them holding the cord and jerking it viciously.

Guy opened his mouth to shout for help and at once one of the half-seen figures moved quickly to his side and stuffed a large wad of material between his jaws to stifle his outcry. Pain shot through him as the cord was twitched again, then more pain as the figure beside him took him by the hair and pulled him into a sitting position, his arms held out stiffly from his body by the board. He was half-pulled, half-pushed off the bed and hauled ignominiously across the room by the cord. He tried to ease the drag on his tender parts by moving quickly to close the gap between himself and his tormentor, only to discover that a second cord, noosed alongside the first, ran back between his legs and was held taut by the tormentor behind him. He could do nothing but obey their silent urgings.

The descent of the stairs was a nightmare for him, held from front and rear and compelled to twist his body sideways to accomodate the long board. Halfway down, the end nearest the wall struck a small picture and sent it crashing to the stairs. He was punished with so savage a jerk on both chords that he screamed into his gag-filled mouth.

Nor were his problems at an end at the foot of the stairs. A door was opened and there were more steps leading down into a cellar. These were of stone, chill to his bare feet. Below him was a gleam of yellow light – at least he would be able to see the perpetrators of this outrage.

Before he could do so, his attention was seized by a frightening contraption in the middle of the stone floor. From a long and low platform two thick wooden shafts stood up to a height of about five feet, their distance apart about the same. Guy was hauled unceremoniously between them, a savage pull of the cord immobilised him while his captors hoisted up the ends of the plank he was fastened to, one after the other, wrenching his shoulder-blades, and fitted them into slots in the top of the uprights.

There were more indignities to come. Wooden poles were dropped into fittings near the base of the uprights, one before and one behind his ankles, immobilising his legs. Then worst of all, his legs were dragged so wide apart that he thought he would be torn in half and fastened with chains to hooks in the poles. He half-stood, half-hung in the grotesque pillory, naked and helpless and in excruciating discomfort.

One of the dark figures took a lit candle from the stone-flagged floor and used it to light others in sconces around the walls. At last Guy beheld his torturers – both black-hooded and black-cloaked. Before he could think much of that, one of them lifted a bucket from the floor and dashed the contents over his face and body – icy cold water that made him start in his bonds.

'That should wake him up,' said the other one, chuckling, and it was a woman's voice, though not one that Guy had heard before, 'I'll change the gag so that he doesn't choke to death before we've finished with him.'

She moved round the apparatus to stand behind him. The material in Guy's mouth had absorbed some of the water thrown over him and he was gulping to swallow it as it trickled down his throat. The cloaked and hooded figure in front of him reached between his distended jaws to take hold of the gag and with horrified amazement he watched a pair of women's stockings being pulled out of his mouth, the length seeming endless to him. As his mouth opened to draw in a deep breath, the woman behind him forced a thick rubber bar between his teeth, like a horse's bit. It was pulled back hard and fastened tightly with cords at the back of his neck.

'Bite on that,' said the voice behind him, 'it will stop you from screaming when we get to work on you.'

Guy's heart quailed. These were merely preparations – what would they do to him when they started in earnest? The cellar was not warm, but he was already sweating.

The two of them faced him, no more than a yard away, to throw the sides of their cloaks back over their shoulders. They were both women, naked except for shoes. He noticed that they wore identical shoes of black glacé kid, high-heeled, open fronted and laced round the ankles with black ribbon.

Their hoods remained on – hoods such as Guy had seen only in pictures of the Spanish Inquisition at its dreaded work – high-pointed black hoods that covered the head completely and had only eye-holes in the front.

The cold water had fully awakened Guy. Humiliatingly pinioned as he was, he observed the two women, his mind functioning again. He was certain that the slightly taller one was Yvette Begard, though he had not heard her voice yet. This was her house, her cellar, and there was a certain familiarity about the heavy swaying breasts and the thick patch of dark hair between her legs. The other woman must be a close friend, he reasoned, brought in to assist in this atrocious farce. In other circumstances he would have been gratified to see her naked body – her breasts were even fuller than Yvette's, quite extraordinary fleshy globes. Under the black hood she was a blonde, he deduced, from the colour of the wispy hair that graced her lower belly.

'Enough of this nonsense,' he tried to say, 'let me go at once,' but the gag reduced his words to mere gurgles.

'Complain as much as you like,' said the unknown woman, 'rattle your chains. You won't break loose. An expert built that simple piece of apparatus that holds you. We are ready to begin now.'

'You are here to be punished,' said the other woman, and it was Yvette's voice. 'You deserve the most rigorous punishment possible for your execrable manners towards women. You are not a man – you are a living insult to women. That thing dangling between your legs is an instrument of frustration, not of pleasure. It will suffer before this night is over, believe me.'

'Are you sure he's awake?' the other woman asked, 'he's very quiet.'

'Make sure for yourself then.'

She approached him and loosened the cords round his maltreated parts, for which he was grateful. His gratitude was short-lived, for she began to pinch his nipples, using her finger-nails cruelly.

'Perhaps we should put the pins through them right away, Solange,' Yvette suggested, 'that livens them up in most cases.'

'Not just yet – he's stirring already. Look at this!'

She seized Guy's member and tugged it hard. He had not realised it until then, but her assault on his nipples had effected a substantial increase in its length and girth. Yvette advanced to examine what her friend was holding.

'Would you believe it? Ready for one of his quick-fire acts, is he? We'll soon put a stop to that. Will you do the honours or shall I?'

'Let me – I've been looking forward to it. Keep an eye on him to see what effect it has.'

A ledge along one wall held a variety of objects. From among them Solange took a broad leather strap as long as her arm and disappeared behind Guy. The crack of leather and a stinging pain across his bare buttocks caused him to rattle about in his pillory to break free. His attempts were unavailing; he could do nothing but shake and suffer as the strap fell across him again and again and a fiery sensation suffused his backside.

'Well?' Solange demanded, pausing in her work. 'Has that done the trick or does he need more, the dirty beast?'

'See for yourself – it's made him worse. He must enjoy being thrashed. Look, it's standing out like a pole!'

'Enjoys it, does he? He's here to suffer, not to enjoy himself,' Solange exclaimed angrily as she grabbed Guy's equipment so hard that he feared she might tear it from his body. 'What a useless thing it is, for all its size. I think we should let the virgin calm him down.'

Uppermost in Guy's thoughts was revenge. However long this indignity lasted, eventually the women must set him free. Then it would be his turn to pay them back. He would have them arrested and charged, they would go to prison for a long time. Another consideration intruded. To follow that course would mean to expose his plight in the newspapers. *Respected businessman sexually abused by two local women* ... how would he ever show his face in Nantes again after that? Worse, a report like that would surely be picked up by one or more of the Paris newspapers. His friends would know, his family, his wife ... they would laugh at him behind their hands while pretending to sympathise. No, he concluded, there could be no official reprisal, he had too much to lose. His revenge must be private.

All such thoughts fled from his mind as Yvette took from the ledge behind her the 'virgin' and advanced on him, holding it before her at the level of her groins.

Guy stared in blank horror at a heart-shaped pad of leather, a loop at the top and two long straps hanging down from its point. The pad bristled with gleaming steel pins, their sharp points towards him.

'Are you experienced with virgins?' Yvette asked him mockingly, 'I am sure that a man like you has torn his way into many a tender little pocket. The name of our virgin is Minette and no man has yet succeeded in making her cry out by his brutal defloration of her. Quite the contrary, men cry out when they feel her embrace. But I forgot, you can't cry out, can you? Never mind, we shall understand your silence.'

She hung the fearsome object by its loop over his hard-standing penis and let it hang there loosely.

'You are not a stupid man,' Yvette continued, 'you will have guessed what comes next. The straps are passed between your legs and then pulled tight, then taken round your waist and tied in front. Those needle-sharp points, thirty-six of them in all, embed themselves in your most tender parts. Imagine it ... the harder the straps are pulled, the deeper the pins go in. Simple, yes? But so effective, we have found.'

Guy shook his head vigorously, pleading with his eyes and

172

with inarticulate croaks. *Anything you like*, he was trying to say, *I'll give you anything you like to let me go.*

'See, he doesn't relish the prospect of making love to Minette,' said Solange, her laughter making her big breasts shake. 'He's begging to be let off. You can see the terror in his eyes. I love it when they beg in absolute terror. Shall I adjust the straps or would you like to?'

'I think I have the right,' said Yvette.

'Of course. If I may make a suggestion, don't pull too hard on the straps the first time. We don't want him to faint too soon.'

'But he's a persistent offender! Why should any mercy at all be shown to him, tell me that.'

'You're right, there's no reason in the world to spare him anything. Pull as hard as you can, make him suffer. When he faints we'll revive him with a bucket of cold water and carry on.'

To Guy they were no longer women, though their full bodies were totally exposed to his sight. The black hoods depersonalised them, the identical pairs of shoes had the same effect. In his blind panic he could not remember their names any longer or which was which. They were torturers about to inflict hideous pain and injury on him.

'On the other hand,' said the one with the dark pubic hair, 'It would be a pity to keep interrupting things by having to revive him. You have a calmer temperament than I do — you must have first turn at adjusting Minette.'

'As you wish,' and the other woman walked around Guy, her high heels clicking on the stone flags. Paralysed with horror, he felt her hand reach between his wide-spread legs to take the long straps. She was standing so close to him that he could feel the pressure of her breasts against his back.

'Minette kisses very gently at first,' she said in his ear, 'her touch is loving and exciting when she begins. Then as she becomes aroused, her embrace tightens. Her love-bites grow more piercing until eventually ... but you will experience all that. Her climax is devastating.'

The straps were drawn slowly between his legs, prolonging his fear. He stared down, praying that his penis would go

173

limp, then the loop would slip off and the torment become impossible. Yet it remained obdurately straight.

He jerked in his bonds as tiny pin-pricks assailed the soft parts between his legs and then stopped.

'You see,' said the voice at his ear, 'she is tender at first, enjoyable even. But next time she touches you ...'

The woman in front of Guy took his oustanding part tightly in her hand.

'It does have a certain use, after all,' she said, 'it is the perfect peg on which to hang our little toy. Do you suppose there is any other use for it, Solange?'

'None that I can think of. Shall I continue?'

'You may well be right, but it seems a pity to abandon so sturdy an implement to the destructive caresses of Minette without one last attempt. What do you say?'

'I think you're wasting your time.'

'We have plenty of that, all night and all tomorrow – as long as we wish.'

'No, only as long as he lasts.'

'True, but he's well-built and strong for a man of his age. He should last till midday, at least, if we rest him now and then.'

'I doubt it. These types that drink too much have little stamina.'

'All the same, I think I might give it a try.'

She put a hand on Guy's shoulder to steady herself, stood on the bars that held his ankles and with her other hand parted the folds of flesh between her legs to steer his upstanding part into her. Guy's arms were strained cruelly as she half-hung on him, her arms around his neck and one leg round the back of his thigh.

'Well, what do you think?' the woman behind him enquired.

'There is a possibility, no more than that. He obviously requires a touch of the strap to get him going.'

'It will be a pleasure.'

The crack of the leather across Guy's backside made him jerk forward, implanting him deeper in the woman clinging to him. He understood what was wanted of him as the strap

174

fell again and thrust with all the strength he could still muster. Sexual connection with any woman was, in the circumstances, very far from his mind. The thought that kept him going was that if he could satisfy this woman, his monstrous tribulations would be terminated.

She was not to be easily satisfied, it emerged. Through the black hood that shrouded her head Guy could hear her sighs and gasps of pleasure, her wordless exclamations. Her finger-nails dug atrociously into the flesh of his neck and shoulders and her body grew hotter against him. Yet still she cried '*More, more!*' and each time that fatigue slowed him down, the strap across his behind stung him to renewed efforts.

Slowly, very slowly, she mounted the heights, her cries becoming louder and fiercer. With the end almost in sight, Guy rallied his remaining forces, sweat pouring down his chest and back, to push her over the edge of delight. When at last her throes commenced, her hips drummed against his and the sharp prickle of points from the forgotten Minette brought grunts of pain from Guy and a fervent hope that it would not be pulled tightly against him while the woman's convulsion was sustained.

After she unwound herself from him and stood back, the woman behind Guy asked, 'Any good?'

'My dear, I've known worse in my time. To be fair to this creature, not that there's any reason to be, the experience was positively enjoyable.'

'Not for him, I hope!'

'Of course not. The presence of Minette so close to his masculinity ensured his acquiescence. Has she damaged him very much, I wonder?'

She unhooked the savage contraption from Guy's still extended penis and squatted to examine his dependents.

'Nothing to speak of,' she reported, 'a pin-prick or two on the skin. Hardly a drop of blood to be seen. We must employ sterner methods to bring him to heel.'

'I like the sound of that. There are several of our toys we haven't tried on a man for ages. But before we proceed with that, perhaps I should also make use of what he has

175

available still.'

'By all means.'

'I'm not tall enough to use him as you did. We'll have to extend him.'

'That should be amusing. I'll release the bolts for you.'

Guy watched in fearful anticipation as the woman who had just violated him went in turn to each of the uprights on which he was supported and did something at their bases that caused metal to clink.'

'Down you go,' said the voice behind him and he was pulled backwards briskly by the shoulders. The vertical posts were hinged at their bases, the board across his shoulders pulled them over, and he was lowered none too gently until he lay trussed on the wooden base of the pillory. He gazed upwards at the woman standing with a foot planted on either side of his head, surveying his extended and helpless body. The vista up her bare legs to the dimly-perceived mysteries of the blonde patch at the join of her thighs appeared tremendously long to him.

The outward curve of her belly and the massy rotundities of her breasts cut off his view of her hooded head. Guy gulped, his fear shading into another and quite different emotion.

'Would you believe it!' he heard the woman above him say, 'that thing of his is waving about as if it wanted me to make use of it. This enthusiasm must be curbed at once.'

'I could apply the tourniquet. That's extremely effective in bringing men under control.'

'We have so many devastating methods at our disposal that it's hard to choose. On balance, I prefer to use our tried and trusted Minette again.'

'The choice is yours, my dear. I'll arrange her for you.'

The loop was put over Guy's standing part again. Lying on his back, he felt the pad hanging down between his legs and the tiny touch of sharp points warned him to remain still. The blonde-haired woman stepped over the cross-bar that held his arms and put the straps beneath his thighs and brought them up under his buttocks. She seated herself on his belly, so that all he could see of her was her black cloak

176

and hood.

The straps were in her hands, he knew. If he incurred her displeasure she could inflict pain on him by tugging at them. He hardly breathed as his captive member was gripped by ungentle fingers and pushed forcibly into a warm place.

'That's good,' said the woman sitting on him, 'it's like mounting a horse and taking hold of the reins.'

'You must put him through his paces,' said the other voice, 'keep him firmly under control, because he's not well trained yet.'

'You may be sure of that. He won't get a chance to bolt while I'm in the saddle.'

She began slowly at first, her hips swaying backwards and forwards lightly as if familiarising herself with the saddle-pommel. When she warmed to her work, her movements became more impetuous and Guy feared that in her enthusiasm she might haul on the straps and damage him. Like the first, she continued for a long time, uttering cries of pleasure, her heavy backside pounding into his belly as she rode on towards her crisis. Long after she had thumped the breath out of him and he was wheezing round his gag, she gave five or six frenzied pushes and then ran down like a clockwork toy until she was still.

'Did you find that satisfactory?' he heard.

'Yes. We've made an interesting discovery tonight – there is a use for him if he's kept under proper control.'

'You didn't permit him the least enjoyment?'

'Most certainly not! Look – hard as a broom-handle still.'

She climbed off him and the two of them, heads masked and lush bodies exposed, stood on either side of Guy, staring down. He lay quietly, beyond fear and beyond humiliation.

'Do you think that a bucket of cold water would put an end to this display now that we have no further use for it?' the woman on his right asked.

'Very possibly, but we must not let him imagine that we have any regard for his drum-stick because we used it to beat a tattoo. Let it remain frustrated while we make him understand the contempt we both feel for him.'

'You're quite right. How about giving it a lashing with the

cords – put a few welts on it as a souvenir?'

Guy was emotionally exhausted. He had surrendered his will to them. He was their creature, to be abused in any manner they chose. So much so that their menacing words of ill-treatment yet to come awoke a fearful pleasure in his heart.

'A lashing? Perhaps. But before that, the final abasement. Remove his gag, Solange.'

'He may scream out in agony if I do that.'

'He's past screaming by now.'

The fastenings behind his neck were untied and the rubber bit taken from between his strained jaws. Yvette – he thought it must be her because of the dark thatch – towered above him, one foot on each side of his head.

'Nothing has changed,' she said to him. 'You are a living insult to women and you have been made to suffer for that, though no suffering is adequate to compensate for the frustration you have inflicted during your lifetime. I despise you. Do you understand – you are despicable!'

Her foot pressed against his face.

'Kiss it as a token of your humiliation,' she ordered.

Guy pressed his lips to the black glacé kid shoe, a curious joy suffusing him.

'That's good,' said the other woman, 'he shall kiss my feet too, both of them.'

Yvette moved away for Solange to present her feet to his mouth.

'You do not escape so lightly,' Yvette said to Guy, 'as a man you are contemptible, and the most contemptible part of you is this.'

The pointed toe of her shoe nudged his still stiff part. As he watched, she put the sole of her shoe against it and pressed it down hard against his belly.

'I trample this despised object beneath my foot,' she exclaimed loudly.

For Guy it was the final push over the precipice of abasement. Under her shoe his tormented member throbbed wildly and then discharged. The black shoe ground into him as he croaked and groaned in the grip of an ecstasy he had never before experienced. The eruption was not his normal single splash but like a hosepipe with the tap turned on full.

He looked up at the hooded women as a dog looks at its master. When they unstrapped him from the pillory, his face was wet with tears of relief and he was so drained, physically and emotionally, that he could not stand unaided.

'We've tamed him,' said Yvette, laughing.

'I doubt it,' said Solange, 'we have taught him a lesson, no more than that. He is cowed for the moment but he will recover in a day or two – animals like him are untamable.'

'See what a mess he has made of himself. Sluice him down with cold water.'

'Willingly,' and Solange flung another bucketful over his chest and belly, making him gasp.

They threw a rough towel at his feet to dry himself with, then his clothes, before pushing him out through the door into the street. Guy was too exhausted in mind and body to do more than make his way slowly and painfully back to his hotel. His arms and back ached from the pillory, his bottom was sore from the strapping and his penis felt as if it had been mangled. It was nearly three in the morning before he reached the hotel and collapsed into bed.

He slept until midday. By then his aches had disappeared and he was able to reconstruct in his mind what had happened to him. He found that his emotions were strangely mixed. The indignity of the proceedings was incredible and utterly monstrous. For naturally, a man in his position in life was not subject to physical outrage from anyone. There would be condign retribution on Yvette Begard and her friend, no question about that. But then, recalling the extraordinary event at the end of the torment, when he had involuntarily experienced a discharge of passion hitherto beyond his experience, he became somewhat confused.

Eventually he roused himself and caught the train for Paris without going back to his factory. On the journey he turned over in his mind various ways of revenging himself on the two women without invoking the forces of the law. The most practical method appeared to be to hire half a dozen thugs in Paris and take them to Nantes. He would watch

179

while Yvette Begard and her friend were hung in their own pillory, one after the other, thrashed with the leather strap until their buttocks bled and then raped by all the men. What had he to fear? They to were most unlikely to complain to the police because that would mean that the way they had treated him would be exposed. And that would make them a laughing-stock.

For a couple of days he did not require his usual marital rights from his wife Jeanne, to her surprise. She wondered if he could be ill – he certainly had returned from Nantes looking somewhat pale and shaken. The only other possibility she could think of was that he had found someone else, more to his way of doing things, and that thought was a pleasant one to her. However, on the third night he was home he seemed to be himself again, in that he rolled her determinedly on to her back the moment she got into bed and performed in the usual way.

Such dreams Guy had that night! Two women in pointed black hoods and high-heeled shoes stood at his bedside and laughed at him while he penetrated his slender wife. Their laughter was loud and mocking and it made their huge bare breasts roll about and their plump bellies shake. 'Look at that,' one of them said between guffaws. 'He's useless. A fourteen year old boy could do better.' In the middle of his nightmare Guy woke up sweating, to find himself physically aroused. He let Jeanne sleep undisturbed, wanting no more mockery in his dreams.

The next day he telephoned Nantes from his Paris office.

'Yvette? This is Guy Verney.'

'You forget yourself, I think. To you I am Madame Begard. What do you want?' she said coldly.

'Ah, excuse me, I was not thinking. Madame Begard, I shall be in Nantes tomorrow. Will you do me the honour of having dinner with me?'

'Surely I made my feelings towards you perfectly clear when you were here last. Goodbye.'

'No – don't hang up, please. Listen to me for a moment.'

'Well?'

All thoughts of revenge had gone from Guy's mind. The

one thing he wanted from Yvette was that astonishing release into ecstasy he had experienced under her glacé leather shoe. The image of that was beginning to obsess him.

'I understand that you do not respect me, Madame,' he said, 'I shall understand if you have no wish to waste your time on a person you despise.'

'Good. You have learned something then.'

'But, Madame Begard ... the fact of the matter is ... I mean ... oh God, it's so difficult to explain. I hardly understand my own intentions in the matter. If only you will agree to meet me, however briefly, perhaps I can make myself clear.'

'Why should I give myself the least concern over you and your intentions?'

'There is no reason, I agree. You revenged yourself on one you believed had treated you with disrespect.'

'And what of it?'

'The revenge pleased you, I believe, isn't that so?'

'It gave me a certain amount of pleasure to give you what you deserved.'

'Yes ... well, would it please you if I were to submit myself without reserve to your revenge again?'

There, he had said it! His secret was out. He waited breathlessly for her reply, his palm sweating on the telephone receiver held to his ear.

'Do you know what you are saying?' she asked.

'Madame, I have given it much thought. I am prepared to submit myself willingly to you and your friend.'

'Perhaps the shock of what occurred has enfeebled your memory.'

'No, I remember everything in great detail.'

'The noose and the pillory, have you forgotten them already?'

'They are vivid in my memory.'

'The strap?'

'Yes!'

'You remember Minette and you wish to meet her again?'

'You and Madame Solange and Minette – would you consider it?'

'I cannot believe this. Are you drunk?'

'I am serious, Madame, I give you my word.'

'Even knowing that we have other little toys and more harsh methods than you have experienced so far?'

'Please tell me about them,' Guy begged.

'We have little clamps to fit on the nipples and tighten with a screw until you scream – except that the gag prevents you. Then we hang weights on the clamps to stretch your nipples, small weights at first, then heavier ones. The agony is atrocious, I believe – judging by the writhings of the victims. Would you offer yourself for that?'

'That and more.'

'More? How brave you are when you are so far away from my pillory. There are things you cannot even imagine.'

'Tell me a little about them, I implore you.'

'Steel pins as long as a finger – do you know what we do with them?'

'What?'

'We pass them through the candle flame until they are very hot, then pinch up a layer of flesh on your body and stick the pin right through. First on your belly where all the fat is. That is only a foretaste. Then we do it on your thighs, on the insides where it is softer. And eventually we put two or three through the loose skin of your worthless fixture.'

'Oh!'

'That frightens you, doesn't it? As well it might. At that point even the strongest man faints. We wake him up with cold water so that he can look down and see his own body stuck full of steel pins – just like Saint Sebastian in the church pictures.'

'How incredible ...' Guy murmured, his mind aflame, 'yet how marvellous.'

'You think so? You still know nothing of how the human body can be tormented exquisitely in every part by the collection of toys I have. Imagine yourself stripped and hanging in the pillory, your whole body on fire with pain while Solange and I use you for our pleasure – for that too is part of it.'

'I will endure anything you care to inflict on me,' said Guy, 'for the simple pleasure of kissing your shoes.'

'Ah yes, you derived some strange pleasure from being trampled on, didn't you? Solange and I were horrified at the sight. But these things happen, unseemly though they are. We accept them as evidence of the final degradation of the victim.'

'Will you meet me?'

'You are making it obvious to me that you derive pleasure from what to me is an act of vengeance against men. Why should I trouble myself to do anything which gives you pleasure? I have had my revenge on you and that's the end of it.'

The image of her black-shoed foot trampling his penis was uppermost in Guy's mind, blinding him to all else.

'I can afford to pay you well for your time. And Madame Solange,' he said.

'What? Do you suppose that I can be bought? Do you think me a prostitute?'

'No, no, no! What I meant was that I will make you a handsome gift as a token of my submission to you. It seems only just.'

'That's better.'

'Then may I dare hope to see you tomorrow?'

'You seem sincere. Very well, you shall have an opportunity to take Madame Solange and me to dinner tomorrow and we will talk. If you are able to persuade us both of your change of heart towards women, you shall make some small atonement afterwards for your worthlessness through suffering.'

'Thank you, Madame,' said Guy fervently, 'thank you.'

CHRISTOPHE AND THE
CONCIERGE'S DAUGHTER

As soon as Jeanne Verney was informed that Christophe was confined to his bed with a high temperature, she sent her own physician to visit him. Dr Fasquelle arrived at the rue Vavin in an automobile driven by a uniformed chauffeur, a circumstance which greatly impressed the concierge, Madame Joligny. She personally escorted him up the four flights of stairs to Christophe's tiny bachelor apartment and announced him grandly. In truth, he was an imposing figure in his superbly old-fashioned frock coat and tall hat. He examined Christophe courteously and diagnosed an attack of acute tonsilitis.

'There is nothing in this to concern you overmuch,' he pronounced. 'You will suffer a certain discomfort from the swelling and your temperature will remain high for a day or two. I will prescribe medicine which, to be perfectly honest with you, will do little more than make you drowsy, to help you sleep most of the time until the malady has run its course.'

'Thank you,' Christophe croaked painfully.

'Don't try to speak, my dear sir.'

Fasquelle turned to address the concierge who was hovering respectfully at the bedroom door.

'He will have difficulty in eating for a time, but it is important to build up his strength. May I rely on you to prepare him a good sustaining soup twice a day and to keep an eye on him?'

'But certainly, M'sieu,' she fluttered, almost curtseying.

'Excellent. I shall return tomorrow about this time to see what progress he is making.'

Jeanne's assurance that his account for attending Christophe during his illness would be paid by her encouraged Dr Fasquelle to visit him for the next three days, by which time Christophe was feeling very much better and was bored by lying alone in bed.

'Do not be too hasty,' the doctor advised him, 'another day of rest in bed will complete your cure. Read a book or ask the concierge to send out for a newspaper if time hangs heavy on your hands.'

An hour or so after Fasquelle had gone, Christophe's lunch was brought up to him by the concierge's daughter, Bernadette.

'May I wait until you have eaten it so I can take the tray down again?' she asked.

'Of course. Sit down, Bernadette, and talk to me for a while.'

Madame Joligny's cooking was simple but good. On the tray was a bowl of thick vegetable soup with an aroma to titillate Christophe's nostrils. It was accompanied by a length of fresh-baked bread, a glass of red wine and, to follow, a handsome portion of soft cheese.

'Why aren't you at school today?' he asked as he ate greedily.

'We've got holidays all this week.'

In the time he had lived in the rue Vavin, Christophe had seen Bernadette about the building many times. She was a friendly child – about twelve years old, he thought. Already she assisted her mother in her duties about the building, sometimes sweeping the steps, sometimes dragging rubbish out to be disposed of. A widow's daughter, born to a life of work and accustomed to it at so early an age, a sad thought for Christophe, for although he too was the child of a widow, his boyhood had been protected and happy. He always made a point of saying a friendly word to Bernadette when he passed her on the stairs or in the entrance.

'Why do I have the privilege of being served by you today?' he enquired. 'Is your mother busy?'

'She's gone out to the shops. Have you been very ill?'

'So-so. I'm feeling much better now.'

'You still look pale.'

'Tomorrow I shall be out of this bed,' he answered, and put the tray on his bedside table now that he was finished with it. 'That was good soup.'

'You don't look very strong yet,' Bernadette said, smiling

at him, 'I bet I'm stronger than you are right now.'

'Is that what you think?' Christophe retorted, smiling back, 'you're wrong.'

'I'll show you,' she said.

In a moment she was on the bed astride him, her small hands gripping his wrists to pin them to the pillow.

Christophe entered good-naturedly into the spirit of the game. He made a pretence of struggling to free himself, not using enough force to unseat her She was laughing in childish triumph all the while, her long brown hair tumbling about her face and shoulders.

'Surrender!' she said.

'Never!'

In the course of their playful wrestling the bed-clothes were kicked half off the bed to the floor and Bernadette's position astride his belly was forced backwards as he pressed against her hands. Inevitably there stirred inside his pyjamas a part of him which had been lethargic for days during his illness. At first, in the mock-struggle, Christophe did not notice what was occurring, but when Bernadette paused for breath he became aware that he was at full stretch. And more – the girl was seated firmly upon his treasure. For an instant he was embarrassed, but the sensation of her warmth through her underwear and the silk of his pyjamas was so agreeable that the embarrassment fled away and he wished only to prolong the contest.

'You think that you have defeated me,' he said, 'but in a moment I shall have recovered my strength and then I shall prove to you that you cannot beat me so easily.'

'That's what you say,' Bernadette answered, 'but I've won.'

'You took me by surprise, that's all.'

'Go on then, try to break loose.'

Christophe recommenced his false struggle. He could have been free in a second, had that been his wish. But after so long an abstinence his desire was to keep the child sitting where she was for as long as possible. He raised his right wrist from the pillow, not too far, with a great grimacing of exertion, then let her force it down again.

'You see!' she giggled.

'I'm not beaten yet,' he said sternly.

He began to twist his hips from side to side in a pretended manoeuvre to dislodge her from his body, being careful not to succeed, for the movement caused a delicious rubbing against his erect part.

'You won't tip me off that easily,' Bernadette told him.

'We shall see,' he answered, continuing the rolling which was giving rise to thrills of pleasure.

Bernadette's face was flushed and her eyes shone. Could it be, Christophe asked himself in amazement, that this child of twelve was secretly enjoying the friction herself? Could she have any understanding of such matters at her tender age? Under her plain grey frock the budding of her breasts was almost imperceptible. And yet, as he twisted his body beneath her, she was without any doubt bumping up and down on his trapped penis! Her action was unconscious, he reasoned, merely a physical reflex. On the other hand, even if one allowed the truth of that, it nevertheless implied that she was deriving a certain pleasure between her legs from the stimulus of his movement there.

'It may take some time,' he said, 'but I shall win.'

'You can take as long as you please,' she said, 'I'm the winner.'

A change in the sensations he was experiencing caused Christophe to realise that his girations had released his penis from his pyjamas. Under Bernadette's short skirt, which concealed all, his swollen friend was jutting out through the trouser slit and was rubbing against the child's underwear.

He stared curiously into her face, pink-cheeked and open-mouthed. Was she aware of his unseen proximity to her ... whatever Parisian children named it?

'Come on,' she said impatiently, 'you're not even trying.'

'On guard then! This is where I tip you off.'

He started to buck upwards with his loins, as if to throw her bodily off him. Not too vigorously – just sufficient to produce the exquisite sensation of rubbing against the soft skin of her hidden thing. Bernadette giggled again.

'You'll never get me off like that. Try harder!'

Christophe's emotions at that moment were overpowering. The impropriety of what he was about – the legality of it even – were far from his inflamed mind. His upward jolting carried him in moments past the point at which he could have stopped himself from what he was doing. He pulled his hands free of her grasp and seized her by the cheeks of her bottom to hold her fast. He thrust three more times and discharged his pent-up passion against her inner thigh. Bernadette squealed and her little hands tugged at his pyjama jacket.

The paroxysm was brief. Christophe released the child and lay still, bemused by what he had done.

'You've wet my leg,' Bernadette announced, still sitting on him.

'A thousand pardons. Take the towel from the wash-stand and dry yourself quickly before it gets on your clothes. Be careful.'

Bernadette pulled her skirt up round her waist to protect it while she examined the damage. By doing so she afforded him a view of her white cotton knickers – and her a view of his deflating penis. She looked and then grinned at him.

'You've been naughty,' she said slyly.

'Yes, you must promise not to tell anyone. Naughty people are punished and neither of us wants that, do we?'

She got off the bed to dry the trickle down her thigh, then came back to the bedside and handed him the towel.

'You must dry yourself too so nobody will know,' she said.

'Thank you.'

'That was a good game,' she said, watching his mopping up. 'Do you want to play it again?'

'Another time. I'm not very strong yet.'

'I won, didn't I?'

'I believe that you did.'

'Do you have any chocolates?'

'Not here, but I'll buy some for you the first time I go out, I promise.'

That evening the concierge herself brought him a light dinner. He had slept for an hour or two after Bernadette's departure and was refreshed and hungry. She had made him a large omelette with grated cheese, a glass of her not very

188

good wine and a peach for dessert. She drew up a chair and sat down while he ate.

'Your appetite is returning, M'sieu Larousse. That's a good sign. Dr Fasquelle is very pleased with your recovery.'

If Fasquelle expressed himself pleased, it went without saying that Madame Joligny was respectfully delighted.

'Yes, he won't be coming to see me any more,' said Christophe. 'I shall be getting up for a while tomorrow and the day after that I propose to venture outside for a short walk in the Luxembourg Gardens and perhaps to sit in the sun for an hour.'

'You must wear a warm scarf around your neck to protect it.'

'You've a kind heart, Madame Joligny. I am very grateful for the way in which you have looked after me.'

'Well, someone had to. It's not right for a young gentleman to be alone and helpless in your condition. You ought to get married to some nice girl and move into a bigger apartment.'

'But I like it here,' said Christophe, smiling at her motherly solicitude.

'You must know your own business best. But if a bit of plain advice from me won't offend you, in your place I'd set less store by visits from your beautiful lady and make a proper life for myself.'

'Why do you say that?' he asked in astonishment.

'You can't marry Madame Verney, that's obvious. She's got a life of her own. She'll look after you because she's fond of you, like sending her own doctor here. But how much time can she spare you? An afternoon a week, two if you're lucky.'

This was plain speaking with a vengeance, Christophe thought.

'You know her name?' he said. 'Have you been keeping watch on me then?'

'It's a concierge's job to know who comes in and who goes out. She hasn't been here for weeks.'

'There is a good reason for that.'

'I don't doubt it. You'd do best to take my advice and find yourself somebody else.'

'But I love her,' said Christophe, thinking to end the conversation.

'I should hope you do after all the times she's been up here in that very bed she bought for you. There's no reason to stop loving her. When she's ready to start with you again, you can carry on as before. But in the meantime, find a young lady of your own age so that you've got somebody to cuddle up to at night.'

'Madame Joligny, that is a most immoral suggestion,' said Christophe, grinning at her.

'I like to be practical,' she answered, 'now if you've finished eating, it's doctor's orders for you.'

'No more of his medicine, I implore you.'

The concierge took the tray from him and put it outside the small bedroom.

'Not medicine,' she said, rolling up her sleeves. 'A wash.'

'Wash? But I managed to wash and shave this morning.'

'An all-over wash,' she said firmly. 'You've been lying there sweating with fever for days. You don't smell of attar of roses. Where do you keep your clean pyjamas?'

'In the second drawer down.'

Madame Joligny busied herself with the arrangements, collecting clean pyjamas, towels, soap and a large basin of hot water. She stripped the bedcovers from him and made him take off his pyjama jacket and lie face down. The sensation of having his back washed was quite pleasant, he found to his surprise.

'Turn over and sit up,' she said.

She washed under his arms and dried him carefully. After that she had him lie down again to do his chest.

'You're lovely hair on your chest,' she remarked, 'like my poor husband, God rest him, only yours is darker.'

'What happened to him? Was he killed in the War?'

'He gave his life for France, you could say. He was a soldier, but it wasn't the Boche who put paid to him.'

By now Christophe was thoroughly enjoying her ministrations.

'Who then?' he asked curiously.

'He was coming home on leave and he got blind drunk as

soon as he reached Paris. When he left the bar to come home he fell under a train on the Metro and was killed outright.'

'My God, that's terrible!'

'He was always fond of the drink so I suppose it was justice of a sort. Now, let's have those pyjama trousers off and do the rest of you.'

'Madame Joligny – you will make me blush!'

'Shall I indeed? Well, you won't make me blush with anything you've got to show,' she retorted and pulled his pyjamas down his legs and threw them behind her on the floor.

Christophe went tense for a moment, then relaxed and closed his eyes as she soaped his belly and thighs. The experience was in truth an enjoyable one. He could almost imagine, behind his lowered eyelids, that Jeanne's hands were caressing him, but for the fact that her hands were soft and smooth and the ones touching him were hardened by housework.

'Well, well,' he heard the concierge say, 'you're really getting better, I see. I bet it hasn't stood up like that for a week.'

Thank heaven that you don't know about this morning, Christophe thought, your cunning little daughter took me by surprise and made it stand to attention for her amusement.

He sighed lightly as Madame Joligny's wet and soapy hand grasped him and slid up and down.

'I can understand why your beautiful lady used to spend hours here with you,' he heard her say, 'you've got the tackle for the job. If you know how to use it, your fortune's made.'

She sluiced him down with warm water and patted him dry the towel.

'Now I've seen that I won't be able to sleep tonight for thinking about it,' she said, chuckling, 'what a pity you're not strong enough yet to give me a demonstration. You owe me something for looking after you and cooking for you.'

Madame Joligny was approaching forty, plump of figure, with coarse black hair and a round chubby face, endlessly smiling. In all the time Christophe had lived in the rue Vavin he had never once thought of her as a desirable woman, nor

191

did he now. But she had unquestionably aroused him with her washing of his body.

'I shall be forever in your debt,' he said, 'but I fear that I am not well enough yet for the energetic demonstration you suggest.'

'All right then, I'll help you into your clean pyjamas and leave you to rest.'

'I beg you, do not leave me in this condition!'

'Like that, is it? Very well, my lad, I know what you want.'

Christophe watched as she unbuttoned the front of her black dress and slipped it off. She pulled the straps of her camisole off her hefty shoulders and lowered it to expose a pair of meaty breasts.

What have I let myself in for, he wondered, aghast at the sight. It would have been better to get rid of her and to relieve himself while dreaming about Jeanne.

Madame Joligny pulled the chair close up to the bedside, sat down and leaned forward over his loins. She pressed her breasts together with her palms, trapping his engorged penis between them. The warm and cushiony touch was altogether agreeable and quickly dispelled Christophe's apprehensions. When she rocked backwards and forwards, he was utterly enraptured by the sensation.

'Just this once,' she said soothingly, 'since you're not up to doing it properly, I'll see to you. Do you like that?'

'You are too kind ...' he murmured.

'A little kindness goes a long way in this world.'

'So true,' he sighed, eyes wide open to miss no moment of the massage of his erect part by the concierge's full bosom.

'You're sure that the excitement won't overtire you?' she enquired, rocking merrily away.

'It will speed my recovery, I am certain.'

'But are you well enough to achieve anything yet?'

'In such expert hands I am sure of it ... please continue ...'

'You must not think that I oblige all my tenants in this way.'

Christophe's loins lifted off the bed in a spate of gratification.

'There's a good boy,' the concierge cooed as if he were a

192

child. 'Such force! You've smeared me right up to my chin.'

Christophe lay watching her contentedly while she used the bowl of warm water to wash herself between the breasts and up her chest. Then she wiped him with the towel and helped him into his pyjamas.

'You enjoy being spoiled,' she said as she tucked him in.

'I admit it freely.'

'Are you more comfortable now?'

'Yes, I can't thank you enough for your kindness, Madame Joligny.'

'I'll leave you to rest. Tomorrow we'll have you out of bed for an hour or two as Dr Fasquelle said.'

On the next day he arose about ten o'clock, shaved and sat in the armchair in his sitting-room to read the newspaper after the concierge had brought him *café au lait* and a croissant for his breakfast. Later on it was Bernadette who came with his lunch and stayed to talk to him. The child was wearing the same frock as the same day before, plain and grey and ending just above her knees, perhaps the only one she had, he thought, apart from the one she wears to go to Mass on Sundays with her mother.

Bernadette admired his crimson dressing gown with the corded collar and cuffs and his dark red slippers of soft morocco leather. No sooner had he finished his meal than she proposed that they should play the 'wrestling-game' again. Christophe had in the meantime reflected on what had taken place at her instigation the previous day and was by no means willing to comply with her suggestion.

'No,' he said, 'if your mother were to find us wrestling together she would be extremely angry with both of us.

'That's all right, she's gone out.'

'But she may return at any moment.'

'She won't be back for hours.'

'How can you be sure of that?'

'She said she was going to visit Auntie Marthe.'

'And where does your aunt live?'

'In Clichy.'

The suburb was a fair journey by public transport, Christophe found himself thinking; Madame Joligny would not be back for some considerable time. But what am I contemplating, he asked himself, it is absurd!

'I'll take my knickers off before we start,' Bernadette offered artfully.

He was startled by the implications of what the girl had said. And undone by it – his heart beat faster and a prickle of sweat in his arm-pits informed him that he was lost. The temptation was more than he could withstand.

'Where shall we wrestle, here?' he asked softly.

'On the bed – that's the best place. Come on!'

He let her lead him by the hand into his tiny bedroom and removed his dressing-gown before he lay down. Bernadette reached under her short skirt to divest herself of her underwear.

'You've changed your pyjamas,' she observed, 'they're nice. You ought to take the bottoms off so nothing happens to them in case you're naughty.'

'Why do you think I shall be?' he teased.

'You were before. I'll help you,' and she undid the waist-tie and pulled the chartreuse-coloured trousers down to his knees.

Christophe was very conscious that the child was staring with avid interest at his exposed equipment. Certain natural changes in its size were taking place rapidly under her scrutiny.

'I know why you're so naughty,' Bernadette remarked.

'Tell me then.'

'Because your pretty lady doesn't come here any more, that's why.'

'You seem to know more about these matters than one would expect in a girl of your age. How does that come about?'

'I know about grown-ups' games,' she answered, her eyes still intent on his elongated part, 'and I know why she doesn't come here anymore.'

'Because I have been ill,' he said quickly, to end the topic.

'No, it's because she's going to have a baby.'

'Who told you that, little fox?'

'My mother.'

The matter was not one which Christophe wished to discuss with anyone, least of all a twelve-year-old girl. For nearly two years he had been Jeanne's lover and in that time he had advanced remarkably in the employ of her husband's business. He now held the title of manager and was the superior of his old ally, Henri Dufour, who had been so understanding about afternoons off in the early days. So far, so good. But Jeanne was by now six months pregnant and while he saw her when he was invited to dinner once a month at Verney's home, it had been a long time since her last visit to his bachelor apartment. For reasons of discretion, she had assured him.

She had also told him that the child was his and that, although she had not intended it, she was pleased by the event. But could he believe her? The question had nagged him a thousand times since her announcement. She claimed that Guy Verney had ceased to perform his marital duties, but was that the truth or a convenient lie? There had been no signs of trouble between Verney and his wife over her pregnancy and so the cessation of dutiful love-making, if a cessation there had been, must necessarily have been recent enough to persuade Verney that he was responsible. They are annoying, these unnecessary confusions, Christophe thought. After considering the whole matter at length, he had decided to suspend judgment upon it until after the child was born. Perhaps it would be possible to detect some resemblance to either himself or Verney and so resolve the issue in his mind. Not that anything would change as a result.

'Your mother told you, did she?' he said to Bernadette, 'I see that I am the subject of discussion between you.'

'We often talk about you because we both like you. Only I like you more than Mama does because I play games with you.'

'That's right,' he said, smiling.

His amusement was due to the recollection of the little game Bernadette's mother had played on him with her weighty breasts the evening before. At his smile the child scrambled onto the bed and took her seat upon his male part pressing it firmly to his belly. She was so young and

195

undeveloped that he felt no touch of hair against his most sensitive member, only warm and tender flesh. Bernadette arranged her skirt so that all was concealed.

'Now I've got you trapped,' she announced and giggled again.

'I believe that you have. I am your prisoner, Mademoiselle. What do you intend to do with me?'

'I'm going to sit on you for as long as I like.'

'How long will that be?'

'Till I squash you flat.'

She began to bounce up and down astride him, sending pleasurable little shocks through his belly.

'That tickles!' she said.

'What does?'

'The hair round your thing – it's tickling me.'

'Only because you have none of your own yet.'

'But I will soon.'

'I am sure of it. You are almost a woman now.'

'What colour do you think it will be?'

'Light brown, like the hair on your head.'

Christophe slid his hands under the child's short skirt to stroke her above the knees in time with her rubbing backwards and forwards along his penis with the soft lips between her thighs. By half-closing his eyes he could blur the image of the girl above him and imagine that it was Jeanne, naked and beautiful, her elegant breasts shuddering as she rode up and down on his upright part embedded within her adorable body. He could hear in his memory her little words of endearment, mingled with sighs of delight. The memory of better days – sweet to recall and yet bitter at the same time, for it was only memory, not actuality. He could almost see Jeanne's graceful arms reaching forward to pinch his nipples and then run her fingernails lightly down his belly towards their deep conjunction. Ah, would those enchanted afternoons with her ever return?

How different was this semi-seduction by a precocious child – this wholly physical act of the friction of two skins together! And yet, what was he to do? The desire was there, always, even if the means to gratify it were unworthy of him.

196

A man must be practical, he told himself. If the best wine was not available, a sensible man did not go thirsty but contented himself with a glass of *vin ordinaire*.

'Am I squashing you flat?' Bernadette asked, her face red and shiny.

'Yes ... I shall be quite flattened soon,' he sighed.

Bernadette speeded up her onslaught. Christophe's hands crept further along her thighs until his thumbs were in her soft groins. His crisis was fast approaching.

'Your skirt,' he gasped, 'raise it, *mignonne!*'

'Why – are you going to be naughty so soon?' she asked breathlessly.

'Very soon!'

She took the hem of her skirt in both hands and pulled it up. Christophe stared agog at the agreeable sight offered to him by her action – the unfledged but pouting lips at the fork of her thighs skidding back and forth along his distended penis. The sight did for him. He uttered a long groaning sigh as he saw the white streaks of his released passion flick out along his belly.

'You're being naughty!' Bernadette yelped, also watching his outpouring.

Her assault became faster and heavier and continued long after he was finished. When she stopped at last her face was bright red and she was grinning contentedly.

'Bernadette, you were naughty too, weren't you,' Christophe asked in amusement.

'No, girls don't make a mess like boys,' she said seriously.

'I know that. What I meant was that what you were doing gave you such pleasure that you continued until it overwhelmed you.'

'What does *overwhelm* mean?'

'That you ...' he groped for words she would understand, 'That what you were doing felt too good to stop. And after a while you couldn't stop. You kept on doing it until something seemed to go pop inside you.'

'Oh that,' she said, grinning at him, 'I've been making myself go off pop for ages. Only it's nicer with you. Let's do it again.'

'Your mama may return soon,' he said to avoid her invitation.

'She won't be back before six o'clock. She hasn't really gone to see Auntie Marthe in Clichy. That's what she tells me when she goes out for the afternoon if I'm home from school.'

'Then where does she go?'

'She goes to visit M'sieu Lafon at the bakery.'

'To buy bread for dinner?'

Bernadette giggled knowingly.

'He's her friend,' she said, 'they play together.'

'What do you mean by that?' Christophe asked, hardly able to believe what he was hearing.

'Like you and me, only he lies on top of her.'

'Bernadette, you're making this up.'

'I'm not! I saw them once, only they didn't see me. I got home early from school and they were doing it in our apartment downstairs. They didn't hear me come in, so I watched.'

'Good God – what did you see?'

'Mama had taken all her clothes off. She was on the bed with her knees up and her legs apart so that M'sieu Lafon could look at her.'

'Are you sure you're not making this up, Bernadette?'

'Honestly – I saw everything they were doing.'

'What were they doing? You said that your mother was lying down.'

'That's right. M'sieu Lafon was standing by the side of the bed with his trousers off and only his shirt on. He was holding his thing in his hand and stroking it and looking between Mama's legs. She's got a great big bush of hair there but you could still see hers because it was open.'

'A curious tableau! Did he touch her at all?'

'Oh yes. He put his hand between her legs and rubbed her and she got hold of his and did the same to him. And then he got on top of her and started huffing and puffing. It was so funny watching his bare behind going up and down that I had to put my hand over my mouth to stop myself from laughing.'

'Did you know what they were doing?'

The twelve-year-old grinned at him.

'Everybody knows,' she said.

'It seems to me that in Paris children learn of these matters at a remarkably early age. Where I grew up it was not so – at least not for me. That little friend of mine upon whom you are sitting used to get stiff and I had no idea why for a long time. A friend at school eventually showed me how to make him go back to sleep again by handling him, but I believe that I was fourteen or fifteen before I learned how men and women give each other pleasure. And it was not until I was eighteen years old that I found a girl who let me experience that pleasure with her.'

Bernadette was looking down at his penis trapped beneath her.

'It's gone stiff again now,' she observed.

'From listening to your story.'

'You want to be naughty again?'

'Why not?' he said in resignation, 'but this time take all your clothes off and lie here beside me.'

'Not if you're going to lie on top of me,' Bernadette said quickly.

'The thought frightens you?'

'Your thing's too big. You'd hurt me.'

'Trust me. We'll cuddle up to each other side by side and you shall clasp my handsome friend between your thighs, no more than that, while I stroke your bottom and make you go off pop.'

'All right,' said Bernadette, 'that sounds nice.'

And so indeed it proved, to the satisfaction of them both. Christophe tickled the girl's ungrown nipples until she became very agitated, then handled the small cheeks of her bottom and caressed between them with one finger until she was in a state to let him do whatever he wanted. He played awhile with the unfledged lips between her legs and when she was shivering all over, showed her how to hold his busy friend between her thighs and rubbed it briskly against her tiny mound until they both went off pop at the same time.

199

And that was all – the complications that might arise from any attempt to explore further were more than he cared to risk.

Next day he felt so much better – recovered almost – that he went for a stroll in the Luxembourg Gardens. He watched the children playing there under the supervision of nannies and mothers and thought to himself how remarkable it was that he had been tempted to do what he had done with Bernadette. Long abstinence and the effects of my illness, he thought to himself, and a child who is more advanced than she should be at her age. He had neither regrets nor guilt about the matter, only a feeling of mild surprise at himself. Now that he was well again he would resume his normal ways. And as an indication that the time to start was that very moment, he lunched in his favourite restaurant and took careful note of the young women he saw there. Only one was interesting in any way at all to him, and even she was as nothing when he compared her with the image of Jeanne in his mind.

On his return to his apartment, Madame Joligny met him at the street door. Evidently she had been waiting and looking out for him to save herself the climb up four flights of stairs. She invited him into her own apartment and said that there was something of grave importance they must discuss.

Damnation, Christophe thought, Bernadette has talked. This will cost me a packet to buy the mother off. And I shall be forced to look for somewhere else to live. It would be impossible to remain here with that memory hanging over me like a cloud.

Imagine then his relief when Madame Joligny told him that she had been giving some thought to his awkward position now that a certain lady no longer visited him. His obvious frustration when he had been washed was testimony enough to his problems. She had been glad to be of service to him on that occasion.

Good God, he thought, she's going to suggest that I sleep with her regularly!

'I suggested that you should find yourself a nice young

woman to live with you and look after you, if you remember,' said the concierge.

'I am grateful for your advice, but it is unfortunately impossible, Madame Joligny.'

'Do not be hasty,' she replied, giving him her endless smile, 'you need someone to take care of your clothes and your laundry and to cook for you and to serve you in bed.'

'I cannot have another woman living with me, you know that'

'But of course. It must be someone of discretion who will make herself scarce when the lady you love resumes her visits to you after her confinement. That way Madame Verney need never know that you have a convenient arrangement for when she is not here.'

'No, it is impossible.'

'Perhaps, but what are the alternatives? You are a young man of vigour and your needs must be satisfied regularly. Otherwise you will find yourself frequenting whores – and that is both expensive and unsatisfactory for one of your refinement.'

'I should not like that,' Christophe agreed, recalling his visit with Gerard to the house in rue St Denis to try out the black girl from Madagascar. How long ago that seemed! It had been interesting, but he had not been tempted to repeat the visit.

'Well, I shall give every consideration to your advice, madame,' he said, preparing to take his leave of the concierge.

'In your own interests, M'sieu Larousse, you must,' she said quickly, 'whores are not the worst that could befall you.'

'What do you mean?'

'A hot-natured young man who has no permanent companion may be led into all sorts of unsuitable situations – dangerous ones even.'

'Dangerous?'

'He might, if he became desperate enough, interfere with children – imagine that! Not that a gentleman of your distinction would so far forget himself as to become involved in police matters such as that. But the dangers of celibacy are very great.'

There was an edge in her voice that warned him that she was aware of his little escapade with her daughter. Christophe sat down again, sweating slightly.

'You must advise me, Madame Joligny. You have convinced me that you have my best interests at heart and I know you to be a practical woman. What do you think I should do?'

She smiled at him again, sure of her victory.

'I know just the person for you,' she said, 'a pleasant young woman who would look after your every need and disappear when you wished her to.'

'Who is she?' he asked curiously.

'My own niece. Her name is Mireille and she lives with her widowed mother, my late husband's sister, at Clichy. You would find her most accomodating.'

'How old is she?'

'Old enough for you. She is eighteen.'

'Pretty?'

'Pretty as a picture.'

'But why would she want to do this for me when she has never met me?'

'Times are hard. There is much unemployment in the country today, especially here in Paris. Her mother has two other children younger than Mireille to feed and keep. What sort of job do you suppose that Mireille can get to assist? Nothing that pays more than a few francs, unless she goes on the streets, and that is unthinkable. With the salary you would pay her she would be able to help her mother and with you she herself would live better than she does now.'

'What sort of salary?'

The figure Madame Joligny mentioned was twice the rate for a maidservant.

'That's a great deal of money,' said Christophe.

'Think of it in this way – it is what one visit to a young whore would cost a week, no more than that. Whereas with Mireille it will buy you her services as a cook, a laundress and a valet. And you will be able to take her to bed as many times a week as you wish. It's not a lot of money at all – it's a bargain.'

'What you are suggesting is extraordinary. I hardly know what to say.'

'There is no need to say anything at all. Naturally you don't want to buy a cat in a bag. As a sensible man you want to know what you are getting for your money. I understand that perfectly.'

'You mean make the acquaintance of your niece before deciding?'

'I mean that you ought to have her on approval for twenty-four hours before you make your mind up.'

'On approval?'

'Why not? This is a serious matter we are discussing.'

'Madame Joligny, you have truly amazed me. What do you propose?'

'Then it is all settled. She will be here before long and I will send her up to your apartment so that you can make her acquaintance.'

Christophe climbed the stairs to his apartment feeling suddenly weary. He slumped into his best chair to think about what had just taken place between him and the concierge, wondering if he could still be running a high temperature and had dreamed it. But no, it was as clear as possible to him that the concierge either knew or suspected that he had played a little game with her daughter. She had not accused him, but her hint was heavy enough. If she had got the whole story out of Bernadette she could cause him serious annoyance. Not that it would ever come to the attention of the police, he was sure, since it was almost certain that a large enough sum of money would keep her mouth shut. The sum might be painfully large – for apart from the police, what he really feared was a threat to acquaint Jeanne with the circumstances. That would end any chance of a resumption of their suspended affaire, of that he was sure, for Jeanne would feel only distaste for the incident. Sensual as she was, he knew her to be also fastidious. The only course appeared to be to go along with Madame Joligny's suggestion for the time being.

He had been sitting in sombre thought for perhaps half an hour when there was a tap at the door. He opened it to find the niece outside, a thin girl dressed in a worn beige coat and an almost shapeless pull-down hat.

'Come in,' he said, his manner not particularly welcoming, 'sit down.'

'Thank you, M'sieu Larousse.'

She sat opposite him in the other arm-chair. Her stockings were of cheap lisle, he noticed, and her shoes scuffed. What a bedraggled sparrow we have here, he thought.

'Tell me about yourself,' he said, not quite knowing how to start a conversation in such unusual circumstances.

'My name is Mireille,' she said, unabashed, 'my aunt has explained to me that you live a lonely life and that you have been ill.'

'I have been ill. As to the rest, that is a matter of opinion.'

She smiled at him nervously and continued: 'My aunt says that you are in need of someone to look after you. She thinks that I may be suitable.'

'So she informed me,' Christophe answered glumly.

'I'm sure she's right, M'sieu. You look tired. You've been out walking too long on your first day up. You should rest for an hour or two before dinner.'

'That was my intention before your aunt engaged me in a curious discussion.'

'Good,' she said and before he could object she was off her chair and crouching at his feet to remove his shoes for him.

'Mademoiselle – I can manage well enough on my own.'

'You say that only because you've never had anyone to take care of you properly since you came to live in Paris. Come along.'

She took his hands and pulled him to his feet with a wiry strength which belied her meagre frame. Somewhere between sitting-room and bedroom she shed her coat and hat to reveal a tobacco-brown frock that fitted none too well. Once in the bedroom she eased him out of his jacket and then his trousers with surprising dexterity. Then his tie and shirt were off and she was on one knee to slip his underpants down his legs.

'But I've been dressing and undressing myself since I was six years old,' he said querulously.

204

'Let's have your socks,' she said, 'left foot up – that's it. Now the other one.'

He stood naked while she held up his pyjama top for him to put his arms into the sleeves, then buttoned it down the front for him, her eyes never once straying to his exposed and pendant parts. She helped him into his pyjama trousers with similar disinterest and he found himself tucked up in bed and Mireille drawing the curtains to dim the room.

'Rest and sleep,' she said, 'I'll wake you for dinner. Is there anything special you would like me to cook for you? You've only to say.'

Christophe looked at her curiously. She stood by his bedside, her arms folded across her body, waiting for his instructions like an attentive servant. She had not touched him during her neat removal of his clothes, she was not physically attractive to him – yet, in spite of all that – he found himself aroused. His unfailing *friend* was giving full proof of that under the bedclothes.

But this is bizarre, Christophe thought, first there is the incident with the concierge's daughter, then that with Madame Joligny herself, when she took me in hand at my own request. And now this! One could say that I am no longer the master of my own emotions. So totally unnerving a proposition should be put to the test without delay.

'Mireille,' he said huskily.

'Yes?'

'Take off your clothes and let me see you.'

Without a word she pulled her frock over her head, took off her plain camisole and knickers and showed herself to him in only her cheap stockings and shoes.

'Does that cheer you up?' she asked as casually as if she were enquiring the time of day.

Without her drab clothes she was more interesting. Her breasts were very small and that made her nipples and the red-brown circles they stood on appear much larger by contrast. Her legs looked strong and were well-shaped. Against her too-pale skin the luxuriant dark hair between her thighs stood out boldly. And that too was unexpected, for the hair on her head was yellowish, cut in an inexpert bang.

'I believe that it does,' he answered, 'one becomes depressed and lethargic after an illness. Both the body and the mind need a tonic. Turn round for me.'

He studied her thin back and small, round buttocks, his glance running down the length of her prominent spine. She was thin rather than elegantly slim like Jeanne, but not to be dismissed out of hand. Perhaps she had potential.

She faced him again, her arms hanging loosely at her sides.

'Shall I get dressed now and leave you to sleep?'

'I would prefer you to get into bed with me, Mireille.'

Her face was expressionless as she got between the sheets with him. Christophe's hands cupped her soft little breasts and one of her hands was inside his pyjamas, squeezing his staunch part.

'You're not a virgin, are you?' he enquired, memories of Bernadette troubling him – though only slightly.

'No, you don't have to worry about that,' she reassured him.

In love-making she was without skill or finesse, he found, whatever her previous experience of men had been. But she was keen to please him. She allowed him to do whatever he chose and instantly fell in with every whim.

'I shall know what you like next time,' she said calmly as he played with her.

The mutual caressing ran its natural course, until at last Christophe mounted her. Her hands stroked his back awkwardly until his busy movements brought about a release of his passion in her narrow loins. He fell asleep soon afterwards, cradled in Mireille's skinny arms.

She woke him up much later with a tray of food – a good nourishing meat stew with fresh bread and a glass of decent wine. She was fully dressed again and sat on the side of the bed watching him while he ate with a good appetite.

'But you must eat too,' he said, when the thought crossed his mind.

'Later, after you've finished. There's more if you want it.'

'Mireille, you are spoiling me. Will you stay with me tonight?'

'If you want me to.'

When she took the tray away Christophe lay propped up on his pillows, arms behind his head. It seemed to him that in some inexplicable way he had acquired a perfect servant – polite, self-effacing, attentive, anxious to please, a reasonably able cook and satisfactory in bed. So many virtues in one eighteen-year-old girl! And ready to disappear from his apartment temporarily whenever Jeanne resumed her visits to him. And be back the next day with his breakfast on a tray before he set out for his office! The concierge's proposition had very considerable merits.

Being young, it did not occur to him that he had acquired a nanny, a wife and a jailer all in one.

MICHEL PLAYS THE MARQUIS DE SADE

To enter Ninette Laval's home was to step back in time forty years to the fussy opulence of the nineteenth century. Michel was astounded by the large salon, overfull of heavy furniture, long velvet drapes, huge gilt-framed pictures and oriental rugs on the glassily polished parquet floor. He looked in questioning surprise at Ninette as she gave instructions to the servant who had opened the door to them.

'Do you like my home?' she asked, 'most people don't.'

'It is magnificent of its style.'

Like a museum, he thought, where everything is lovingly preserved for the edification of posterity.

'My parents furnished it when they were first married. I've allowed nothing to be changed since their death, nothing at all.'

Ninette Laval was in her early thirties, about the same age as Michel himself. Unlike the setting in which she lived, her own appearance was modern in every way. Her dark hair was expertly bobbed, her short evening gown was an expensive creation of turquoise and gold, her stockings very fine and as transparent as a grapeskin. She was not exactly pretty, Michel thought, nor would one have called her plain. Her figure was good, her carriage excellent. Her nose was perhaps a trifle too long and her jaw a touch too square. Neither would have mattered but for her habitual expression, he decided. Throughout the evening, whether she was eating, drinking, talking or dancing, she preserved an expression of undefined slight hostility. Even when they were dancing the tango together her expression had not wavered.

The expression revealed to the world an innately unfriendly nature or masked a deep timidity, he concluded. A better acquaintance with her would enable him to determine which it was.

'When did your parents die?' he asked politely.

'In 1912. They were among the tragic victims of the *Titanic* disaster.'

'Good God – how awful for you!'

The servant poured chartreuse into tiny crystal glasses and stood silent. He looked nearer seventy than sixty.

'You may go to bed, Gaston,' said Ninette, 'I will let Monsieur Brissard out myself.'

'I was twenty at the time,' she told Michel, 'and engaged to be married to a young man they had chosen for me. He was the son of an old friend of my father's.'

Michel sipped the liqueur.

'Was he in the War, your fiancé?' he asked.

'He was killed very early on. Not that we were engaged by then. Soon after my parents' death I came of age and could direct my own life. I sent him away.'

Her tiny glass was empty. Michel moved from his chair onto the sofa next to her in order to refill it from the heavy decanter.

'When you telephoned this morning,' he said, 'did you really not know that my wife was away in the country with the children?'

'Of course not!' she answered sharply, 'otherwise I would hardly have wasted my time telephoning her.'

'As things have turned out, I hope you will not regard it as a waste of time. The evening has been most enjoyable.'

'Yes,' she said softly.

The moment seemed right. Michel put an arm around her waist and drew her to him to kiss her. His lips touched only the corner of her mouth before she pulled away and would have risen to her feet but for the restraining arm about her.

'Not even a kiss?' he said in astonishment, 'but that's ridiculous.'

He held her tight and her exclamation was cut off by his lips finding hers and stifling the protest. Her mouth was closed and unresponsive under his but she did not struggle. She sat passive and unresisting as Michel kissed her mouth, her cheeks, her neck and her mouth again. Encouraged, he slid his hand up her side to her breast and held it gently.

209

To that Ninette responded instantly. She flung herself away from him and her hand swept round to deliver a violent smack to his face.

'How dare you touch me!' she shrilled, her face flushed with anger. 'How dare you!' and her other hand swung across to land resoundingly on his cheek.

'What the devil do you think you're doing!' Michel exclaimed, rubbing his stinging cheeks, 'I've a good mind to teach you a lesson!'

'Don't you lay a finger on me, you pig,' she hissed, her hands raised ready to strike him again.

Infuriated by her barbarous response to his advances, Michel grabbed her by the nape of her neck and jerked her forward with such force that she lost her balance and fell face down across his knees.

'You must be taught how civilised people behave towards each other,' he said.

While he held her head down by the back of her neck she was helpless, for all her kicking. He pulled up her skirt and under-slip to reveal a rump clad in almost transparent rose-pink silk. Her struggles became more frantic and her hands were pulling at his fingers to release herself. When that failed, she scratched at the back of his hand with her nails.

'Ah, would you!' he said, gripping all the tighter and wrenching her flimsy underclothes down to expose the pale-skinned cheeks of her bottom.

'You behave like a badly brought-up child and you will be disciplined like one,' he said loudly.

He raised his hand and smacked her hard. Ninette squealed and lashed out futilely with her feet. Michel was thoroughly caught up in the comedy. He laid into her soft bottom with his open palm, changing its pallor into red blotches. How many times he spanked her he did not know. He stopped only when her struggles ceased and she lay across his knees sobbing quietly. His irritation was gone and he felt in control again. And more, he realised as he stared at Ninette's reddened bottom, he was sexually aroused. He straightened his legs so that she slid down them and lay on the rug at his feet, face-down and still sobbing faintly. Her disarranged frock covered only one cheek of her bottom and left the other exposed to his sight. The transparent pink underwear was bunched round her thighs above her stocking-tops.

The evening was not to end without entertainment, he thought, though it would differ from what he had anticipated. She was lying on one of his feet. He heaved it upwards and rolled her over onto her back. Her bare arms covered her tear-stained face but the hitched-up skirt gave him a pleasant view of her thighs and a patch of short brown hair.

'Stop that noise,' he commanded, 'You're not hurt.'

'You brute,' she said from under cover of her arms, 'you have no right to treat me like that.'

'I have the best right in the world.'

'What do you mean?'

'Sit up and I will inform and educate you.'

She uncovered her face and sat up, then gasped when she found what she had been displaying to him. Her face blushed a fiery red as she tugged her skirt down.

'Don't get up,' said Michel forcefully, 'I prefer you on the floor.'

'I won't be treated like this in my own home,' she protested weakly, but she stayed on the oriental rug. Under the skirt her hands tried to wriggle her underclothes back into place.

'Stop fidgeting at once! Cross your hands in your lap and pay attention.'

Her normal expression of hostility was gone. She looked subdued and a little apprehensive. Michel felt that he understood her nature now. She was a deeply timid person who would respond only to domination by a man.

'Have you read any of the works of the Marquis de Sade?' he asked peremptorily.

'What? No, of course not.'

'You're lying, naturally. I'm pleased that you are acquainted with the Marquis' works because they will have given you some idea of what I am going to do to you.'

'No ... I beg you ...'

The grand gesture to dominate her imagination and

211

subdue her will, Michel thought, casting about in his mind for something suitable. So many years had passed since he had himself read de Sade's stories that he could scarcely recall what the villainous heroes did to their shrinking virgin victims before ravaging them with sexual organs the length of a forearm.

'You asked by what right I chastised you for your bad behaviour,' he said, an idea forming in his mind, 'observe my right!'

Legs stretched out and apart, he slowly unbuttoned his trousers, pulled up his shirt-front and let his erect member jut out through the slit in his underwear. Not as long as a forearm, he thought, but of a serviceable size which, to Ninette's timid eyes, will no doubt appear huge.

'Oh my God!' she cried and covered her eyes with her hands.

'Put your hands down at once,' Michel said firmly, 'look at me!'

She lowered her hands, glanced quickly and then stared down at the patterned rug.

'No ... this is absurd,' she said, 'you believe *that* gives you the right to beat me?'

'You were spanked, not beaten,' Michel corrected her, 'and yes, this emblem of manhood displayed for your better education gives me certain rights and privileges.'

'We live in the twentieth century, not the Middle Ages,' she answered, rallying a little now that the memory of the smacked bottom was fading. 'Has it escaped your attention that I am a citizen of France and protected by its laws, not at the mercy of any passing rapist.'

'There are laws more ancient than those of the Republic-laws which cannot be changed or repealed by female emancipation. You see before you the living symbol of the oldest law of all.'

If a third person had been secretly present in Ninette Laval's salon, the scene being played out would have appeared ridiculous in the extreme. There was Michel in his evening clothes, stiff collar and bow-tie, legs sprawled out and his pink column boldly exhibited against the black of his

212

trousers. Before him, crouched on the floor awkwardly because her legs were hampered by her displaced underwear, there was Ninette, her lowered eyes flickering up from time to time at the object presented for her inspection. To neither of the participants in this little drama was the scene at all ridiculous. They were fully engaged in their own strange version of the eternal negotiations between men and women.

'Respect the law now it is revealed to you,' said Michel, amused by the way she kept stealing brief glances at him.

'In your arrogance,' she countered, 'you would like to believe that fifteen centimetres of flesh give you the right to summon any woman to your bed. I despise you for this naive assumption and for the coarseness of a nature which impells you to expose yourself in so gross a manner.'

'Listen to the words of outraged modesty,' he sneered, 'if the sight were so repulsive to you, you would surely not keep glancing up at it under your eye-lashes. Admit it now, you are delighted and fascinated by what you see. Abandon this false shame and look frankly and openly.'

'Very well,' she fought back, raising her head, 'what am I supposed to admire? The miserable sexual organ you are so proud of? It is an insignificant length of flesh which has been made temporarily hard by an inflow of blood and which will soon be limp again. Do you think me a young girl to be impressed by it?'

'Insignificant? Evidently you have little experience of men if you use that word. You speak from inexperience and ignorance. The correct word is magnificent, *Mademoiselle*.'

His emphasis on the word brought a blush to Ninette's face.

'You believe that I am a virgin,' she said, 'that is the reason for your audacity. You forget that I was engaged to be married before I was twenty.'

'So you told me, and broke off the engagement. Why was that – was your fiancé not a satisfactory lover, *Mademoiselle*?'

'That's no concern of yours.'

'How many lovers have you had in the years since then? Any at all?'

'Why will you humiliate me with your rudeness? Cover

yourself and go away.'

'If I had something appropriate to cover myself with, perhaps I might.'

'What do you mean?'

'Give me that fragile under-garment I pulled down to bare your bottom for chastisement.'

'Your impudence goes too far!'

She started to rise from the floor. Michel put the sole of his patent-leather evening shoe against her shoulder and pushed sharply. Ninette tipped over backwards.

'I am waiting,' he said loudly, 'do not try my patience or I shall apply my hand to your bottom again.'

'Damn you!' Ninette gasped.

She kicked her legs in the air and struggled to get her knickers off, affording Michel a fine view of her bare backside and brown-haired secret place. He caught the warm silk she hurled at him.

'Observe,' he said calmly as he draped it over his upstanding part, 'your wish is complied with.'

The look on Ninette's face was indecipherable as she stared at the rose-pink tent he had fashioned.

'I am trying to understand you,' she said at last. 'Why do you come into my home and behave as if you were a Turk in his harem. What do you expect me to do – go to bed with you?'

'Have I suggested that?'

'You have not said it, but all your actions point in one single direction. Understand once and for all that I have no intention of going to bed with you.'

'Nor I with you.'

That surprised her.

'Then what is the purpose of this charade?' she demanded.

'You must not interrupt me,' said Michel, 'I was saying that I have no intention of taking you to bed, to use your delicate phrase for what we both know to be an insertion of this veiled part of mine into the soft place between your legs, until you beg me to.'

'If that is what you are hoping for, you will wait a long time,' she answered, her cheeks again a faint pink from the

214

image of conjoined parts he had planted in her mind.

She was becoming too argumentative, Michel thought. The initial shock had worn off. He must act to frighten her back into submissiveness. If only he could remember more of what the Marquis' violaters did in these circumstances. They menaced their victims with their monstrous cudgels... yes, that part worked well enough. Perhaps a continuation would have the desired effect on her.

He swathed her pale pink underwear round his hard member and moved his hand up and down a few times.

'How very exciting,' he said, looking her full in the face, 'the delicate touch of this fine silk against my penis. I can well appreciate the enchanting sensations you experience from its soft rub against your most tender parts when you walk or sit with your legs crossed.'

Ninette's mouth was open as she watched the slow movement of his hand.

'It would be the simplest thing in the world,' he continued, 'to release my desire into this pretty morsel of silk which has enclosed your loins and has kissed you between the thighs so often.'

'Stop it,' she gasped.

'I have warned you before not to interrupt me, Ninette. You will make me angry. What a pity it would be to see your precious little garment soaked with a sudden overflow of passion. Don't you agree?'

She nodded nervously, her eyes intent on his caressing hand.

'Now answer me a question. Did you enjoy being spanked?'

'Of course not. You hurt me.'

'And excited you at the same time.'

'No!'

'You are lying again to disguise your fear of your own natural responses. Watch my hand and in a few moments you will see something I am sure you have never seen in your entire life.'

'No – please don't – I implore you.'

'Then tell me the truth.'

'It aroused me to some extent when you beat me – is that what you want me to say?'

'That's better. Now take your clothes off.'

'What did you say?' she exclaimed.

'I wish to see you naked.'

'Certainly not!'

One must be overbearing, Michel reminded himself, in order to make her submit.

'You are being absurd,' he said, 'I saw your bottom clearly enough when I warmed it for you. And you gave me a fine view between your legs when you were rolling about on the floor with your skirt up. I have seen all that you most wish to protect.'

'Then be content,' Ninette pleaded.

'Many women have afforded me the pleasure of viewing their naked beauty. What I glimpsed of your body was unremarkable,' he answered in his best domineering tone, 'nevertheless, it amuses me to inspect the rest of you. Off with your clothes.'

'You gave me your word – does that mean nothing?'

'My word is inviolable, you may be sure. Before this fellow I am holding makes any approach to you it will be necessary for you to request his attentions.'

'But I don't want to undress.'

'Liar!' said Michel, 'you are unwilling to admit it, that's all. I know perfectly well that you want me to see your body. You desire the thrilling sensation of my eyes caressing your breasts and belly from a distance. So take your clothes off.'

'And if I refuse?'

'Do it!' he commanded.

Ninette stood up, trembling slightly. Slowly she undid the fastenings of her turquoise evening gown and removed it to appear before him in a thin and clinging slip of *crêpe de Chine*.

'Hurry,' Michel spurred her on.

He had recognized her true nature. Her upbringing had made her a person afraid of her own natural instincts and incapable of giving expression to them. She could release them only by transferring the responsibility to another and so

216

absolve her conscience. To be forced by a man to do the things she secretly wished to do but dared not do – for Ninette this was the ideal.

'And the stockings,' he ordered.

In moments she was completely nude. She stood facing him, arms at her sides, her eyes averted from his. She was waiting for words of admiration, he guessed, now that she had revealed all. She must be kept subdued.

'Do you admire your body in your mirror before you dress each morning? he asked.

'Of course not!'

'Then I shall be a mirror for you now and reflect back to you what you show to me, so that you may know yourself better.'

'Not that!'

'I see a woman with dark hair, bobbed and parted off-centre,' he said in a tone of indifference. 'A square-jawed face with a mouth that has not learned what delight there is in kissing. I see a well-formed body, pale of skin, with long and delicate arms that do not know how to hold a lover close. I see slender thighs and pretty ankles. Do you recognise this picture?'

'That's not what I see in the mirror,' she whispered.

'Ah, then you have stood naked before your mirror to admire yourself. I thought as much. You cannot deceive me with your false modesty.'

Her face blushed pink at his words.

'You are before a mirror now,' Michel continued, 'not a cold surface of glass but a living mirror which describes what it sees. For example, I see a pair of breasts, not too large, not too small, their tips of dark cherry red pointing towards me. I guarantee that the touch of a man's lips is completely unknown to them. And there, below them, the slight *embonpoint* of your belly, set with an unusual navel of upright-oval shape. Has a tongue ever touched it? Of course not. Then lower still – I see a triangle of curly brown hair, no bigger than the palm of your own hand, ensconced between white-skinned thighs. And where I cannot see, I can imagine the small and secret alcove which you have preserved untouched for so many years. There – that is the portrait of yourself which I reflect back to you.'

'You are laughing at me,' she murmured, eyes downcast.

'I tell the truth as I see it, as a good mirror should. Do you contradict me?'

'No ...'

'You are beginning to learn. Watch now.'

Michel tucked his standing part, still in its pink silk wrappings, into his trousers and fastened the buttons over it.

There was a certain amount of humiliation of the young women in de Sade's tales, he seemed to recall, to break their will and render them pliable. It was worth a try. After all, there was nothing to lose except an amusement with which he was becoming slightly bored.

'Kneel before me,' he said menacingly. 'Closer – between my legs.'

The expression in her brown eyes told him that she had relinquished all responsibility for what happened. Yet she must be pushed further if anything was to come of the comedy. He took her hand and placed it on the bulge in his trousers.

'Trace the outline with your fingers. Learn to know its size and strength,' he ordered.

'I can't!'

'You can do whatever I tell you to do.'

He reached forward to grasp her breasts tightly, one in each hand.

'Don't hurt me,' she whimpered.

'Then obey me. Use both hands.'

Her fingers travelled lightly over him, the touch almost imperceptible.

'Grasp it with both hands,' he said, 'move it up and down quickly.'

'But ...'

'Do it!' he insisted, his hands clamping harder on her soft breasts as if he would squeeze them like oranges for their juice.

Ninette obeyed him urgently. Her face was still turned up to his and was pale, but in her eyes he could detect a strange mingling of horror and desire.

'How close, yet how distant,' he said, 'my penis wrapped in your underwear, your hands on me. Between your hands and my flesh two layers of clothes – yours and mine – only millimetres thick. So close, yet so distant that there is no contact of flesh on flesh. Yet I feel the effect of your hands even through these barriers. Consider that effect. Consider what you are now doing to me. Let the image of it fill your mind and fire your imagination. Faster now!'

Ninette's mouth was open in a silent scream of protest and pleasure. The friction of her hands through the silk flung Michel headlong into a furious emission. At the climactic moment Ninette squealed and jerked her hands away sharply to dissociate herself from what was happening to him. At once Michel caught her by the back of her neck and forced her head down between his thighs so that her cheek was pressed hard against the throbbing package inside his trousers. He held her prisoner there until his delicious throes faded.

'Poor pink knickers,' he said with a chuckle, 'violated and soaked through.'

'Beast! Let go of me.'

He released her head and took hold of her wrists to keep her kneeling before him.

'Is that what you wanted?' she asked, her courage flickering again now that she thought that he was satisfied.

'I wanted to know whether you are capable of giving me pleasure.'

'You call *that* pleasure?'

'Of a minor kind. As it is the only kind you have experienced, I suspect, you need not denigrate it.'

'How dare you suggest such a thing!' she shrilled.

'Be quiet. You claim not to be a virgin. Very well then, you allowed your fiancé to make love to you in order to discover whether you enjoyed the experience. Evidently you did not.'

'You are guessing.'

'The facts are clear. When your parents no longer controlled your life and you were independent, you wanted no more of this fiancé. Therefore you did not enjoy his love-

219

making. Was he too hasty with you? Was he clumsy? The fault may have been as much with him as with you.'

'You are completely wrong. He was kind and tender, not an animal like you.'

'Much good it did him,' said Michel, releasing her left wrist, 'reach behind you on the floor and hand me your petticoat.'

'What for? Haven't you ruined enough of my lingerie already?'

'Will you forever argue with me! Give it to me at once.'

His tone startled her and she did as he said. He wrapped his legs round her thighs and crossed his feet to prevent her from rising and moving away from him when he let go of her other wrist. She watched anxiously while he folded the flimsy *crêpe de Chine* lengthways.

'What are you doing?'

'You will see.'

'I'm tired and you've had what you came here for. I want you to go now.'

'How will you make me? You are helpless and at my mercy,' he taunted her.

'Am I?' she said in a sudden burst of fierceness, her face mottled with anger.

Her hand clenched into a fist and struck down hard between his parted legs. Fortunately for him, Ninette's understanding of male anatomy was sufficiently defective for her blow to fall upon his now limp part, swathed in her own underwear. Even so, he yelped in shock. Before another and perhaps more damaging blow could be struck he propelled himself forward from the sofa and carried her to the floor with him. She kicked out and hit at him until he succeeded in rolling her over face-down on the rug and sat on the small of her back to hold her down.

'You are a savage,' he said, 'you meant to disable me. You deserve to be punished severely for that.'

'Don't beat me again,' she begged.

Michel reached out for the lace-edged petticoat he had dropped in his sudden evasive manoeuvre, finished folding it into a long strip and blindfolded Ninette with it.

'For God's sake ...' she gasped.

From the floor he took one of the silk stockings she had discarded at his insistence earlier and used it to tie her wrists together behind her back.

'Release me,' she begged, 'I promise not to try to hurt you again.'

'Why should I trust your promise? You are safer as you are.'

Did the Marquis ever let his ravagers tie up their young girls, he wondered. There was one story where the heroine was suspended by her neck with her feet just touching the floor while she was sexually abused. That seemed a little extreme for Mademoiselle Laval's salon. Something less dangerous and more amusing was called for. He climbed off her back and hauled her to her feet, then picked her up and put her full-length on her back on the red plush sofa.

'You promised not to!' she exclaimed, made fearful by the blindfold.

Michel picked up her legs, seated himself close to her bottom and pulled her legs over his lap.

'What are you doing?' she asked anxiously.

'I am still your mirror,' said Michel, 'or had you forgotten so soon?'

'But I can see nothing.'

'There is no need. This mirror speaks. When you stood before me earlier I had no view between your thighs, for you kept them pressed together.'

She gasped loudly as he prised her legs apart but she made no attempt at resistance. As he had guessed, with her hands bound – however lightly – and her eyes covered, she felt no sense of responsibility for whatever might occur. She thought of herself as a helpless and bound victim at the mercy of a brutal man's lust and she lay still in tremulous anticipation. Michel could take her now if he wished and she would co-operate and then afterwards claim that she had been violated by force. That was not his intention. He would play the comedy through to the point where Ninette of her own free will asked him to do it to her. That would eliminate all possibility of equivocation in future.

221

'The mirror speaks,' he said, 'it gives you back a picture of what is displayed to it – the join of two slim and alabaster thighs, well separated. I see a patch of light brown hair, short and curly, hardly covering the small lips of your secret place, your well-guarded treasure.'

Her chest rose and fell rapidly at his words. Michel explored with his fingers.

'They are warm and soft, these lips,' he said, 'and by parting them a trifle I can reflect the interior. Ah, all is pinkness and moistness – something has aroused you, I fear. Can it be my animal brutality? Now I open this pretty entrance wider to lay all bare to the view. At least you told me the truth about not being a virgin. I shall open you wider still, right to the limit ...'

Before he could proceed further with his game Ninette's legs drummed across his lap, her back arched off the sofa and ecstasy took her. Michel watched and was entertained by the twitching of her body and the rasp of her breathing. He waited for her to become calm again.

'Now you have repaid me by showing me something I have never seen before,' he said. 'A spontaneous discharge of passion. It happens at times to men in their sleep – but to a woman wide awake? All I did was to look, not to caress. Has it happened to you before?'

'Not like that,' she answered. 'You can untie me now – you've achieved what you wanted.'

'But we are only beginning to know each other, you and I. We shall continue.'

'There's no point. You've done what you wanted in my underwear and you've made me do what I had no wish to do. We're both finished.'

'By no means. You know nothing of men if you believe that.'

'Then what more do you want of me?'

There was no hostility in her tone. Her release had made her tranquil and her bonds and blindfold comforted her. Michel took advantage of the moment and slid his forefinger deep into her.

'Not that!' she gasped, 'anything but that. You promised.'

'Your lack of experience of men does you no credit. It is only my finger. Had it been something else, you would have appreciated the difference in length and girth, I assure you. You are familiar with the sensation of a finger in you, though only your own.'

'You mustn't say things like that,' Ninette murmured.

'Between you and me, why not? There is no embarrassment in speaking of it. You are a grown woman with normal appetites, without husband or lover. Therefore the natural thing is for you to pleasure yourself.'

'You talk about private things with such ease,' she said hesitantly. 'How can you?'

Michel's finger twitched inside her and the ball of his thumb began to rotate slowly on the small rosebud under it.

'I speak naturally of natural things,' he answered, 'it is you who are tongue-tied and unable to express your desires and emotions. Why is that?'

'Some matters are too private to speak about,' she sighed.

'The whole world experiences these desires and emotions. What you regard as private is in reality public.'

'That can't be so. My friends know that I have no lover. As for strangers, what they believe doesn't matter to me.'

'Every man you pass in the street,' said Michel, 'assumes that you have a lover to kiss those little breasts and caress you between the legs until you yearn to feel him enter you.'

'But that's dreadful – to think like that about someone you don't know!'

'As for the friends who know you have no lover, they naturally guess the truth – that your own fingers are your lover.'

Under the blindfold Ninette's cheeks were scarlet, partly from shame and partly from arousal under Michel's slow caress.

'No,' she moaned, 'if I believed that I could never face my friends again. They cannot believe that I do that to myself.'

'Why not? Accept the truth about yourself and stop pretending.'

'But it's wrong,' she gasped, her legs beginning to tremble across his lap.

'A view imposed upon you by your parents. You are a grown woman and can think for yourself. How often do you pleasure yourself?'

'Every day ...'

Michel's finger fluttered inside her and his thumb rubbed quickly as her belly thrust upwards and she moaned in delight. Her spasms this time were longer than before.

When she could hear him again, he asked, 'You enjoy it greatly, whatever you pretend. When was the first time – when you were a child?'

'No, it was after my parents died and I broke off my engagement.'

'You knew nothing of the pleasures of your own body until you were twenty? Tell me the circumstances.'

She could talk easily to him now after what he had done to her. Her bandaged eyes gave her the illusion of being alone, he guessed, and she was relaxed mentally by the satisfaction she had enjoyed.

'I was in bed one night,' she said, 'I was lonely and restless. I didn't want my fiancé because I never liked what he made me do. The idea of love-making was abhorrent to me – to let a man lie on me and push his way into my body. I was hot so I took off my night-gown and lay naked above the sheets. I would never have dared do that when my parents were alive. In my restlessness I found myself stroking my thighs and I was shocked. I stopped at once. But after a while I found myself doing it again and my fingers even touched the hair between my legs. I tried to make myself stop. In fact, I did stop, several times. But there was no hope of sleep and as the night wore on my hands strayed back again and again and eventually they were caressing me *there* where I was so hot and wet. I was lost then, utterly lost – half a dozen quick strokes and it was too late to stop. Afterwards I fell asleep almost at once and in the morning I woke up feeling guilty.'

As she related her experience Ninette's voice became faster and jerkier. Michel recognised the signs; his thumb, still in position, rotated swiftly and Ninette uttered a long groan as she attained yet again her culmination and dissolved in ecstatic sensation.

'That too was almost spontaneous,' he observed, 'it would have occurred without assistance from me. All I did then was to accelerate it. I am seeing you in a very different light from an hour ago.'

'You are reflecting my impure soul back to me now, not just my body,' she said.

'Impure is a foolish word. After that first time, did you feel guilty again?'

'Every time.'

'That means every day.'

'Yes, since I am confessing everything to you. I do it myself every night when I go to bed, otherwise I cannot go to sleep. And I wake up each morning regretting it.'

'Do you feel guilty now?'

'Why no,' she answered in a surprised tone.

You feel no guilt, Michel thought, because you are sheltering behind the thought that it is I who am making you experience pleasure against your will. Yet if it were really against your will, how easily you could stop me – you have only to call out loudly enough to awake your servants and they will come running into the room. That has been so ever since we commenced this game – even when I was spanking your bottom.

Aloud he said, 'The mirror has not yet completed its task. There is more of you to reflect.'

Ninette made no reply. He bent her legs and pushed her knees up to her breasts, then stood to lift her and turn her over so that she was kneeling on the red plush seat with her head on the arm of the sofa. Her wrists were still pinioned behind her back by a stocking, though the folded petticoat had slipped from her eyes and was hanging loosely round her neck.

'What are you about?' she asked, her voice full of curiosity.

Michel knelt behind her on the sofa, still the picture of elegance in his formal evening attire. He was experiencing some small discomfort from the clammy touch of the silk wrappings around his alert member. He opened his trousers and liberated himself, dropping Ninette's violated pink knickers to the floor.

'Tell me what you are doing?' she repeated.

'Positioning you before your mirror.'

'Like this? Ah, no!'

'Most assuredly yes. Another part of you is revealed to the mirror now. It sees and reflects back to you the two cheeks of a round bottom, once pale but still faintly pink from the smacking they received.'

He put his hands on them and squeezed.

'Plump and pliable,' he said, 'and if I part them like this ...'

'No, for shame!'

'And wider still – yes, I see a tiny russet flower, its petals furled.'

'Oh my God!' Ninette gasped as he touched it.

'Ah, it contracts when it is touched. This is worthy of further investigation.'

One finger-tip caressing it lightly, he inserted his other hand between her thighs to immerse his fingers between the open lips there and massage her tender rosebud.

'You will kill me,' she sighed as his manipulations rekindled her passions.

'And if I do? You are at my mercy to kill with sensation if that is my wish.'

'You are cruel ... a cruel devouring beast ...'

'I am merciless and I shall devour you with my animal lusts.'

'Have pity – do not make me do it again.'

'You say that to me, little hypocrite, when you are already trembling at the prospect of the climactic delight which you are slowly approaching? Cease this idle pretence. It is too late for me to stop. If your body were denied the touch of my hands it would of its own accord carry you the remainder of the way as it did before. You are lost, Ninette, just as you were that first time you caressed yourself in bed and experienced a great surge of delight.'

'Don't torment me with that memory, please.'

'Here is no torment, only pleasure. And here is no guilt, only joy. You cannot prevent me from forcing you into this delight. Accept the sensations, welcome them, enjoy them,

226

for you are going to feel them whether you will or not.'

'I shall die,' she moaned softly, shudders running along her bare back.

'Then die of delight!'

Ninette's earlier satisfactions had slowed down her physical responses. Though she was thoroughly aroused, only very gradually did she approach her natural culmination. Michel observed her with an experienced eye as he continued to caress her, front and rear at the same time, restraining her just short of the brink over which her body was striving to leap. Her breath came and went in long sobs, her rump bucked under his hand.

'I can't stand any more,' she gasped, 'kill me if you must, but do it quickly.'

'Why should I hasten to end a spectacle which is giving me such enjoyment? You must endure until I choose to terminate the performance.'

'Fiend!'

'What a sorry plight you are in. You have advanced much too far to retreat now, isn't that so? And I have no intention of permitting you to leap forward to the conclusion you crave with every fibre of your being. An hour of this will prove most instructive.'

'Finish, I beg you ...'

'No, no – I am getting to know you better as time passes and to understand you. And we have so much time – all night.'

'I can bear no more – do it properly if that is the only way to put an end to this!'

'What do you mean by *properly?*'

'I can't say it,' she moaned, 'you know what I mean.'

'Unless you say what you mean how can I understand you?'

'Put it in me,' she said desperately, as if the words were torn reluctantly from her mouth.

'What do you wish me to put in you – my finger?'

'Monster! Your ... penis ... put it in me before my heart collapses.'

'Have I understood you correctly? You are asking me of

your own free will to put my penis inside you? Is that what you mean?'

'Yes,' she wailed, her entire body shaking furiously with pent-up desire.

'In which entrance, Mademoiselle – the front or the rear?'

'The front!' she shrieked, her face and neck fiery red.

'Then since you request it, I shall oblige you.'

Her threshold was hot and slippery, her vestibule agape to receive him. But beyond that the corridor was narrow and tight. Michel ventured only part of the way before commencing the reciprocating motion which is the cause of pleasure in men and women when they are conjoined. His arousal was at its height from the strange game that he had been playing with her. Now that he had docked in the forbidden haven, his cargo would soon be unloaded.

'I am inside you,' he informed her, 'as you requested.'

'Brute!' she groaned.

Excited though he was, Michel was conscious of the ridiculous aspect of the act they were performing together. As who could not be? There was he, fully dressed in evening attire, from bow-tie and wing-collar to patent leather pumps. And by contrast, below him knelt Ninette completely naked with her wrists tied behind her back by a silk stocking and with her own petticoat dangling round her neck. I shall most certainly describe this scene to Monique, he thought, for she can make a picture of it from her own imagination that will serve as illustration to one of the books that interest her.

Not only was the coupling ridiculous from the visual aspect – psychologically it was quite grotesque. Michel had played being the Marquis de Sade, menacing a helpless young woman, abusing her, humiliating her. All this was far from his normal personality, a complete aberration for him – and yet he found a perverse enjoyment in it. As for Ninette, the frightened semi-virgin, she had played at submission, she had exaggerated her own fears. And eventually she had given free rein to her own long-frustrated desires. Although she did not know it, Michel was smiling in amusement as he pumped away steadily.

228

Ninette's cheek was on the cushioned arm of the sofa as she tried to see over her shoulder the man who was violating the sacred altar of her body – the altar which for so many years had been tended only by her own hands. The turmoil in her mind was as great as that in her body. Her eyes were glazed and she shuddered continuously. Michel had her by the hip-bones to steady himself as he edged his way deeper within.

This path has been trodden only once before, he thought fleetingly, and that by the dismissed fiancé. How little he understood her nature if he was as kind and considerate as she claims. If only he had thought to roll her on her back and take her by force, she would have loved him forever!

He would have taunted her aloud with the thought, but passion welled up in him so impetuously that words were impossible. Oblivious of Ninette's squirming, he plunged to the hilt as fierce spasms seized him. His final violence brought on Ninette's throes of gratification and her satin-skinned bottom rammed against him in frantic release.

'You have ruined me,' she said when she could speak again.

'With your consent,' he agreed, feeling pleased with himself, 'and by your own request.'

For the rest of that month, while his wife was away from Paris, Michel was a frequent visitor to Ninette's home, to re-enact with her their private extravaganza. Certain dramatic conventions were observed by both of them. It was understood that she was an unwilling victim and that he was ravishing her by force. These conventions were never stated, but both adhered to them with care. To extend and improve the game Michel bought and skimmed through the most notorious writings of de Sade and came across many scenes which could be adapted to Ninette's old-fashioned reception room. She never invited him into her bedroom, for that would be to acknowledge that she wished to participate in what took place between them. No, their stage was always the reception room, late at night, after the servants had gone to bed.

A heavy light-fitting on the wall proved useful on one

229

occasion. Michel found that by knotting two stockings together he could attach Ninette to it above her head so that she stood helpless against the wall while he handled and used her body as he chose. Another time the piano was pressed into service and gave out a crash of discord as he violated her on it, hastily silenced by closing the lid! Ninette herself hinted at some variations, for she never spoke out frankly for fear of spoiling the game, but it emerged that she found a fearful joy in being compelled to kneel before him, her wrists bound behind her back, and kiss his upright part in submission before it entered its natural home. Each of their encounters necessitated the destruction of her knickers – that aroused her inordinately as a symbol of her own fate to follow.

They enjoyed themselves greatly in their curious games, which continued after Michel's wife returned home, though less frequently then. But alas, misfortune was not slow to manifest itself. By reason of her strict upbringing and lack of experience, Ninette had not the least idea of what women did to avoid the normal consequences of regular love-making. And Michel never thought to raise the matter. Less than three months after their first encounter, Ninette informed him, with bitter tears, that she was pregnant.

ADRIENNE AT A MUSICAL EVENING

One of those who continued the civilised tradition of arranging musical *soirées* for their acquaintances was Madame Floquet, a lady who regarded herself as a patron of the arts. It was at one of these evenings that Adrienne Dumoutier and Maurice progressed from friendship to something quite different – to being lovers, one might almost say, as the world views these things. But *lovers* in its ordinary sense does not adequately define the complications of their emotions.

Adrienne and her husband Edmond were present because Madame Floquet was an aunt of hers. Maurice and Marie-Thérèse were invited at Adrienne's suggestion so that they could go on as a foursome afterwards to dance to music of a less pretentious kind at the *Jardin de ma Soeur*. They met first at the Brissard's home for a drink and arrived at Madame Floquet's a little late. The music had started and the salon was full. The servant responsible for seating the guests could find space only for two, right at the back.

From such casual chances often spring the most astonishing results. Marie-Thérèse and Edmond took the remaining chairs, both of them having an interest in modern music, while Maurice and Adrienne descended the grand staircase again to chat over another drink until the performance was finished.

'Thank heaven we are spared that awful music,' said Adrienne, 'my aunt must be quite mad to think that it is of any value. And her friends are complete idiots to sit through it.'

'But isn't this fellow Milhaud supposed to be a shining light of modern French music?' said Maurice, 'I mean, I don't know anything about music but I seem to have heard his name.'

Adrienne was wearing a short evening frock of peacock blue, backless and sleeveless, supported over her fair-sized

231

bosom by a *diamanté* halter-strap. Her bare shoulders were finely rounded. Her hair was the most striking thing about her, being shiny and rich red, elegantly shingled and set in soft waves. The contrast between her and Marie-Thérèse's style of dark-haired beauty was piquant.

'The critics write him up in the journals,' said Adrienne, pouting her bright scarlet lips at Maurice. 'He's one of the so-called 'Six' who are bringing about a renaissance of French music. Or so they claim.'

If Adrienne had not been his wife's closest friend, Maurice might long ago have permitted his admiration of her to become apparent. She was altogether a stylish modern woman and an intimate encounter with her might well be exceptionally rewarding. These things were not difficult to arrange. A drink together in a discreet place and some exploratory talk. A luncheon – that was how one proceeded – to see if the attraction was sustained. If the outcome of that was satisfactory to both, then a private meeting, to ascertain whether a full love affaire would develop. Of course, many an encounter of that type ended when the couple put their clothes on again and parted with a kiss. But some endured.

'Do you suppose he'll be playing for long?' Maurice asked, glancing around the small reception room in which they sat, 'if so, I'll ring for someone to bring us another drink.'

'He'll go on for hours,' said Adrienne, 'they all do.'

She set her glass down and touched and then gripped the hem of her skirt, paused for one breathless moment and drew it upwards over her silk-clad knees. Maurice could hardly believe the evidence of his own eyes – what man could in such circumstances? Yet there, uncovered for him to admire, were her garters, jet-black and threaded through with pale green ribbon. The effect on Maurice was as nature decreed. It declared itself by a growing tightness inside his underwear.

'Pretty, aren't they?' Adrienne asked, her head tilted to one side.

Whether she meant her knees, her thighs or her garters was not at all obvious, nor was it of any importance.

'Very chic,' said Maurice.

She smiled sweetly at him and drew her skirt a little higher. Maurice gazed at her enchanting thighs above her garters, bare and smooth. And – what he had never expected to see – in the deepest recess between those thighs he glimpsed the flimsy band of lace-edged *crêpe de Chine* which covered her most secret place. His heart leaped in his breast, drowning out the distant music from the salon.

What was in Adrienne's mind to shamelessly reveal so much to Maurice? Not only was his wife her dearest friend, they had been lovers since they were at boarding school together. There, perhaps, was to be found the reason. Between these two beautiful women there was a certain rivalry in all that they did. It could be discerned through the years they had known each other in various manifestations – in excelling at their lessons, then in marrying well, in dressing elegantly, in the style and decor of their homes, in the esteem of the parties and dinners they gave. Even in their love-making there had always existed a spirit of each striving to impress and vanquish the other.

All that was unsuspected by Maurice, eyeing with delight Adrienne's raised skirt and the vision presented to him. For a moment he glanced up into her face to let her see his appreciation. The tip of her tongue slipped out for an instant between her scarlet lips and with a gesture of her head she directed his glance downwards again. Maurice's hand found its way without his conscious knowledge to his own lap to press against his aroused male part. Adrienne drew her skirt even higher and parted her knees to give him a clear sight of the little strip of material that only just concealed so dear a secret.

'Ravishing!' he exclaimed.

'Thank you,' she said coolly.

'You must know what effect you are having on me, Adrienne.'

Most assuredly she knew – and she was enjoying her role of temptress. She had transfixed the attention of her dear friend's handsome husband by showing him her legs, no more than that. She could guess what was in his heart – a raging desire to kiss her thighs, and an even more ardent

233

desire to tear away the narrow strip of silk between them. How easy it had been to wipe away all thought of Marie-Thérèse from his mind, devoted husband though he was supposed to be. Could he be led into the final act of infidelity to his marriage vows, she wondered. It might be amusing to find out.

She lightly caressed the inside of her own thigh with her finger-tips and heard him sigh.

'Do you think I've got good legs?' she asked.

'They are quite perfect!'

Her finger-tips slid upwards into her soft groin and pulled aside the last thin veil. Maurice gasped as he saw the patch of bright ginger hair between her legs. He was fascinated by the fiery colour of it. He rose to his feet and stumbled one step towards her, the only thought in his mind to possess that glowing jewel. Adrienne chuckled and stood up, allowing her frock to descend her thighs and conceal what he had been privileged to view, just as the door opened and one of Madame Floquet's servants ushered in two latecomers to the *soirée*.

When he was dancing with her at the *Jardin de ma Soeur*, Maurice pressed Adrienne for a meeting. He was eaten up by desire, his hand feverishly hot against her bare back. But all that she would say was that he should telephone her sometime.

After that evening she let him stew. She had established to her own satisfaction a position of superiority. What more was there? She was extremely fond of Marie-Thérèse, a point of great consideration. Rivalry was one thing, to risk hurting her friend was quite another. What was to be gained by allowing Maurice to consummate the desire she had aroused in him?

She was cool when he telephoned to arrange a rendezvous. She put him off with excuses, time after time, never entirely discouraging him. For in truth his persistence day after day amused her at first and then flattered her. It was a tribute to her attractions, what else? Very well, she decided after a week of telephone calls, you shall advance a little further, Maurice, though not to the goal you are aiming at.

It went without saying that the meeting-place must be far away from those parts of Paris where he and she were known and could be recognised together. She specified the Bois de Vincennes in the east of the city, a park she had visited only once before in her life and that as a child. One afternoon, in the weak winter sunshine, she and Maurice strolled along the edge of the lake on which a few swans and a multitude of ducks busied themselves in the search for food.

Adrienne looked very chic in a wrap-over coat of moss green, furred at the collar and cuffs. Her deep cloche hat was of the same shade, with a broad band of damson silk tied round it, the long ends fluttering in a light breeze. She looked utterly delightful, yet from the moment Maurice met her at the entrance to the Bois and kissed her gloved hand, he was blind to what she wore. His mind was obsessed by one image alone – the bright ginger tuft between her thighs which he had glimpsed so briefly during the recital. Since that evening he had thought of it almost continuously, at night he had dreamed of it. He had attempted to free himself from its power by making love nightly to Marie-Thérèse with the intensity of a newly-wed. Yet the image was undimmed in his mind. When he looked at Adrienne, it was almost as if that patch of colour shone visibly through her fashionable clothes!

They walked slowly under the trees and he declared his fervour and used all his powers of persuasion on Adrienne. She prolonged his suffering by seeming almost to agree and yet never finally consenting to a meeting in some more convenient place. There was nothing he could do in the Bois except talk, which was the reason she had chosen it.

Even so, he surprised her. They reached the furthest point of the walk at the narrow end of the lake and turned back along the other side. Maurice glanced about quickly to see that they were unobserved and steered her off the path and under the trees.

'I must kiss you,' he explained, pulling her behind a broad trunk.

'Such devotion!' she said, smiling, 'One kiss, then.'

While their lips were pressed together she felt his hand insert itself within her winter coat and feel for the join of her

235

thighs. She broke off the embrace at once and pushed his hand away.

'Really!' she exclaimed, 'am I a little shop assistant to be fondled in a public place!'

'It was hardly a private place where you set me on fire, Adrienne.'

'My aunt's salon is not a public park.'

'Nevertheless, you showed me a glimpse of Paradise, and that was a garden.'

'I do not carry Paradise about with me between my legs – only that which every other woman has,' she mocked him.

'You are wrong. You have something special and magnificent.'

'Poor Maurice! I was only amusing myself the other evening because I was bored. You must not take it so seriously.'

'Bored or not, your little amusement lit a fire in me which only you can extinguish.'

'You may put your arms around me and kiss me, but no more than that.'

He did so gladly. This time it was her hand which found its way inside his overcoat and touched him.

'Heavens!' she said, ending the kiss, 'it is obvious that you are in a state of dangerous over-excitement. What is to be done?'

'If you refuse me, Adrienne, I shall go insane!'

His senses whirled as she tugged at his trouser buttons. He drew in his breath sharply as her kid-gloved hand clasped his ravenously erect penis.

'You are as eager as a young boy,' she said, 'how old are you, Maurice – thirty-five, thirty-six?'

'At this moment we are both eighteen. I adore you, Adrienne.'

'The evidence for that is impressive.'

Then her hand was gone.

'There's a man walking his dog this way,' she said calmly, 'we must stroll further. And I must leave you. I'm expecting Marie-Thérèse at four and I don't want to be late.'

Their next meeting was nearly a week later. Adrienne

chose the Eiffel Tower, a tourist attraction none of her friends, or Maurice's, was likely to visit. Like the Bois de Vincennes, it was too public a place for Maurice to be led into displays of ardour too vehement for her to deal with. They met on the second platform and stood side by side looking out across the Seine to the Trocadero gardens. Maurice put his arm round her waist and told her that he adored her.

'How long have we known each other?' she asked.

'Six or seven years. Why do you ask?'

'And for how long have you adored me? Two weeks?'

'I cannot explain it rationally to you. Reason does not enter into it. If you could look into my heart you would be dazzled by the brightness of the devotion you would see there.'

'Perhaps. Do you love Marie-Thérèse?'

'Naturally.'

'How do you reconcile these two passions, dear Maurice?'

'There is no need. They do not impinge on each other in any way. My feelings for her and my feelings for you are entirely separate. I love both of you to distraction.'

'Strange! I could never love more than one person at the same time. But then, I am a woman.'

'And a most fascinating one,' he agreed.

'Any fascination I may exercise over you is less over your heart than over another organ, I believe.'

'Put your hand inside my overcoat and you will have tangible proof of the devastating effect you have on me. I have only to think of you and a certain part is alert.'

Adrienne glanced over her shoulder to make sure there was no one near them on the platform and then complied with his wish.

'Marie-Thérèse must be enjoying a second honeymoon,' she said, laughing at him while her hand made matters worse, 'I thought she looked a little pale and tired when she called on me last week. Let us hope that she does not guess the reason for your fervour.'

'You are cruel to laugh at me when it is you who are responsible for my condition. But all beautiful women are cruel.'

'Am I cruel, Maurice?' she teased him, her hand caressing him slowly through his trousers, 'or am I being kind to you just now?'

'You are beautiful and cruel,' he sighed, 'say yes to me, I implore you. We have so much to gain by being lovers.'

'And to lose.'

'What is there to lose?'

'I might lose my dearest friend.'

'No, I swear! We will be discreet. Your friendship will not be harmed.'

'Perhaps.'

She removed her hand before things went too far.

The day arrived when Adrienne almost forgot that she was involved in nothing more than a teasing game. A slightly malicious game, one might say, to prove to herself her superiority over Marie-Thérèse. Yet as the drip of water will at last wear out the stone upon which it falls, Maurice's persistence eventually had its effect upon her. In short, she agreed to meet him in private for a fuller expression of his urgent emotions.

She was fully aware of the particular nature of her allurement for him. She thought it strange that he could be so strongly impressed by a mere accident of natural colouring, but she knew enough of the world not to be surprised. After all, it was known on good authority that the Emperor had fallen in love with Josephine de Beauharnais and married her for her pretty bottom. *She has the sweetest little backside in all the world*, he said of her to others. And it was sure that Josephine wiggled it to good effect.

There was no question of allowing Maurice to take instant possession of the coveted treasure. This was one little red fox which could outwit any hunter until it decided to let itself be caught! She had not entirely lost sight of the purpose of her game with Maurice. She proposed to tease him to the very limit. The episode would be marvellously amusing – for her.

The location was important. She refused outright the half dozen discreet little hotels he named. She also refused to drive out of Paris to a hotel in the country. Every one of them will be full of people we know committing adultery with each others' wives, she declared.

Moreover, so unique an occasion demanded sumptuous surroundings.

Maurice suggested the Hotel Ritz. Adrienne turned it down flat. She would be recognised there and compromised. Poor Maurice was in despair.

'I know of a place,' she said.

'Name it! Anywhere you choose!'

'The Delaunys are in South America for the winter. We could use their house.'

'But the servants will be there.'

'Only one or two to look after the place.'

'But what are you suggesting? That we break in?'

'That butler of theirs is a rogue. If you offer him a big enough bribe he will give himself and the rest of the staff an afternoon off. Next Tuesday would be convenient for me.'

'But we've both been guests in that house. He will know who we are.'

'Of course. You surely don't imagine that he would let perfect strangers use the house. Because he knows who we are he will be certain that we are not thieves.'

'But ... he could blackmail us afterwards.'

'Who would believe such a story?'

'I confess myself uneasy about the suggestion.'

'Very well, forget that I suggested it. You are evidently not so interested in me as you have pretended.'

'But I am!'

'Then prove it.'

'I shall go and talk to the fellow immediately. Tuesday you said?'

Filled with trepidation at the outright madness of what he was doing, Maurice checked that he had plenty of money with him and took a taxi to the Delaunys' imposing house on the Avenue Foch. On the way there he calmed himself by looking at his mission in the light of a business transaction. His experience of that was extensive. Acting for his father he had negotiated many quite difficult deals with all kinds of people, in France and abroad. Very well then, here was a quite extraordinary transaction confronting him. Like any

239

other, what was needed was tact, diplomacy, persistence and enough money. In his mind it became a most interesting challenge.

On the following Tuesday he rang the doorbell at two in the afternoon, a smile on his lips. The butler opened the door himself, his face impassive, took Maurice's hat and overcoat and showed him up to the magnificent salon on the first floor. Not one word was spoken by either of them on the negotiations that had taken place the week before.

Alphonse Delauny was very rich indeed, though no one had ever heard of him before the War. Even now the origin of his wealth was a subject of unkind gossip and speculation by those invited to his house. In a sense, thought Maurice, following the butler up the ornate curving staircase, there is a certain poetic justice in putting this house to the use I have in mind for it.

The salon was decorated in the style of Napoleon III, furniture, mirrors, pictures, every single item genuine, to be sure. The room itself was impressively large and took up the whole of the first floor of the house. There was a huge carved fireplace in rose-pink marble and, above it, right up to the high ceiling, a gilt-framed mirror the whole width of the fireplace. On the mantle stood a large clock with a pair of nudes in gold draped round the dial and holding hands above the twelve. The clock was flanked by a pair of gilt candlesticks, each holding three virgin candles.

On either side of the fireplace there were conversation corners, each of four heavy gilt and red armchairs grouped together. At the opposite end from the doors stood a grand piano, and in spite of all the furniture, the room gave the appearance of being half-empty.

'I have removed the dust-covers, as you requested, sir,' said the butler gravely, 'is everything to your satisfaction?'

'Yes,' said Maurice, handing over a thick wad of banknotes.

'Thank you, sir. If you will excuse me I shall station myself by the door so as not to miss the bell. There is no one else in the house.'

Maurice sat on one of the chairs and wondered for the

hundredth time if he had lost his wits. Would Adrienne really come here, or was this just a stupid trick she was playing on him? With her, how could one tell? He sat and worried for a quarter of an hour before the tall door at the end of the room opened again and the butler ushered in Adrienne. Maurice stood up and waited while she made the long walk across the salon to him.

The butler bowed.

'If you will excuse me, sir, I must go out on household business. I shall not return until after six o'clock. May I request you to make quite sure that the door locks behind you when you leave the house?'

'I will attend to it.'

Side by side he and Adrienne watched the butler's retreating back down the salon. When the door closed behind him, Maurice tried to take her into his arms to kiss her.

'Not so hasty,' she said with a smile, 'let me take in the surroundings.'

'Yes. Do you find this place sufficiently sumptuous for our purpose?'

'It's very grand, isn't it? What a joke that the Delaunys are thousands of miles away and we are in their house alone. And with a particular intent! I really am delighted that you were able to arrange it, Maurice. I shall be grateful.'

'Then may I kiss you?'

'How impatient you are. Sit down over there, Maurice. You have much to learn about me.'

'Whatever you wish. I will do anything you say.'

'Then sit down.'

He seated himself upon a priceless chair and awaited her pleasure. She looked very smart indeed in a honey-coloured afternoon frock with a big collar and a flowing chiffon scarf tied loosely under it.

'That's better,' she said, 'now, answer me a question. Do you still adore me?'

'To distraction!'

'Good. You want to see me naked, yes?'

'But of course.'

'And so you shall.'

241

Before his astonished gaze she undid the fastenings down the side of her frock and wriggled it over her head. Her hat, which she had forgotten, came off with it and fell to the rich carpet. She stood for his inspection in pale tangerine cami-knickers decorated at yoke and hem by a band of net and hand-embroidered appliqué.

For a while she posed for him, letting him admire her shapely legs. Then the tangerine came off and she was naked but for her stockings and a tight satin brassiere. Before Maurice could catch more than a glimpse of the object of his desire, she was sitting in an armchair opposite him, her legs crossed. She fumbled behind her back for a moment to unhook herself and the brassiere joined her other clothes on the carpet. Her breasts were plump and round now that they were released from their tight confinement, Maurice noted.

'Is that what you wanted?' she asked.

'My dear Adrienne, your body is superb. I could study it for hours and rhapsodise on its magnificence.'

'What would you say?'

'I would praise the delicacy of your skin, your graceful shoulders, the elegance of your legs ...'

'My big bosom? You seem to have left that out in your rapid passage from shoulders to legs.'

'I was leaving the more intimate parts until the last. Yes, I would praise the symmetry of your bosom. I find your breasts enchanting and not in the least too large.'

'Flatterer!'

'I do you no more than justice.'

'Is there any other part of me you would care to see?'

'One in particular,' he replied huskily.

'Namely?'

'The magnificent part of you which is modestly protected by your crossed legs.'

'Modestly? Is that what you believe? Perhaps provocative would be a more apt description than modest. What do you think?'

'Provocatively modest, then,' he said, grinning at her teasing.

242

'Or modestly provocative?'

'That too.'

Adrienne leaned back and put one stockinged foot up on the chair seat she occupied, so that her knee was on a level with her shoulder. She clasped the raised shin in her interlaced fingers and moved her other leg to the side, so presenting to him a complete view of the brilliantly coloured patch of hair between her thighs. Maurice gestured briefly in admiration.

Her eyes studied him thoughtfully.

'Once the clothes are removed,' she said, 'these scenes are frequently so predictable that they become boring. Hot hands and heavy breathing obliterate style and wit. The brevity of the pleasure a man can give a woman is a small recompense. I like to be amused, Maurice, or I become bored and lose interest. Tell me some amusing adventure of yours.'

'You mean with a woman?'

'What else?'

Maurice thought for a moment, his eyes fixed on the exposed acme of his desire. He related to her his curious adventure with the two sisters on board ship for America. Adrienne laughed.

'Extraordinary,' she said, 'you thought you were making love in the dark to Michelle and all the time it was Antoinette. They fooled you.'

'Only once. When I was sure what had happened I paid Michelle back.'

'How?'

'I made her come to my cabin and let me make love to her. I felt that she owed me that much.'

'How did you force her to agree?'

'By threatening to let her mother find out about her little trick.'

Adrienne laughed again and her thighs moved even further apart. The soft lips beneath the ginger fleece were clearly visible and slightly open.

'You really paid her back,' she said, 'when you made love to her, did she enjoy it or did she hate it?'

'She hated it at first because it was under duress and not of her own free will. Then she began to enjoy it despite herself, and that made her hate it even more.'

'Did she reach a climax of this hateful pleasure?'

'Yes, and that was the final insult for her.'

'A very confusing experience for a young girl. You have amused me, Maurice. You may kiss me.'

He slid forward from his gilded chair to kneel and press his lips to the silky skin of her inner thighs, high up near the prize he wished to win. Her groins carried the delicate fragrance of Chanel 5. Adrienne's hand pressed lightly on his head and he heard her say: 'Perhaps you do know how to please me, after all. Try.'

Maurice flicked his tongue into her until she sighed gently. Encouraged by that, he boldly kissed the object of his obsession. Under the ginger fur her mound was full and prominent. In moments, under his attentions, the plump lips were parted fully and through the expensive perfume with which she had dabbed herself he savoured the hot scent of her own eroticism.

'Kiss me,' she murmured.

Her tiny bud was already swollen with desire as his tongue caressed it to new heights of sensation. She was responding so rapidly to his tender ministrations that he knew that he had discovered the key to her secret entrance and he was confident that he could make use of it to gain admission.

'It is strange that it is you pleasing me,' he heard her murmur, as if to herself, 'one could say bizarre almost ... but how very amusing ...'

Then she gasped as her crisis overtook her and she squirmed ecstatically under his busy tongue. When she was finished, Maurice sat back on his heels and studied her face. Her eyes were closed, but there was a satisfied half-smile at the corners of her mouth.

'That was remarkably quick,' she said, her eyes opening, 'either you are the greatest expert in Paris or there is something about this little interlude of ours which aroused me formidably. Which do you think it was, Maurice?'

'How can I say? The important question is – was the

outcome satisfactory?'

'Entirely. You have earned your reward, my friend.'

Maurice shed his jacket and tie and opened his trousers. Adrienne eyed his stiff part casually.

'What do you prefer?' she asked. 'Do you want me to lie down for you? The floor or a sofa?'

'No, stay as you are. I have to see.'

He knelt upright between her splayed legs and positioned himself at the open portal presented to him.

'To see,' she said, smiling, 'yes, I understand.'

Maurice grasped her thighs and initiated a very gradual penetration of her ginger grotto, staring downwards the whole time, watching his centimetre by centimetre insertion. When he was fully in place he remained still, looking at what he had achieved. Adrienne stretched out her arms to clasp him to her full breasts, but he shook his head.

'I want to see what I am doing to you, Adrienne.'

'Then see all you wish.'

To observe himself embedded in that brightly-coloured nest filled Maurice with such elation that he hardly dare move for fear of precipitating an instant emission. His body shook at the surge of his emotions and the movement almost betrayed him. His hands squeezed her thighs hard and he knew that whatever he did it was only a matter of seconds before his torrent would burst through the dam and flood the valley below. In an attempt to hold back the climactic moment for as long as he could he looked away from the fascinating sight between Adrienne's thighs and up into her face. Her mouth was drawn back in a smile that displayed her white teeth, her eyes gleamed with triumph. But Maurice was so fraught with passion that he missed the mockery of her smile and took it for pleasure.

'Look down, Maurice,' she whispered, 'feast your eyes on what you have desired for so long. At this moment it is yours to do what you like with.'

For Adrienne, the satisfaction she was then experiencing was far keener than the purely physical satisfaction she had enjoyed minutes before. Here was Marie-Thérèse's husband, the brilliant Maurice Brissard, on his knees to her. And he

245

was so bemused by the sight of her carrot-coloured bush that he was trembling like a leaf. In two more seconds it would be over, to judge by his flushed face and uneven breathing – a man of the world behaving like a young boy approaching a woman's commodity for the first time. Adrienne found the thought incredibly amusing. She was sure that Marie-Thérèse had never brought her husband to such a pitch of frenzy during her years of marriage to him. What a rare triumph to savour and remember! And one day, when it no longer mattered, perhaps to tell?

Maurice's eyes moved slowly down from Adrienne's mocking face to her plump breasts, lingered for a moment at her dark, almost brown, nipples, then down further to the deep-set navel in her soft belly and so back at last to the ginger patch of curly hair surrounding the warm lips into which his fleshy shaft was thrust. He smiled beatifically and commenced a short to and fro movement, neither slow nor fast, staring hard at what he was doing.

Adrienne was unaffected physically by the use he was making of her body. She watched his face, secretly exulting in her victory. She curled her legs around his waist to hold him fast until the moment of her final triumph.

How simple to make a fool of a man, she thought, even Maurice. All it required was to open her legs. As soon as his penis stood up, his senses left him. Even a young girl on board ship had known that and had taken advantage of her knowledge. Had he really turned the tables on Michelle, she wondered, or had he made that part up to save face?

She felt her breasts bouncing as Maurice's thrust became faster and rocked her body on the chair. What a pity they had grown larger than was fashionable and needed to be tightly bound and flattened before she could wear really elegant clothes, she thought. She had heard from a friend about a surgeon in Switzerland – immensely expensive of course – who was believed to be able to reduce oversize bosoms without leaving visible scars. Perhaps it was worth while to make closer enquiries into the matter, though in all honesty it sounded like a drastic remedy. The most sensible course would be to find someone who had undergone the

246

operation and persuade her to describe it and to allow her to inspect the results.

Her reverie was interrupted by a wordless cry from Maurice as he lunged hard and delivered himself of a stupendous outburst within her.

'Ah!' Adrienne exclaimed.

Her little cry was not of rapture but of final triumph. Now I have you, she thought gleefully. After this you will implore me to give you this satisfaction again and again, my dear Maurice. I shall dole it out to you just often enough to keep you at fever-pitch, but never enough for you to become accustomed to it and to take it for granted. You do not know it, my friend, but you are going to be a source of great amusement to me for as long as I find the game interesting. And before you get this pleasure from me the next time, I shall think of somewhere even more outrageous for you to arrange.

But if she could have seen inside Maurice's head at that moment and read his thoughts, her elation would have been swept away like dust before a strong wind. He had known for a long time that Adrienne and Marie-Thérèse were lovers – ever since the day he had visited his cousin Monique and seen the painting in her studio of the two women posed together. There was no mistaking its significance, even though Monique had insisted that it was only a little joke, the picture.

By her unconsidered escapade at Madame Floquet's musical soirée Adrienne had presented him with an opportunity to get even with her. The victory was his. Nor was this the end of the matter. However difficult Adrienne might make their meetings, as she had this first one, he intended to persevere. Each time he used her body for his gratification, the thought of revenge would bring him the same supreme satisfaction.

As for Marie-Thérèse, tonight he intended to penetrate her with the same sturdy instrument of vengeance which he had just employed on Adrienne.

It was going to be very amusing.

247

JOIE D'AMOUR

PARIS IN THE 1920s

The interest which greeted publication of a small selection of Anne-Marie Villefranche's stories under the title of Plaisir D'Amour has encouraged me to persevere with the translation of another selection. As before, these candid tales of her friends are by turns tender, comical and outrageous, depending on the reader's own attitudes towards sexual encounters between men and women.

There is no need to repeat here how these stories were written or how they became my property after the author's death, since that was set out in the preface to Plaisir D'Amour. What may be of interest to those few who read prefaces is to learn of the large number of letters I received after the publication of that little volume, from people who still remember Paris as it was between the two Wars. The majority of my correspondents were amused by Anne-Marie's stories, but a few professed to be offended by such intimate revelations. Plus ça change, plus c'est la même chose, as the French say: the more things change, the more they stay the same.

For any clumsiness of translation in the present volume I can do no more than offer my apologies. The spirit of the French language is unlike that of English and the author's style is all her own, sometimes breathless, sometimes reflective, sometimes humorous. I hope that I have done it some measure of justice.

Anne-Marie's stories were written to amuse herself. If this new selection gives as much pleasure to readers as the first, it may be that eventually she will be accorded the esteem she merits as an observer of the follies and caprices of her friends.

Jane Purcell
London 1983

GINETTE ON THE METRO

For Michel Brissard to travel on the Metro was an unusual occurrence. Not that he had any strong antagonism towards it – indeed, he supposed it to be a most useful means of conveyance for the many who needed to travel about Paris quickly and cheaply to reach their place of work or to return to their homes in the evening. For himself he prefered something more suitable, more convenient, more comfortable and more exclusive.

Yet one spring day he found himself, for reasons which are of no consequence to what took place, standing in a crowded carriage of a Metro train down below street level. He was thankful that his station was the one after the next. Little did he imagine that he was about to embark upon a curious adventure – an adventure which would involve two things of great importance to him – a pretty girl and money.

The train rattled to a halt on the track between two stations, evoking a chorus of dismayed groans from the passengers. After it had been at a standstill for a minute or two Michel addressed himself to a young woman standing next to him – one might almost say pressed against him by the crush of home-going passengers.

'Excuse me, Mademoiselle – do you think that we shall be here for long?'

She looked over her shoulder at him and smiled.

'A few minutes, perhaps, who knows? It is not unusual, Monsieur.'

Until that moment Michel had paid no great attention to her since her back had been presented to him, so that his view of her had been only of her hat and coat. She wriggled herself round to face him and he saw a pretty face with high-arching eyebrows and a little pointed chin. Her eyes were large and lustrous, their colour a dark velvety brown. In short, she made a deep impression on him with no more than a glance. He put her age at about twenty-five or six – ten years younger than himself.

'Are you in a hurry, Monsieur?' she asked, 'an urgent appointment, perhaps?'

Her smile of amusement indicated what sort of appointment he might be hurrying to – an hour or so with a charming woman friend to enjoy the pleasures of love before going home to dinner with his wife and family. Michel smiled back and removed his hat as he answered her.

'No, it's not that – just the inconvenience of being stranded here.'

'Obviously you are not very familiar with the ways of the Metro,' she said. 'How far are you going?'

'The stop after the next, if we ever get there. And you, Mademoiselle?'

'Alexandre Dumas,' she informed him.

To Michel that seemed almost as remote as Indochina. It was somewhere out in the east of Paris, out beyond the Place de la Bastille. Yet the young woman on her way to so outlandish a place was dressed pleasantly enough in a green woollen frock and a three-quarter length jacket. Department stores clothes, he noted, but chosen with an eye to style. Her shoes were good of their kind, so far as he could make out in the crowd.

'A long way,' he said sympathetically, 'at this rate it will take hours.'

She shrugged.

'No one is waiting for me,' she said.

To a man of Michel's temperament the words were virtually an invitation.

'If I may make a suggestion,' he said 'let us get off this miserable train at the next stop and have a drink together. You are in need of some refreshment to fortify you for your long journey.'

She studied him carefully – his face, his expression, his dark and waved hair, his expensive suit and silk shirt, his tasteful neck-tie, the gold wedding ring on the hand with which he was holding on to the overhead strap. All this took no more than three seconds and Michel was aware that she was making an assessment of his standing in life.

'Thank you, Monsieur,' she said, smiling at him in the most charming way, 'I would like that.'

Eventually the train clattered into the next station, they got off together and walked side by side up the steps to the street, Michel's hand placed courteously under her elbow to assist her. He took her into a cafe nearby, ignoring the pavement terrace and leading her inside in case anyone he knew might pass by and see him with her.

Her name, he learned, was Ginette Royer and she worked as a sales assistant in a big store in central Paris. She was unmarried and lived alone. Her father had been killed in the War and her mother lived with a sister near Orleans. By then she and Michel were on first-name terms, naturally, and both understood what was going to take place after they left the cafe. After all, this was the most natural thing in the world and far from the first time for either of them.

'If you will excuse me for a moment,' said Michel, glancing at his watch, 'I must make a telephone call. After that I shall escort you home, if you will permit me.'

He made his call and his arrangements, explaining most convincingly that urgent business would prevent him from being home for dinner that evening – the usual convenient little lies which husbands make use of on these occasions. That done, and with a clear conscience, he paid the bill and found a taxi. No more standing on the Metro for Michel that night!

During the time the taxi was travelling through the evening traffic along the rue de Saint Antoine he put an arm about Ginette's waist and kissed her. She responded warmly to his advances and after another lengthy kiss he went so far as to stroke her breasts lightly through her woollen frock.

'Michel,' she murmured, 'you are an impatient man.'

'And you, chérie?'

'You have guessed it – I am an impatient woman.'

'Then we shall get on well together.'

3

By the time the taxi reached the Avenue Alexandre Dumas Michel's hand was up her skirt, stroking her bare thigh above her stocking-top. The touch of her skin aroused him enormously, it was so smooth and soft. He slid his hand higher up her thigh towards her warm sanctuary.

'That's what I want,' he said, kissing her neck.

'You shall have it,' she answered, turning her head so that her mouth could find his and cling in another long kiss.

Once off the Avenue, the taxi threaded its way through narrow streets and stopped at the address Ginette had given the driver. In his mood of exhilaration Michel added a more than generous tip to the fare and was rewarded by an insolent wink from the driver. In this high state of arousal the stairs up to Ginette's apartment seemed endless – flight after flight – yet with a pause on each landing for him to hug Ginette to him and kiss her, his hands on her bottom to press her close to him.

But at last they were there. She opened the door and led him into a sparsely furnished yet very clean and neat room – her sitting-room, dining-room, bed-room and kitchen all in one. Michel would have pulled her to him again to resume his kissing but she slipped from his grasp to pull off her hat and coat and drop them on a chair as she went across to the divan bed. She had her dress off in a moment, then her knickers, and sat on the side of the bed wearing only shoes, stockings, and a pale green chemise, her arms stretched out towards Michel. He moved towards her, his breath rasping in his throat. As he reached the bed she let herself fall backwards, so that she was half-lying on it, her feet still on the floor. She pulled her chemise up round her waist and spread her knees to expose herself.

'That's what you said you wanted,' she gasped, 'it is yours to take.'

Michel stared round-eyed at her parted thighs and the brown-haired nest between them, enraptured by the pouting lips at the entrance to her shrine, yet amazed at the eagerness with which she had made herself available. For

4

a moment he wondered whether he had been picked up by a professional, but commonsense told him that, if she were that, she would have asked for money first. And confronted by an offer so tempting as that spread before him – a warm and fleshy place in which to satisfy his desire – what man could turn away? Certainly not Michel. He shed his jacket and tie and was fumbling at his trousers as he fell to his knees on the thin carpet beside the bed. His fixture was hard and strong and sank into her easily. At that moment he expected no more surprises from Ginette, only the vigorous climb together to an apex of delight. Yet once again she amazed him. Before he had attained the full length of his forward thrust she gasped and shook in a manner that warned him that she was about to reach the culmination of her pleasure! He pressed on, her reaction grew stronger until, at the moment his hardness was fully inserted, she reached an abrupt climax of passion. Her clenched fists beat against his back and her loins jerked furiously upwards against him – so furiously that he was compelled to seize her by the shoulders and hold on tightly until her violent shuddering ran its course and ceased.

'Oh, that was good,' she exclaimed, 'thank you, Michel.'

'You have been without a man for a long time,' Michel observed, smiling at her pink-flushed face.

'Far too long. I am so glad that I met you this evening.'

'And so am I. Do you want to rest a little?'

'No, no – I am ready for you. Do it to me, please.'

No further encouragement was necessary. In truth, it was remarkable that he had been able to contain himself for so long after entering her, but his astonishment at her instant response had temporarily suspended his actions. But now, her hot body under him and her moist flesh clasping his male part like a soft glove, he gave full rein to his natural ardour.

It must have been that Ginette's unexpectedly fast response had aroused him more than he realised. Or perhaps it was her little cries of pleasure as he burrowed between her legs. Whatever the cause – or combination of causes – the act of love was briefer than usual for him. Though not the outcome – his vital essence rushed from him a flood of voluptuous sensation.

'There,' said Ginette, stroking his face, 'now you have caught up with me.'

'But this is terrible,' said Michel, 'you did not share the pleasure with me.'

'It was too soon after the first time. But it doesn't matter – I am content.'

'But of course it matters. I am mortified!'

'We were not synchronised either the first time or the second time, that's all,' she said with a smile.

'Synchronised – what a strange word to use,' said Michel, 'yet it is apt.'

He eased himself away from her and planted a light kiss on her little patch of brown fur before attending to his underwear and trousers. Ginette closed her legs and sat up on the bed so that the pale green chemise slid down her body to cover her belly.

'I hope that you will dine with me,' said Michel. 'Is there a good restaurant anywhere near here?'

'There's a place within walking distance which serves good food. At least, I think it's good, but to you it may not seem so.'

The restaurant was a quarter of an hour's walk away on the Avenue Alexandre Dumas. It proved to be small, but the food was acceptable, though simple. The wine was drinkable. Michel enjoyed his dinner less for the fare than for the company of Ginette. For the outing she put on her new frock, tidied her hair and face to make herself as pretty as possible, and kept him amused by stories of the peculiar ways of customers in the store where she worked. He wondered whether, just possibly, one of the customers at whose mannerisms he was laughing might be his own wife, her demanding manner in shops being a longstanding cause for irritation with him.

After the meal they strolled back under the street-lamps to her apartment. They sat together on the bed and kissed

6

nd Michel began to undress her. The entire scene had
been played so swiftly before that there had been little
opportunity to admire her body – or even to see it
properly – apart from the exciting little entrance between
her thighs. Matters were less urgent now. Michel stripped
her completely naked and touched her all over – her small
round breasts, flat belly, the soft cheeks of her bottom –
he enjoyed every morsel of her to the utmost.

'Off with your clothes too,' she said as he nuzzled her
breasts for the hundredth time, 'let me see you.'

Then it was her turn to get to know his body. She ran
her finger-tips over his broad and hairy chest and found
words of admiration for all of him, above all for his
upstanding part, though with as much modesty as becomes a woman naked with her lover. In this respect, of
course, women are at a certain disadvantage, for while it is
accepted that a man will praise the entire delicious body of
his mistress, for a woman to appear too enthusiastic about
the fifteen centimetres of a man's body which bring her
the greatest pleasure may awake in his mind a suspicion
that she has been familiar with more of those invaluable
parts than he considers fitting in one on whom he is
bestowing his intimate affections. For as all the world
knows, the standards set by society for men are not those
set for women.

Such considerations apart, Ginette's careful approval of
the strength and appearance of his cherished organ won
Michel's heart. Matters proceeded between them in the
most natural and pleasurable way, to the moment when he
rolled her onto her back and was poised to make his grand
entrance.

'This time we shall be *synchronised*, I hope,' he said,
smiling.

'This time, yes,' she answered, spreading her legs for
him.

So it proved. There was no premature crisis on her part
as he slid into place. What occurred was well-managed
and afforded them both equal delight, if intensity of
delight can be compared. The climax of passion was

7

perfectly timed – Ginette shuddered in ecstasy and drum med her heels against his bottom at the instant he discharged his spasms of gratification into her.

In the weeks that followed, Michel regarded his chance meeting with Ginette on the Metro as a most fortunate event. Unlike the other woman who had played an important role in his adventures away from his wife, Ginette had no extensive social life and was always available when the mood took him. She did not ask, much less insist, on being taken to chic restaurants where he might be recognised – she was content with the small and unknown establishments he took her to. She did not expect expensive presents from him – on the contrary, she expressed touching gratitude for whatever small gift he brought. From his point of view it was an ideal liaison and Ginette was a perfect mistress, always pleased to see him, always good-humoured, always ready to make love and totally undemanding. This affaire of the heart had an idyllic quality which Michel had never before encoun- tered.

Perhaps that itself should have cast a faint shadow of doubt on his new-found happiness. Or at the very least, it should perhaps have occasioned the raising of an imagin- ary eyebrow in his mind. Yet the longer he knew Ginette and the better he got to know her, the more he esteemed her. But neither women nor men are perfect, for this is a very imperfect world in which we live, however Mother Church may try to explain that inconvenient fact. The relations between men and women are, of necessity, never perfect – and almost never uncomplicated. While Michel was getting to know Ginette, she was getting to know him, and this knowledge she intended to use to her advantage. And why not? He was a rich and clever man, one of the Brissard family, beholden to no one. She was a poor young woman, likely to remain poor all her life unless she did something to change her fortunes. That she proposed to do, for she was ambitious, besides being pretty.

She revealed her ambition to Michel cleverly, not all at once, but bit by bit over several weeks, over meals and in

8

the intervals while they were resting between love-making. In this way he accepted it as the most natural thing possible. He was himself imbued with the entrepreneurial spirit of his family and he recognised and respected this quality in others – especially when it appeared that a share of the profits might fall into his hand.

'A fashion boutique, Ginette? No doubt there is money to be made from such a venture, as you say. My wife spends a fortune on clothes. So do all her friends. But this is a business I know nothing about.'

'But I do,' she said, 'my job for the last five years has been observing women's taste and selling them clothes in the store. Now I'd like to do it for myself.'

On another occasion, as they lay relaxed together on her bed, her head on his chest, she took the matter further.

'You remember we talked about opening a fashion boutique – well, I've found the right premises to let.'

'Really?' he said lazily, 'where?'

'In the rue Cambon.'

Michel blinked. That was in the most fashionable part of Paris, running between the Boulevard de la Madeleine and the rue de Rivoli. The rent of a shop there was likely to be exorbitant. And to stock a boutique with clothes that would be interesting to the women who shopped in that district would be very expensive. He said so.

'Not nearly as expensive as you think,' she answered, 'I know where to buy everything at very good prices – I have made a point of this. In the fashion business one buys cheap and sells very dear.'

Eventually they reached the point where they talked money. The sum she named was very much less than he had expected, well within his means if he were to dispose of some other investments that, as Ginette explained it, produced a much lower level of profit than her projected venture. In the end she persuaded him. He put up the money, she left her job and opened her boutique on the rue Cambon.

From the very beginning it was successful. The first time he visited it he was delighted by the taste and variety displayed in the choice of its wares – frilly silk blouses, pencil-slim skirts, beautiful stockings, delicious under-wear – a profusion of women's apparel to send a man's imagination racing and his heart to beat a little faster. Sales were brisk and it was obvious to Michel after only a month that Ginette had found her metier and that he had made a very good investment. Whenever he had the time during the day he strolled round to the rue Cambon for the double pleasure of observing money being made for him and of fondling Ginette in her small office at the back of the boutique. This had become important , for now that she was running a business she had much less time and was not so readily available as she had been in the past. However, she was always delighted to see him and, even when busy, she would leave the customers in the care of the two assistants she had engaged, so that she could retire into the office with him for half an hour.

There was a morning in July when he found himself at liberty for an hour before a lunch appointment. He made his way to Ginette's boutique, noted with satisfaction that there were three or four ladies of fashion examining expen-sive items, said 'Good-day' to the assistants as he passed through and into the office. It was a tiny office with hardly room for an Empire-style table against one wall to serve as a desk, and two small chairs. But within this confined space a scene was being played which struck Michel dumb with astonishment. Ginette was standing at the desk, her hands flat on it so that she was bent forward at the waist in a manner to thrust her rump out to the rear. Her pleated silk skirt of lime green was hitched up her back to expose the plump cheeks of her bottom, innocent of any covering of underwear. Behind her, standing between her widely parted feet and clasping her tightly by the waist, was a man in a beautiful grey suit. That is to say, he was partly in his beautiful grey suit, for his trousers were down around his ankles and his jacket had slipped from his shoulders and hung halfway down his back from the vigour of his exertions! And those exertions – a fast plunging of his hips – were proof enough, if any proof were needed, that his male part was deeply embedded in Ginette.

Michel stared with bulging eyes at the pair of them, still oblivious of his presence, for they were sideways on to him and very much involved just then with their own emotions. Ginette's eyes were closed and on her face was an expression of exquisite pleasure. The man's eyes were open but they saw nothing, for at that very instant his final thrusts caused him to convulse in climatic passion.

Michel spoke acidly:

'Good-day Ginette. I regret to interrupt your *business meeting* but perhaps you will be so good as to explain to me what is going on.'

Two startled faces turned towards him.

'Who the devil are you?' the other man demanded angrily, 'Get out!'

'Michel,' said Ginette, recovering from her surprise, 'I did not expect you until after lunch.'

'Obviously!'

'But it was time that the two of you met,' she continued with a sang-froid which amazed him, 'Monsieur Michel Brissard – Monsieur Armand Budin.'

To introduce a lover who had discovered her in an act of infidelity to a lover still embedded in her warm body – and her own spasms of delight not long past – this required such remarkable self-composure on the part of Ginette that the two men were at first astounded and then amused.

Michel held out his hand and grinned.

'Monsieur Budin, it is an honour to make your acquaintance,' he said with heavy irony.

Armand took the offered hand awkwardly, being still pressed firmly against Ginette's bare backside.

'If you will excuse me for a moment, Monsieur Brissard,' he said.

'But of course,' and Michel turned his back politely while the two lovers at the desk disengaged themselves. When he turned again, Ginette was sitting on one of the small chairs, her skirt just covering her knees. Armand

11

was leaning elegantly against the wall, perfectly decent again and lighting a cigarette.

'I know your face,' Michel said, 'where have we met?'

'We have never met formally before, to the best of my recollection – if you regard this occasion as a formal one,' said Armand, smiling, 'but I am a friend of your sister Jeanne.'

'Of course! I remember you now. But what are you doing here? I was under the impression that I had an understanding with Mademoiselle Royer.'

'I had the same impression,' said Armand, 'I am a partner in her business.'

'But so am I!'

The two men glared at each other for a moment and then laughed as the implications became clear to them.

'It would seem,' said Armand, 'that our little Ginette has a more highly developed sense of commerce than either of us suspected.'

Michel seated himself on the other chair and looked at Ginette thoughtfully.

'Tell me, my dear,' he said, 'are there any other partners we don't know about?'

'Only one other,' she answered calmly, 'Monsieur Falaise.'

'And who is he?'

'He is the director of the department store where I used to work – a most charming man – and enormously useful in advising me on establishing and running the boutique. As you are aware, we are making very good profits and some of this is due to his advice and experience.'

'So we are a partnership of four?' Armand asked, 'Does Monsieur Falaise also drop in from time to time to . . . discuss business matters with you, Ginette?'

'Of course, though not as often as either of you. He is much older, you understand.'

'There is one other matter which Monsieur Budin and I ought to know about,' said Michel, 'is it your intention to offer any more partnerships in the business?'

'No,' Ginette said with great sincerity, 'I find that three

partners are enough for me in a venture of this kind. Of course, if either of you desires to withdraw from the arrangement now that you are in possession of the full facts, I am sure that it would be no particular problem to find someone to buy out your interest.'

'Not I,' said Armand at once, 'the boutique is an excellent investment. And besides, I enjoy our little business discussions.'

'I am very pleased,' said Ginette. 'How about you, Michel?'

'I am in complete agreement with Monsieur Budin. There is no question of withdrawing from the arrangement. However, it seems to me necessary that we should reach a more businesslike agreement as to when we each call to discuss our interests with you, dear Ginette. To prevent any embarrassment in future, you understand.'

Armand nodded his approval of the suggestion.

'It is difficult to know which is the more inconvenient,' he said, 'to be interrupted in conversation with Mademoiselle Royer and perhaps to lose the thread of one's discourse, or to interrupt by chance a conversation between her and another and be a reluctant witness to another's private concerns.'

'For myself the inconvenience is equally unfortunate both ways,' said Ginette. 'How shall we arrange matters? Alternate days or mornings and afternoons?'

'I propose mornings and afternoons alternating weekly,' said Michel.

Armand was looking a trifle puzzled.

'Not so fast,' he objected, 'let me be certain that I have understood what it is that you are suggesting.'

'Of course,' said Michel. 'This week, for instance, you make your visits here in the mornings and I make mine in the afternoons. Next week I have the mornings and you have the afternoons. Then the next week we change back, and so on. Does this suit you?'

'An excellent proposal, very convenient and admitting of no misunderstandings. Ah – but what about our other

13

partner, Monsieur Falaise. We must not overlook him in our arrangements.'

'As to that,' said Ginette, 'he is an extremely busy man and is only able to call here on Mondays. So if that is satisfactory to you both, neither of you visits me on Mondays – but of course you have Saturdays, when the boutique is open for business all day.'

'That seems reasonable to me,' said Michel.

'And to me,' Armand agreed, 'but what about the evenings – how do we arrange that?'

'I must have my evenings free,' Ginette said quickly, 'to be with my fiancé. Otherwise he would only see me on Sundays.'

Michel and Armand looked at each other over her head, their eyes wide with surprise. Michel recovered his voice first.

'Your fiancé – how full of surprises you are, Ginette. Have you been engaged to be married for long?'

'Since just before the boutique was opened.'

Armand shrugged and smiled broadly.

'Yes, you must have your evenings free to be with your fiancé. It would be unthinkable to keep a young woman apart from the man she loves and intends to marry. I am sure you agree with me, Monsieur Brissard.'

'Unquestionably. But if I may be permitted a question on behalf of both of us – is it possible that he may wish to become a partner in the business?'

'No, not in the business,' Ginette assured them both, 'he has no talent for commerce. He is a teacher at the lycée.'

Then all seems to be settled,' said Michel.

'Excellent, then I will take my leave,' said Armand, bowing slightly. 'To be quite certain that I have it right – it's the mornings that are mine this week, yes?'

'Yes,' said Ginette as he kissed her hand. 'I shall expect you tomorrow morning. Au revoir, dear Armand.'

When he had gone Michel sat down again on one of the chairs and looked pensively at Ginette!

'This has been a day of surprises,' he said, 'not entirely pleasant, I fear.'

14

Ginette raised her eyebrows at that.

'Really? Do you feel that I have in some way deceived you, Michel? Tell me truthfully what is in your mind – let us dispose of this matter fully.'

'By chance I have learned things in the last half-hour which I feel that I should have been told before.'

'Let us be practical, my friend – you would probably have refused to participate in my business plans if I had disclosed certain other interests.'

'That is possible.'

'And that would have been to your disadvantage.'

'Perhaps you would explain that to me.'

'Does it need explaining, Michel? You are a partner in a very promising business venture. The money you have invested will produce good profits, year after year. That must please you.'

'In that matter I am content.'

'That there are others concerned in this business – well, I doubt very much if you would have been willing to subscribe the whole of the money. One-third was a reasonable sum for you.'

'I have already told you that I have no complaint about the business aspect of our arrangements.'

'Then it is as I thought – you are troubled by the more personal aspect. But dear Michel, where is the problem? You and I have been intimate friends for months now. As far as I am concerned we shall continue to be so.'

'How can you say that? Two other men have the same privileges as I have. I say nothing of your fiancé, since that is another matter altogether.'

'But what has changed? Whenever you want me, I am yours, just as before.'

Michel's experience with the many women who had played important parts in his life, and his experience with his wife, had long ago led him to the inescapable conclusion that it was futile to argue against feminine logic. A sensible man proceeded differently.

'I came here today because I have not seen you for two

days and I wanted you,' he said. 'What did I find? I found you in the intimate embraces of another man.'

'That was most unfortunate,' Ginette said at once, 'I shall never forgive myself. But can you forgive me, Michel?'

'I am heart-broken,' he said, 'you in the arms of a stranger!'

'Not entirely a stranger, as it proved. At least, not a stranger to your sister. And you recognised him.'

'That has nothing to do with it,' said Michel, feeling that he was on uncertain ground.

'Of course not. But let us be frank with each other. You and I have given each other a great deal of pleasure. For my part I would like that arrangement to continue. As for the others – well, you are not my fiancé. He perhaps has a right to complain, except that he knows nothing of my personal friendships and never will. Even now you know everything, do you not still love me a little, Michel?'

She looked so charming as she held out her arms towards him that his heart was touched. He rose to his feet and embraced her, holding her slender young body close to him as he kissed her.

'Ah,' she said between kisses, 'something hard and strong in your trousers is pressing itself against me. Am I forgiven, then?'

'Of course,' he breathed, 'I am on fire for you, Ginette.'

She knew better than to propose an encore of what he had observed taking place between her and Armand. She moved back a short step or two, pulled her slim pleated skirt up around her waist and seated herself on the short side of the table-desk. Michel's glance travelled in admiration slowly up her shapely legs in their fine silk stockings to where her garters held them above her knees, then on up the smooth white flesh of her thighs to the brown-fleeced treasure between them.

'Adorable,' he said.

'Then come to me.'

He stood between her knees, his hands fondling her breasts through her thin silk blouse while she occupied

16

herself with unbuttoning his trousers to extract his stiff part and handle it in a most friendly manner.

'Dear Ginette, your touch is unmistakable,' he said softly.

'And so is yours,' she sighed as his finger-tips caressed her nipples.

Their touching of each other's bodies continued in the most natural way in the world, to signs of contentment and little gasps of pleasure, until the imperious throbbing of the fleshy protuberance in her hands advised them both that the moment was fast arriving for a closer embrace. Ginette released the cherished part she held and used her pretty fingers to open for him the soft lips between her legs, showing him her moistly-pink interior and her little bud of passion. Then as Michel steered his prow into it, she lay back on the neat stacks of invoices and delivery notes and paid bills which covered her desk and brought up her knees to grip him by the hips as he leaned over her and plunged within.

She had been well prepared by her earlier encounter with Armand. The way had been made smooth and slippery by the exertions and emissions of love. The sensations imparted to Michel by the clasp of her supple sheath of warm flesh caused him to utter a long sigh of delight. And Ginette, her earlier pleasure having been cut short by the appearance of Michel almost at the very moment when Armand was lifting her to the heights of passion, she too sighed in deep delight to feel within herself that sturdy male baton. Almost at once Michel was intensifying their mutual pleasure by means of long and slow thrusts.

'Oh yes,' she murmured, 'that's marvellous!'

His hands were on her breasts, squeezing them through the thin silk in rhythm with the swing of his loins. Ginette's head rolled from side to side on the desk-top, her face pink with emotion. She was content – a difficult situation which could have turned into angry drama between the two men had been so well managed that no better outcome could be imagined. And as proof of that,

17

here was Michel bestowing on her with great eagerness the pleasure she most enjoyed in life!

As every lover knows, it is ordained that such transports of joy cannot be long sustained. Michel's slow probing transformed itself all too soon into a series of short and fast jabs and these brought about an ecstatic convulsion in Ginette and an outburst of hot passion from Michel, to their mingled gasps and sighs.

'You were magnificent, Michel,' she said at last.

'And you are adorable, chérie,' he answered, smiling at her as he withdrew from her satisfied body.

Ginette sat up and got off the desk to adjust her creased skirt and blouse.

'I must change these clothes,' she said, 'it would never do for customers to see me crumpled from the tender embrace of love.'

'Yes, it would be a poor advertisement for your boutique,' he agreed.

'Then you must leave. I shall see you tomorrow, I hope.'

'You may rely on it,' and he kissed her hand and left her to repair the damage.

As he passed through the boutique he noted that one of the assistants was dealing with a customer and the other was carefully folding a delicious little garment to return it to its box – a pair of camiknickers in ice-blue silk with broad lace bands at the legs and bodice. Michel paused to smile at her.

'A charming little fantasy to grace a beautiful woman,' he said.

'You like it, Monsieur Brissard?' she asked, holding it up so that he could appreciate it fully.

Naturally she knew his name. Ginette had instructed her assistants most carefully so that they would recognise her three wealthy backers when they visited the boutique.

'I am sure that it would look very chic on you,' he said, a wealth of implication in his tone.

As her sales assistants Ginette had engaged two very slim girls of about eighteen. Both were this day dressed in

18

the same modish skirt and blouse which Ginette herself was wearing and which she was now changing in the privacy of her tiny office – evidently this must be a style which the boutique was promoting. The girl Michel was talking to had a *gamine* look about her which Michel found provocative. Her dark brown hair was cut very short, her little nose was slightly turned-up and her eyes were bold.

'Do you think so, Monsieur?' she asked, giving him a tiny impertinent grin, 'it is not really my colour.'

'What is your colour, Mademoiselle . . .'

'Gaby.'

'Well then, Gaby, which colour suits you best?'

'We have this chemise-culotte in damson-red also, and that is utterly beautiful.'

'Especially if you were to wear it,' he suggested.

'There is little chance of that, Monsieur – it costs as much as I earn in a month.'

'Perhaps something could be arranged.'

She smiled and shrugged slightly – just enough to make her pointed little breasts move excitingly against the thin material of her blouse.

'Would you care to see it?' she asked.

'By all means.'

When she held the garment up in front of her by its shoulder-strings Michel could hardly repress a sigh of admiration. The silk was so fine that it was almost transparent and the rich colour against bare skin would be incredibly provocative. The top was cut so low that, held against Gaby's body, he observed that her breasts would be scarcely covered at all if she were to wear it.

'It is charming,' he said, 'it would suit you admirably.'

The pink tip of her tongue showed for a moment between her lips.

'A marvellous gift,' she said, 'one which no woman could refuse.'

'Wrap it for me,' he answered, reaching for his money, 'you know Fouquet's on the Champs Élysées, about ten minutes walk from here?'

'I know where it is.'

'If you were to meet me there soon after five this :vening for a drink, I will have this beautiful little gift with me. We could discuss going on to a suitably private place where you might be disposed to let me see the effect of this damson-red creation against your skin.'

Gaby hesitated for a second before replying.

'If Mademoiselle Royer were to find out,' she said, 'it would be most unfortunate – she would dismiss me instantly.'

'Have no fear of that,' he assured her, 'I shall be very discreet.'

'Then until later, Monsieur Brissard,' she said, handing him the neat little package.'

Michel left the boutique well pleased with himself. He adored Ginette, of course, and he anticipated years of profitable and pleasurable partnership with her. But he felt that she owed him something more in return for her lack of frankness over the business arrangements and the personal arrangements. He intended to repay himself, without her knowledge, by making full use of her staff, starting with Gaby that evening.

A LESSON FOR BERNARD

As all the world knows, male pride is usually based on possessions, such is the illogicality of men. Possessions of wealth, of a superb house, of a country estate, of a fast automobile, of a beautiful wife or mistress – the list could be extended without end. For some men it lies in possession of a fine physique, inherited, one need hardly say, from their parents. Or even a portion of themselves, for it is well known that some men are excessively proud of the part of themselves which is at its largest during the encounters of love.

Bernard Gaillard was such a man. He was of no more than average height and had averagely handsome features. His station in life was assured and might yet become distinguished. He was thirty years old, unmarried, had many friends and an active social life. None of which explained a certain air of pride about him, which impressed most of those who knew him, an aura of self-assurance no one could miss.

The cause of his pride lay between his thighs. This particular possession set him above the average, a fact known to a large circle of married and unmarried women. A whisper had been set in motion years before by Marie Gauquin, his mistress at that time. In discussing Bernard with a woman friend she had referred casually to his physical attributes. The word had been passed on from woman friend to woman friend until it became a topic of almost open discussion among the women of the social circle in which he moved. This worked greatly to his advantage – after all, women have a highly developed sense of curiosity. There were many who would not have considered him more than an acquaintance or a friend of their husband's, who could not resist the urge to find out for themselves whether all they had heard about Bernard was true, or merely exaggerated gossip.

In consequence, Bernard never lacked for female companionship and was never tempted into marriage. His affairs of the heart were usually of no more than a few months duration, but their termination had never prevented the continuation of the friendship between him and the woman concerned. The truth was that when their curiosity had been amply satisfied, women found him more entertaining as a guest at their dinner-table or receptions than as a lover.

It was at a large party at the home of Maurice and Marie-Thérèse Brissard that Bernard first met Madame Lebrun. The contrast between her shiny black hair and her pale ivory complexion was the first thing about her to catch his eye, then he found himself drawn by her vivacious manner. She was standing near the grand piano in the Brissards' salon, a glass in her hand, two or three male admirers about her, when he was introduced by Marie-Thérèse.

Her lustruous eyes, so dark-brown as to be almost black, blinked once when Marie-Thérèse spoke his name. Bernard kissed Madame Lebrun's free hand and smiled at her. He knew the significance of that blink – he had observed it many times in the past. It meant that his name was not unknown to her and that she had been made aware by some friend of his endowment. He joined in the conversation and as more and more of Madame Lebrun's attention centred itself upon him, the other men about her took the hint and moved away to find other companions to talk to.

'Have you known the Brissards long?' Bernard asked.

'No, we met only recently when my husband became involved in some business venture with Maurice.'

Bernard glanced around the salon for faces he did not know.

'Is that your husband over there talking to Jeanne Verney?'

'Oh no, he has a dreadful cold and dare not come out tonight. Do you know a friend of mine, Marie Derval?'

That was the information Bernard had been fishing for.

Marie and he had been lovers for five months the previous year. Without question it was she who had passed on to Madame Lebrun the secret – or perhaps one should say semi-secret. To judge by her manner, Madame Lebrun's dormant curiosity was fully awakened now that she was face to face with the possessor of so fortunate an attribute.

For his part, Bernard found Madame Lebrun very desirable, since his affections were not engaged elsewhere at that moment. Under her elegant black frock her body was lithe and graceful. He put her in her late twenties, though the diamonds round her neck were worth a fortune. That was to be expected – the Brissards were not likely to involve themselves in financial ventures with men who had not already demonstrated their ability to make money. Madame's jewellery testified that Monsieur Lebrun had that ability.

When a man's imagination is truly captured by a woman, his whole manner reveals it. He stands a little straighter and taller, speaks with more than his usual confidence, his gestures become more animated and his conversation more lively, even if he is speaking of nothing more than social trivialities. He is hardly aware of the others in the room – if you ask him the next morning who was at the party, he will not remember speaking to his closest friends. All his attention is concentrated on one person – he sees no one else – but he sees her in extraordinary detail. Everything about her is totally fascinating! The sheen of her hair, how delightful! The shape of her face, the colour of her eyes, how perfect! Her clothes and jewels – chic beyond belief! The soft skin of her bare arms, her slender wrists and long fingers – marvellously elegant! Her perfume – sensuous and modest at the same time!

His desire conjures up visions in his mind of the loveliness concealed by the clothes that suit her so well. She has small soft breasts, of course, just the right size to fill his hands if only he were permitted! And naturally, her hips are narrow, her buttocks taut and pert, the skin of her thighs as smooth and pale as alabaster! And between

23

them, inside her delicate silk underwear – a treasure to make a man's mind reel in delight at the mere thought of it!

All this the would-be lover discerns, which is to say that Bernard discerned, through thousands of francs worth of expensive clothes – or if not discerned, at least imagined.

And she – Simone Lebrun – the object of his ardent imagining, knew exactly what was in his mind, because women always know, and his every gesture proclaimed it as clearly as any words. She knew that she had made a conquest, if one may employ the normal, banal expression. She was amused and flattered. Like all women, even while preening herself before him, she was considering whether her conquest was worthy of further encouragement or whether it would be more sensible to disengage herself gracefully from the conversation and move away. This question of where the balance of advantage lies is usually decided by women in a very short space of time.

Bernard smiled at her again – not a polite smile but one that hinted at much more – that he was interested in her, that he knew she might be interested in him, that he would welcome her interest with every fibre of his being – and so on, for the routine is known to all. Simone understood his smile, glanced down for a moment as if in modesty – or in thought – then met his gaze fully and smiled back in a manner that indicated that she was as eager to proceed as he was.

When the party dispersed, it was unthinkable that Madame Lebrun should make her way home unescorted. As one of the few unaccompanied men present, it was only courteous for Bernard to escort her. She told him that she lived quite close to the Brissards, close enough to walk, she insisted, rather than bother with taxis.

It was a pleasant enough evening for a stroll – pleasant enough for October, that is. The early evening rain had stopped at last and the pavements glistened under the soft golden lights of the stree-lamps. The breeze was very cool, but Simone was fully protected from it by a magnificent full-length fur coat.

Not far from the Brissards' home she slipped her arm familiarly into his and walked close enough to him for his hip to press into the luxurious fur that enswathed her.

'That look you gave me!' she said, 'I almost dropped my glass.'

'A glance of admiration,' said Bernard, 'a heart-felt tribute to your beauty.'

'It was more than that and you know it,' she said, speaking quickly and with evident emotion, 'it was as if you were kissing my breasts!'

Her lack of restraint pleased Bernard. The preliminaries required by Simone would be brief, the conquest certain.

'It was inevitable,' he said, 'we looked at each other and knew in an instant that we were meant to be lovers. To deny this would be like denying that there is a moon in the sky.'

'Perhaps. But if my husband had been present and seen that look, he would have killed you.'

'Then he must never know. This formidable secret of the emotions you and I feel for each other must remain ours alone, my dear Simone.'

'I confess to you,' she said as they turned into the street on which she lived, 'my legs are trembling. I feel as if I have been struck by lightning.'

'We have both been struck by the same lightning-flash,' Bernard told her. 'Come home with me now – your breasts need to be kissed and I need to kiss them.'

'That's impossible. Léon is waiting for me. He will not sleep until I am home.'

She stopped outside a modern apartment building and unlocked the street door with a key from her tiny evening bag.

'I must kiss your lips at the very least,' said Bernard.

'Then come in off the street.'

Inside the wrought-iron and glass street door they were in a small courtyard, surrounded by the six-storey apartment building. At that late hour of the evening many

25

windows were dark and the rest obscured by drawn curtains. All was quiet.

Bernard drew Simone close in against the wall and kissed her ardently.

'When, when, when?' he murmured.

'Very soon, I promise.'

'Tomorrow?'

'Perhaps.'

'Even tomorrow is too long,' he said, his hands groping in the dark until he had her fur coat open and could take her by the waist to press her to him. His celebrated part was at full stretch, its entire length against her belly through his clothes and hers.

'I must know!' she sighed as his hands caressed her breasts through her frock.

'What?'

By way of answer she unbuttoned his dark double-breasted overcoat. Her hand slid down between the waist-band of his trousers and his shirt, seeking a route for itself. Baffled at first by the complications of his clothes, she resumed her assault avidly until she had his shirt-front up out of his trousers and could force her hand down inside his underpants until she touched the object of her curiosity. Her hot palm enclosed the swollen head, her long fingers stretched down the hard stem.

'You are thoroughly excited,' she whispered, ' and, my God, how dramatic the result!'

'Now do you believe how desperately I want you?'

'I see that I shall have to be very careful in future about letting you kiss me,' she teased, 'anything could happen if you are so susceptible.'

As she spoke her awkwardly placed hand was gently massaging what she held and Bernard, shaken by tremors of delight, was attempting to stroke her nipples through her clothes.

'It is you,' he sighed, 'there is something about you that threw me into a frenzy even before I kissed you . . . I shall die if you say no to me . . .'

'My poor Bernard,' she said, 'tonight I must say no to

26

you because there is no way I can say yes. But tomorrow afternoon, perhaps . . .'

'Yes, I implore you. You cannot be in any doubt of the strength of my passion for you.'

'No doubt whatsoever,' she whispered, 'and getting stronger all the time! Heavens, I shan't be able to sleep or rest until I have seen this with my own eyes!'

'Tomorrow for sure – at three – say yes!' Bernard implored her, half-delirious with the pleasure suffusing his body from the jerky caress of her hand.

'Such strength!' she exclaimed incredulously, 'I do believe that in another instant you will make a protestation of your passion.'

Her free hand whipped the silk handkerchief from his breast pocket and pushed it down the front of his trousers as his legs shook and his hands gripped her tightly by the waist.

'Simone!' he gasped, the evidence of his desire pouring into the ready handkerchief.

'Magnificent!' she crooned to herself. 'Oh, magnificent!'

At last Bernard sighed contentedly and was still. She removed the handkerchief from its guard-post and stuffed it into his overcoat pocket.

'I must kiss you,' he murmured.

'One moment,' and she tucked his shirt-front down his trousers before letting him take her in his arms and press his lips to hers fervently.

'You have given me a foretaste of Paradise,' he said.

'Then tomorrow we will enter the gates and enjoy the full joys,' she said, 'but for now I must leave you, my dear. My husband is waiting. Au revoir.'

'Until tomorrow.'

She patted his cheek and walked away across the courtyard.

With what joyous anticipation Bernard prepared for Simone's first visit to his apartment can scarcely be imagined. His two servants, a middle-aged married couple

27

well accustomed to his ways, grinned and winked at each other behind his back as he paced about giving them instructions. They knew well that a new woman in his life meant a good many afternoon and evenings off for them while he entertained in his bedroom.

'Put the best sheets on the bed, make sure that there is a full bottle of Eau de Cologne in the bathroom, fresh flowers in the sitting-room, all the furniture to be dusted, polished and shining, check the stock of champagne' he reeled off the list of preparations which his servants knew as well as he did (if the truth were told, even better than he did).

'Well!' said the maid to the valet after he had gone out, 'I've never seen him this excited before. It must be someone special he's met. Do you think he's fallen for this one?'

'Hope not,' said the valet, 'working for a married couple is a lot more hard work than working for a bachelor.'

'We don't have to worry about that,' the maid said scornfully, 'he only goes for married women.'

'Not always – there was Madame Vosges the summer before last. The tall woman who wore pearls all the time – you remember.'

'Oh, her – that was Madame Toussaint. What makes you think she wasn't married?'

'Because she often used to stay all night here and sometimes he stayed overnight at her place.'

'She was separated from her husband, but she wasn't divorced.'

'She was the one you used to complain about leaving lipstick on his underpants.'

'No, that was the one after her – Madame Benet. Madame Toussaint broke one of her necklaces in bed with him. I was on my knees half the morning looking for loose pearls.'

'If you kept any you didn't tell me about it.'

'Not a chance! Rich women know exactly how many pearls or stones there are on every piece of jewellery they own.'

'A pity. Still, it's interesting, what you said, about him being so steamed up over the new one, whoever she may be. I wish some rich and beautiful woman would lie on her back and wave her legs in the air for me.'

'Just let me catch you!' the maid said tartly, 'rich or poor, you'll soon regret it. Now get on with your work, he wants us out of here straight after lunch.'

Simone arrived a little after the appointed time, as was her natural right as a woman. She was well wrapped against the inclement autumn weather in a superb astrakhan coat, with a toque of the same fur on her head. To enhance her appearance she wore on her wrist, outside her fine black glove, a bracelet of golden yellow topaz stones.

The greetings were warm, and as swift as good manners permitted. Bernard kissed both of her gloved hands and helped her out of her coat. Simone took off her hat and expensive gloves and embraced him. They held each other close and kissed with passion. Less than three minutes from the time she entered the apartment she was in Bernard's bedroom. He assisted her to undress, murmuring words of heart-felt praise as her slender body was progressively revealed to him, then flung back the impressive Gobelins tapestry bedcover so that she could slip between the sheets.

She lay propped on one elbow, a tender smile on her face and one pretty breast exposed, waiting for him to join her in bed.

After so much anticipation, after so much fervour, there at last she lay! What man's heart would not beat like a drum sounding the charge at such a moment! Alas, the chagrin of love pierces more keenly in such idyllic circumstances, when all seems perfect and yet there is something concealed which is less than perfect. In the next quarter of an hour Bernard was to learn that Simone's approach to love was not his! Romantic that he was, his concept of love-making was traditional, even stereotyped, one might say. He desired above all else to lie in close embrace with her, to feel her warm body beneath him, her

29

arms about his neck and her mouth seeking his while he plunged and plunged again in the motion that would launch them both into climactic rapture.

Stripped of his clothes, he posed with one knee on the bed, fully aware of the effect which the sight of his proud staff of flesh had on the hearts of women. Simone stared at it, her dark eyes gleamed and her lips were trembling as she whispered, 'Stupendous!'

She took it in both hands and planted a kiss of homage on its tip. Matters were progressing extremely well, thought Bernard, easing himself into bed beside her. His arms reached out to clasp her to him, but she twisted in the bed until her head was at the level of his loins and her hands were gliding up and down the impressive length of his hard pride.

'I never imagined . . .' she murmured, 'not even after last night. Oh, Bernard, this is magnificent beyond words!'

He let her have her way, flattered by her reaction and her almost incoherent words of admiration – above all by the look of rapt attention on her face as she stared at what she was caressing so expertly.

'Take care,' he murmured after a time, 'you are giving me such sensations of delight that things might go too far.'

'I want to give you the most marvellous sensations you have ever experienced, Bernard. It would be a pity to hide it away inside me before I have expressed my admiration fully.'

'Yes, yes . . . but if it were inside you it would also give you such sensations of pleasure as you have never known.'

'Later,' she breathed, 'ah, it's bigger than ever – look at the size of it now!'

Bernard stared through half-closed eyes at his mighty part and what her delicate hands were doing to it.

'It's time,' he gasped, 'I must put it in you now!'

'It jumps and throbs in my hands!' she exclaimed, 'like a trapped animal struggling to be free!'

'Simone!'

'Yes, a strong and fierce animal that I have caught.'

By then, of course, nature was taking its appointed course and it was too late for Bernard to make protestations. He moaned and twitched, lost in ecstasy.

'Oh, what a fountain!' Simone cried aloud joyfully, her busy hand manipulating him, 'again, again, again!'

To Bernard the rapture seemed to last forever, wave after wave of bliss rolling through his shaking body, until at last her hands were still. He stared at her face, aglow with pleasure, her eyes intent on his impressive part in open admiration.

'I must confess that I do not understand why you did that,' he said when he was capable of coherent speech.

'But why not?'

'It is not the usual way in which lovers pleasure each other.'

'Perhaps not, but why must we follow the usual way? After all, to observe so magnificent a fellow as yours performing the entire cycle of love is a sight not to be missed. Do you object? Has it never been done to you by a woman before?'

'That's not the point, Simone. Certainly I have no objection – but that was not what I expected from you.'

'How can I know what you expect of me – and does it follow that we shall only do what *you* expect? Have you not considered what I may expect from you?'

'That is my only desire,' he said, taking her into his arms while he wondered where this conversation was leading him.

'What is?'

'To give you pleasure by demonstrating my passion for you.'

'Good, you succeeded very well. Your passion gave me extraordinary pleasure.'

'I can understand that you . . . how shall I put it . . . that you feel a certain admiration for me . . .'

'Yes,' she sighed, hugging him close, 'I have never seen one that size before – I am lost in admiration!'

'Then we must put it to its proper use. That will give you even greater pleasure than what you just did to it.'

31

'Impossible,' she said, 'there cannot be any pleasure greater than that I have just experienced.'

'You mean that only by playing with me you achieved a climax?'

'Yes, of course.'

Bernard was bewildered by what he heard.

'The mere sight and touch did that for you?' he asked, wondering if he and she were talking about the same experience.

'Yes!'

'I find that extraordinary,' he said.

'Do you? Perhaps your experience of women has been limited to those dutiful ones who lie passively on their backs.'

'By no means.'

'Then you have encountered something which for you is new and different – are you not grateful?'

'But of course,' he replied, stroking her breasts, 'you are beautiful and very exciting, Simone.'

His hands strayed down her body and between her thighs. The touch told him that she had been aroused to the full – confirmation, if it were needed, of what she had said.

'Let us now do it my way,' he whispered amorously, 'I promise to give you such pleasure that the memory of what has gone before will be as nothing.'

'I doubt it,' she said, 'but I see that you won't believe me until you make the attempt.'

At a measured pace Bernard went through his customary repertoire of kissing, touching, fondling, stroking, until the moment arrived for him to assume his normal position above her. Simone smiled and placed herself on her knees and elbows, her black-haired head down on the pillow and her bottom up in the air.

Yet another caprice, Bernard said to himself, an astonishing one perhaps, but Simone was proving herself to be altogether an astonishing person. He stationed himself behind her on his knees, the better to observe the charms offered so generously to him.

His heart skipped a beat and a tiny moan of sheer delight escaped his lips at the sight of her bottom. The cheeks were so perfectly rounded, the skin so deliciously silky. And there below, between her well-parted thighs, a tender mound covered with black fur as fine as astrakhan! In an instant Bernard presented the head of his beloved appliance to the pink cleft marking the entrance to Simone's secret boudoir and eased himself into it. He need not have feared – no constriction impeded him. On the contrary, he was accepted and contained as comfortably as if he were of no more than average dimensions.

Simone's head was turned to look at him over her shoulder.

'Are you happy now that you've got what you wanted?' she asked.

'You are divine,' he murmured, 'I adore you.'

She said no more as he rocked to and fro, his hands grasping her tightly by the haunches to steady her. In short, he did what any man does when he is lodged in a woman, until an involuntary cry of triumph announced that he had reached the peak of physical sensation and was presenting her with his bodily tribute.

As soon as his spasms had ended Simone pulled away and rolled slowly over sideways to stretch out her legs. Bernard sank back onto his heels and regarded her in confusion.

'That pleased you?' she asked.

'Never mind that – it obviously did not please you.'

'I did try to warn you.'

'You gave me your body and nothing else!'

'But my impression was that it was my body you wanted, Bernard. What else did you expect?'

'Lovers give their hearts along with their bodies. You gave me only your flesh.'

'I gave you pleasure. Is that not enough?'

'Not nearly enough.'

She slid round on the bed so that she could reach between his thighs and take hold of the limp part dangling there.

'The pleasure seems to have been sufficient, to judge by the condition of *this*,' she said, 'I do not understand what is troubling you. Should I have gasped out *I love you* at your critical moment?'

'You are laughing at me.'

'No, I am trying to ascertain why an experience which produced the desired result for you was apparently unsatisfactory.'

'Because it was entirely physical and had no element of emotion in it.'

'Ah, you require every woman who goes to bed with you to be in love with you – is that it?'

'Not in love, that would be absurd. But unless there is a mutual affection the true pleasure is absent.'

'But I do feel affection for you, Bernard, a great affection – otherwise I would not be here with you now, naked in bed.'

'I am confused,' he confessed.

'Evidently. I think you are mixing up love and pleasure.'

'But if there is no love at all, only pleasure, then all that remains is the satisfaction of a physical need.'

'And what is wrong with that?' Simone asked. 'This fellow here in my hand is big enough to have the most urgent needs to satisfy.'

'You are confusing me further.'

'Surely we want as much love as is necessary to enhance our pleasure, not to invade and confuse our hearts?'

Her fondling was causing strength to flood back into his deflated part.

'My God – how superb!' she exclaimed, 'how can you sit there fretting yourself about nonsense while this giant is rearing up again like a flag-pole?'

'Simone! I forbid you to do that until we have discussed this matter and reached an understanding of each other.'

'Don't be silly,' she replied, her hand caressing his elongated shaft, 'first things first – we can talk all you like

34

after I have given this fellow what he is sitting up and begging for.'

About a month after he first met Simone, Bernard invited his friend Jean-Albert Faguet to dinner in his apartment. The food was well-chosen and lovingly prepared, the wines were very fine. Faguet, a man devoted to good living, fell to with a hearty appetite.

'So what do you want my advice about?' he asked when they reached the *caneton à l'orange*.

'Why do you think I want your advice?'

'My dear Bernard, why else would we be dining here like a pair of old bachelors? If this were a social occasion we would be in a good restaurant with a couple of pretty women. What's the problem – you've made your mistress pregnant and you want me to relieve her of her guilty burden? That's no trouble – send her along to my clinic. Twenty per cent discount for an old friend like you. Thirty per cent if you pay me cash.'

'That's not it at all,' said Bernard, 'it's a much more complicated and delicate matter.'

'Really? You'd better tell me about it.'

As they ate Bernard described the strange course of his month-long *affaire* with Simone. Naturally he did not mention her name, for that would have been the height of indiscretion. Jean-Albert Faguet listened in mounting amusement and finally broke into loud laughter, much to Bernard's embarrassment.

'Forgive me, Bernard,' he said, dabbing his eyes with his table napkin, 'A thousand pardons! I can see that this is not comical from your point of view. Have you told me everything?'

'I believe so.'

'Then let me see if I have followed you properly. You have a new mistress, beautiful and elegant, as you have said. In your lovemaking her pleasure is in handling you, not in sexual connection. Correct?'

'Yes.'

35

'She does not deny you her body, so long as you comply with her desires at other times.'

'But she does not participate, Jean-Albert. She lets me have my way when I insist, as if she were a cocotte I was paying for her services.'

'So you tell me.'

'What shall I do?'

'Find yourself another mistress, of course.'

'But I want *her*.'

'Ah, I see – you love her.'

'Love her?' said Bernard in surprise, 'I've never given it a thought. But now that you raise the question, I suppose I must love her in some strange way. That first time I saw her at – never mind where – there was an odd and magnificent sensation in my heart. I thought it was desire, yet now I recall it, perhaps it was something more.'

'Then the case is altered.'

'Oh, this is infuriating!' said Bernard. 'Do you think that I am making a fool of myself?'

'Without question.'

'What do you suggest?'

'I am puzzled as to why you should seek my advice, Bernard. My experience of love is no more extensive than that of any man of my age.'

'But your experience of women is prodigious.'

'As to that,' said Jean-Albert, helping himself to more wine, 'it is perfectly true that in the course of a month's work I have the honour of putting my fingers between the thighs of more women than you can hope to in a lifetime. I am better informed about what women have under their skirts than any doctor in Paris.'

'Exactly!'

'I venture to say,' Jean-Albert continued, 'that if my patients visited me wearing masks, I know them so intimately that simply by raising their clothes I could identify each of them by name. Could you do as much with all the women you have made love to?'

'But this is mere boasting,' Bernard objected.

'You think so? Let me assure you, since it seems that

you have been most unobservant, that these tender parts you love and which provide my living are infinitely variable. I approach my work in a truly scientific and professional spirit. I observe, I note, I compare, I remember.'

'The fur varies from blonde to black,' said Bernard, 'and the texture from silky to bristly. That much is true.'

'Any fool knows that after he has been with two or three women. In reality there are many more variable factors and each woman presents a different combination of these factors. I assert without fear of contradiction that no two women in Paris are identical in this important respect.'

'Be more specific, if you please.'

Jean-Albert rolled his eyes upwards in mock-despair.

'What sort of lover are you?' he demanded. 'Are you so unaware of the individual charms of your mistresses? To cite an obvious example, in some women the insides of the thighs touch all the way up to the top, whereas in others there is a gap between the thighs at the top. In the first type, all but the hair is more or less concealed until she opens her legs for you. In the second type the soft lips remain visible even when she is standing upright. Which type is the lady we are discussing?'

'Now that you have directed my attention to the question,' said Bernard thoughtfully, 'she is of the second type you described.'

'At least you have noticed that much about her. We may proceed then to the size of the Mount of Venus itself. In some women it is markedly protruberant and fleshy, in others it does not exist at all. Between these extremes there are innumerable graduations.'

'Jean-Albert . . .'

'We may consider the shape and size of those fascinating outer lips, ranging from luscious to elegant, naturally pouting or delicately closed until aroused. Nor must we overlook the . . .'

'Jean-Albert!' Bernard interrupted, 'your disquisition on the appearance of the female apparatus of love can be

37

postponed until a more appropriate time. My problem is urgent. Without regard to the lusciousness or elegance of the object of my desire, how am I to persuade its alluring owner to let me make regular use of it?'

'But that is a matter of the heart, not of the anatomy.'

'I know that. I am asking for your advice.'

'Why me? My knowledge of women is confined to the expanse between navel and groin. About that I know everything. As to what goes on in their hearts, I know as little as you.'

'I cannot believe this. The two areas are closely connected.'

'So much I have observed. But I am far from understanding the nature of the connection.'

'But if you fail me what am I to do?'

'Either say *Adieu* to her or accept her as she is, what else? Women have their reasons, whether they understand them or not, for the multiplicity of ways in which they seek pleasure. Oh, the stories I could tell you! But the point is this, my friend – these reasons are her own business and no one else's. The person who has captivated you lives her life in her own way, not yours. If she is satisfied by what she does, it is not for you to object.'

'I am sure that if I can hit on the right method I can assist her to fulfil herself in love.'

'Good God, what arrogance! You are not her doctor, her confessor or her husband. If you wish to be her playmate, then you must play her game. If her game does not please you, find another playmate. There, that's all I intend to say on the subject.'

'But . . .'

'Not another word!'

Bernard shrugged, deeply disappointed.

'Do not behave as if you were playing in a tragedy,' Jean-Albert reproached him, 'life is given to us to enjoy – good food, good wine, pretty women. We are enjoying two of these gifts of God at this moment. After dinner I propose that we enjoy the third.'

'What is it you have in mind?'

'Though you are of the wrong sex to be a patient of mine, for the sake of our friendship I am prescribing a course of treatment for you. There will be no fee.'

'I am listening, doctor.'

'A short time ago I had the good fortune to make the acquaintance of a young woman who appears nightly on the stage at the Moulin Rouge. She is amazingly pretty and only nineteen years old.'

'I congratulate you.'

'I suggest that we conclude this excellent dinner you have provided with a glass or two of cognac and make our way to the Moulin Rouge to arrive at the moment when this dear friend of mine has concluded her performance for the evening and is ready to be entertained. A little light supper, a bottle of champagne – and so on.'

'Jean-Albert – this is true friendship – to offer me your little friend to cheer me up,' said Bernard, his eyes moist with tears of affection.

'Are you mad? Offer her to you? Certainly not!'

'What then?'

'I have no doubt that Mademoiselle Gaby will bring along one of her friends from the dancing troupe to be your companion. There – what do you say?'

'You are a good friend. I will follow the course of treatment you prescribe.'

The outing planned by Jean-Albert was uncomplicated and entirely pleasing. Gaby did indeed have a friend in the chorus line willing to complete the party, a fluffy-haired and pert-nosed blonde of nineteen or twenty who called herself Mademoiselle Lulu.

After the sumptuous dinner they had enjoyed, Bernard and Jean-Albert ate sparingly in the restaurant with the two girls, though Gaby and Lulu proved to have voracious appetites which belied their slenderness. It was a most convivial supper, Jean-Albert footing the bill. Afloat on half a dozen bottles of champagne, they decided to make a whole night of it and eventually found themselves in the rue de Lappe, drinking cognac in a cheap establishment

39

where they danced to the music of an accordion. Around three in the morning they had progressed to Les Halles, where amid the noise and bustle of the market what seemed to be enough food for the whole of Paris for a week was being bought and sold. In a tiny restaurant in the nearby rue Coquillière they ate onion soup with grated cheese on top and rubbed elbows with market porters bracing themselves with a tot of spirits.

In due course they found taxis and parted, Jean-Albert with Gaby, Bernard with Lulu, she to offer what recompense she could for her supper, he to complete his therapy. That too was uncomplicated. Mademoiselle Lulu stripped naked the instant she was in Bernard's bedroom and slid between the sheets.

His evening clothes scattered across the floor, Bernard joined her. They kissed and fondled each other for a few moments and she murmured,

'Don't keep me waiting, chéri!'

She had a dancer's body, slim and yet muscular. Bernard would have preferred to have paid it more attention. Now that Jean-Albert had planted in his mind certain lines of enquiry about the interesting area between women's thighs, there was much that he desired to examine and classify. But Lulu was impatient.

'My God!' she exclaimed as he inserted himself, 'What have you got there – a truncheon?'

'Something worthy of you,' said Bernard, not over-pleased by her reaction, 'do not be alarmed, I know how to use it to please you.'

'Do it slowly then, or you'll maim me for life!'

He proceeded with care and eventually made her cry out in rapture. Even so, when he finally delivered his compliment, she uttered a sigh of relief.

'Was that good?' he asked, lying beside her again.

But she was already asleep.

When Bernard woke it was after midday and Mademoiselle Lulu was gone from the bed. He rang for his maid, but it was the valet who came into the room and drew the curtains.

40

'Pierre, I brought a young woman home with me last night. What happened to her?'

'She left about ten, Monsieur. She said not to wake you.'

'Did you give her breakfast before she left?'

'I served her myself in the kitchen.'

'In the kitchen!'

'It was her own suggestion,' said Pierre, picking up the clothes strewn across the carpet, 'and it seemed appropriate. Would you like your coffee now?'

'Yes, just coffee.'

Bernard sat up in bed, realised that he was naked and got into pyjamas before the maid brought in his coffee. She had a most disapproving expression on her face, but said nothing.

My domestic staff believe that I behaved foolishly in bringing that dancer home last night, he thought, yet Jean-Albert thought it was a good idea. In retrospect, what do I think about it myself? She had an attractive body, but she did not encourage more than the minimum use of it. Well, after all, she had been dancing on the stage all evening and then we were eating and drinking until nearly dawn. Without doubt she was tired. She offered me what she had as quickly as possible so that she could go to sleep. An honest enough creature in her way, but hardly what I am used to.

For Jean-Albert that sort of adventure may be satisfactory, he thought, but he is looking for light relief and quick thrills after the heavy emotional burden of comforting some of his most important patients, who probably find him irresistible after he has had his fingers between their legs in the line of duty. For me that sort of thing is unsuitable. I need an intelligent, educated and charming woman as an intimate friend. I shall telephone Simone and try again with her.

She accepted his invitation readily enough and came to his apartment. But then she sat in his drawing-room and said that she wanted to discuss matters with him.

'I am amazed,' said Bernard, 'when you were here

41

before and I wanted to talk to you about my feelings you completely diverted me. You can't have forgotten what you did.'

'We were in bed then,' she said, smilingly at him, 'that is no place for discussion.'

'I see. What do you want to talk about now that we are not in bed?'

'My impression on that occasion was that you were dissatisfied with me in some way. That is an impossible position for a woman to find herself in. Let us be clear about each other, Bernard, so that we do not involve ourselves in stupid and futile arguments, if we are to continue meeting.'

'That is in doubt, is it?'

'You know it is.'

'On what does it depend?'

'On a sincere exchange of views. What is it that you want from me? Tell me that and I will respond by telling you what I want from you. Then we can each decide whether there is any sensible basis on which to continue meeting each other. Or if our aims are incompatible, we can say *Goodbye* now and go our different ways.'

She looked so desirable, sitting on a chair with her legs crossed at the knees and a few centimetres of silk-clad thigh showing where her skirt had ridden up that Bernard was almost at a loss for words to answer her.

'With you it seems to be a question of logic and not of the emotions,' he said. 'Well then, I want to be your lover, Simone.'

'That is not very precise, my friend. Try again. Do you want me to love you or do you want me to give you pleasure?'

'Cannot the two go together?' he asked in astonishment.

'You are a most conventional person. Do you never examine your own motives? Is there no moment when you are totally frank with yourself?'

'I gave up going to the confessional years ago. You are suggesting that I should be my own priest and hear my own sins – is that it?'

42

'Perhaps,' she said, smiling at his manner of expressing himself.

'But to what end?'

'In order to give yourself absolution, perhaps, and cease to be either guilty or confused about your own life and desires.'

'I feel no guilt, I assure you. I live my life without harming anyone. What more is there?'

'Yet you are not honest about your feelings. You deceive yourself.'

'About what?'

'At this moment, about me and about what it is that you want from me.'

'Does it seem like that to you, Simone, tell me honestly.'

She smiled and stroked her knee with her finger-tips.

'You have answered your own question,' she said.

'You are telling me that it is clear in your mind what you want from me,' he countered.

'Certainly. What I want from you is pleasure, Bernard. What I do not want from you is love. I have that from my husband. I have no wish to complicate my life by attempting to love two men or be loved by two men.'

'That's frank enough! And so what you offer me is pleasure, that and no more?'

'Exactly so.'

Bernard breathed out heavily while he thought about her proposition. She watched him in amusement and waited.

'You are an extraordinary woman,' he said.

'Look at it this way – you and I are negotiating in the hope of reaching an arrangement satisfactory to both of us, not an arrangement which favours one at the expense of the other. To me it appears simple.'

'So be it,' said Bernard, 'the contract is that we each provide the other with pleasure and no more. Do you want it signed and sealed.'

'You may take me to bed,' she answered, 'we will seal the contract there.'

* * *

For months they persevered with each other after that day. They had reached a compromise and both made an effort to make it work. Simone had her way with him and he had his way with her alternately. Each tried to enter into the spirit of the other's pleasure and in this they succeeded to an extent which surprised them both. Bernard gradually lost his feeling of being cheated when Simone took hold of his proud implement and put it through its paces so that she could closely observe the final outcome. By reconciling himself to her desire he was able to take great pleasure in the extremely skilful way in which she handled him. For her part, Simone by stages lost her impatience with him when he inserted his fleshy stamen into her and slid to and fro. She took no pleasure from the process but it was her side of the bargain and she kept it faithfully.

Bernard came to know a good deal about her in time – her parents and background, her devotion to her six year old son, named Léon after his father. About her husband he learned little and asked less, though he was introduced to him at a reception soon after the New Year. Monsieur Lebrun was a short and heavily-built man who wore a white carnation in the lapel of his expensive suit. His manner with Bernard was somewhat unfriendly and he gave him a stare which made Bernard wonder for one atrocious moment whether Lebrun suspected anything.

Simone laughed at his fears the next time she came to visit him. Her marital relations with her husband were a subject of occasional speculation to Bernard, but it would have been unforgivably impolite to ask her. Had Lebrun lost all interest in her, perhaps, except as the mother of his son and organiser of his household? Or was his desire for her still active? Did he insist that she lay on her back for him, which might go some way towards explaining why she preferred other ways of pleasure with Bernard?

There was a particular Thursday in April when Bernard was expecting Simone to visit him after a parting of almost a week. He was in a very good humour that day and decided to give her a little surprise. After his servants had left the apartment with instructions to return between six and seven o'clock, Bernard went into his bedroom and took off all his clothes. The afternoon was to be one of mutual pleasure – very well, it would start that way. He would encourage Simone to gratify herself in her individual manner and then claim his own satisfaction from her.

She was due at three. Ten minutes before the hour Bernard was seated naked on a chair in his entrance hall. He stroked his impressive part with warm affection, his thoughts intent on the anticipated delights of Simone's beautiful body. The truth was that he no longer found anything untoward in the position she favoured when it was his turn to enjoy her – head down on the pillow and pale-skinned bottom up in the air. There was much to recommend it, he had found. For one thing it facilitated his admission into her tender entrance and made it possible for him to plunge as deeply as he wished without causing her discomfort. And for another thing, it gave him the joy of caressing her belly and breasts throughout the act of love.

He sat enthralled by a delicious fantasy – Simone would enter the apartment to find him naked and ready for her. At once she would fall to her knees in admiration and, still wearing her hat and coat, would take his magnificence between her gloved hands and kiss it fondly. Then, all else forgotten, she would stroke it to a superb discharge of passion! And to save her clothes from being splashed, at the critical moment she would open her pretty lips and take the shiny red tip into her mouth!

After that he would lead her into the bedroom, undress her slowly and have his fill of her. Twice at least – perhaps more – for she knew how to keep him aroused. Ah, what pleasures lay ahead in the next hour or two!

Hastily Bernard took his hand away from his trembling part and switched his thoughts away from Simone. He had been so lost in his reverie that he had almost gone too far. Another few moments and he might well have scattered his compliments before Simone was there to appreciate

45

them! He was aflame! He prayed that she would not be late. Every second now seemed to him like an hour – a lost hour that could be an hour of delight.

The bell rang at last. With almost unbearable joy in his heart he went to open the door, his proud appurtenance waving about in front of him. He flung the door wide, a welcoming smile on his face as he exclaimed:

'Simone, chérie – see what I have for you!'

Simone's husband, in a black homburg hat and a dark overcoat, stood facing him. There was an expression of deep anger on his face. The anger turned to shock and then, as Lebrun's gaze travelled down Bernard's naked body to the mighty baton sticking out from between his thighs, to black hatred.

THE ITALIAN COUSIN

On the other side of the Alps, as all the world knows, the Italian sun ripens women into early bloom and then into luxurious physical maturity. For this best of all reasons the four Brissard brothers were greatly interested when their mother informed them that a cousin of theirs from Italy was shortly to visit Paris with her husband. Naturally, they had heard of this cousin before – she was a daughter of one of their mother's sisters, Aunt Marie, who had married a wealthy Italian about thirty years before. Only their parents had made the journey to Rome the year after the War ended to see Aunt Marie's daughter married in sumptuous style to the Marchese di Monferrato by no less a dignitary than a Cardinal. The Cardinal was, of course, the brother of the Marchese, since the Monferrato family maintained the tradition of putting one son into the Church in each generation, leaving to the first son the management of the estates, so that in this time-honoured way the family retained a hold on both spiritual and temporal influence.

The first introduction of the Monferratos to Paris society was at a reception arranged at the home of the Brissard parents. The four brothers were there – Maurice, Michel, Charles, all with their wives, and Gérard, the youngest and as yet unmarried son, their sisters Jeanne and Octavie – Jeanne with her husband Guy Verney and Octavie, widowed tragically early by the war, alas alone. Then there were the brothers and sisters of Monsieur and Madame Brissard senior, with their spouses, their sons and daughters and their spouses – in all, over forty members of the family assembled in the salon of the Brissard home to make the acquaintance of their noble Italian relations.

Teresa di Monferrato, it must be said plainly, was not beautiful, as had been expected. She was marvellously

47

well-groomed, expensively dressed, spoke French well with only a slight accent – but . . . what subtleties, what worlds of implication are carried by that little word *but*! She was a little too short and certainly a little too plump for her lack of height – a result perhaps of over-indulgence in Italian cuisine. Her complexion was a little too olive, her expressive mouth a little too wide – a stern critic could endlessly catalogue her tiny shortcomings. Perhaps they can best be summarised by saying that there was no visible trace of French descent to be discerned in her -- and when one has said that of a person, all has been said!

The contrast between her and the Brissard wives present was very marked. Her raven-black hair was longer than their fashionable bobs. Her bosom was fuller than was considered chic. Her frock was *haute couture*, but by no means Parisian *haute couture*, for it relied less on purity of line for effect and more on the dramatic. To the women present she appeared somewhat unstylish.

That being the case, after close inspection and discussion between themselves, the Brissard wives exhibited every sign of affection towards Teresa. They arranged to take her on shopping expeditions, recommended their own hairdressers, shoemakers, glovemakers, dressmakers and other suppliers of luxurious goods and services so essential to the woman of fashion. This affection for Teresa was based, very naturally, on a certain feeling of superiority on their part. Their cousin may have married into the Italian aristocracy but, when all was said, she was not a Parisian and therefore lacked style. From that it necessarily followed that she represented no possible threat to themselves and she could safely be patronised, shown around and befriended.

Such are the vagaries of human nature – and the important differences between the mental processes of men and women – that in the matter of Teresa di Monferrato the views of the Brissard men were diametrically opposed to those of their women. As men of the world they kept these views to themselves, there being no reason to become involved in any kind of disagreement with their wives over the visitor. Yet the plain fact of the matter was that there emanated from the charming Marchesa subtle waves of sensuous magnetism that drew to her the interest of every man at the reception, as unerringly as a flower draws to itself bees by means of its colour and scent – bees eager to enjoy the delicate nectar in the secret recesses of the blossom. This magnetism could be discerned – by men, that is – in the way she gestured with her hands as she talked, the way she sat, above all in the manner in which the cheeks of her generous bottom rolled under her frock when she walked. In short, all four of the Brissard brothers judged their Italian cousin very desirable and each secretly determined that he should enjoy her most intimate favours during her stay in Paris.

But how was this to be arranged? In the evenings the Monferratos entertained lavishly in the grand house rented for their stay on the Avenue Carnot. They gave receptions and dinners, were invited to other people's receptions and dinners, they attended the Opera frequently, they dined out in those restaurants which had established a reputation with gourmets – Androuet's, Lapérouse, Maison Prunier, Joseph's on the rue Pierre Charron off the Champs Élysées. They visited the well-known places of entertainment which every visitor to Paris knows of – the Moulin Rouge, the Folies Bergère and the rest of them. In all, a strenuous round of social activities. During the daytime the Marchese himself, Rinaldo, was off to see other amusements of Paris, generally accompanied by one of the Brissards, their father assigning them in turn to the task of being Rinaldo's guide and companion. He, this plump nobleman of fifty, wanted to see everything, from the Tomb of the Emperor Napoleon to the Flea Market at St Ouen!

Rinaldo was not the problem. As for Teresa herself, every morning seemed to be devoted to another shopping excursion with one of the Brissard women. That left the afternoons, yet her Italian dedication to the siesta appeared to be total. For more than a week the brothers, each acting independently and in secrecy from the others, tried to pierce this apparently impregnable barrier of lack of time.

It was Charles who won this extraordinary race – Charles who combined in his person the stylish masculinity of his father with the gentle grace of his mother and who was, by common consent, the best-looking of the four handsome men. By diligent bribery of Teresa's personal maid he gained her mistress's ear – and in due course certain other and more interesting parts of her pampered body.

On the appointed afternoon the maid, whose name was Caterina, admitted Charles surreptitiously by the servants' entrance of the grand house. She was a plump woman of fifty who wore ankle-length black and spoke hardly any French at all. But her eyes, as shiny as the black buttons on her clothes, saw everything and understood everything – especially the power of banknotes of large denominations. She led Charles up back-stairs to the door of Teresa's boudoir, tapped gently and nodded to him to go in.

The room was charming – not too large to inhibit expressions of close affection, not too small to make such expressions seem furtive. The floor was richly carpeted, the long windows hung with curtains of emerald-green tussore silk. The door beyond, which evidently led into the Marchesa's bedroom, was discreetly closed, as one would expect. In this elegant boudoir, reclining on a chaise longue, was Teresa, Marchesa di Monferrato. In preparation for her customary siesta – or so she would have said if anyone had been discourteous enough to ask her – she had removed her fashionable clothes and was wrapped in a flimsy peignoir of dark orange silk. Charles advanced to her side and bowed to kiss her hand, his heart joyful at the sight of how very lightly she was clad – for her peignoir was so loosely and negligently tied that her round breasts were exposed almost to her nipples.

'Dear Charles,' she said, 'it is kind of you to call on me.'
He responded gallantly that it was kind of her to receive

him and, so as to lose no moment of this precious meeting, launched forth at once upon an account of his devotion to her, his enslavement to her charms and the many nonsensical things that men feel obliged to say at such moments. Teresa listened to him with a smile of interest and pleasure until, greatly encouraged, he went down on one knee by her chaise longue to kiss her bare foot in token of his homage. She had a fine little foot, high-arched, the toe-nails beautifully manicured and tinted pale pink. As he raised it carefully in his hand, a few centimetres only, the better to press his lips to it, the smooth silk of Teresa's peignoir slipped from her legs and she lay open to his gaze of admiration to mid-thigh.

Immediately Charles pressed his advantage, as what man in his position would not! From her foot his lips moved upwards to her knee and then, as he trembled in anticipation, he moved higher and kissed her delicately on the silky smooth inside of her thighs.

'I have heard about French gallantry,' she sighed, 'but I have never experienced it. Oh Charles, is this how Frenchmen make love?'

'It is how I make love,' he said, kissing her thighs again.

He turned back the silk folds of her wrap to reveal a thick bush of jet black hair at the join of her legs.

'How adorable!' he murmured, running his fingers through it as if combing it for her.

He unknotted her belt-tie and opened the peignoir fully, feasting his eyes on the comfortable embonpoint of her belly and then the enchanting domes of her breasts. He covered them lightly with his palms and squeezed gently.

'This familiarity between cousins,' she said, her lustrous dark eyes on him, 'Is it usual in Paris?'

'Between you and me it is a necessity,' he answered, 'you must feel that yourself or you would not have agreed to receive me here.'

'A necessity, I agree,' she sighed pleasurably and, as he bent over her to kiss her firm nipples, her hand touched the front of his trousers and opened the buttons one by

51

one. She groped under his shirt until she could take hold of his stiffness and fondle it with vigour.

Lips still busy with her breasts, his own hand passed slowly down her warm belly to the dark thicket below. He parted the soft petals of flesh and found that she was quite ready for him. In the emotions of their encounter, Teresa began to lose her grasp of the French language and lapsed into her native Italian.

'*Ah, che bello*!' she exclaimed as his finger-tips brushed over her tiny bud of passion.

The words were sufficiently like French for Charles to understand that it was an expression of pleasure. He continued his tender manipulation for some moments until she tugged his upright part out into the open and stared at it in affectionate anticipation.

'*Mettimelo dentro*!' she implored him.

Charles kissed her breasts again, not knowing what her words might mean. She repeated what she had said, this time more insistently.

Her splendid legs parted wide as she spoke and she pulled his projection towards her in a manner that left no room for doubt. Charles shrugged off his jacket and obligingly spread himself over her on the chaise longue and sank the object of her desire deep into the welcoming furrow between her thighs.

'*Adesso . . . prendimi! Sfondami tutta*!' she exclaimed joyfully.

The words meant nothing to Charles, but what need is there of words in any language, when a man and a woman have joined their bodies together in the most intimate and exciting way possible? Teresa's movements, her sighs, the tight grip of her hands on his shoulders – these told Charles all that it was necessary for him to know at that moment. The lady was enjoying his close attentions as much as he was enjoying paying his tender respects to her. If the whole truth were told, to judge by the enthusiasm with which her splayed legs were grasping him and her hot loins lifting rhythmically to meet his thrusts, her enjoyment was perhaps even greater than his!

'Teresa . . . I adore you!' he murmured as the delicious sensations coursing through him became ever stronger and more irresistible.

'*Più forte, caro!*'

The bucking of her body told him that she was urging him to increase the intensity of his attack. He lunged and plunged and revelled in sensation.

'*Sto venendo!*' she shrieked, bouncing up and down on the chaise longue so furiously that Charles was compelled to cling tightly to her as he approached his climatic moment.

'*Dio!*' she moaned as he poured out his silvery treasure into her tender purse, '*Dio!*'

There were tears of ecstasy on her face, something Charles had never seen before. He kissed them away and stroked her hair until she was calm again.

'There is much for me to learn in Paris,' she said, smiling at him.

'It will be my pleasure to teach you,' he replied, easing himself away from her.

After a while he was able to sit in a relaxed manner on the chair facing her, his trousers decently fastened, to tell her of his endless admiration and devotion to her. Teresa, her peignoir modestly rearranged to conceal all, stretched out a languid arm from where she half-reclined on the chaise longue and rang a little silver bell. Almost at once the black-garbed maid entered the room with a huge silver tray.

'Will you take a little refreshment?' Teresa asked. 'Coffee? Lemonade? Or something stronger?'

'Coffee,' said Charles, thinking to himself that the timing of the maid's entrance signified that she must understand very well the space of time her mistress required for the completion of a passionate episode and could be punctually at the door, her tray prepared, waiting for the tinkle of the little bell. Yet since Teresa seemed to find nothing remarkable in that, he concluded that the Italian way with servants was perhaps more familiar than was ordinarily the custom in France.

He sipped his coffee and chatted politely to Teresa as if this were no more than a social visit. But the respite was brief – as soon as the maid was gone, Teresa set aside her cup and stretched out her arms towards Charles. The loose sleeves of her dark orange wrap fell back, showing him her fine wrists and slender forearms.

Charles perched on the edge of the chaise longue and took her in his arms to kiss her. Through the thin silk the warmth of her flesh enchanted him, his hands glided appreciatively over her shoulders, down her back, along her sides – and returned inevitably to her breasts. For a while he contented himself with caressing her firm nipples through the silk, and this she obviously found extremely arousing, for her palm was laid on his thigh and stroked upwards. Afire with emotion, Charles opened the loose top of her peignoir to gaze fondly on her domed breasts in wordless admiration before pressing his lips to their delicate skin.

Teresa's preference in love-making, he discovered that afternoon, was not for long-drawn-out encounters of tender passion leading to an overwhelming discharge, but for a series of short and forceful episodes, with little periods of rest and refreshment in between. This he attributed to her Italian temperament – the fiery spontaneity which impelled her to urge him on with staccato expressions the moment he was lodged in her beautiful body and which forced such uninhibited shrieks of delight from her lips in her ecstatic crisis.

He gave her three proofs of his devotion that afternoon before she suggested that it was time that he left so that she could make herself presentable before her husband returned. The suggestion appeared to be a sensible one. Charles adjusted his clothes and kissed her hand in farewell.

'When may I see you again?' he asked.

'Very soon, I hope, dear Charles.'

'Tomorrow?'

She smiled at that.

'Tomorrow I cannot. Let me think . . . Friday. Yes, Caterina will arrange everything.'

Before he had time to protest that he could never survive for three whole days without her company, she tinkled the little bell and at once the maid came into the boudoir.

'Au revoir,' she said sweetly.

She had pulled her peignoir loosely over herself to cover her thighs and most intimate parts – though one delicious little red-brown nipple was peeping above the orange silk. Even so, the slight dishevelment of her hair, her faintly flushed face and the contentment of her attitude as she half-lay on the chaise longue spoke eloquently of what games she had been playing, and since she made no effort whatsoever to disguise any of this from her maid, Charles wondered if the faithful Caterina had been listening outside the door throughout!

'Au revoir, Teresa,' he answered, bowing slightly.

Charles had reason to congratulate himself in secret on his achievement. It was the first time he had made love to an Italian woman and the experience had been very rewarding. It was also the first time he had made love to a Marchesa and that conferred a certain prestige on their encounter, he thought. It was not the first time he had made love to a cousin – Marie-Véronique had that honour, the wife of a nephew of his mother. On the other hand, Marie-Véronique was only a cousin by marriage, so perhaps one ought not to count that. It could be said that Teresa represented a triple success!

But, all unknown to Charles, his brother Maurice was pursuing the same quarry. By temperament Maurice was more forthright and more formidable than Charles, there being more of their father in him. For Maurice there was no question of slipping into a house by the servants' door and climbing back-stairs. That would be an impossible affront to his dignity! When the Marchesa was at last persuaded to meet him in private, he escorted her to a small furnished apartment he maintained in the rue Lafitte. He had acquired this useful pied-à-terre some time before so as to have a suitable place in which to entertain ladies in comfort and privacy. Its existence was unsuspected, needless to say, not only by his wife but even by his brothers.

One result of Teresa's innumerable shopping trips around Paris was that she looked incredibly chic that day in a winter coat of black vicuna with huge astrakhan cuffs that swept back almost to her elbows and a broad trim of the same fur round the hem – the creation of a master of haute couture! With it she wore a little black cloche hat with a diamond spray pinned to the side. Even as he congratulated her on her appearance, Maurice thought to himself that the visit to Paris was costing Rinaldo di Monferrato an amazing amount of money. His estates must surely be far more productive than one had imagined! But of that Maurice knew nothing – all discussions of matters of business had been confined to close discussion between Rinaldo and Brissard senior.

As soon as the apartment door was closed and secured behind her, Teresa threw herself into Maurice's waiting arms and kissed him hotly.

'Dear Maurice,' she breathed, 'Show me the bedroom. I cannot stay with you for very long.'

Maurice discarded his hat and overcoat and led her to where she wanted to be.

'But how charming!' she exclaimed, glancing round the room, which was elegantly furnished in the modern style, 'this is where you bring your mistresses – this pretty little room?'

'My dearest Teresa,' he replied, helping her off with her beautiful coat, 'there are no mistresses. This is all for you.'

He lied, naturally, as a man must on these occasions. Teresa knew that he lied and accepted it, as a woman must in these circumstances. She smiled and took off her hat and shook out her jet-black hair. Then with a gesture that delighted him, she kicked off her expensive black lizard-skin shoes, sending them sailing across the room towards the broad and low bed.

'Help me off with my frock, Maurice.'

'Perhaps you should have brought your maid,' he said,

feeling for the fastenings down the side of her tight-fitting peacock blue creation from Patou.

He was joking, but she took him seriously.

'I almost did – but then I thought that her presence might embarrass you. But I am sure we don't need her – you must have long experience of assisting women to undress.'

The frock came off over her head to reveal her standing in a crêpe-de-chine slip which terminated well above her knees and was trimmed at top and bottom with ecru lace on which were set tiny pink rosebuds. At this point she twined her bare arms around his neck and pressed against him while she kissed him, the warmth of her soft belly through his clothes causing his male part to stiffen itself against what would shortly be required of it. When she released him Maurice shed his jacket and waistcoat hurriedly, and by now the carpet was strewn with discarded garments.

'You are very beautiful,' he said.

'But you haven't seen me yet, Maurice, only my clothes,' and she took the hem of her slip in both hands and pulled it over her head.

'More beautiful than I imagined,' he continued.

She sat on the side of the bed and smiled at him affectionately, wearing only stockings and the smallest silk knickers he had ever seen on a woman, cut to cover only her most secret delight and fully exposing her belly and thighs to the groin.

'An Italian style?' he asked, 'It is very charming.'

'Will you take off my stockings or should I have brought my maid?' she asked.

'I shall take them off with pleasure, dear Teresa.'

She posed voluptuously for him, half-reclining on the soft bed on her elbows, one stockinged foot up on the edge of the bed to raise her knee high, the other leg outstretched. *Such* legs she had, Maurice observed with approval – and with the experience of a man who had been privileged to see, and to caress, the legs of a very considerable number of pretty women. Such legs! From her well-rounded thighs down to her knees, her perfectly-shaped calves and her slender ankles surely a subject for a painter! Except that Maurice would not trust any painter to observe Teresa in a state of near nakedness without being quite sure that the man was securely tethered to the wall and unable to throw himself at her feet and swear eternal devotion in return for the honour of kissing her foot!

Teresa's garters were the same shade of peacock blue as her frock and delicately frilled with fine lace. He removed her silk stockings with finesse and left the garters on, for the pleasure of seeing the contrast with the smooth olive skin of her bare thighs. Naturally, from his vantage point at her feet the sumptuousness of Teresa's body was overwhelming. Those magnificently full round breasts – so tantalisingly close and so generously offered for his delight! Even Maurice's ready tongue was at a loss to find words that had sufficient emotional force to describe them or to praise them. It would have required a poet in the highest order of talent to find a phrase that would do justice to those enchantingly firm-pointed playthings! To say nothing of the satin-skinned expanse of her belly, displayed so freely – the felicities of language necessary to convey its attractions would be beyond the capabilities of even the Académie Française in plenary session! And there below, at the join of one upraised thigh and one outstretched thigh, a little triangle of peacock blue silk which covered but did not quite conceal her most secret treasure. The thin material was stretched in a delicious outward curve that hinted at a plump mound – and through the translucence of the silk there was faintly visible the dark shadow of her jet-black fleece.

Between almost inarticulate murmurs of admiration Maurice kissed along the warm inside of her raised thigh until he reached her groin and the silk-covered bulge that aroused him – all unaware that his brother Charles' lips had followed this same golden route only the day before.

'Ah, Maurice,' she whispered, 'how marvellous is this moment!'

58

In a state of high exhilaration he pulled off the remaining tiny garment that protected her modesty and rained kisses on the gently pouting lips he had unveiled.

'*Madonna mia!*' Teresa sighed, her legs opening wider.

Exquisite though the moment was for them both, there was still more of her ripe body to be adored. Maurice took hold of her hips and rolled her over on the bed until she was face down and the elegant rotundities of her bottom were in plain view. He ran his hands over the silk-skinned cheeks, enraptured by their supple fleshiness. He squeezed them, he kissed them – he bent over her to bite them gently, causing Teresa to utter little cries of pleasure.

It continued, this most enjoyable lovers' game, until Maurice was impelled to tear off his clothes and get onto the bed with her to seek even more exciting forms of play. He kissed his adorable cousin from the tip of her straight Roman nose to the tips of her beautifully-tended toes, missing out nothing in between – curves, plains, protruberances, hollows, smooth parts, fleecy parts – not one enravishing centimetre was left unkissed. By then the hot-blooded Teresa had temporarily forgotten her French in the tremors of pleasure he was provoking and, his stiff part a willing captive in her hand, she was murmuring '*Oh, si . . . ancora . . . di piu!*'

Maurice threw a leg over hers and rolled into position on her belly, the upstanding tips of her breasts pressing against his dark-haired chest. Teresa's hands were between their thighs before his could get there, to open her portal wide for his entrance. In an instant Maurice was deeply embedded, Teresa exclaimed '*Meravigliosa!*' and crossed her ankles over the small of his back to pull him tightly into her. The only question at that moment left to be answered was which of the two of them, he or she, would reach the apex of passion first, for they were both thrusting furiously against each other. In the event it proved to be Maurice, but an instant later Teresa shrieked in ecstasy as she felt him discharge his rapture within her.

After that they rested for a while and exchanged endearments over a glass or two of champagne from

Maurice's well-chosen supply in the apartment. All too soon for him Teresa enquired what the time was and explained that she had to go home to prepare for dinner that evening with Michel and his wife.

'So soon?' said Maurice, 'must you really go so soon, dearest Teresa?'

She relented and said that she could stay another quarter of an hour, but no more. Maurice was not a man to let time slip past and opportunities to run to waste. His hand insinuated itself between her legs to seek and caress her dew-soaked rosebud and at once she was ready for a repetition of their earlier delights. This time he turned her over on her front, three soft pillows under her belly, so that he could lie on the voluptuous cheeks of her bottom and feel them bounce under him as he pierced her from behind with his sturdy probe and brought on a second ecstatic crisis in her and himself.

'Tomorrow?' he asked when they were dressing to leave.

'No . . . that's not possible . . . Wednesday. I shall come here at three.'

Maurice bowed to kiss her gloved hand.

'I shall be here waiting for you,' he promised.

The visit to Paris of the Marchese and Marchesa di Monferrato lasted for more than three months – the whole of the fashionable autumn season. Towards the end of December they returned to Italy, the end of their stay marked by a magnificent reception in their grand house, at which flunkeys in green and gold livery served chilled champagne and a string quartet played music which was lost in the high-spirited chatter of the hundred guests present. A day later the Monferratos took their departure by train, accompanied by four servants and a mountain of baggage.

In the autumn of the following year Aristide Brissard entertained his four sons to lunch at his favourite restaurant. From the tenor of the of the invitation they surmised that he had news of importance to communicate to them – perhaps, they speculated, he intended to retire from active participation in the daily affairs of the family business and hand over to Maurice. If that were so, then it was understood that Maurice would appoint Michel as deputy head, thus giving more scope in turn to Charles. The prospect was an interesting one, Only Gérard, still intent on his studies at the University, would remain unaffected by such an announcement and so, though he was present at the lunch, he was the least concerned and probably the one who enjoyed his lunch most.

In the event, Aristide's news was to affect Gérard also, for the old man had not the least intention of handing over responsibility – at least, not of the financial type.

'My dear sons,' he said at the end of the meal when a fine cognac was being served, ' I have something to tell you which will give you occasion for rejoicing. Your mother has received a letter from her sister Marie to inform her that the Marchesa di Monferrato has been delivered of a son, an heir to the title and estates. Will you join with me in drinking to the health and prosperity of the child, his mother and our good friend Rinaldo.'

Glasses were raised in salutation, even while silent calculations counted back the months and established the uncomfortable fact that Teresa must have conceived during her stay in Paris with her husband. On the other hand, the fact that she was with her husband gave some reassurance.

'But how solemn your faces are!' said Aristide, 'even you, Gérard, our family joker! Is anything wrong?'

'No, no,' a chorus of voices answered from around the table.

'Rinaldo is naturally delighted to have at last a son to carry on the name of Monferrato,' said Aristide, 'as you know, he is very much older than Teresa. There is also the consideration that before his marriage his life was one of extreme devotion to the pleasures of love. He indulged himself with a formidable number of women, from princesses to peasants, not to mention women of a certain profession – of the highest sort, you understand. But there were fears that the well had run dry, if I may express myself plainly. The extended stay here was obviously most fortunate in its outcome.'

'Ah, Paris – city of love and pleasure!' Gérard commented with hidden irony and Maurice shook his head at him warningly to shut him up.

'A fortunate outcome indeed,' said Charles carefully.

'My opinion exactly,' said Maurice.

'I am perfectly aware,' said Aristide, 'that your cousin Teresa is a very desirable woman. And being far more Italian than French, it may be that her blood is hotter than is seemly in a married woman.'

'Really, Papa – how can you suggest any such thing!' said Maurice.

'I am also aware,' Aristide continued, ignoring him, 'that during her visit to Paris last year her intimate friendship was bestowed upon – well, let us say that her husband's privilege was extended to . . . someone not her husband. No, do not trouble to deny it, I am not a fool.'

'Of course not, Papa,' said Gérard, the only one of them grinning.

'We are men of the world,' said Aristide, 'I have educated my sons to conduct themselves with courtesy and discretion in matters of the heart. Even you, Gérard, I hope.'

'I hope that I have not disappointed you, Papa.'

'Not in the least. I am proud of all my sons.'

'There is something I must tell you,' said Charles. 'Naturally it would have remained a secret forever, but after the news you have given us, I feel it is my duty to advise you that I am the father of Teresa's child. I confess this with pride.'

'You?' Maurice exclaimed, 'impossible! It is I!'

Gérard howled with laughter, drawing attention to himself from all parts of the restaurant.

'What is ridiculous in that?' Maurice demanded angrily, 'do you think I am unacceptable as a lover to a woman of charm and rank?'

'No, not that, Maurice,' Gérard said, struggling to control his mirth, 'but the fact is that I too was honoured in the same way by the lady. That makes three of us – so how about you, Michel – were the same privileges bestowed upon you?'

'Yes, by God!' Michel said, red-faced. 'It seems to me that our Italian cousin distributed her favours very liberally.'

'The little devil!' said Maurice, 'she was hot-blooded to an extent I for one did not envisage. Yet perhaps the signs were there all the time – her enthusiasm and her desire for more and more embraces.'

'The warmth of those embraces!' said Michel, 'how inspiring, no matter how often repeated.'

'How delightful she was, even in her most eager moments,' Charles said reminiscently.

'And that magnificent backside!' said Gérard.

'Enough!' Aristide said in reproof, 'we are speaking of a lady who is distantly related to our family. Let us choose our words with decorum, if you please.'

'Tell me one thing,' said Maurice, his agile mind working, 'was the purpose of the visit to Paris for Teresa to become pregnant?'

Aristide tapped the side of his nose with one finger.

'No indiscreet questions. Be content, all of you. While you were paying your respects to your cousin I was able to make certain arrangements with her husband in regard to part of his extensive holdings, and this will not only increase his income substantially – it will also return a handsome profit to us for many years to come. In all, the visit to Paris may be counted a success, for everyone has benefited from it in various ways. There is to be no more discussion of it, do you understand?'

'The secret is safe with us,' Maurice answered him on behalf of them all.

'That I do not doubt. It is, after all, a proud secret – that one of you is the father of the next Marchese di Monferrato.'

MONIQUE AND GÉRARD DISCUSS ART

The official attitude, had there been such a thing, of the Brissard family towards Monique Chabrol was one of formal disapproval and regret that a woman of her background should live her life in an uncompromisingly bohemian style. It was fortunate that she was not a blood-relation, for that would have made matters even more serious. It was bad enough that she was a Mont-Royal, a family allied to the Brissards by marriage.

Monique lived alone in Paris and painted. Sometimes her paintings were hung in the important exhibitions and on such occasions the Brissards would make a point of going there – partly to see what new scandal she was perpetrating and yet partly, it must be said, to demonstrate family support for her, even though they disapproved. Undeniably Monique had talent. Thankfully she painted in the traditional manner, not the slap and daub rubbish produced by the modernists. But, and here lay the problem, the subjects she chose seemed to the discreet Brissards unsuitable for public exhibition. Monique's interest in sexuality, it had to be admitted, was a little too open. What was done in private was a man or woman's own concern, that was understood, however strange or improbable the paths they followed to their pleasure. But a painting in a gallery was a public statement of private matters, and that they could not approve. At least she had the good sense to change her name to Chabrol.

A portrait had been commissioned from her some years ago of the head of the family, Aristide Brissard, and even that was a cause of some annoyance. It depicted him in classical portrait style, wearing a formal dark suit, wing-collar and cravat, his features caught to the life. Yet in some way that was hard to put precisely into words, Monique had managed to convey a lurking twinkle in the eyes that did not exactly conform to the image of a serious-minded and distinguished man of business and devoted father of seven children. It was more the twinkle of a man who would not hesitate, away from his home and family, to slip his hand down the top of a young woman's frock. If the truth were told, Aristide himself was secretly pleased with the picture, but as his dear wife was not, he held his peace about it.

Aristide's four sons firmly supported the official line of disapproval of Monique and all her doings, family loyalty being bred into them. Privately they found Monique amusing and interesting and called upon her from time to time for a glass of wine and some spritely conversation. Needless to say, the wives were not informed of this. The youngest son, Gérard, still a student at twenty-three, had no wife to concern himself about and was the most frequent caller of them at Monique's apartment. He had the additional interest of a great liking for art and music and, perhaps most important of all, he admired the way in which she set the pattern of her own life and refused to fit into anyone else's pattern.

Naturally, as an admirer of the surrealist painters, he deplored the fact that she persisted in painting in what he regarded as an outmoded style. Her men and women were always anatomically correct – a trifle no modernist would bother himself with – and she put them in recognisable settings – rooms, parks, riverbanks – copied from nature. For this he chided her sternly and she retorted in the same vein, describing his contemporary heroes as purveyors of the grotesque and unintelligible. In short, Gérard and Monique had a good-natured affection for each other.

He was in her sitting-room one evening, a glass of good Beaujolais in his hand, taking her to task for faults he discerned in a new painting of hers which hung on the wall.

'As a piece of work it must have taken you Heaven knows how long to complete,' he said, 'and what is the result – a pastiche of a well-known picture by Ingres, painted eighty years ago. As such it has no aesthetic purpose.'

'I painted it as a joke,' said Monique, 'you take it too seriously.'

'Then explain the joke to me, if you can.'

'Why don't you look at it more closely.'

Gérard got up and walked across the room to study the picture close up. It showed a low sumptuous divan covered in turquoise damask, on which lay a naked and beautiful woman. Her arms were behind her head on the cushion and her body was half-turned towards the viewer to afford him the sight of her young breasts and smooth belly. Behind her on the floor sat cross-legged a young man in Turkish costume – baggy orange trousers, an emerald green tunic and a bright red fez, playing a curiously shaped musical intrument something like a slender guitar.

'It is copied from Ingres' *Harem woman and slave*,' said Gérard, 'and yet there is something different about it. Of course – you have made the slave with the guitar a man instead of the original woman! And good God – you have given him the features of my brother Charles! What does this mean?'

'Do you notice anything else?' Monique asked.

Gérard scrutinised the colourfully-dressed slave closely and grinned broadly as he discovered, pressing outwards against the baggy trousers, the unmistakable shape of an erect penis.

'This picture hints at events of which I know nothing,' he said, returning to his seat, 'Charles and a Turkish slave – what can it signify? Tell me, dear Monique, before I explode with curiosity.'

'Ah, Gérard,' she teased him, 'I cannot reveal to you a secret concerning another. If Charles has not told you of this adventure, then I certainly will not.'

'Charles and a naked slave woman – surely this is impossible. He has never said a word to me about this. It must be connected with his visits to Istanbul. Did he tell you, Monique?'

'I will answer no more questions.'

'But who is the woman? – she is delightful.'

66

'I said no more questions. You either like my picture or you don't – to me it is a matter of indifference.'

'I like it more now that I understand a little of what it is about. For you it seems that art copies life.'

'Not always. Sometimes life copies art.'

'How?'

'To explain that to you would take forever and you are an impatient young man, Gérard. Perhaps the time has come for a demonstration of what I mean. If you dare, that is.'

'If I dare? Of course I dare! You would be astonished at some of the things I have dared.'

'Student pranks,' said Monique condescendingly.

'You insult me,' Gérard exclaimed. 'Try me! What is your proposal?'

'A small experiment, no more than that, to ascertain the relative merits of my old-fashioned style, as you call it, and the modern style you admire.'

'Go on then – how?'

'I will arrange two little experiments here in my home. Afterwards we will discuss which had the greatest effect on you.'

'I am ready for anything. I must warn you before we start that you will never change my views.'

'Perhaps. We shall see. Let us say tomorrow at eight in the evening. One thing – I must have your word that you will engage yourself fully in the spirit of the experiment and not attempt to change the course of things, however bizarre they may seem to you. Is that agreed?'

'Agreed.'

In this way it came about that promptly at eight the next evening, intrigued by the prospect of adventure, Gérard presented himself at Monique's apartment in Auteuil on the western edge of Paris. He had been instructed by telephone that morning to dress in a dark jacket and grey trousers, though the purpose of the mode was beyond him. Monique opened the door to reveal herself wearing a long-sleeved Persian-style caftan of red and gold.

'An Arabian Nights party? Then what am I – the European traveller?' he asked in amusement.

'Certainly not,' she answered, offering her cheek to be kissed, 'I have arranged an evening that is to be essentially French, though perhaps not typically so.'

While he was puzzling over that she led him into her sitting-room, where two other guests were sipping champagne and conversing with each other.

'Mademoiselle Marchand, allow me to present my cousin, Monsieur Brissard,' she introduced him formally.

Mademoiselle Marchand was in her early twenties. The expression of her classical features was calm and dignified as she held out her hand for Gérard to kiss. Her red-brown hair was worn long, not cut short and waved in the modern style, and it was drawn back from a central parting to an arrangement at the nape of her neck. She was sitting straight-backed in her chair, her legs crossed elegantly. Apart from her grey suede evening shoes she was completely naked. As Gérard bowed to kiss her hand and murmur *Enchanté, Mademoiselle* it required a most determined effort of will to prevent himself from staring at her alluring bare breasts.

The other guest, a man in his thirties, rose to his feet to bow and shake hands as Monique introduced him as Monsieur Creux. Like Gérard, he was wearing a dark jacket and grey trousers.

Gérard sat on the sofa by Monique and was handed a glass of chilled champagne.

'Monsieur Brissard has some claim to being a poet,' Monique announced to the company, 'unfortunately he has fallen under the malign influence of the anarchists who describe themselves as Surrealists, whatever that may mean.'

'Opinions differ on these matters,' said Gérard stiffly, 'and you, Monsieur Creux, are you also a painter like my distinguished cousin?'

'I have that honour,' Creux replied, 'evidently you are not acquainted with my work.'

'To my regret, no. Have you exhibited recently?'

However much Gérard tried to stop himself from staring at Mademoiselle Marchand, it was becoming almost impossible to ignore her rounded breasts and the tuft of red-brown hair showing above her crossed thighs. Especially when she spoke to him.

'I had the pleasure of posing for one of the pictures which Monsieur Creux exhibited in last year's Salon,' she said.

'If only I had seen it!' he said, 'I could never have fogotten so beautiful a woman.'

She accepted the compliment with a graceful inclination of her head.

'The time has come for our picnic in the woods,' said Monique. 'Come with me, Mademoiselle, while the gentlemen finish the bottle before they join us.'

To observe Mademoiselle Marchand rise and follow Monique out of the room was an enchanting experience. The rounded cheeks of her bottom swayed in a motion that was the purest poetry. Gérard's male part, already stiff inside his clothes, trembled with excitement.

'Mademoiselle Marchand is a friend of yours?' he asked as Creux poured out the last of the wine.

'A friend? Perhaps. A model from time to time. I have known her for some years. She has a good body for painting, very well-proportioned. Had you noticed?'

'A little fuller of bosom and rear than is considered chic,' said Gérard, attempting to be nonchalant.

'Chic!' exclaimed Creux contemptuously, 'that word has no place in the vocabulary of an artist. It is a word for dressmakers and magazine writers. Finish your wine and let's go.'

'But where are we going?'

'To a picnic, of course, you know that.'

'At this time of day?'

In effect, they went into Monique's studio. All the clutter of her work had been removed and she had procured ten or twelve shrubs and small trees in tubs, arranged round a central clearing. A large green rug covered the open space and on it sat the naked Mademoiselle Marchand unpacking food from a wicker basket. Monique had shed her caftan and wore only a thin linen chemise that came halfway down her strong thighs and did little to conceal her big breasts and width of hip. She was busy pulling the cork from a wine bottle.

'But of course!' said Gérard as he and Creux seated themselves beside the women, 'I have it now! This is Manet's *Dejeuner sur l'Herbe* brought to life!'

'I told you that we are to have an essentially French party,' said Monique.

'In spite of your admiration for the modernists,' said Mademoiselle Marchand, 'it appears that you are acquainted with the work of our great French painters of the past.'

'Naturally, Mademoiselle,'

In the circumstances it seemed oddly appropriate to him that they should address each other formally.

'And is Monsieur Manet's celebrated picture one of which you approve?'

'I have been told that it caused a certain amount of unease when it was first shown. People asked themselves by what extraordinary train of events did two fully dressed men find themselves at a picnic in the woods with two unclad women. What was to happen next, they speculated. The picture was judged scandalous by polite society.'

'Perhaps we shall find out what happened next,' said Monique, 'we have recreated to what extent we can the setting and the characters. Let us hope that the spirit of what the artist intended may inspire us.'

'The experiment has a certain interest,' said Creux, raising his glass, 'Manet, dear departed master, in whatever heaven you now pursue your work, I salute you!'

'To the illustrious past,' Gérard joined in the toast generously.

'My role is only to take off my clothes and stand or sit or lie while artists paint pictures with me in them,' said Mademoiselle Marchand, 'yet it seems to me that the untalented daubers who now pass for artists have in their blind arrogance kicked away all the support of the past and wish to pretend that they and they alone have just invented art. Is that not so?'

While he was answering her, Gérard could not avoid

70

observing that Creux had pressed Monique onto her back, pushed her chemise up to expose her generous belly and filled her naval with wine from his glass. Gérard's words trailed off as Creux leaned over Monique to lap up the wine with the tip of his tongue. That pleasant task completed, he hitched the chemise higher and with fingertips dipped in wine set himself to tickle Monique's nipples.

Gérard was stretched out on the green rug on his side, one knee up to relieve and disguise the urgent pressure of his penis inside his trousers. Mademoiselle Marchand sat facing him, one leg tucked under her and the other extended gracefully, the whole of her beautiful body from breasts to furry groins presented to him. Her face was serene as she contemplated what Creux was doing to Monique.

'Are you lovers, you and Madame Chabrol?' she asked.

'Why no – our pleasure together has been solely that of conversation,' Gérard answered, a little surprised by the question.

'Your preference is perhaps for the fashionable women one sees window-shopping in the rue de la Paix?' she continued, 'flat-chested, no more behind than a boy and hair cut as short as a convict's?'

In truth Gérard was beginning to ask himself, as he watched Creux handle Monique, why he had never taken the opportunity on a visit to her apartment to make advances to her. Those full and fleshy breasts Creux was rolling in his hands – the sensation of fondling them must be marvellously sensual! As Creux moved back to push up Monique's knees and transfer his attentions to the captivating area between her thighs, Gérard was overwhelmed by the sight of the neat strip of hair that covered her plump mound. He sighed loudly as Creux stroked it for a moment or two before splitting it with his thumbs and inserting two fingers.

'Monique is beautiful,' said Gérard thoughtfully, 'I wonder that I never noticed it before.'

'You lack the artist's eye,' said Mademoiselle Marchand simply.

She reached out casually to unbutton Gérard's trousers and take out his straining erection.

'Now you have seen her through Monsieur Creux's eyes,' she added, fingering him gently, 'therefore you have become aware of her beaty – as this indicates.'

'To be truthful,' he said, 'I have been in this condition since the moment I saw you. Without in any way detracting from Monique, my salutation is for you rather than for her.'

'I find that difficult to believe,' Mademoiselle Marchand retorted, her hand moving pleasurably up and down his stiff part, 'you have scarcely looked at me – your eyes have been entirely for Madame Chabrol.'

'As to that, I did not wish to embarrass you by staring directly at your loveliness.'

'How could you embarrass me? I make my living by posing nude for art classes and painters who can afford to pay me. It does not embarrass me in the least to have men stare at my body.'

Creux opened his trousers and mounted Monique, his distended part positioned to drive into her.

'But these artists and students see you perhaps as a subject for their work,' said Gérard, fascinated by the penetration of his cousin by Creux, 'they do not regard you with the eye of a lover?'

'As to lovers, I am not without experience of them.'

Gérard reached out a trembling hand to caress Mademoiselle Marchand's superb breasts and their delicious pink tips.

'Then you must recognise the desire in my glance,' he murmured, 'you must feel the fire in my touch.'

'There is something in what you say,' she replied calmly, 'if indeed this that I have in my hand is displaying its strength for me and not for Madame Chabrol.'

'It is, I assure you!'

'Then courtesy demands that I should respond. Lie on your back, Monsieur Brissard.'

He did so and in an instant she was kneeling astride him, one hand steering his boisterous part in the direction he ardently wished it to go and the fingers of her other hand opening wide the soft entrance to her dearest sanctum.

'There,' she said as she impaled herself on his rigid projection, 'is that what you want?'

'Ah, chérie – that is most agreeable!'

'Really!' she said, a little offended, 'we have only recently been introduced, Monsieur Brissard. Endearments such as chérie are over-familiar and in poor taste.'

'I beg your pardon, Mademoiselle Marchand,' he gasped as her slithering up and down his shaft sent shivers of delight through him, 'I must mend my manners.'

'Most certainly you must, if we are to continue our conversation.'

'I would not have it interrupted for all the world, believe me.'

'Heavens!' she exclaimed, her attention distracted from his lapse of manners, 'Look at Monsieur Creux!'

Gérard turned his head on the rug and saw Creux's grey-trousered bottom thumping up and down like a great steam-engine piston. Beneath him Monique was uttering little squeals of pleasure and urging him on by thumping him with her heels.

'Such transports!' said Mademoiselle Marchand as she carried on bouncing gently up and down on Gérard, 'How exhilarating! Would you like me to do the same?'

'I would be most obliged,' he gasped, almost at the limit of his endurance.

At that she set to with a will, her breasts jerking up and down in the most luscious way to the rhythm of her movements.

'Oh!' she said in a tone of surprise.

'What is it?'

'I'm about to . . . no, it is too soon . . .'

From Gérard's right came the long-drawn '*Ah*' of Monique attaining her climactic release under Creux's pounding. Mademoiselle Marchand's mouth opened wide in a silent echo of that cry and her hot loins thrust at Gérard in a sudden flurry of movement. Ecstasy coursed

73

through him as he fountained his appreciation into her wildly shaking body.

After a while they sat and talked normally again, the two men fully dressed, Monique with her shift down to conceal the contours of her voluptuous body, Mademoiselle Marchand stark naked and utterly composed. They drank more wine, they sampled the food – excellent slices of cold roast duck, crusty fresh bread and good Camembert cheese.

'Are the possibilities of Manet's picture becoming apparent to you?' Monique asked Gérard.

'I already see it in a new light.'

'Then it seems we are making progress. Do you suppose that Manet would have approved of the manner in which we interpreted his intentions just now?'

'I feel certain that he would have approved of an intention which has formed in my mind.'

'Which is?'

For answer he put his hand on Monique's bare thigh and slid it upwards to the hem which just concealed her most secret citadel – a citadel which had been stormed by Monsieur Creux only a quarter of an hour before. His finger-tips touched the fleece on her warm mound.

'Until this evening I had not appreciated the bounties of your body,' he told her, aware that Creux and Mademoiselle Marchand were listening and watching. A curious situation, yet he could do no more than trace to its end the pattern that had been set – the soft and moist lips under his fingers made any other course of action impossible. He moved closer to her to remove her chemise, but she prevented him.

'That is out of the scope of the original picture,' she said, 'Manet painted two men fully dressed, one woman naked and one in a chemise. It would be unthinkable to change his concept.'

Gérard pulled her down to lie facing him and put his hands up inside the loose chemise to play with her abundant breasts.

'Perhaps you should have chosen another picture as our model – one in which all the figures are without clothes.'

74

'Perhaps, but I like this one. There is a touch of perversity about it which gives a certain thrill.'

Between his fingers the tips of her breasts were very firm. His hand moved down to massage the satin-smooth skin of her belly for some considerable time before at last seeking the wet entrance between her legs.

'You are ready for me,' he whispered.

'I am ready more often than you or any other man will be,' she said, smiling at him.

'We shall see about that,' he anwered, his pride stung.

He rolled her onto her back and her legs parted wide as he got on top of her. She undid his trousers for him and in an instant he slid deep into her pliant opening with a single push.

'Slowly, dear Gérard,' she murmured, 'do not exhaust yourself too quickly in an attempt to demonstrate your virility. Mademoiselle Marchand's little gratification was proof enough of that. Delight us both, but conserve your strength, for we are only at the beginning of the possibilities of the masterpiece we are exploring together.'

He took her advice and probed in a stately motion which set up enravishing tremors of pleasure in her and him alike. He noted that Creux had set Mademoiselle Marchand on her hands and knees and was behind her, thrusting his taut stem into her with what appeared to be his customary vigour.

'No, no,' Monique sighed, 'slow down, Gérard, do not imitate him. He will be done for after that, but you must last a long time yet. Mademoiselle Marchand will want you again, and so shall I.'

Gérard slowed his pace, to the extreme delectation of his cousin. But when he observed Mademoiselle Marchand shaking in violent ecstasy as Monsieur Creux discharged into her, the sight was too much for him. Gérard cried out in joy as he delivered his copious compliment to Monique, while she sobbed and bit into the shoulder of his jacket.

It was as she said. Creux took no more interest in the proceedings after that. He settled comfortably on his

75

back, his eyes closed, and dozed off, the picture of respectability in his dark jacket neatly buttoned and his grey trousers. Gérard poured more wine for the two women and for himself and resumed the conversation on art.

'Now that you have opened my eyes to the possibilities of paintings,' he said, 'the scope seems boundless. There are thousands of famous paintings one could live through.'

'For example?' said Mademoiselle Marchand, self-composed and formal again after her energetic interlude with Creux.

'Well, a picture I have always liked very much is Boucher's portrait of Louise O'Murphy – that delicious fifteen-year-old girl face-down and naked on a chaise-longue to show off her pretty bottom for King Louis.'

'There is no man in the picture,' said Monique, 'and the rules of the game preclude any additional persons. If we stage that, the young lady would have to pleasure herself with her fingers. I can arrange that for you with an enchanting girl who poses for me sometimes.'

'No, that would be too frustrating, just to watch,' Gérard admitted, 'I know – Fragonard's woman on a swing! There is a man in that – lying on the grass to look up her petticoats as she swings up into the air.'

'That might be interesting,' said Mademoiselle Marchand, 'yet I wonder how one makes love on a swing? A way could be devised, I am sure.'

'Or Poussin's *Bacchanal*,' Gérard suggested, 'half a dozen men and women enjoying a naked romp round a statue of the god Pan. What do you think, Monique?'

'It has possibilities. Any others?'

'Do you know a woodland picture by Wateau which shows five or six women sitting under trees and a man of distinction strolling past to admire them?'

'You flatter yourself,' said Monique, 'five or six women! Two will be more than enough for you.'

'I am certain of it,' Mademoiselle Marchand agreed with a little sigh.

Her long fingers had worked their way into his trousers as they were talking and she teased his limp penis.

'Do you not find it significant that all the artists you have named are from the glorious heritage of the past?' Monique asked, 'not one dadaist, cubist, futurist or surrealist among them. Why is this?'

Mademoiselle Marchand's delicate stroking was having its intended effect on Gérard. His sleeping adjunct awoke, stirred itself and began to stretch.

'I cannot deny what you say,' he answered Monique, 'the images that came into my mind were all of pictures I have seen in the Louvre Museum and other galleries.'

The hand clasping his treasured possession was now sliding briskly up and down it, rousing wild emotions in him. His own hand found its way between Mademoiselle Marchand's naked thighs so that his fingers could feel for her tender bud of passion and caress it.

'Do you not agree that Mademoiselle Marchand has the perfect face and body for an artist's model?' Monique enquired, observing their amorous progress. 'Her features are the classical type one sees on ancient Greek statues. She has very well-shaped breasts, with nipples pointing forwards and upwards, not outwards as one sees on so many women – my own, for instance, point slightly outwards, though, thank God, not downwards! Her thighs and legs are marvellously proportioned and her bottom is exactly the right size to balance the swell of her breasts. Her skin is a joy to paint – it is so smooth and unblemished that it has a certain sheen when the light reflects from it. It is no wonder that she in in such demand.'

Mademoiselle Marchand had never in all her life been in greater demand than she was by Gérard at that very moment. He scrambled to his knees between her spread legs, his extension pulsating visibly as he aimed for his target. She brought her knees up to her breasts to aid his ingress and he paused, entranced by the vivid contrast between her widely-split pink notch and the serenity of her beautiful face. But the pause was only of an instant's

77

duration – the image was one to savour in recollection later on, when his urgent passions had been slaked.

She gasped pleasurably as he struck home, rocking on her back to his fierce thrusting. Moment by moment as he plunged deeply within her, the composure of her face was annihilated, to be replaced by an expression of uncontrolled rapture. At the very last she was uttering little staccato screams of delight, which blended into a long wailing climax when Gérard's passion erupted into her.

'Your stamina is admirable, dear cousin,' Monique said when Gérard and Mademoiselle Marchand were lying side by side on the green rug, recovering their breath.

'Thank you,' he answered politely, 'I am impressed by your deep understanding of art, as demonstrated here this evening.'

'My understanding of art? Is that all.'

'By no means,' he said, sitting up, 'pour me another glass of wine and let us continue our discussion. There is much that I want to say to you, Monique.'

'Much? That is surely an exaggeration.'

'To you,' he said, raising the glass she handed him.

Like Monsieur Creux, Mademoiselle Marchand had dozed off, he on his back and snoring lightly, she curled up on her side with one arm under her head as a pillow.

'We are the survivors, you and I,' said Gérard, 'did you expect that?'

'I thought it possible. I am familiar with Monsieur Creux's capabilities. As for Mademoiselle Marchand, she has had a tiring day posing for a life-class and your most recent efforts evidently fatigued her unduly.'

'She participated with great enthusiasm that time.'

'And why not? You are a vigorous young man and you gave her good reason to participate fully.'

'She is, as you said, a delightful creature,' Gérard said, eyeing the sleeping Mademoiselle Marchand's long thighs and supple bottom.

'Do you want her as your mistress? It can be arranged and she will not be too expensive for you. Her tastes are simple.'

78

'I am grateful for the offer, Monique, but the encumbrance of a regular mistress is not for me. What I would like is something quite different, but also within your power to arrange.'

'Tell me what it is you want.'

'The privilege of visiting you.'

'But you have that already,' she said, pretending not to understand him.

'Visits of love, not social visits.'

Monique was lying on her side facing him, propped on one elbow. She smiled enigmatically at his words and stroked one of her breasts thoughtfully through her chemise.

'A man as handsome and enterprising as you can find all the young girls he wants,' she said, 'I am fifteen years older than you. Outside the scope of our experiment in art-appreciation, why would you seek pleasure from me? Mademoiselle Marchand would be more suitable in every way.'

'She is adorable, of course, but I have made love to scores of women like her.'

'Then are you suggesting that there was something out of the ordinary about out little entracte a while ago?'

'How can I explain it except by telling you that it was an experience I would like to repeat.'

'You shall – as soon as you are able,' she answered.

Her hand moved down to her thigh and Gérard's dormant interest began to rise again as he watched her caress herself lightly.

'Let me do that for you,' he offered.

'Certainly,' and she raised one knee to permit his hand free access.

'You are handling my most precious *objet d'art*,' Monique murmured. 'One which gives me unfailing delight, day by day, sometimes many times each day. Yet to you it can seem nothing more than that which you find between any woman's legs, indistinguishable except for the shade of the hair from the scores you have fondled.'

Gérards fingers played delicately within the pink and

moist folds of flesh and over the rose-bud just beginning to flower into crimson passion.

'I understand your meaning well, Monique. To me also the fifteen centimetres of flesh between my legs is a marvellous object, the source of all pleasure and inspiration. Yet to a woman it must seem no more than another ordinary stiff thing to put inside her.'

'Perhaps you do understand,' Monique sighed, her plump belly heaving with exquisite emotion under his careful manipulation.

'We are discussing the difference between subjective and objective perception of the same data,' he said gravely.

'Is that what we're doing? To me it feels far more interesting than that.'

'Is is a very interesting topic for discussion for it leads to the question of whether subjective and objective perceptions can be reconciled satisfactorily.'

'Does it?' she panted. 'The Sorbonne is turning you into a philosopher, Gérard, but a most satisfactory one – Oh!'

Her breasts shuddered under her chemise and she pressed herself hard against his fingers as she reached the culmination of her desire and dissolved into quaking gratification.

'We understand the value of each other's prime possession,' he said, 'you can hardly refuse me the right to visit you from time to time to attempt a reconciliation of our assessments of each other.'

Monique rolled slowly over onto her back and pulled her chemise up above her breasts.

'We shall see about that later,' she whispered, 'for the present, why not put your jewel into my jewel-box so that we can compare sensations?'

'With the greatest of pleasure,' he said, climbing aboard her.

Gérard's second lesson in art-appreciation took place a few days later at three in the afternoon. This time he was given no instructions on how to dress and when Monique opened the door to him he noted that she was wearing a not very new peasant-style blouse with a draw-string neckline and a loose skirt of shiny black. She led him straight into her studio.

'This is Denise,' she said, gesturing towards the girl lying on an old red blanket on the studio floor, 'Denise, this is Gérard, a sort of cousin of mine.'

Denise was thirteen or fourteen years of age, Gérard judged. She was totally naked and her body was too thin, her breasts only just starting to grow and only the wispiest of floss showing between her thighs. She was on her side with one knee up to expose herself and beside her lay a battered and stringless Spanish guitar, evidently a prop.

'You are working?' Gérard asked after greeting Denise politely.

'Yes, would you care to inspect my work?' Monique replied.

On the easel was a large sheet of white paper on which she had been making a water-colour picture of the girl. With surprise Gérard saw that it was in the modern style – the body of Denise was distorted and her skin colour was depicted as pale green. The guitar, oddly misshapen, appeared in dark blue.

'Very good,' Gérard said, 'you really can do it when you try, Monique.'

'I find it excessively boring, but it is in a good cause.'

'What cause?'

'The furtherance of your education in art, of course. Denise, it is time for a rest. Join us for coffee.'

Monique's studio was one large room of her apartment. The side nearest the window was where she worked and the other side, in contrast, was furnished for her comfort when she gave herself and her model a break. A sofa and a pair of chairs were grouped round a small table on which a spirit lamp kept a large pot of coffee permanently hot.

Monique sat on the sofa and poured coffee. The girl, wrapped in a thin and almost shabby pink kimono which

81

was part of Monique's clutter of equipment, seated herself next to her. Gérard took one of the chairs and smiled at the young girl.

'Do you pose often for Madame Chabrol?' he asked.

'Yes, sometimes,' she said, almost shyly, glancing towards Monique for support.

'What is the picture you are working on to be called?' Gérard asked.

'If it were a sensible study,' said Monique, 'it would have a sensible title such as *Young girl with guitar*. But in this modern style it must have a title as absurd as the picture itself. Do you have any suggestions?'

'I will put my mind to the problem before I leave. It is a truism, of course, that the shape of a guitar echoes, in its double curves, the shape of a woman's body. But you have chosen so young a model that the truism does not apply. I wonder what was in your mind?'

'Perhaps you will find out. More coffee?'

'Thank you, no. Do you play the guitar, Denise?'

'No, it is only for the picture.'

'I shall teach you how to play,' said Monique, her dark eyes lighting up.

'Oh Madame – will you really?'

'Certainly. You shall have your first lesson now while Monsieur Gérard is here. He may be able to assist.'

'But it has no strings,' Gérard objected.

'No matter. There is much theory to be taught before we reach the practical part.'

What strange fancy had entered Monique's head? her cousin wondered. He had good reason to know that her imagination was both fertile and vivid.

'The first thing you must understand, Denise,' she said, 'is the importance of delicacy of touch. To obtain the best results you must treat the instrument as the living creature it is and handle it with love and respect.'

'Yes, Madame,' the girl said dutifully.

'There is only one certain way in which to impress this upon you. I shall demonstrate it, using you as my guitar.'

'But how can you do that, Madame?'

'You will see. Lie across my lap on your back,' and Monique spread her legs under her loose skirt to provide a broad base for the girl.

'Like this?' Denise asked, taking up the position suggested, the pink kimono held tightly around her.'

'Exactly. Now, I support your head with my left hand, as I would hold the neck of the guitar. Do you follow me so far?'

'Yes, Madame.'

'Good. Put your arms straight down by your sides – guitars do not have arms. That's it.'

Gérard watched in fascination as Monique parted the untied kimono to reveal Denise's flat little belly and over-prominent hip-bones.

'With my other hand I play across the strings,' said Monique, trailing her finger-tips across the girl's belly. 'Do you feel how very delicately I play?'

'Oh, yes!'

'Later on, as the music progresses, my touch will become firmer and eventually, at the very end of the piece, we shall reach a crescendo. But for now the fingering is extremely gentle.'

Her hand was sweeping lightly across the tops of the girl's thighs in a butterfly caress.

'Musicians call this mode of playing *pianissimo*,' she continued, smiling at Gérard over the exposed body of the girl in a manner that could only be described as conspiratorial, 'is that not so, Gérard?'

'I believe that is so,' he replied, keeping his voice calm even though his male part was at full stretch inside his clothes.

'It is an Italian word which means *very, very softly*,' said Monique, 'you must remember that, Denise.'

Her fingers had strayed to the small mound between the girl's legs and were stroking the tender lips under their thin covering of light-brown fluff.

'Oh, Madame,' Denise gasped, 'what is this music called?'

'It is a piece by a modern French composer,' Monique

answered with a faintly malicious smile, 'its title is *Pavane for a dead Princess*.'

'Maurice Ravel,' said Gérard, his mind still functioning in spite of the strong emotions aroused in him by the scene he was witnessing, for Monique was stroking lightly upwards along the soft lips of Denise's small inlet, to part them.

'She must have been beautiful, this princess, to have such music,' Denise murmured, her thin thighs trembling.

'The music becomes a little stronger now,' said Monique, her finger-tips fluttering within the girl, 'do you feel the change?'

'Yes! Oh, Madame!'

What emotions were coursing through Gérard at that moment as he observed the proceedings in growing discomfort of body and agitation of mind! Denise was three or four years too young and undeveloped to be sexually attactive to him, but to see her used in this way by Monique as an object of sexuality was unbelievably arousing in its perversity. Especially now that Monique's strumming of her living instrument was eliciting moans of pleasure like chords of music! Denise was squirming on her player's lap, her thin legs shaking wildly, the pink slit between her thighs open and wet – and Monique was staring defiantly at Gérard, daring him to relieve his passion by forcing his way into that tender aperture.

'No!' he gasped, his face flushed red with emotion, 'she is too young.'

'So much the worse for you,' said Monique, 'you must endure your suffering then until I am prepared to assist you.'

Denise squealed in rapture and collapsed limply across Monique's lap.

'Good,' said Monique, 'you have learned your first lesson well, Denise. Sit on the sofa now and rest for a little while.'

The expression in her eyes as she stared at Gérard was unfathomable.

'A few days ago I gave you a lesson in art-appreciation,'

she said, 'today I am giving music lessons, it seems, and it is time to move on from the beginners to the more advanced players. Are you as much interested in music as in painting and literature, Gérard?'

'My interest is intense,' he assured her and she chuckled.

'I have no doubt of that,' she commented and rose from her place on the sofa to seat herself cross-legged between his widely-parted feet on the rug.

'A guitar lesson?' she suggested, reaching for his trouser buttons, 'I think not.'

'My own strong preference is for a duet,' he said as she brought his hard-straining part into the light of day.

'That may be, but I am the teacher here and it is for you to obey me unless you wish to discontinue the lesson. How proudly it stands, Gérard! Tell me what has put you in this condition – surely not the sight of the girl's body?'

'Not her but what you did to her,' he answered, watching her fingers glide lightly up and down his pride.

'Naturally. Perhaps if we become very close friends I may allow you to observe me do it to myself. Would that interest you?'

'Dear Monique – what is of supreme interest to me at present is to make love to you, as we did the other evening.

'Is that so? But have you never strayed from the beaten path to explore any of the amusing byways of love? You boasted to me not so very long ago that you had dared many extraordinary feats.'

'I must confess that they were all adventures along what you are pleased to call the beaten path,' he murmured as she continued to manipulate him most pleasantly.

'How strange – and you a devoted follower of the bizarre imaginings of the surrealists! You seemed to me to be very comfortable in the nineteenth century setting of Manet's picnic, which is surprising, in view of your artistic beliefs. Admit it, at heart you are a traditionalist.'

'But that is entirely another matter,' he objected, 'you are confusing art with the pleasure of love.'

'You find them easy to separate and distinguish, then?'

With her free hand Monique plucked at the bow holding the draw-string of her peasant blouse, then pulled the blouse itself right off her shoulders and down below her full and dark-nippled breasts.

'Ah,' Gérard exclaimed in appreciation, but she was just too far away for him to touch them.

Monique turned her head to speak to the girl curled up on the sofa watching the proceedings.

'Denise, bring me the guitar.'

Obediently Denise fetched it from the other side of the studio and stood by the side of Monique. She had not bothered to tie the belt of her borrowed pink kimono and the delicious little mound between her thighs was clearly visible to Gérard. For her part, Denise stared unashamedly at his upright and twitching device in Monique's hand.

'This is your second lesson, Denise,' said Monique, 'watch closely and you will learn the action of a man's musical instrument.'

'Yes, Madame,' the girl answered.

Monique's fingers played crescendo until Gérard's body started to tremble in incipient deliverance. At once she seized the stringless old Spanish guitar from Denise and pushed it between his thighs so that his leaping part entered the round hole in the instrument's belly, into which he poured his sudden passionate outburst.

'You understand now the purpose of the male instrument?' Monique enquired of Denise.

Gérard stared down in amazement at the guitar between his legs – this fragile wooden instrument which had received his offering.

'What is the name of the music this time?' Denise asked with a knowing smile.

'It is another very modern piece – by Schoenberg, I think, though I am not an expert in these matters,' Monique answered with a broad smile, 'it is called *Sonata for flute and guitar*.'

DR FAGUET AMUSES HIMSELF

According to Jean-Albert Faguet it was during his service as a surgeon in an Army hospital during the War that he made a great decision about his future. On his return to Paris he put this decision into effect and became a happy and fulfilled man – in addition to being a fairly wealthy one. Not all of his friends believed this story, partly because he told it in a frivolous manner and partly because he was a frivolous person. Or if not entirely frivolous, he was at least a constant pleasure-seeker and his most important interests were known to be women and the theatre.

These interests he succeeded in combining very cleverly with his profession by specialising in the intimate problems of women and making himself well-known to female members of the theatrical world. In less than ten years from the end of the War he was recognised as an outstanding and sympathetic practitioner. His patients were not merely the wives of well-to-do men but, by deliberate choice on his part, a great many actresses, singers, dancers and show-girls. Some of these entertainers were considerably better-off than their salaries suggested and some of them only pretended to be so. Nevertheless, they were all content to pay Jean-Albert's higher than average fees, such was the confidence he inspired.

It is not hard to discern the reasons for this. The greatest asset of any young woman, it goes without saying, is her appearance. If a kindly Providence – and her parents – have endowed her with a beautiful face and an elegant body, then the gift is one of inestimable worth in a world where men, to an unneccessary extent, are in possession of wealth and influence. Why this unequal state of affairs exists, and whether it should continue to exist in the twentieth century, is a question for philosophers and theologians to answer, but as a fact it is undeniable.

Clever women may deplore it and argue against it, but until the world changes, beautiful young women have an obvious advantage over their plain sisters.

That there are successful actresses of no great beauty is true enough, as anyone who has observed Madeleine Lambert or Edmée Favart on the stage will acknowledge. Even so, the vast majority of young women seeking an independent career as entertainers are provocatively pretty.

To any woman, the most important part of her body – the part to which men are drawn as a compass needle is to the North – is the intimate area between her thighs. All the rest – hair, face, bosom, legs – are signposts, as it were, to steer men, or at least one chosen man, in the direction of the eventual goal. Needless to say, the importance of this area to a stage entertainer cannot be stated too highly, for it is an essential part of her success, if she is to achieve any success in her career.

To cast no aspersions on the many talented women who at present grace the stages of the places of entertainment and drama, one may take as example a name from the classical French theatre of a century ago – the illustrious Rachel herself! As all the world knows, she found her way onto the boards of the Théâtre Français before she was twenty years old only because she had attracted the interest and aroused the passions of Louis Véron, a man more than twice her own age. From him she progressed to the even older and very much richer Baron Hartmann. While it may be said that Véron admired Rachel's acting talents equally with her slender body, the interests of the Baron lay entirely in the secret shrine of passion between her legs and, for the sake of that, he backed her acting career with his money.

Jean-Albert Faguet, doctor of medicine and specialist in the intimate problems of women, numbered among his patients a great many of the pretty young women who may be seen on stage at the Casino de Paris, the Folies Bergère – and even such establishments as the Théâtre Daunou and the Théâtre de la Madeleine, where the performers keep all their clothes on and declaim lines of dialogue written by a dramatist!

Nothing has changed in a hundred years, except perhaps that France has become a Republic instead of an Empire. And from the example of Madame Rachel it may readily be understood that the most intimate parts of actresses and entertainers require constant supervision. The young women who consulted Jean-Albert made very frequent use of their most precious asset in the furtherance of their careers and, at times, a little carelessness could produce unfortunate results. Jean-Albert was known to be highly expert in correcting such undesirable errors.

A favourite patient was the well-known entertainer Mademoiselle Renée Lelouche, at that time enjoying her most successful season ever at the Casino de Paris, where her sultry Mediterranean charm and her appealingly husky voice had won instant acclaim. She paid little heed to the dictates of high fashion – her raven-black hair was full and long, she made no attempt to disguise the fullness of her breasts – indeed, on stage she revealed quite three-quarters of their rotund charm by the extensive décolletage of the gowns she wore.

Apart from her beauty, which all the world admired, what Jean-Albert found particularly entrancing about her was her secret tattoo – a most inappropriate decoration for a woman! On the inside of her shapely left thigh, high up where the public never saw it, there was tattooed in red and blue against her creamy skin a butterfly with exquisitely spread wings! The first time he saw it, when Mademoiselle Renée bared herself for his examination, Jean-Albert was astounded and entranced. When he knew her well enough to enquire about it, she explained with her famous throaty chuckle – for by then she trusted him completely – that her career as an entertainer had commenced not upon the stage but in an establishment of a certain type in Marseilles, she being fifteen years of age when she made her debut. The majority of the establishment's clients were sailors, and since tattooing is popular among men of that calling, she had swiftly come to accept it as a normal form of personal decoration. It seemed to her the most natural thing in the world to visit the tattoo artist who had his studio next door one day after she had enjoyed a bottle or two of wine.

'It is beautifully done,' said Jean-Albert. 'The man was a true artist. How much did you have to pay?'

'Don't be a fool,' Renée said, 'I didn't pay money for it.'

'Of course. But tell me, now that your lovers are no longer sailors but men of wealth and style, how do they respond when they catch their first glimpse of this delicate little fantasy on your thigh?'

'The same way you did – it fascinates them. Men are all the same, even you.'

During this conversation she was lying on Jean-Albert's examination couch without her frock and shoes, wearing only silk stockings and a thin slip of hyacinth-blue – and that pulled up round her waist to expose for his attention the dark-haired little mound on which her career had been founded.

'There is much in what you say,' Jean-Albert admitted, his sensitive fingers slowly caressing the little butterfly.

'It's the plain truth,' she asserted, 'I've known them all, from sailors to Cabinet ministers, and there's only one thing on a man's mind most of the time.'

'You exaggerate a little,' Jean-Albert protested with a smile.

'Is that so? Well then, tell me what you're doing at the moment – examining me or feeling me?'

Jean-Albert smiled more broadly and brought his mind back to his work.

'Examining you, of course. I was checking to see how the tattooing process had changed the texture of the skin, that's all.'

'Really? Listen, doctor, I don't mind if you do both. That way I won't have to pay you any money.'

'I appreciate your generous offer – believe me I do – but I have an inflexible rule which prevents me from accepting the favours of my patients in return for my professional services. Even, alas, a patient as alluring as you.'

'What a pity,' Renée said with regret. 'But surely you allow a discount for cash?'

'For you, naturally.'

'Good – to work then, dear doctor,' she said, satisfied that she had obtained at least some financial benefit from him.

Jean-Albert examined her tender shrine with loving care and was able to reassure her that her fears of pregnancy were unfounded and that he could prescribe for her irregularities. He wondered briefly, while his fingers were within that cherished entrance, which minister of the Government was indulging his delight with Mademoiselle Renée – and what it was costing him, in money or in favours, or both.

A patient of a different sort was Madame Marie-Paule Boyer, a talented actress of about thirty, who had aspired to the heights of playing in real drama at such theatres as the Boulevard Repertory and the Châtelet. Not for her the sequins and daring costumes of Renée Lelouche; Marie-Paule's appeal to her audience was not based on the allure of her body. Nevertheless, she had looked after that body well and had been married and divorced twice in ten years, on both occasions to actors.

Jean-Albert found it pleasing to examine her – from a strictly medical standpoint, of course. He adored her extravagant personality, though he was secretly wary of her high opinion of herself as an actress. He did not find in her the frankness which delighted him in Mademoiselle Renée, for instance. The truth was that Marie-Paule had convinced herself that her skills on the stage were the sole reason for her success. She had conveniently forgotten that the role which had launched her career before she was twenty had been offered to her by a theatrical producer whose interest had been aroused by the charm of her lustrous brown eyes and her neatly rounded bottom. This particular man was notorious, even in theatrical circles, for his rate of consumption of aspiring young actresses, yet Marie-Paule had been able to retain his interest for several months and had emerged at last from his embraces as a rising stage star.

Her clothes were always high fashion – she had arrived on one occasion in a frock of moss-green with thirty-five buttons down the back, from the collar to a point between the cheeks of her bottom – that foundation of her success! Jean-Albert employed no female attendant to be present during his examinations and this, though unethical, was part of the reason why he inspired confidence in his patients – for there was no second pair of ears present to listen to potentially embarrassing secrets. He assisted Marie-Paule out of her frock with the ease of long practice, discovering in the process that only the top twelve buttons could be opened and the rest were decoration.

'Why have you come to see me?' he asked when she was stretched out before him, her ivory silk and lace cami-knickers unfastened from between her legs and pulled up round her waist, 'some particular reason – or merely a routine check?'

Marie-Paule kept herself in trim. Her breasts had the firmness that daily applications of cold water produced, her belly was flat enough to be chic and just round enough to be desirable. The little fur coat between her legs was rich brown in colour and neatly trimmed.

'I propose to marry again,' she announced grandly, 'perhaps you have heard?'

'No, I assure you. I have seen nothing in the newspapers yet. But my congratulations! Who is the man to be honoured so greatly?'

'Then it is still a secret! There are certain difficulties, you understand. His process of divorce is not yet final – I cannot name him for that reason.'

'I understand. He is someone of importance.'

'Naturally,' Marie-Paule said, amazed that so obvious a statement was necessary.

Jean-Albert made a mental note to ask his many friends in the theatrical world who Marie-Paule had been sleeping with recently. Someone would know – there were no secrets at all behind the scenes.

'Then if you will raise your pretty legs, I will check that all is well for the delights of married life,' he said. 'Good – but wider apart, if you please. I am sure you are familiar with the position.'

'I doubt if that remark is in good taste,' Marie-Paule said, but she smiled as she complied with his request. 'Let me take you into my confidence a little. My fiancé has no connection with the theatre. I wish to give him children – is there any reason why I should not?'

'None that I know of. Has he children by his first wife?'

'No, it seems that she is infertile.'

'That is very sad,' said Jean-Albert, palpating her smooth belly thoughtfully.

'And I – am I infertile?' she asked.

'As to that, there is only one way to find out,' said Jean-Albert, 'and you need no intruction from me in that, I am sure.'

She chose to ignore his remark and asked if he had seen her in her latest role at the Théâtre Antoine.

'I was there for your first night,' he replied, 'you were superb!'

She took praise as her natural right and Jean-Albert knew that he could keep her soothed with flattery for as long as he chose.

'The clothes you wore were enchanting,' he continued, 'most particularly the tango frock in the last Act.'

'I selected that myself,' she informed him. 'The director wanted me to wear something absolutely unsuitable – I put my foot down very firmly, I can assure you. I simply refused to wear it.'

'Naturally,' said Jean-Albert, folding back the petals of her secret rose with tender care, 'he must have been a fool to argue with you.'

'Ah, you understand me so well,' she said approvingly.

Another of Jean-Albert's patients with somewhat elevated pretensions was Mademoiselle Blanche Pasigny, a tall and slender woman who pretended to be twenty-eight

93

but who was five years older. She appeared with reasonable frequency on the stages of the better-known theatres, as did Madame Boyer, though in less important roles. Her face and nose were a trifle longer than was generally thought beautiful but she was undeniably charming, if at the same time a little eccentric.

Whenever she found occasion to visit Jean-Albert, she invariably stripped herself completely naked except for her stockings and shoes. Jean-Albert had no objections, though it was by no means necessary. Mademoiselle Blanche had a secret which she revealed only to her lovers and to her doctor. A secret which Jean-Albert respected – and more than that, which he cherished. When she disrobed her secret was revealed – the pink tips of her pretty breasts had been pierced and thin gold rings inserted! Gold loops as wide across as the first joint of Jean-Albert's thumb, for he used that as a unit of measurement.

'Was it a doctor who did that for you?' he asked, the first time he was privileged to see this truly astonishing mode of adornment.

'Naturally,' said Blanche, glancing down at her ornaments.

She was standing in only her silk stockings by the side of his couch and the movement of her body caused the gold loops to sway.

'But – if I may ask – why?'

'You don't like them?'

'As for that, I find them enchanting. But the idea is an unusual one, even among people of the theatre.'

'Have you never seen a woman with gold rings in her breasts before?'

'Never, I must confess. I have a patient who is of the Indian nobility and she has a diamond set in one side of her nose – it would seem that her husband the Rajah likes it. But jewellery for the breasts!'

'Then you know something now you didn't before.'

'I am grateful to you for that. But do they not cause you discomfort?'

'Not the least. Naturally, it was painful when they were pierced, but that wore off in a few days.'

'But – how shall I put it to make myself clear – when you are with a lover and become aroused, so that those little buds become firm – is there no discomfort then?'

'The sensation is very pleasant – not precisely pain, not even discomfort, but a certain tingling which makes me even more aroused.'

'You surprise me.'

'I see that you do not believe me,' said Blanche amiably, 'then see for yourself.'

She took his hand and put his palm against her left breast – a delicious handful of smooth-skinned flesh. Jean-Albert instantly forgot his medical ethics without the least qualm as he took up her offer to see for himself. He used both hands to delight his senses by the feel of her pliant breasts until, before long, her rose-bud tips were pointing proudly outwards and the gold rings hung clear of her skin.

'Evidently there is no discomfort,' said Jean-Albert in delight.

'On the contrary, I assure you,' Blanche replied, her dark eyes half-closed.

He continued his gentle massage, the reason for her presence forgotten.

'Now what am I to do,' Blanche sighed, 'once I am aroused like this the rings make it impossible for me to stop. I was a fool to let you touch me there. An application of cold water is the only way to calm them down.'

'There is another way,' said Jean-Albert, who had thoroughly aroused himself by caressing her oddly-adorned breasts.

'What do you mean?' she asked with a touch of slyness.

'Cold water on such enchanting breasts is cruel – a denial of their natural rights and a frustration of their ordained pleasure. The better and kinder way is to continue with what we have commenced, you and I, to the culmination of the desire which fills us both.'

'But you – a doctor – can suggest this to me?' she

sighed, moving her body so that her breasts rubbed against his hands.

'Chérie – I am a man and you are a beautiful woman. What more is there to be said?'

'I always believed that the medical profession were able to preserve a distance between themselves and their women patients,' said Blanche, her finger-tips stroking Jean-Albert's face.

'Do not be deceived – being a doctor is how I make my living, not how I live my life.'

'I cannot resist you,' she sighed and draped her naked body across his examination couch, her legs widely parted.

Jean-Albert stood beside her, his hands roaming freely over her body from her slender neck to her dimpled knees, his emotions aflame. The smoothness of her belly and the satin skin of her thighs caused his senses to whirl and it was the hand of a lover, not that of a doctor, which touched her dark-fleeced mount of Venus. He perceived that she had told him no more than the truth about the effect of the gold rings – the entrance to her tender alcove was open and ready to receive him. He shed his jacket quickly and lowered himself onto her as she lay on the narrow examination couch, his virile part at full stretch. He tugged at his trouser buttons and felt them give – then without any guidance from his hand or assistance from Blanche his trembling stem of flesh found its way to the portal it sought and, with one easy push, he lodged it fully in her moist warmth.

'That's so good,' Blanche murmured. 'Ah, chéri, if you knew how good that feels!'

This was not, by any means, the first time that Jean-Albert had made love to a patient on his couch. Some of the younger women who came to consult him were so disarmingly enticing that he was unable to prevent himself from bringing into play all his considerable charm to persuade them to share this great pleasure with him. Usually this happened with show-girls, whose youthful grace of face and form was, it must be confessed, their only talent for the stage. The process of persuasion was rarely difficult, as these young women generally had the same casual attitude towards love-making as Jean-Albert himself. Besides, from their point of view it made good sense to cultivate his friendship – after all, who could tell what misfortune might arise to threaten a budding career – and who better than Jean-Albert to deal with such annoyances expertly and in confidence?

When a woman proved to be exceptionally pleasing on the couch, Jean-Albert continued the liaison in more regular surroundings – suppers in good restaurants after their performance, dancing at interesting and fashionable night-clubs, scenes of delicate passion in his apartment. These intimate liaisons never lasted more than a few weeks, neither party being deeply involved, but they afforded pleasure and entertainment of a high level at the time and frequently led to lasting friendships of a semi-platonic type.

In due course many of these beautiful showgirls formed more permanent relationships with men of wealth and status after a year or two on the boards. Occasionally one even managed to marry well, usually to a rich foreigner – South American millionaires were popular for this purpose. Jean-Albert experienced feelings of pride – an almost proprietorial pride – in these circumstances. When the beautiful Madame Santa Cruz came to consult him, for example – he had first made her acquaintance as Mademoiselle Josette Leduc, an elegant twenty-year-old dancer at the Folies Bergère. He and she had been lovers for a whole month, a time he recalled with extreme delight. She had succeeded in marrying one of her stage-door admirers, an amazingly rich though not parti-cularly intelligent foreign land-owner. Naturally he pre-ferred the civilised life of Paris to the simplicity of his ancestral hacienda and peasants.

That all of Jean-Albert's tender encounters were enjoy-able, it goes without saying, though some were perhaps less so than others. A few of his non-theatrical patients, women who had passed their fortieth birthday – passed, not celebrated – a few of these pressed their favours upon him as soon as they had bared their intimate parts for his professional inspection. He was, it has to be said, a man of distinguished appearance and wide-spread reputation. It may be that the husbands or lovers of these unhappy ladies were remiss in their attentions. Whatever the reason, the touch of Jean-Albert's hands on their inner thighs, as he prepared to examine their secret shrine, brought long sighs of tremulous anticipation and murmured invitations to set aside the Hippocratic conventions for the time being, to make at that warm shrine the offering which the promptings of passion readily suggest.

These were women of elegance and influence. Age notwithstanding, Jean-Albert obliged them cheerfully. To make love was to make love. A simple closing of the eyes took away the need to contemplate little lines about the eyes or mouth, incipient wrinkles on the neck or thinning hair. To his burrowing part the sensation was the same, whether the receptacle which contained it snugly was twenty years old or forty-five years old. The pleasure was the same and, since ladies like this never queried the specially high fees he charged them, it could with truth be said that to make money in this way was better than working for a living.

The moment that Jean-Albert had inserted himself fully into Blanche Pasigny's delicious little pocket, he knew that she was worth cultivating further. Her legs were crossed over his back and her dark-brown eyes were half-closed as he slid in and out at a measured pace. Her soft breasts were flattened under his chest and he could feel, even through his shirt, the pressure of the gold rings against him. How would it feel if he were naked, like her, he wondered – would they be cold on his skin at first or did her own body heat affect them? How strange a fancy for a pretty woman to have her nipples pierced with loops as if they were her little ear-lobes! He must find out why she had done it.

Such speculations were no more than fleeting and exciting images in his mind, suffused as it was at that time

98

with sensuous pleasure – nothing more than tiny irridescent bubbles in a mounting wave of passion. He thrust more urgently at Blanche, feeling her grow hotter beneath him as she sighed continuously and dug her fingers into the tight cheeks of his bottom. The tidal wave of emotion reared itself up to a vast height, hung trembling for the interval between two heart-beats, then broke and crashed over in a fury of white spray.

'Yes!' Blanche shrieked as her back arched off the couch.

'Yes!' Jean-Albert gasped as he delivered his ecstatic tribute.

That night he took her to supper and dancing at the Acacias and afterwards, in the comfort and privacy of his own bedroom, made some interesting discoveries about her gold loops. Blanche had a way of trailing then down a man's bare belly that was remarkably exciting. When he had suitably rewarded her for that by sending her into squirming ecstasy, she reawakened his passion by dangling her pretty breasts over his limp part and shaking them in such a way that the gold loops beat gently against it and roused it from its lethargy to such effect that his essence gushed tumultuously over her breasts and made her laugh. Thus was initiated a friendship which endured for a very long time, even after they both had moved on to other lovers.

In the natural order of things – for who can ever say with complete sincerity that life has given everything the heart desires – not every desirable young woman who sought Jean-Albert's professional advice was susceptible to his virile charm, however much he might desire her. There was Mademoiselle Christiane Cartier, for example – oh the names theatrical people give themselves! There is a quality of hallucination about the theatre that transforms a girl born in a back-street and baptised plain Jeanne or Marie by her parents into a creature of glamour and excitement with a name to match! Mademoiselle Christiane was in her third season at the Folies Bergère, though, it must be admitted, only in the chorus line as yet.

She was a tall, exquisitely formed creature, still only nineteen. Her hair was by nature a very light brown and she had improved upon this by becoming blonde. In order to maintain this pleasing illusion, the neat little fur coat between her legs was bleached to the same shade. Stretched out for examination, her long dancer's legs up and apart, she was one of the most desirable sights Jean-Albert had ever enjoyed in his years of viewing beautiful women. He never failed to express his admiration, in words of total honesty, for he thought this no more than her rightful due.

But, even as he spread her blonde-flossed and delicate pink petals to commence his internal inspection, he knew with great sadness that only his fingers would ever enter Christiane's endearing little pouch of love. No man had ever been privileged to worship there. The truth was that Christiane had no liking at all for men in that respect – she sought and found her delight in the arms of other women.

A tragic waste, that was Jean-Albert's secret opinion, but naturally he kept it to himself.

'Who is your friend now?' he enquired casually as he paused to admire for a moment the enchanting pink shade of her interior, 'When I saw you last it was a night-club singer from Lyon.'

Christiane shrugged as prettily as she could, lying on her back.

'She's with someone else now. I cannot tell you the name of my present friend – it would to too indiscreet.'

'Ah, little mysteries,' said Jean-Albert, 'well, at least tell me whether she is a singer or a dancer, then I can have the pleasure of guessing.'

'Neither.'

'An actress, perhaps?'

It is difficult for a woman to refuse anything to a man who has two fingers inside her secret place, even if he is not a lover but a doctor – especially if the fingers were those of Jean-Albert, who behaved like a lover and a doctor at the same time.

'It is a great secret,' said Christiane, 'but I will tell you this – she is the wife of a very important person.'

'Important in the theatre?'

'What else?'

'A director or an impressario?'

'I'm not going to say any more.'

'There is no need. I am pleased for you, Christiane. I can already see you as the star of your own show before long, with a connection like that. But please assure me that she is kind to you, your new friend.'

'She adores me.'

'Naturally. But is she kind to you?'

'Kind and tender. When we are together she covers my body with little kisses, right down to my toes. Before she touches me, she looks at me with pleading eyes for permission. And afterwards, when she has done everything she wants to me, she asks me in a soft little voice whether she has really pleased me. Ah, you cannot imagine how marvellous it is to be with her.'

'That's good to hear. Your last friend treated you roughly – you came here once to seek my assistance for an unpleasant bite-mark on this little blonde treasure of yours.'

'Don't remind me! It was sore for a week. I had to go without underwear.'

'It was an act of cruelty, to bite you so fiercely.'

'Ah, yes,' Christiane murmured, 'but at the time, it was incredibly exciting!'

Jean-Albert laughed at that.

'Put your clothes on,' he said, 'everything is in good order. I do not understand why you came to see me.'

Christiane sat up on the coach and crossed her long legs, her flat belly and slender thighs still on view to him – and her little blonde tuft.

'For advice,' she said, 'I have heard that a woman can become pregnant if she makes love with another woman who has been with her husband. This worried me. Is it really possible?'

101

'I have read this myself in medical journals,' said Jean-Albert, 'but I have never encountered such a case.'

'But surely there are well-known instances of women conceiving without the direct aid of a man – everyone knows that.'

'Then everyone does not include me. It is true that over the years I have examined more than one young woman – usually very young – who has insisted that she has not been with a man, even though she was obviously pregnant.'

'There you are then!'

'But the tearful insistence was really for the benefit of the angry mother who brought her here. Not one of these sad young girls was a virgin, I assure you.'

'Then you are saying that there is no risk?'

'Only the Church knows of examples of virgins becoming pregnant. For the rest of the world, including you, it is necessary for a man to insinuate his penis between your thighs, if not actually inside you.'

'There is no danger of that,' Christiane said firmly.

'Then enjoy yourself with your new friend. Accept her kisses and her . . . whatever else she bestows on you. I shall follow your career with interest. I saw your performance at the Folies only a month ago and thought that you were marvellous. Ah, those beautiful long legs of yours, those slender thighs! You stood out from the other dancers like a rose in a cabbage patch. I fell in love with you all over again and, if you had the least interest in men, I would be at the stage-door waiting to take you out every night.'

Mademoiselle Christiane leaned forward to kiss him on the cheek.

'You pay the nicest compliment,' she said, 'if ever I wanted a male lover, you would be the first.'

Mademoiselle Nadine Vallette, a ballerina of some distinction and public acclaim, was a performer in a more elevated category of art with whom Jean-Albert enjoyed a brief, though memorable liaison. She was a lean and dark-haired woman with enormous lustrous eyes. It must be said that, perfect as was her face, she had hardly any bosom worthy of the name and her hips were as narrow as those of an adolescent boy. In her favour, however, was the indisputable fact that she adored making love and she had beautiful thighs, their sinewy development speaking eloquently of her years of training from childhood on. If that were not enough to endear her to a man, her entire body was so supple that Jean-Albert was able to devise extraordinary ways of making love to her.

Nadine could, for example, stand with her legs apart and bend forward to put her hands flat on the floor – all this without the least inconvenience! In this stance, totally naked, she presented from the rear to a discerning lover the taut cheeks of her bottom and, set between her long and strong legs, a tender fruit about the size of a large peach, ripe for splitting.

Jean-Albert found great interest in approaching her closely from behind when she assumed this posture for him, to steep his stiff appendage in the sweet juice of her fruit and enjoy the pulpy feel of its warm flesh enclosing him. Nadine, steady as a rock, withstood all the amorous pounding which his male part subjected her to – more than that, she found it most gratifying. She took the view that any woman could lie on her back for a lover but only she, Nadine, could offer herself to love's pleasure in this unusual way. From the standpoint of Jean-Albert, she was somewhat less than a real person in this position, for her head was down between her knees and all that she presented to him was the essential channel of love. He accepted that quite cheerfully, Nadine being not entirely his ideal of a woman, for reasons which became more and more obvious during the course of their affaire.

Apart from the the delights of this acrobatic trick of hers, Nadine was very willing to follow all Jean-Albert's suggestions. The truth was that she found interesting the variety he introduced into their encounters, being herself too unimaginative to have until then explored the astonishing possibilities of her own lithe body.

She was also able, Jean-Albert ascertained when they

103

had known each other for some time, to cross her leg
behind her head! On the first occasion she demonstrated
in a state of total nudity, this rare feat to him, Jean-Albert
was astounded – and fascinated – as who would not be?
While she was locked in this bizarre position he picked her
up from the bed and carried her to an armchair, there to
balance her upright on the cushion. The exertion caused a
charming crease across her flat and muscular belly and
below that, she gave the impression of being totally open
to him – as indeed she was! Her great shining eyes stared
at him in urgent invitation as he stood imprinting on his
memory the unique spectacle before him.

'Jean-Albert – do not keep me waiting,' she whispered.

He was already as naked as she was, one tender passage
between them having taken place earlier that evening. He
knelt before her chair almost in reverence, took her high-
arched feet in his hands and penetrated her secret recess
with a skilful push. Nadine put her hands on his shoulders
– she could reach no further round her upright thighs –
and closed her eyes in anticipation. The subtle pressures
on her nervous system brought about by her posture
seemed to accelerate her sensual feelings remarkably –
she shrieked out twice in delicious crisis before Jean-
Albert attained his rapturous release.

The problem with Nadine, from Jean-Albert's point of
view, was not that she had no imagination – he himself
had enough of that for them both, as he demonstrated
during their liaison. It was rather that she was completely
without humour. To another man this might not have
been of the slightest importance when weighed against the
satisfying pleasures her body afforded. But there was an
element of frivolity in Jean-Albert's character that predis-
posed him towards laughter, even in the most serious
moments of love. He alone understood the slightly ridiculous nature of their love-making in the extraordinary
positions Nadine's suppleness permitted. He alone appreciated the comic grotesquerie of it. Poor Nadine was far
too intense to be aware of the piquancy of the ludicrous.
She could not share the joke with him. Inevitably,

104

Jean-Albert began to experience a slight boredom after some weeks, when the novelty of what they could do together wore off.

In consequence he was more than pleased – he was also relieved, the day she confessed to him in her very earnest way that she had met another man and had fallen in love with him. As befitted the occasion, Jean-Albert played the comedy through to its end with all the correct emotions. He told her of his undying devotion to her, of the true joy she had brought into his life, of the memories of her he would treasure until his dying day. He assured her that he would not reproach her, for love strikes like a thunderbolt and no one can say where it will strike next. He said with great nobility that it was her happiness that must come first. Nadine took all this nonsense at face value – she was, after all, without either imagination or humour – and they parted the best of friends.

If, in some impossible tribunal, Jean-Albert had been questioned on solemn oath and required to name the person for whom he had done most in his professional capacity, he would have answered '*Madame Pascal*' – and this without any serious pause for reflection.

Charlotte Pascal had been long retired from the stage when she consulted Jean-Albert. He was recommended to her by friends who knew of his connections with the theatre and his sympathetic handling of the annoying little problems which can complicate matters for entertainers. Fifteen years or more had passed since she last performed in public, but her legend endured and Jean-Albert was honoured when she arrived for her appointment with him. What he knew of her was no more than all the world knew, that she had been born in the Dordogne, the seventh or eighth child of miserably poor parents. At fifteen she had run away from home to seek her fortune – or so her publicity said – and on her own had secured a job in Paris in a cheap cafe-concert. She could sing a little and dance a little in an untrained manner, but above all, her engaging personality, vivacious and impudent, shone out boldly and enchanted all who saw her little performance.

Better offers were not long in presenting themselves. She sang and danced in more impressive establishments for more money, her path ever upwards. Only five years after her first appearance in Paris she enjoyed a season of phenomenal success at the Moulin Rouge! Her fortune was made, even though she was never outstandingly pretty and her talent on the stage was limited. She was of middle height, with light brown hair, and her figure was the ideal of the Belle Époque – full-bosomed, tiny waist and well-rounded hips and bottom. Rich men were soon jostling each other for the privilege of being her companion – and for that she had real talent. From her throngs of admirers she acquired over the years property, money, furs, jewellery – all the trappings of success. Her tours of New York and London were triumphs, from which she returned with millions of francs.

The War changed all that, alas, as it changed so much else. The public which had once delighted in her type of entertainment wanted something modern and different. The directors of the Moulin Rouge, the Casino, the Folies Bergère, gave it to them – pretty young girls with bare bosoms, tall head-dresses of ostrich plumes and a narrow band of glittering rhine-stones to conceal the genuine bijoux between their thighs. Madame Charlotte retired to live on the income of her considerable investments. Unlike some of the stars of those far-off pre-War days – Polaire and Caterina Otero, to name but two – Charlotte had not gambled away her vast earnings from performances on the stage and in bed.

Her loves were also legendary. She had married three or four times – Jean-Albert could not remember precisely – and her lovers had been too numerous to count, even by her. The thought in Jean-Albert's mind as he contemplated with respect the tender parts bared for examination on his couch – the thought was of the formidable legion of important men who had entered this little pleasure-palace and revelled in it. If only it were possible, he thought, to preserve it forever as a monument to the Golden Age of France! He touched it with great reverence, almost as if it were a holy relic in a church.

'I find nothing wrong with you, Madame. Why have you come to consult me?'

There was an expression of dejection on her famous face and dark shadows under her eyes, as if she had not slept properly for some time.

'For the best reason in the world,' she said, 'I can no longer enjoy the pleasures of love.'

According to Jean-Albert's secret calculation she was about fifty. Apart from the air of dejection, she seemed to him to be in good health.

'For how long has this unfortunate condition persisted?' he asked.

'Nearly a week! Tell me candidly – am I too old for it?'

'Of course not. You have twenty years yet of the pleasures of love ahead of you.'

'But I cannot do it anymore, that's the problem, however hard I try.'

Jean-Albert arranged her legs flat on his couch and pulled her skirt down over her thighs – still firm and unblemished, whatever her age. He pulled up a chair to sit beside her and talk.

'Tell me about your usual range of amorous activities, Madame, so that I can form a picture as a preliminary to diagnosis.'

Madame Pascal talked to him very freely, as women always did, and it was with a feeling approaching awe that he came to understand the force of her sexual drive. After parting from her last husband, five or six years ago, the poor man being depleted in body and purse by the continuous demands she made on him, Charlotte had made provision for herself by installing in her home a succession of strong young men – sometimes Spanish, sometimes Italian. Each lasted, as far as Jean-Albert could ascertain, no more than six months at the outside. In turn, each was sent away with the fine clothes and trinkets Charlotte had bought him, and a parting gift of money. The arrangement seemed a most sensible one for a woman in her circumstances and Jean-Albert offered his congratulations on its logical simplicity.

'Since I must know everything in order to determine where the problem lies,' he said, 'Tell me how often you require the services of these young stalwarts.'

'Not as often as when I was in my prime,' she answered sadly. 'It is a melancholy truth that middle-age slows us all down. Even so, the young men of today lack stamina – a few months and they are useless.'

'Your present companion – how long has he been with you?'

'Manuel? A month or so, no more than that.'

'And are his abilities satisfactory to you?'

'In the sense that he is ready at any time to carry out the little duties I require of him, he is satisfactory – so far. But he can no longer satisfy me, whatever he does. Nothing happens, you understand.'

'To you, to him, to both?'

'To me, of course. He is only a good-looking animal. He does it on command.'

'How frequently do you command him to perform this little duty?' said Jean-Albert, coming back to the question she had earlier evaded.

'Since you insist on knowing my personal affairs, no more than three or four times, in general.'

That number of times a week was good for a woman of her age, Jean-Albert considered, for surely her ardour had been cooled somewhat by the years.

'Every week?' he asked.

'What are you saying – week? I am not a decrepit old woman yet. Every day, I mean.'

The revelation explained for Jean-Albert why her young men were dismissed after a few months – they were probably too worn out to carry their own luggage when they departed!

'I see,' he said thoughtfully, 'and until quite recently you were able to enjoy the full delights of love as regularly as that?'

'Of course I was!'

'Some years ago, Madame, when you were twenty-five for example, what then? Much the same?'

'Ah, those marvellous days when my name was on posters all over Paris! My appetite for love was larger then, I assure you.'

'How large?'

'I needed to be loved six or seven times a day, at the very least.'

'Not by any one man, I am sure of that.'

'I never met a man who could satisfy me for more than a day. I always needed several lovers to keep me happy. Because of that I met so many charming men – dukes, bankers, industrialists – and everyone of them insisted on making me the most interesting presents! A house here, an apartment there, a small chateau in the country, a race-horse or two, diamonds enough to fill a bucket – it was an enchanted time for me! But see what I am reduced to now – a useless body that does not respond to a man's touch.'

She wept a little and Jean-Albert patted her hand to soothe her distress.

'Calm yourself, Madame. Did this misfortune occur gradually or suddenly?'

'All at once! It was incredible. Last Thursday Manuel was particularly vigorous – he surpassed himself that day, the dear boy! He transported me to Paradise again and again, then we fell asleep in each other's arms and I remember that I promised him a solid gold cigarette case with his initials on it as a special reward. In the morning . . .'

'One moment,' Jean-Albert interrupted. 'Had you been making love all through the day?'

'Naturally! In the morning before we got up. Then again while I was in my bath. And after lunch when we returned home, and before dinner while I was dressing for the evening. And naturally when we went to bed that night after an hour or two dancing in the *Boeuf sur le Toit*. It was a marvellous day.'

'I see. Please continue.'

'Where was I? Ah yes, the gold cigarette case. I fell asleep with that thought in my mind. I was so happy. Then in the morning, after my maid had brought in the coffee, I turned to Manuel and he loved me with passion, as he always does. But I – I lay there absolutely numb, feeling nothing at all! Imagine my horror!'

Jean-Albert nodded sympathetically.

'What then, Madame?'

'I was terribly upset – I cried for an hour! Then I pulled myself together and told myself that it meant nothing, that it was a small reaction from a surfeit of love the day before. I kept away from Manuel all through the day – I think that was the hardest thing I've ever done in my life – and at ten that evening I took him to bed, certain that all was well again.'

'And was it?'

'No – it was exactly the same as in the morning. Nothing!'

'Since then you have tried again, of course?'

'Naturally – three or four times every day, hoping desperately that the ability to enjoy the sensations of love would be restored to me. But my body remains numb and unfeeling.'

'Yet you still feel the urge to try?'

'More than ever before! You must understand that this rapture of the senses has been the most important thing in my life since I was sixteen. To be deprived of it so cruelly after all these years is more than I can bear! For the past five days I have hardly slept more than an hour or so at a time and I cannot eat at all from nervous anxiety. I am totally exhausted and I cannot go on. If you cannot cure me, I shall kill myself.'

'There is no need for that,' said Jean-Albert firmly, 'I am certain that a cure can be effected if you will place yourself in my hands.'

'You have my complete confidence! Cure me and you may charge any fee you like.'

'As to that, we shall see,' said Jean-Albert. 'First we must make you well, then we can discuss fees. But understand me, Madame, when I said that you must place yourself in my hands, I mean without reservation. The treatment, you see, will be unpleasant.'

'Not a surgical operation!' Charlotte exclaimed in horror.

'Nothing so drastic, I promise you. But once started, you must go through with the treatment, even if you are tempted to abandon it halfway. And to that end I shall require you to sign certain legal documents giving me permission to proceed with such treatment as I think best, with no possibility of action by you in the courts.'

'Good God,' she whispered, 'Your words terrify me.'

'Let me assure you that in all that happens I shall have your best interests at heart,' said Jean-Albert with his most engaging smile.

'Can you guarantee a total recovery?'

'What doctor can give a guarantee in so serious a case? But I will say this, Madame, I have every confidence that your powers of love can be restored.'

'Tell me about the treatment, so that I can gather the courage to stand it.'

Jean-Albert shook his head gravely.

'You have my word that it will not be painful,' he said, 'apart from that I can say nothing.'

'How long will it take – at least tell me that much,' she pleaded.

'A week, perhaps, no more.'

'I will bear anything that will restore me to normal,' she said with determination, 'when can we begin?'

The following day Jean-Albert escorted her to an establishment owned by a medical colleague of his, where special arrangements had been made for her reception. It may be thought ironic that the place in question was a residential clinic where well-to-do families concealed young daughters who had the misfortune to become pregnant without the benefit of marriage. That was not Charlotte Pascal's problem, to be sure, but the clinic was discreet, secluded, well-managed – and in so distant a

111

suburb that no person of style would regard it as being a part of Paris at all.

Madame Pascal was installed there in a small but charming room, well away from the young ladies awaiting their big event. She was put to bed with a sleeping-draught prescribed by Jean-Albert that kept her soundly asleep for the next twelve hours. She awoke to find herself in the care of a woman of thirty who wore a plain grey frock and was burly enough to be a Grenadier! This woman, Ernestine, supervised her regime – which consisted of nourishing food, two glasses of wine a day and plenty of sleep, either natural or induced.

There was nothing seriously wrong with Madame Pascal, Jean-Albert knew, only a nervous exhaustion brought on by years of excessive indulgence in the pleasures of the bedroom, too many late nights, too much champagne – and all this made worse by her own natural anxiety and insomnia when her body failed the first time to respond to the touch of a lover. In the clinic she had no choice but to rest, eat properly and remain chaste. Ernestine was with her throughout the entire day, seemingly a companion and maid but in truth a jailer. At night, to her chagrin, Charlotte's body was enclosed in a thick quilted bag that fastened above her breasts and her hands were enclosed in similarly thick gloves, tied at the wrists! This, she realised with some embarrassment, was to prevent any attempt on her part to ascertain whether the power of sensation had returned between her legs!

Jean-Albert visited her twice a day, morning and evening. On each visit he asked her to lie naked on her bed while he took her temperature, checked her pulse, palpated her breasts lightly, opened the tender petals of her sex and probed delicately inside with his fingers. None of this had the least medical significance, of course, but it reassured Charlotte that she was receiving constant expert attention. As the days passed, the feel of his fingers on her breasts and, even more so, between her thighs, became increasingly exciting – and increasingly frustrating!

On the sixth morning, as he started to go through his routine, he asked, as usual, if she had slept well.

'No,' she replied, 'I had such dreams that I kept waking up all the time.'

'What sort of dreams?'

'They were so vivid – yet I can remember only the final one. Isn't that strange?'

'Then tell me that.'

'But it concerns the most intimate matters!'

'So much the better – it may be a sign of recovery. Tell me about it.'

'If you insist. I dreamed that I was on stage at the Moulin Rouge, just like the old days – playing to a packed house. How they clapped and cheered when I made my entrance! There was a man in full evening dress on stage to greet me and introduce me – as if *I* needed any introduction to audiences! But he was tall and very handsome and he took me by the hand and presented me to the applauding audience as if I were an unknown. I found this very strange and puzzling, though I did not become angry, as I would have done in real life.'

'Was this man someone you knew?'

'I thought that I knew him but I couldn't think of his name.'

'What happened then?'

'There was a divan on the stage. He led me to it and I sat down, then he stood behind me so that we were both facing the audience – it was so strange, and yet it was as if we had rehearsed all this together. He put his hands on my shoulders and made me lie down – with my legs up in the air! My frock slipped to my waist and I knew that I had no underwear on! And he, the man who was making me exhibit myself in this way, he announced loudly that here at last the management of the theatre presented, regardless of expense, the sight which all Paris had been waiting to see! Ah, how they clapped and shouted their appreciation – what a triumph!'

'A most interesting dream, Madame,' said Jean-Albert, smiling as he looked down at the naked body of Madame

113

Pascal on the bed. Her breasts had lost the firmness of youth and lay slackly, spreading outwards, but her skin, through continual massage and treatment with lotions, preserved its smooth sheen. Her thighs were good, only a little fleshier now than when in her great days she had clasped many a rich admirer between them. The little tuft of hair that covered her much-loved treasure-box was a rich brown colour, though that might have been aided by a touch of colouring, as on her head. But what of that?

Within her curly fleece Jean-Albert's sensitive fingers encountered the soft lips which had been the object of so much desire – and a certain moistness that informed him that in relating her dream she had become aroused. She sighed very softly, her eyes half-closed, as he felt a little further inside. Beyond all doubt, she was distinctly aroused! That was to be expected – she had been compelled to remain chaste for a longer period than at any time in her life since she attained the age of sixteen.

'Jean-Albert,' she murmured, using his name for the first time, 'I shall die if you don't let me do it!'

His finger-tip was on her firm little bud of passion.

'The course of treatment should last a full week,' he said, 'To cut it short now might undo all that we have achieved. Have you considered that?'

'I don't care!' she exclaimed, 'I'm cured – I know I am. You must not torment me any longer, I implore you!'

Tiny tremors ran across her belly and her thighs were trembling.

'Then you are of the opinion that I should let you return to your home to resume your pleasures with your Spanish friend?' Jean-Albert asked.

'I cannot wait that long! It must be now!'

'Like this?' he asked, his fingers moving in her open furrow.

'You are a man – do it properly!'

Madame Pascal was almost at her last gasp as Jean-Albert positioned himself, fully clothed, between her wide-spread thighs. Her fingers tore at his trousers, pulling off three buttons in her haste. Then she had him by his rigid part and pulled it into her, her loins rising to meet him. A dozen fast strokes – no more – and she shrieked and thumped the bed with her heels and fists in ecstasy. There was no more for Jean-Albert to do but wait for her long and profound transports to end in shudders and sighs.

When at last she was calm again, she looked up into his eyes with an expression of deep gratitude.

'You have cured me,' she said, 'there are no words adequate to thank you.'

'The restoration of your abilities is thanks enough,' he said.

'But you, dear friend – you were not satisfied. How could you be – it was so fast.'

'As to that,' said Jean-Albert, easing himself off her, 'do not disturb yourself on my account. What I did was in my capacity as your doctor, to find out in the only possible way whether the proper sensations had returned.'

'I understand. But it would be ungrateful of me to permit you to depart in a condition of frustration. Take off your clothes and lie here with me and we will do it again.'

Jean-Albert stroked her hand and smiled, trying as best he could to make his trousers cover him decently, even though buttons were missing and his part was upright and prominent. He had no intention of remaining frustrated for long, but Madame Pascal's kind offer was not to his inclination. A scientific experiment was one thing, but to do as she proposed would imply another sort of relationship between them. He had no wish to become one of those hard-worked persons who relieved her emotions on a regular basis.

'Let me give you some advice,' he said to her, in a manner that was equally friendly and professional, 'all is well now – you may leave her as soon as you are ready. They will order a taxi to take you to your home. But – please listen to me carefully – you must regard yourself as cured but convalescent for the next few weeks and not overtax yourself. Otherwise, who can say what might occur?'

'What are you saying?' she asked in evident dismay. 'That I must live like a nun even though I am well again?'

'Not at all. What I want you to do is to reduce the frequency of your lovemaking for the next month or so, that's all.'

'Reduce! Good God – I really am getting old!'

'You're still in your prime, but you must take care of yourself a little. Come and see me in four weeks and tell me how things are with you.'

'But to what must I reduce?' she demanded. 'Tell me!'

'I suggest to not more than twice a day for the present.'

He could hear her moaning softly to herself as he left the room.

Perhaps she would follow his advice – she had been deeply shocked by what had happened to her and would not want to risk a repetition of that sad condition. But Madame Pascal's future behaviour, now that she was fully recovered, had little interest for Jean-Albert at that moment. Despite all his talk of scientific methods, the truth was that it had aroused him to touch her – and had aroused him even more to penetrate her, however briefly. It would have been simple enough to continue from that position of advantage, but his fantasy required another type of realisation just then. Madame Pascal was, after all, an averagely attractive woman of fifty or thereabouts. Jean-Albert's fancy embraced other possibilities.

He had it in mind – bizarre though it may seem – that he would find it prodigiously interesting at that moment to roll about on a bed with Ernestine, the muscular woman attendant who had taken care of Madame for the past few days. Through her grey frock Jean-Albert had discerned breasts as big and round as water-melons – and haunches that would not have disgraced a blacksmith. Her thighs – ah, they must be like the trunks of smooth trees, he thought, columns of marble to support so magnificent an edifice. To revel in Ernestine's mountains of flesh – what incomparable joy! To lay bare that which was concealed between her thighs – unimaginable pleasure! Would it be on the same heroic scale as the rest of her – a fleshy mound as big as a clenched fist, covered by a mat of hair? He wanted very much to find out, and from the glances he had exchanged with her on his daily visits to Madame Pascal, he guessed that this Amazon would deny him nothing.

THE SELF-ESTEEM OF MARCEL CHALON

When a woman changes lovers, it may mean little more to her than changing her stockings – and perhaps for much the same reason. But the shock to the discarded lover's self-esteem may prove to be catastrophic. At first he refuses to believe what she has said, then, when he realises that she is in earnest, he becomes angry. Many crimes of passion have been committed in these moments, no one can be unaware of that, though the average man does not murder his former beloved out of hand but contents himself with shouting at her before he storms out of the door. Anger is a fatiguing emotion and after a time the discarded lover subsides into bitter disappointment. Eventually he recovers and finds another mistress, so that life and love may continue.

Marcel followed the classic route after Yvonne Daladier informed him that their affair of a year was at an end. With him the anger continued for three days, during which time he roamed around the Grand Boulevards, getting drunk in bars, smashing glasses and insulting complete strangers. More than once he was evicted by force, until at last he went home by taxi, dishevelled and bruised, his anger spent and bitter disappointment setting in.

Why had she done this to him? he kept asking himself. He was a good-looking man of twenty-six, he dressed well and was a lively companion. In bed he was more than adequate to make a young woman happy. He had independent means and had maintained her in good style. Their months together had been happy for them both. In short, there was no possible reason for her to have behaved in so disgraceful a manner.

Yet she had abandoned him for someone else! Indeed, she had moved out of the apartment where they had enjoyed many delightful hours together and had taken up residence elsewhere! It was incomprehensible – and it was intolerable!

After he had slept off his drunkenness and changed his clothes, Marcel made his way with a sad and heavy heart to what had been Yvonne's apartment for one last time. What was in his mind, who can say? Perhaps he would die there alone of a broken heart. Perhaps he would get drunk again there in order to forget her. Anything was possible.

He let himself into the deserted apartment with his key and looked around. It was only three days since she had told him of her decision and already half the furniture and pictures were gone. She herself had not been there in all that time, he knew, having made innumerable telephone calls from public bars to vent his rage. The maid had answered once or twice and had told him that Madame was away. Away she certainly was! Away somewhere with her new lover – perhaps in a hotel, perhaps in the country. Not, surely, at Deauville, where at the start of the relationship Marcel had taken her for ten days of interrupted delight together! But, perfidious as she had shown herself to be, he told himself painfully, she might well be at Deauville with her new admirer, leaving the maid to pack up and move her belongings to her next apartment.

He wandered into the bedroom. The bed was still there – that piece of furniture on which they had given each other so much pleasure. A groan of agony escaped Marcel's lips as he stood and looked at it, recalling happier times. The fragrance of Yvonne's perfume still clung faintly, making the scene unbearably poignant.

He pulled open a drawer of the dressing table, expecting to find it empty. To his surprise it was half full of her things – stockings, underwear. Yes, he concluded mournfully, she had taken only a small suitcase of clothes with her – enough for a brief stay in a hotel somewhere until everything had been transferred to wherever she was going.

In a sudden burst of anger, Marcel pulled out every drawer and spilled the contents on to the bed. There was a dazzling profusion of elegant lingerie – little silk chemises

119

and lace-edged knickers in rose-red and dusky-pink, myrtle-green and eau-de-Nil, hyacinth blue and cornflower blue. There were sleek pairs of camiknickers with hand-embroidery at the yoke, inlet with Chantilly lace. There were at least a dozen pairs of silk stockings, of every shade from flesh to dramatic black.

He plunged his hands into the sumptuous array of intimate finery piled high on the bed, his mind ablaze with confused emotions. He had adored her so much – her soft skin and tender thighs, her pouting mouth and little face, her delicious breasts . . . poor Marcel thought he would go insane with these reminders of what had once been between him and Yvonne. Three days without her! Even worse – three nights without her and the pleasures of her body! It was more than he could bear.

He hardly knew what he was doing as he tore off his jacket and threw himself onto the bed, his fingers fumbling with his trousers and underpants until he wrenched up his shirt front and pressed a handful of Yvonne's silk underwear to his hot belly. The thrill of that moment made him gasp aloud. His male part stood stiffly erect, trembling of itself even before he began to caress it with the coloured silks he held.

'Yvonne . . . Yvonne . . . I adore you . . .' he groaned aloud, feeling himself to be within instants of fountaining his desperate passion for her into a fistful of her underwear.

In the madness of longing that had seized him he was deaf and blind to the whole world, unaware that someone else had entered the apartment and, attracted by his moans, was heading towards the bedroom. How could he? He was at that moment of divine folly when the body knows that it is committed to a convulsion of ecstasy that nothing can prevent.

In that very moment Yvonne's maid entered the room and halted, wide-eyed with amazement at the spectacle before her. There lay Marcel on the bed, his trousers round his knees and his shirt round his waist, rubbing a double handful of Madame's underwear against himself!

Marcel stared back, open-mouthed, at the maid in her hat and street-clothes, her hand still on the door-handle. It was a moment of incredible tension for both of them.

Embarrassment, shame, anger – a most complicated mixture of emotions coursed through Marcel's mind at this ill-timed intrusion – but it was beyond human remedy to avert his oncoming crisis. His distended part twitched furiously and discharged into the wad of flimsy underwear that concealed it from the maid's view. He attempted to suppress the spasms that were racking his body, but he was helpless until at last the process was completed.

The maid watched him shake and gasp through his anguished climax, her agile mind at work on the question of how to turn this astonishing event to her own advantage.

'Wait outside, Cécile,' said Marcel when the power of rational speech was restored to him, 'I will explain everything to you in a while. Just go outside. You will not be the loser, I assure you.'

'But Monsieur Marcel,' she answered, advancing into the room, 'there is no need for you to be embarrassed. I can understand your feelings and I am not in the least put out. Besides, it seems to me that at this moment you are in need of some assistance to clean you up.'

Her sympathetic manner soothed Marcel's agitation at being discovered in so unlikely an act. He had got to know Yvonne's maid well enough during his short liaison and had always found her to be an understanding woman. Moreover, he had been accustomed all his life to being waited upon by servants who prepared things for him and tidied up after him. Not that one had ever performed this particular service for him before, but there was a first time for everything.

He lay back easily on Yvonne's bed and closed his eyes while Cécile removed the sodden pad of tangled garments from his belly.

'My,' she said, 'you have given me a lot of extra washing and ironing to do, Monsieur Marcel. You must have been in a terrible state.'

'To think I have been brought to this,' he murmured in self-pity, 'she knows that I love her with all my heart and yet she denies herself to me for the sake of another man. It is too much!'

'Heart-breaking,' Cécile agreed, 'lie still while I fetch a towel.'

She brought a cloth dipped in warm water and a fluffy towel. While she was attending to him she said in a friendly way:

'May I ask you something personal, Monsieur Marcel?'

'Of course. I know that I can trust you, Cécile.'

'It's easy to see why you did what you were doing when I came in just now unexpected. To have Madame's underwear against your skin was the next best thing to having Madame herself, yes?'

'A poor substitute,' he said.

'That's what I wanted to ask you. It produced the right result, but was it any good? I know I came in at the wrong moment and took your mind off things, but suppose I hadn't – what then?'

Her ministrations were not unpleasant. She washed Marcel's deflated part as gently as if she was bathing a baby and patted it dry with the soft towel. Marcel began to appreciate her attentions.

'Your entrance made no difference, Cécile. As soon as those moments of madness were over I would have lain here in an agony of disappointment. To tell you the truth, I might have burst into tears of frustration. You have saved me from that and I am grateful.'

'Oh Monsieur – it is too sad to think about! Don't you feel any better for the relief you gave yourself?'

'Worse, now that it is over. For a few moments those delicate underclothes gave me an illusion of her presence, but at the critical moment, I was alone.'

'Even though I was here?'

'I think that made my loneliness even more unbearable, Cécile. My heart is broken – what more can I say?'

'It is tragic,' she sighed. 'What will you do now?'

'I? There is only one course of action open to me to

calm down my jangled nerves and bring tranquillity to my mind and body.'

'What's that?'

'There are certain establishments men visit – I am sure you have heard of them – where a dozen obliging women are available at a price. I shall go to one of them and stay there, paying woman after woman, until I faint from total exhaustion. Then at last my broken heart will be at peace.'

'You mustn't do any such thing,' Cécile said firmly, 'Have some regard for your health, I beg you.'

'There is no other way.'

'Perhaps there is. I have an idea. If it fails, nothing is lost. If it succeeds, calm will be restored to you.'

'Tell me!'

'Will you trust me, Monsieur Marcel?'

'Implicitly. You have shown yourself to be a person of profound sympathy.'

'Then close your eyes and keep them closed. This is most important, Raise yourself a little so that I can remove the rest of Madame's underwear from under you.'

She gathered the frothy little garments he had strewn on the bed and went to the dressing-table to fetch a perfume spray.

'Are your eyes closed? Now stay still and accept whatever happens.'

She draped an item or two of silk and lace over his face and gave them a quick spray of expensive perfume.

'Ah,' Marcel murmured, 'that fragrance! I could almost believe that she is here with me.'

Cécile said nothing. She stood beside the bed observing the effect on him. His limp part was stirring – that being the art of the perfumer, to arouse a man's feelings. She dangled a black silk stocking so that the toe just brushed over the head of his lengthening and thickening staff. As it grew stronger yet and raised itself from his belly, she trailed the stocking along its whole length.

'Oh my God!' Marcel whispered through the scented garments over his face.

Cécile continued, trailing a dainty chemise over his bare belly to make the lace hem tickle him delicately.

Ah . . . ah . . . ah . . .' he sighed.

She wadded up the black silk stocking and pushed it gently between his thighs so that he would feel the touch of it against his dependents and then flicked at his jutting part with a pair of eau-de-Nil coloured knickers. Only a few moments of this were needed to render Marcel incoherent with pleasure. She wrapped the garment loosely round his trembling part, so that more sensation woud arise from the intermittent contact and so carry Marcel further towards his goal.

That done, she stood back from the bed to remove her hat and outdoor coat – and then her skirt and knickers – very plain and uninspiring when compared to Madame's frilly silks. She was ten years older then Yvonne Daladier, which made her thirty-four. She was not unattractive, in her way, but as a servant she had little time to herself and her pleasures had necessarily been with men of her own class and therefore lacking in finesse. She envied her mistress the succession of handsome and elegant young men to whom she formed attachments.

No one can say, of course, what was uppermost in her thoughts as she got on to the bed to straddle Marcel. The opportunity to try out for herself the joys of one of Madame's lovers – it may have been partly that – in addition to her natural desire for money. Pleasure and greed are two strong motives which frequently march together.

Because he was blindfolded by the underwear draped over his face Marcel saw nothing of her broad bared belly and its thick muff of black hair, nothing of the fleshy lips she drew apart with her fingers. He felt the caress, as soft as a whisper, of the silk draped around his upstanding part gently pulled away, to be replaced by warm flesh that slowly took him into itself.

'Yvonne!' he exclaimed, 'I adore you!'

Cécile was careful not to touch him directly with her hands in case he could distinguish between Yvonne's skin and her own work-hardened skin. She balanced herself above his loins and rode gently up and down, hearing him babble on and on as his excitement grew stronger.

Men are complete idiots, she thought; show them a pair of drawers and they take leave of their senses. What stupidity!

'Yvonne!' Marcel moaned.

'Yes, chéri, yes,' Cécile whispered back, making her voice as much like her mistress's as she could in the circumstances.

She need not have given herself the trouble. Marcel was far beyond the point at which he could distinguish between one woman's voice and another. She continued to ride him slowly and his loins rose by degrees from the bed, pushing deeper, as he hung tremulously on the brink of rapture.

'Oh yes . . . oh yes . . .' he whispered, until his words changed into a long muted wail as he discharged lengthily, deep inside Cécile's convenient receptacle.

Though she was only mildly aroused until then, Cécile gasped and clutched at her own breasts through her blouse as Marcel's warm douche flicked her into a brief climax.

Still riding up and down easily, she waited for his spasms of delight to fade, watching his quivering belly in surprise at how long they were lasting. The men she had known until then were finished in five seconds when their emission began. Marcel continued to shudder and gasp in ecstatic release long after he had emptied himself into her. Now that, she thought, would do wonders for a woman properly prepared in advance to share it with him. Perhaps she had discovered the secret of Madame and her lovers – perhaps it was an intensity of passion prolonged for a long time.

Only when Marcel at last lay still did she climb with care off the bed, to wipe herself before donning her underwear and skirt in silence. An occasional tremor still shook Marcel's body, she noted, as, properly dressed again, she slowly removed the chemise from his face.

His eyes opened slowly to take in his surroundings

before focusing on the friendly face of the maid standing beside the bed.

'Oh, it's you, Cécile,' he said, smiling at her, 'I had a most marvellous dream.'

'Did you, Monsieur Marcel? What was it?'

'She was here with me and we made love. It was incredible! I feel so good – so calm.'

'I'm very pleased to hear that. Do you want to sleep for a while?'

'I believe that I will. You won't go away, will you?'

'No, I have plenty of work to do around the apartment. I shall be here when you wake up. I'll draw the curtains to help you sleep.'

For the next couple of hours Cécile busied herself with hand-washing and ironing the expensive underwear which Marcel had made use of for his first solitary attempt to summon up the remembrance of past pleasures. Her little ruse had proved to be a success beyond her expectations. It had calmed Marcel down and without question that alone had earned her a considerable tip from him when he woke up. In passing, he had given her unawares a brief pleasure which she had not expected – and an insight into the ways of those with more money and leisure than herself. But that apart, she was cheered by the thought that Marcel would without doubt be generous to her and that led her to speculate on the possibility of making more money from him to add to her savings, before the lovelorn young man recovered his wits and found himself another woman – a matter of a week or ten days at the most, in Cécile's estimation. Madame Daladier had never been a generous employer and there was little to be squeezed out of the household budget. Cécile's savings came from tips given to her by Madame's admirers for little services.

She woke Marcel at six in the evening with a glass of tea with a thin slice of lemon in it. While he was sipping at it gratefully she attended to his exposed part, now soft and small, washing and drying it in the most matter-of-fact way.

'Has your sleep refreshed you?' she asked.

'Yes, I am eternally in your debt, Cécile. When you found me here, I wanted to die. Now I am ready to live again. I can never repay you for your kindness.'

'As to that, Monsieur Marcel . . .'

'Of course! If you will be so good as to pass my jacket to me . . . there, I know that mere money can never repay the devotion you have shown me today in my hour of need, but I hope that you will accept this as a small token of my gratitude.'

'You are too kind,' Cécile said politely, tucking the bank-notes quickly down her blouse. 'If only I could do more to help you through this time of anguish.'

'Perhaps there is a way to help me,' he said slowly, 'though I hesitate to impose my misery on you.'

'You have only to mention it.'

'Because of you I enjoyed a dream of such exquisite pleasure that I shall never forget it. I would like to dream that dream again, if you could bring yourself to assist me.'

Between them it was arranged that Cécile should return to the apartment on the next day at three. She left her hat and coat in the entrance hall and went to the bedroom, where the door stood slightly open. Inside, the curtains were drawn to dim the room and Marcel was in bed, his eyes closed as if he were asleep.

'Yvonne – it's you at last,' he whispered, not stirring.

Without a word, Cécile took from her capacious handbag a tiny chemise the colour of Parma violets and spread it gently over his face. She had already sprayed it with Madame's perfume and the familiar fragrance caused Marcel to sigh loudly.

'You are so adorable, Yvonne! To be with you is happiness beyond imagining.'

Cécile had brought the spray with her. She squirted a cloud of fragrance on to the silk to intensify its effect.

'Chérie!' Marcel moaned.

She drew the coverlet and sheet away from him and down to the foot of the bed. He was naked and his projection was at full stretch.

'See how impatiently I have been waiting for you,' he murmured.

Cécile delved into her bag for a pair of silk stockings and trailed them slowly the length of his body, from throat to thighs, then upwards along his strong shaft from base to tip. This caress, many times repeated, brought about a trembling in his limbs and made his upstanding part twitch.

'It is so thrilling when you tease me,' he whispered, 'you will drive me mad with pleasure. Don't stop!'

She continued the treatment until she judged the moment right – Marcel was squirming in delight and muttering little endearments. She wound the stockings loosely around the portion of him that throbbed so urgently, gripped it high up between thumb and forefinger and flicked a few times.

The result was dramatic. Marcel convulsed as if an electric wire had touched him and a torrent into the stockings announced the arrival of the climax of his pleasure. But, Cécile observed, the duration of his passion was much shorter than the day before. Evidently he required something more to bring him to full release.

His words confirmed her deduction.

'Ah, chérie,' he said, 'No one has ever aroused me as you do. I dream incessantly of your beautiful body.'

As before, Cécile bared herself below the waist and took up her position, kneeling above his loins. His firmness had only partially relaxed and a few flicks of her short finger-nails on his nipples soon restored it sufficiently to guide into herself. The warmth of that contact brought back Marcel's vigour in full measure.

It was in Cécile's mind that on this occasion she might benefit equally with Marcel from the union of bodies. She therefore slid up and down very slowly so as to give herself time to respond physically to the feel of what was inserted in her. Marcel trembled and sighed as she worked away steadily – his satisfaction was assured and she could take thought for her own.

She had been told that the positions of love are numerous. She had seen illustrations in a book of engravings that demonstrated the possibilities that existed when a man and a woman had the time and inclination to experiment with such diversions. Nevertheless, the only ones Cécile had experienced herself were two in number – flat on her back or standing against a wall, according to circumstances at the time. To find herself sitting above a man on his back was unfamiliar, of course. She experienced a strange sensation – not of doing it to him instead of him doing it to her, which she would have expected – but almost of doing it to herself! That was of no importance, however, for she was pleasing him and at the same time she was giving herself pleasure.

When the spasms in Marcel's body warned her of the imminent arrival of his spate of passion, she thought that it was too soon for her. This momentary disappointment proved to be false – his prolonged quaking brought her to a turbulent climax. She heard herself squeal in gratification as her eyes bulged and her nipples tried to burst through her blouse.

So that's what Madame enjoys two or three times a day, she thought when the exquisite sensations died away.

The bizarre liaison between Marcel and Cécile continued for three more days. The routine was not changed. He was there naked and in bed by the time she arrived. She covered his closed eyes with perfumed lingerie and teased him with silk stockings on his skin until he discharged for the first time, then prepared herself and mounted him to give him – and herself – a great felicity. After that she became the attentive servant again, properly dressed and polite as she washed and dried his satisfied part. And each time, before she departed, Marcel made her a handsome present of money.

On what proved to be their final meeting in Yvonne's abandoned apartment, matters proceeded differently. The customary sigh of pleasure was absent when she covered his face with a pair of lilac silk camiknickers and sprayed on the perfume. He said nothing and did nothing. There was a tiny frown on Cécile's face as she drew down

129

the bed covers to expose his naked body. He was aroused, that was a good point, she thought. Yet he seemed to be ill at ease. No longer was he allowing himself to be enchanted by the illusion of Yvonne's presence.

His first gratification was unusually slow to arrive, however long Cécile trailed the edges of soft underwear over the skin of his belly and along his rigid part – not even when she made it sway from side to side by flicking at it with a pair of cyclamen red knickers. His continued silence was a further indication which she could not fail to understand – his mood of the past few days was changing. All the same, there was a service to be performed if she hoped to benefit again financially from his gratitude.

Eventually, to facilitate matters, she drew a silk stocking over his stem to encase it and his bulbs fully, then took it boldly in her hand and stroked up and down in a fast rhythm.

That had the intended effect, to be sure! He gasped and writhed in pleasure and then squirted his passion into the stocking. But, Cécile's watchful eye noted, compared with what she had seen him do before, his climax of delight was brief. His body had responded to her stimulation, but his heart and mind were untouched.

Since he made no comment of any kind but just lay on his back as before, she prepared herself to complete the regular performance. There too she encountered a new problem! By the time she was in position above him she found that his hitherto unflagging part had become limp and small.

Yes, she thought, we are fast reaching the end of the little comedy we have played out together!

Even so, the only indication she had of his desires was that he lay waiting for her to continue. Now assuredly Cécile did not possess one-tenth of the skills of her mistress in arousing the passions of a failing lover. She did what she could, guided only by her instinct – rubbing, squeezing and tugging – until at last the sleeping part was awakened and rose up. In great relief she inserted it into the portion of herself ordained by a kindly providence for that purpose. At once she began to move up and down forcefully, her consideration being that brisk stimulation seemed to be necessary to retain the interest she had stirred with much difficulty. It would be a catastrophe if she permitted this interest to droop before the final act was accomplished!

Marcel raised his hand and pulled the lilac silk underwear from his face and stared her full in the eyes.

'But this is ridiculous!' he exclaimed, 'I'm doing it with you, not *her*.'

Cécile said nothing, for there was nothing to say. The dream was evidently at an end and Marcel had woken up from his torpor. His next words surprised her.

'So then, if it's you, it's you – and why not? We'll do it properly this time, Cécile.'

He reached out to unbutton her plain white blouse and in his hurry he pulled one button right off. His hands went up under her chemise to take hold of her breasts and squeeze them.

'Not a bad pair at all,' he commented, speaking more coarsely than would have been suitable if he had been with Yvonne.

Cécile shrugged. It wasn't much of a compliment but it was the only one she had ever been paid on her bosom.

'You've done me a favour or two these last few days,' he said, 'now I'm going to do you one. Swing your backside – let's have some action to warm you up!'

It was true that he was hard inside her and for any man that meant that he would want to complete the process that had been commenced. So much was obvious to Cécile, but beyond that she wondered what she had stirred up in him. This was a new Marcel she was seeing – vigorous, demanding – one might even say dominating. She obeyed his instructions and moved her hips to and fro hard, becoming more and more aware of the fleshy protruberance on which she was impaled – and of the pleasant sensations it was giving her. Under her chemise Marcel's hands kneaded her breasts and tugged at her nipples to intensify her passion. Before long, Cécile was

131

out of control. She moved fiercely, her whole being straining towards the point of rapture which she felt was very close.

'That's good,' Marcel urged her on. 'Faster! I want to see it happen to you.'

The tightness of his grip on her breasts was almost painful, except that even pain was a pleasure to her at that moment. She thumped down on him another six or seven times and his wish was fulfilled – he saw it happen to her. Her head went back until her face was directed towards the ceiling, the muscles of her belly clenched like a fist – and from her wide open mouth there came a long throaty groan of pure ecstasy.

'More!' Marcel commanded her, jerking himself sharply upwards into her.

Without question it was the best she had ever experienced. It was in a totally different category from the pleasure other men had given her and it took some time for the tremors in her body to cease. Her head fell forward and she was looking into Marcel's face and there she saw a smile of triumph.

'Good enough for a start,' he said to her. 'Now I'm really going to show you what it's like.'

'Oh, Monsieur Marcel! I'm as limp as a rag already.'

His hands left her breasts and took her by the hips. An agile twist of his body reversed their positions, so that she was underneath him, her thighs outside his legs and his belly pressed flat to hers – and this he accomplished without losing his place in her fleshy cleft.

She thought that he would attack her as if with a battering-ram and had no relish for it. Here again he surprised her. He pulled her chemise up around her neck to expose her breasts and stroked them softly.

'Did I treat them roughly?' he asked, smiling down at her.

'It felt nice, whatever you did.'

'You must understand, Cécile, the moods of love change quickly. After the wild pleasure you have just experienced you need a different sort of approach.'

132

'Do I?'

'Believe me, I understand these things.'

He moved inside her with long and slow strokes to give her a little time to recover from her recent exertions, but not too much for her to go cold. She appreciated the tenderness he was showing her, though in her heart she did not believe that it would do anything for her. In this she was judging from her own limited experience, in which the few men she had been with had wanted to do it fast and hard and then go to a bar for a drink. Marcel had been taught the ways of love by a succession of beautiful young women who knew how to savour love to the very last drop – women like Yvonne who expected a lover to be able to entertain them in bed for several hours at a time.

It was not until sighs of pleasure from Cécile indicated that she was responding correctly to what he was doing that Marcel changed his pace from a gentle canter to a brisk trot.

That Marcel, an average selfish man, devoted all this attention to the sensual gratification of a maidservant was an indication of his unusual frame of mind at that time. As she lay on her back with her clothes round her neck and her legs encased in cheap black stockings, she was not beautiful. Her face was broad, her eyebrows unplucked, her complexion uncared-for. All this he had seen for himself when he had removed the blindfold from his face and stared at her. Her breasts, it must be said, were flabby, she had no discernible waist. Worst of all, the unkempt bush of black hair that grew from her groins halfway up her belly demonstrated that she was devoid of the slightest idea of how to make herself attractive to a lover.

Truth to say, Marcel did not understand his own motives in making love to her as if she were the most desirable woman in the whole of Paris. He was obeying the promptings of his own heart and it was not necessary that he should understand them. What he was doing made him feel good, that was what mattered. Not just physically good – that was the result of the exciting friction of joined sexual parts – but good in his heart.

'Oh my God!' Cécile moaned, 'It's incredible!'

'Ah, but it gets better still,' Marcel gasped.

It was as he promised, until she was reduced to a body quivering uncontrollably at the spasms of pleasure that shook her. But there is a limit to the intensity of pleasure a man or a woman can sustain. Of this Marcel was well aware, and in good time his measured trot became a gallop. The bed on which they lay was creaking to their efforts. His belly smacked against hers again and again and by now Cécile was thrusting upwards simultaneously with Marcel to plunge him to the limit each time.

When the moment came she screamed in delight and Marcel cried out aloud with her as the surge of his passion flung them both into ecstatic release. For Cécile it was as it she were watching a Fourteenth of July firework display – the whole night sky ablaze with exploding rockets, blinding white star-shells and coloured rains of fire.

For Marcel it was his ticket to freedom from Yvonne and he revelled in the relief of it, his movements extending Cécile's pleasure beyond anything she thought possible. He was still pumping away at her, though more slowly, long after she was lying limp and almost unconscious beneath him.

On this occasion it was she who wanted to doze for a while. Marcel was too exhilarated to think of sleep – he wanted to go out into the street and see people and visit friends and reactivate his life.

He roused Cécile by shaking her shoulder gently. She opened her eyes and saw that he was fully dressed and ready to depart. A moment later she remembered that she was lying naked on her back and she closed her legs modestly – though what *modesty* signifies after what had taken place between the two of them, who can say? Marcel smiled briefly, at her reaction.

'Cécile,' he said, 'I am going now and I shall never come back to this apartment. I want you to have this,'

'Thank you,' she said, taking the money without even looking at it, 'if there is any way in which I can be of

134

ervice to you in the future, Monsieur Marcel, please let
me know. I mean that.'

'You have done more for me than you realise. The rest I
shall do for myself.'

'Then good luck, Monsieur.'

Almost six months passed before Marcel and Yvonne
spoke to each other after their parting. Of necessity they
caught sight of each other by chance from time to time,
now could it be otherwise? They had the custom of dining
in the same half dozen restaurants favoured by good
society, they frequented the same half dozen theatres.
And being young, they danced in the same half dozen
fashionable establishments. On these occasions Marcel
made no attempt to avoid Yvonne, but it was obvious to
him that she was avoiding him. She pretended not to
notice him, or looked the other way – or even became
engrossed in conversation with her companion whenever
Marcel was within ten metres of her. She was always with
her new lover – a dark-complexioned man with shiny
black hair parted exactly in the middle. Marcel knew that
his name was Pierre Aubernon and he had learned a little
about him but had never made his acquaintance, nor
wished to.

Imagine then Marcel's astonishment when out of the
blue one morning Yvonne telephoned him at his home
with the suggestion that he should take her to lunch. He
gave the suggestion a little thought, but not too much,
before deciding that he was free to meet her. After all, he
was not a complete fool. If she wanted to meet him then
she had some sort of plan into which she hoped to fit him.
To her own advantage, naturally.

They met and talked over a particularly good meal.
Yvonne was wearing a simple green frock of panné velvet
and a hat with a turn-down brim. She looked remarkably
chic. She behaved towards him quite charmingly and
displayed not the least sign of embarrassment at what had
happened. Indeed, an observer at another table in the
restaurant might well have received the impression that an

135

affair of the heart between these two was about to commence!

'Are you happy?' Marcel enquired, not greatly interested in the matter, one way or the other.

'But of course. And you?'

'As always.'

'I thought I saw you in the crowd at the theatre last week. Were you there?'

'I was twice at the theatre last week. Which one were you at?'

'The Champs-Élysées.'

'Yes, I also caught a glimpse of you. With Monsieur Aubernon, I believe.'

'Ah, is that a reproach?' she asked with a smile. 'Since we parted I've seen you in public with at least three different women.'

'It was not a reproach, merely an observation. If it is of any interest to you, though I cannot imagine how, then there have been four women in my life since we parted, as you so tactfully put it.'

'Four in less than six monthes! You certainly have been amusing yourself, Marcel.'

'Of course,' he said, smiling back at her.

Towards the end of the meal she said:

'You still live with your mother? I don't know why, but I half-expected not to reach you there when I telephoned.'

'It would be too cruel to leave her alone.'

'What happened to the little apartment I lived in? Do you still have it?'

'I gave it up after you moved out.'

'Really? Then where do you take all these new friends of yours?'

Marcel shrugged and made no reply.

The lunch ended and still nothing of significance had been said. Marcel paid the bill and the head waiter bowed them all the way from their table to the door. They stood on the pavement outside and both knew that the moment of truth had arrived.

'Shall I put you in a taxi?' Marcel asked politely, leaving the initiative with Yvonne deliberately.

'A taxi? Yes,' she answered, seeming a little put out that he had not offered to escort her home.

'There's a cab rank on the corner. Let's walk down to it. Where do you live now, Yvonne?'

'Rue Bosquet. Don't tell me you didn't know.'

'I didn't know. That must be off the Avenue Bosquet, I suppose.'

'Yes – a charming little street, very quiet and peaceful.'

They were at the taxi. Marcel opened the door for her to get in and remained on the pavement himself.

'Au revoir, Yvonne,' he said, 'it has been delightful to see you again.'

'Oh!' she pouted, 'come with me. You must see my apartment.'

'But what of Monsieur Aubernon?'

'He is in Brussels. Come with me, Marcel, there is something I wish to ask your advice on.'

The taxi driver was an unshaven individual, slumped behind the steering wheel. He had heard similar conversations between men and women a million times and they bored him.

'Well . . .' said Marcel, 'only for a few moments though. I have an appointment later on.'

He got in the back of the taxi with Yvonne and told the driver where to go.

'This matter on which you want my advice,' he said, taking one of her gloved hands into his, 'is it important?'

'Very. And most confidential.'

To see what her reaction would be, he slipped a hand under her skirt and gently stroked her thigh. She smiled at him and sighed as if in pleasure.

Her apartment was on the first floor. Cécile opened the door to them and stared in surprise at Marcel. When she took his hat he winked briefly at her and she gave him a quick grin, unseen by Yvonne, who was taking off her hat in front of the hall mirror.

Cécile followed them into the sitting-room.

'Is there anything you would like, Madame?'

'No, thank you. I have important matters to discuss with Monsieur Chalon. Please see that we are not disturbed for any reason.'

'Very good, Madame.'

'You have a nice apartment,' said Marcel.

The furniture was all new and expensive. Two of the pictures on the wall were presents from him to Yvonne and had previously hung on the walls of the other apartment.

Yvonne was at last betraying signs of nervousness now that the moment had arrived for her to come to the point.

'You know that Monsieur Aubernon has been a dear friend of mine for some time now,' she began.

'I am aware of the fact,' Marcel answered non-commitally.

'He is involved in high finance – did you know that?'

Marcel shrugged his shoulders.

'I had heard something to that effect from a friend who is an expert in such things,' he said, 'but I did not pay much attention.'

'What expert?' Yvonne asked quickly.

'Why do you ask? It cannot be of any importance.'

'Perhaps it is. Will you tell me, Marcel?'

'Certainly. It was Charles Brissard. Do you know him?'

'I have met his wife and I know a little about the Brissard family and their financial interests. What did your friend say about Pierre Aubernon?'

'That he was involved in high finance.'

'No more than that?'

'Yvonne – what is this about? Surely you did not invite me here to cross-question me about the business activities of a man you know much more about than I do? Tell me the point of your questions and perhaps I can be of some assistance.'

'Did your friend mention that Pierre is involved with Alexandre Stavisky?'

'Stavisky?' said Marcel thoughtfully. 'Yes, I seem to recall that the name did crop up in the conversation.'

138

'What was said of Stavisky?'

'Yvonne, this is becoming an irritating conversation. I am not a witness in a court of law.'

'Please – I have a reason for asking. What did Charles Brissard say?'

'I don't think that I should repeat it. After all, it was a confidential conversation.'

'Tell me, I implore you!' she exclaimed.

'Since you wish it . . . he said that Stavisky is a swindler on a big scale and that he will end his days in prison. Unless . . .'

'Unless what?' Yvonne asked breathlessly.

'Unless his secret partners in the government have him murdered first to save their own necks. Understand me, I know nothing of these things, I repeat only what was said to me.'

'Oh my God!' Yvonne gasped and burst into tears.

Marcel moved across to perch on the arm of her chair. He put an arm about her shoulders to comfort her and pulled the silk handkerchief from his breast pocket to give to her.

'I'm lost!' she sobbed mournfully.

'What do you mean? How does this affect you.'

'I will tell you everything.' she said through her tears, 'Aubernon has gone – run away before the scandal breaks. He is deeply implicated in Stavisky's business affairs. He went without telling me – it was only yesterday that I discovered that his clothes are gone and his other belongings. He said nothing to me except that he had to go to Brussels on business. But he's cleared out and left me behind.'

'Good God,' Marcel said as sympathetically as he could.

'He'll never dare show his face in Paris again. He has left me nothing – not even my jewellery – that's been taken too. I don't know what I am going to do. This morning I learned that the rent of this apartment is already overdue. And there are outstanding debts every-where.'

'Can you return to your parents at Ivry and live with them?' Marcel asked.

'It is out of the question . . . you see, on my advice they allowed Aubernon to invest their money for them in Stavisky's bonds. They will have nothing – and it's all my fault!'

'How very awkward,' said Marcel, 'I don't know what to advise.'

At that she uttered a heart-rending sob. Evidently she expected him to resolve her pressing problems for her.

'You must stop crying,' Marcel said firmly, 'or you will make yourself ugly.'

That dried her tears at once. She dabbed at her eyes with his handkerchief and gave it back to him.

'I have ruined my make-up. Excuse me while I repair the damage. I will only be a minute.'

While she was gone Marcel resumed his seat and pondered the implications of her position – and his own. Her desertion of him had caused him to suffer atrociously. He still recalled the numbness of heart and the sense of futility that he had felt. By good fortune, the services of her maid had been of tremendous assistance in reviving his normally robust vital forces. Plain though she might be, the maid was a woman who understood a man's grief and offered practical comfort. In retrospect, the afternoons he had passed with Cécile in the abandoned apartment seemed most strange – yet undeniably the touch of her hand on his masculine part and the use of her body had been extraordinarily healing to his bruised heart.

Now, it seemed, he could have Yvonne back for the asking – if she didn't do the asking first! That surely was the entire purpose of the meeting. The question was, after so much had happened, did he truly want her back? She was beautiful, that went without saying, and very desirable. When he put his hand on her bare thigh in the taxi, above her garter, the touch of that delicate skin had brought back a flood of very tender memories. But then,

Paris was full of beautiful and desirable women. He had enjoyed the intimate friendship of four in the past six months: And at no greater cost than that of entertaining them to dinners and theatres and a shopping trip or two – a frock for one, a dozen pairs of silk stockings and gloves for another, a string of pearls, some frilly underwear – nothing very serious.

That was not Yvonne's style at all. She expected far more. This apartment, for example, she would surely not want to move out of it and the rent was bound to be higher than he had paid before to house her. She was expensive to dress too, and she had a collector's instinct for pictures, not to mention jewellery.

To set against that was the fact that she was adorably entertaining. Not today, perhaps, because she was immersed in her troubles. But ordinarily, her wit and charm were unfailing. In bed she was unparalleled, at least in Marcel's experience. To explain why was not easy. Her body was pretty, though perhaps not exceptional. She had little pointed breasts set high and a narrow waist. Her arms and legs were very slender – if ever she lost any weight they might even become thin. No, it was the instinctive use she made of her body that was so enchanting, the sophisticated enthusiasm she brought to the act of love, however often repeated.

Alone in her bedroom, Yvonne did far more than touch up her tear-ravaged make-up. When her mirror told her that her face was perfect again, she took off all her clothes and sprayed herself from head to foot lightly with the perfume that Marcel found so exciting. She checked that the lacquer on her carefully groomed toenails was unblemished and brushed the small patch of russet hair between her legs downwards into a neat little point.

She put on her newest négligée, a flimsy creation of silk and lace so fine that her body was almost visible through it. A little experiment with the tie-belt produced the effect she wanted – a deep décolletage that exposed enough of her breasts to rouse a man's interest and still

141

left something for him to uncover for himself when matters had proceeded that far. The négligée had another advantage – she could make it fall open when she was sitting in a way that exposed one leg to halfway up her thigh.

Marcel still desired her, she knew that for certain, as women always know these things. She had known it in the restaurant while they were eating, though nothing had been said by him that would reveal his feelings. In the taxi, when he had slipped his hand up her skirt to feel her thigh – an old gesture of his from the time when they were together – that had only confirmed what she already knew. Perhaps she should have moved her legs slightly at that moment, in a manner she understood well enough, to bring his finger-tips into fleeting contact with the soft hair that graced the tender lips between her thighs. That used to have a most encouraging effect on him in the old days.

Yes, he still desired her. Very well – the time had arrived for her to show him how very desirable she could be when she put her mind to it. He would go hard in his trousers the moment he saw her enter the room dressed as she was – or should it be undressed – in her enchanting négligée. A few moments sitting on his lap, her bottom rubbing against his hardness, a hand inside his shirt to tickle his nipple – and he would beg her to return to him. She would appear to hesitate, saying that her problems were too great to impose upon a friend, even so intimate a friend as he had been. He would be so eager by then to get inside her that he would sweep away her objections and insist that they resume their affaire.

She returned to the sitting-room, having been away for no more than ten minutes to make her preparations. Marcel was not there! Yvonne rang for her maid.

'Cécile, where is Monsieur Chalon?'

'He's gone, Madame.'

'Gone? But that's impossible!'

'He asked me to give you a message.'

'Then give it to me at once.'

'He said that he regrets that he had to leave for his appointment elsewhere.'

'Is that all?' Yvonne demanded in a shrill voice.

'No, Madame. He also said that he hoped you would be able to settle your problems satisfactorily.'

NICOLE LIBERATED

The first time that Nicole Brissard permitted another man to enjoy the intimate privileges reserved by decree of Church and State for her husband alone, she was acutely nervous. So much so that she was not able on that memorable occasion to attain the climactic release which is the natural result of the exercise of those intimate privileges.

The setting was too unfamiliar, perhaps – not the comfortable security of the marriage bed but the rear seat of Pierre de Barbin's shiny automobile, parked under the trees of the Bois de Boulogne after dark! For a woman of Nicole's station in life such a setting for an act of passion might seem extraordinary – grotesque even – but then, de Barbin was an extraordinary person. From the moment he had been introduced to her, not more than two weeks before, he had been most persistent, calling on the telephone to propose little meetings, as if she were unmarried and he a suitor. At first Nicole was surprised, then she was flattered. Eventually she agreed to meet him for lunch. He was amusing and charming – so much so that she fled away quickly after lunch before he could suggest a visit to his apartment, if that was what was in his mind, as she supposed. For at that moment she was not certain that she would have the good sense and prudence to say 'No'. And if she were to accompany him to his apartment and he embraced her, would she have the strength of character to resist temptation? The answer to that question being unclear in her mind, Nicole decided that discretion was the better part of valour and so she took her leave of him.

That afternoon, safe in her own home, she recalled a conversation she had had perhaps a month previously with her sister-in-law Jeanne Verney. They were drinking coffee together on the terrace of the Café de la Paix, two beautiful and elegant women pausing for a moment during

144

a shopping expedition. Their conversation had turned to the subject of the less than satisfactory ways of husbands in general.

'But why do they do it?' Nicole demanded.

'It is their nature,' Jeanne replied, amused by the question.

'That's no answer. Why do married men chase after other women?'

'Really, Nicole – it is the way of the world. You speak like a convent girl. How long have you been married to Michel now – it must be seven years.'

'Yes, but that is no reason. Am I ugly? Am I cold-blooded? Am I undesirable?'

'That has nothing to do with it, as you well know. In all those seven years have you never enjoyed a little adventure of your own? Be truthful now.'

'Of course not!' Nicole exclaimed, 'what are you suggesting? That I have been unfaithful to my husband?'

The word that best described Nicole was *appetising*. At all times she looked sleek, well-fed and healthy, her chestnut-brown hair shone, the skin of her broad-cheeked face was flawless. When she was pink with indignation, as now, she was so attractive that men sitting at nearby tables turned to stare at her in open admiration.

'My dear, be calm,' said Jeanne. 'You believe that Michel has a little friend he visits. That does not surprise me in the least. Michel is a Brissard, and so am I. We share the same passionate nature.'

Nicole pursed her red-painted lips and stared hard at Jeanne.

'I've certainly heard rumours about *your* little adventures,' she said virtuously, 'though naturally I refuse to believe them.'

Jeanne laughed at that.

'Perhaps someone has been indiscreet,' she said, 'but it is of no importance.'

'No importance? How can you say that? Suppose that these rumours came to the ears of your husband – what then?'

'Who would tell him? And if someone did, do you think that he would pay any attention to them? His interest in my charms was never very strong and it expired some time ago. What is of importance to Guy is to be married to me.'

'Because you are a Brissard, you mean?'

'Precisely. Guy cannot afford to offend my family.'

'That hardly applies to me,' said Nicole, 'I am a Brissard only by marriage to Michel.'

'Then discretion is even more important.'

'Discretion in what?'

'In any little adventure you may decide to embark upon.'

'Jeanne – what are you saying? I have no such intention, I assure you. I am a married woman with children.'

'You, me, Marie-Thérèse, Lucienne – we are all women with good marriages and children. If our husbands have a roving eye – well, that's the way of things. They never stray far and they preserve the decencies. There are no scandals, no dramas. Why should we complain?'

'Because we are wives, not kept women!' Nicole replied hotly.

'Assuredly, but since the world is not perfect, we must be practical as well as virtuous.'

'Ignore a husband's infidelity, you mean?'

'Ignore it, of course. And arrange one's own little pleasures. What could be less chic than a wronged and grieving wife?'

'But I could never bring myself to contemplate going with another man. I am a good Catholic.'

'We are all good Catholics – it is expected of us. I must arrange for you to meet some charming and unattached men to take your mind off Michel's little arrangements.'

'Never!' Nicole declared, and she meant it.

That notwithstanding, it was through Jeanne that she met Pierre de Barbin not long afterwards – that extraordinarily persistent man who had taken her to lunch and charmed her with his conversation to the point where she fled in dismay.

Unabashed, de Barbin tried again, this time proposing

an afternoon drive. Nicole accepted, for on reflection she was sure that she could deal with him if he attempted to extend their friendship into forbidden territory. Pierre's automobile was impressive – a great gleaming maroon-coloured Panhard-Levassor open tourer. It had huge lamps on the front like the eyes of a predator and the strength of a score of horses to speed it along. Nicole sat beside Pierre on the black polished leather upholstery, warmly wrapped against the wind, as he drove out of Paris in the general direction of Alençon. It was a fine day in early autumn and, once clear of the suburbs, Pierre put the big machine through its paces for her. The engine roared its bass note of power, the trees on either side of the road whipped past them and Nicole's long silk scarf trailed behind her like a banner in the slipstream. How exciting it was, that headlong rush! And when Pierre, his leather-gauntleted hands clamped to the steering-wheel, put back his head and howled out a song to the open sky – ah, what intoxication! Nicole's heart fluttered wildly in her bosom as if she were a young girl again.

When the exhilaration of speed at last burned itself out, they turned back towards Paris, but by a different route. Pierre drove more reasonably now, maintaining a ready flow of amusing conversation which Nicole found irresistible. When the light began to fade he switched on the big headlamps and sent long lances of yellow light piercing the darkness before them. That too was fascinating, though in a different way from the outward journey.

As it happened, Nicole's husband was away from home that day, on business of some importance in Bordeaux, or so he had said, and there was no need for her to be home in time for dinner. When they reached Chartres Pierre stopped and they dined together in a restaurant he knew there. Before they resumed their journey towards Paris, he put up the folding hood of the car to protect Nicole from the night air. By the time they reached the outskirts of Paris it was after nine o'clock and Nicole was thinking that her children would have been put to bed by the servants and she would not see them that night.

They were passing through the Bois de Boulogne when Pierre pulled off the road, set the hand-brake, switched off the engine and headlamps and, before Nicole was completely aware of his intentions, had assisted her out of the car and back into it in the rear seat. In the dark his arms went round her and he kissed her passionately. Replete with good food and good wine, Nicole allowed him to do so, for the experience was undeniably pleasant. But when she felt his ungloved hand on her thigh under her coat and skirt, naturally she protested at once. But not too much. After all, her heart said, the man embracing her in the dark might almost have been her husband. The hand stroking the soft skin of her bare thigh above her garter might almost have been Michel's hand. Her conscience insisted that it was not, but the touch was so *interesting* that she listened to her heart. After all, nothing irrevocable was going to take place here in the open air, of that she was sure.

But in fact, the moment was a critical one for Nicole, whether she chose to recognise it or not. Almost without her awareness the hand that was touching her thighs so tenderly soon gained ground and arrived inside her silk underwear! And in another moment or two it was caressing her closely-guarded *bijou*! She uttered a little gasp and tried to squeeze her thighs together, but Pierre's hand was too well-placed to be so easily dislodged.

'No, no!' she exclaimed. 'you must stop that !'

Pierre silenced her protest with a long kiss, while his fingers gently parted the soft lips they had caressed and touched her tiny bud as delicately as a bee kisses a flower in its search for nectar.

'Ah,' Nicole sighed.

An idea had become fixed in her mind, one which grew ever more obsessive as her passions kindled under Pierre's sure touch. In the whole of her adult life she had known only one male part – that of her husband, of course. The question in her mind was – were all men the same in this respect, or were there differences? What sort of differences could there possibly be, she wondered as she

148

thrilled to Pierre's intimate caress – differences of length, of thickness? An opportunity to find out might never again present itself!

She put a trembling hand to Pierre's lap and encountered a hardness through his trousers. But that told her nothing except that he was in a state of acute arousal, as was to be expected in view of what he was doing to her with his fingers.

Her determination grew. She hooked her fingers into the opening of his trousers and jerked the buttons open in one hard pull. Then it was Pierre's turn to gasp as she delved under his shirt and into his underwear until she held his stiff pride firmly in her kid-gloved hand.

Nicole's mind was ablaze with her new-found discovery – yes, there was a difference! In her years of marriage to Michel she had come to know his body well, especially that part of it which gave her the greatest delight. Of course, when they were first married her girlish shyness had permitted her to glance at it only surreptitiously during their love-making. To reconcile her deepening affection for that upstanding part with her modesty had been something of a struggle for her. But as she became on terms of familiarity with it and her appetite developed for the pleasures of the marriage bed, she soon learned to look at it openly, to touch it, to caress it affectionately and then to kiss it.

The darkness prevented her from seeing what she held in her gloved hand but she knew it to be different. To avoid the possibility of mistake in this, she hastily removed her gloves and grasped it again in her bare hand. Yes, it felt somewhat thicker than the one she knew best. A little shorter, perhaps, but thicker. That being established, the next question that formed itself in her excited mind was – if simply by holding it she could distinguish a variation of shape and size, would the sensations it gave her also be different? In the hypothetical and unthinkable event of it being permitted to enter her, that was, her prudence hurriedly added.

While Nicole debated this question in her mind, Pierre

was sighing with pleasure at the touch of her hand on the part of him which formed the subject of her speculation.

'Nicole, chérie,' he murmured between kisses.

'Oh,' she said in disappointment as his hand withdrew from between her thighs.

But it was only to unfasten her coat. Then he had her by the waist with both hands and lifted her from the seat beside him as if she weighed no more than a feather. He seated her across his lap, facing him, her legs straddled wide.

'What are you doing?' she gasped as he groped between them to pull aside the loose leg of her expensive silk knickers and so bare her *bijou*.

Even as she asked her wholly unnecessary question, a wicked little voice in her mind was suggesting to her that it was a great pity that because of the darkness Pierre was unable to see and appreciate the sheer beauty of her silk underwear – the delicacy of oyster-grey crêpe-de-chine patterned all over with charming pink rosebuds and trimmed around the wide legs with a narrow band of fine lace. And before the little voice could be suppressed, it went on to add that it was an even greater pity that for the same reason Pierre was equally unable to see and admire the elegance of the *bijou* he was stroking so ardently, with its tender pink lips and neatly clipped tuft of dark brown fur.

That such thoughts should enter the mind of a happily-married young woman may be thought utterly reprehensible – worse than that, sinful if one is a good Catholic, as Nicole undoubtedly was. But as all the world knows, such thoughts do enter the heads of even the most happily-married women, though naturally they never admit this to anyone else. Even more reprehensible – or sinful – according to how one looks at it, is that a beautiful young woman like Nicole should find herself in the back of an automobile in the Bois, with a man not her husband – and he with his fingers caressing her inside her secret feminine sanctum! Yet such things happen, not rarely, but with great frequency, most especially in Paris, though undoubtedly in every other city in the whole world.

Something warm and firm pressed against the delicate skin of the lips between Nicole's thighs, and this time it was not Pierre's fingers. What a short time ago had been merely hypothetical now became reality, and what had been unthinkable was now fact as Pierre slid his stiff part into her. Nicole's conscience complained bitterly that she should never have allowed matters to reach this stage. Moreover, it insisted that she must take immediate action to prevent the natural outcome. 'Smack Pierre's face and get off his lap at once', her conscience shrilled.

But really . . . the unfamiliar male part moving boldly inside her was extremely pleasant – thrilling, one could say. And if the question was to be answered completely as to whether lovemaking with another man was truly different, than a little more time would be necessary to appreciate the subtler point of difference. These matters could not be decided in an instant.

Pierre's hands were up her skirt, clasping her by the cheeks of her bottom, to pull her closer into his lap. To drive himself in deeper, Nicole thought. The plan was a logical one – after all, if his part were a little shorter, as she suspected, then she would need to get closer to him to experience it to the full. In the interests of the experiment, she assisted him by pulling her skirt up around her belly and eased herself forward with her feet up on the car seat on either side of him, her knees up level with his shoulders.

One difference was already noticeable. Michel talked almost without stop when he made love to her – little endearments and words of admiration and pleasure. In contrast, Pierre had hardly uttered a word since they had got into the rear of the car. Now that was interesting.

'But you must stop him at once,' said the voice of conscience in Nicole's ear. 'This is infamous! If you allow him to continue doing that to you for one more minute it will be too late! Just feel how tightly he's gripping your bottom – he's nearly ready to do it!'

The insertion of Pierre's slightly shorter, though unde-niably slightly thicker, part had imparted a most exquisite warmth to Nicole. She could sense her face glowing pinkly in the darkness, while inside her clothes her body seemed to be bathed in delicious heat. The rhythmic motion to which Pierre was subjecting her initiated tremors of delightful sensation that sped from her spread thighs up through her belly to her breasts, making their engorged tips tingle. How very enjoyable it was to make love, she thought, even with a comparative stranger.

'Stop him,' her conscience exclaimed in alarm. 'He's going to do it now!'

'*What if he does?*' Nicole replied silently and she shrugged, so silencing the voice of conscience.

Her shrug achieved more than that. The movement transmitted itself from her shoulders through her body to Pierre's busy male part and brought on his crisis. His fingernails dug into the soft flesh of her bottom as he cried out and discharged his rapture forcefully.

When the power of rational speech was restored to him, he protested that it was little short of tragic that she had not shared in his momentous delight. With a thousand apologies and expressions of self-blame, he withdrew from her frustrated body his limp sprig, replaced it with his agile fingers and in seconds had her gasping in her emotional crisis, determined that he should not leave her unsatisfied.

Nicole was to learn in due course that Pierre de Barbin was a most unusual man. All that she knew of him at that moment was what she had observed and what she had been told – in short, his outward characteristics. He dressed well, was a clever and amusing conversationalist, had a large circle of friends, he was to be seen at all the appropriate parties and entertainments. For years he had been a target for many a mother with a daughter to marry off. But at thirty he was still sauve, still charming, still amusing – and still unmarried.

To doting mothers of eligible daughters he was an enigma. All the world knows that a man of means requires a suitable wife to manage his household and to give him children. His avid and continuous interest in pretty women was no secret. Well then? To those who knew him well, Pierre was also an enigma. Outwardly he conformed to the manners and customs of polite society – yet he readily explained to his intimate friends, men and women, that he despised all that. His intention was to break every rule, to defy convention – and never to be discovered doing so. The reason he gave for this curious intention was that if he were to be recognised for the social anarchist he was at heart, then he would be indistinguishable, except for his income, from the shabby crew of bohemians who haunted cheap cafes and changed their women more often than they changed their shirts. The *rabble*, as he described them.

'I shall destroy the system from within, by bringing as many young women as possible to my way of thinking' – that was his boast. When asked who was to know that he was destroying the system if he always stayed in the shadows, he answered with pride: '*I* know.'

In short, Pierre was the worst kind of romantic, lacking even the usual excuse of being a writer or dauber of some sort.

A day or so after the drive in the country he invited Nicole to accompany him on an afternoon walk along the riverside. That, at least, was what he said on the telephone. When she accepted and asked where they should meet, he at once proposed his apartment in the rue de Cléry. Nicole's analysis of the situation was that the suggestion of a walk was merely a ruse to get her into his bedroom. In this she was mistaken, for she as yet knew nothing of his secret life of rebellion. She agreed to meet him that afternoon at three.

Naturally she had her reasons, though she would have died rather than admit them to anyone. During the encounter in the Bois de Boulogne she had detected, she believed, certain variances in the configuration of men's proudest parts. The belief – perhaps half-belief would be more precise – had been to some extent confirmed by tender connection with her husband since then. During the mutual caressing which preceded the marital act, she

153

had made a point of handling Michel's stiffness for some time, to impress its general size and shape on her memory. In due course it had made a deep impression on her elsewhere, an event which she remembered with pleasure and, in addition, with a detailed review of the sensations it had provided.

An opportunity now offered itself to investigate further – to formulate a definite opinion about the comparison. In effect, it would be interesting to determine if the comparison was valid or not, this affair of the length and thickness of two different stems of hard flesh. More important still, this was an opportunity to discover whether Pierre's adjunct produced sensations of pleasure more intense or less intense that that of Michel. Of that she was far from certain – in the unfamiliar confines of the rear seat of a car she had not responded fully. In Pierre's apartment, in the comfort of his bed, she would be at ease and therefore able to concentrate her mind on the matter in hand – and after it had been in hand long enough, between her legs.

From these secret speculations it may be judged that Nicole had passed beyond the ordinary considerations of a married woman's duty to her husband and that she was already contemplating the commission of actions which may be described as – if not immodest – then indiscreet.

She arrived at Pierre's apartment a little after three, not wishing to make herself appear too enthusiastic, yet telling herself that politeness dictated that she must not be more than ten minutes late. The autumn afternoon was almost at an end, the street-lamps were already lit. Pierre greeted her with kisses on both hands and then on her lips. She had dressed with care for this meeting – her impressive full-length silver fox coat over an afternoon frock in pale turquoise that looked simple yet had the touch of a master couturier in its cut, the ensemble topped by a pretty little close-fitting hat of the same delicate turquoise.

Pierre maintained a ceaseless flow of compliments as he drew her into his bedroom and began to undress her as if he were her maid. After the hat and coat were off he unbuttoned her frock at the back of her neck and lifted it

154

with great care over her head so as not to disarrange her hair.

'But how elegant!' he exclaimed, studying her tangerine-coloured silk slip, 'an adorable thought that, to wear this audacious colour hidden from sight under a modest frock!'

Then that too came off to expose her round little breasts with their pink tips – and the lace and silk knickers she wore, of the same colour as her slip. Pierre stood back a pace or two to study her better, his eyes lingering in hot affection over the gentle curve of her belly under the thin silk.

'Truly beautiful,' he said, profound admiration in his voice.

He knelt at her feet and gently eased down her legs the flimsy garment which alone concealed her secret treasure. Words seemed to fail him momentarily – he bowed his head in respect and kissed her warm belly, his hands smoothing over the cheeks of her bottom.

'You are enchanting,' he murmured, his voice returning.

Nicole, standing in only her shoes, stockings and frilled garters, appreciated his compliments – what woman would not? But secretly she was waiting for the moment when Pierre would discard his own clothes and, together on the bed, she could satisfy herself by touch and vision as to the shape of that most important part. By now, she thought, it must be fully extended.

To her amazement, Pierre rose from his knees, took her fur-coat and held it out for her to put on. She looked at him questioningly and his words almost took away her breath.

'For our walk,' he said, 'you promised to go walking with me.'

'Like this?' she exclaimed, unable to believe what she had heard.

'Certainly. Only you and I know that you are naked inside your fur coat. It will be very exciting, I promise you.'

'But you're mad!'

'Not in the least. Trust me, Nicole – it will be an experience never to be forgotten.'

'It is impossible!' she said, her mind in a whirl of confusion at the mere suggestion – a confusion, it must be admitted, which was not entirely unpleasant.

He had captured her imagination by the audacity of his proposal and, well aware of this, he pressed his advantage quickly. Calmly and logically he began to tell her of his secret life of anarchy and she, bemused by what she heard, allowed him to slip on her fur coat and fasten it about her. They were out of his apartment, down the stairs and almost in the rue de Cléry before her senses returned.

'No!' she exclaimed at the street door, 'what am I doing, for heaven's sake?'

'Not for heaven's sake – for your own sake,' Pierre replied with an encouraging smile, 'you are on the threshold of a voyage of discovery about yourself. Be bold – take just one more step.'

They were in the street, walking arm-in-arm along the pavement. A passer-by approached them and without thinking Nicole flinched and tried to hide behind Pierre. He laughed.

'Don't be afraid,' he said, 'no one can see through your beautiful fur coat. To all the world you are fully dressed. Only you and I know the truth.'

Her mind was numb as he found a taxi and settled her into it. Nicole kept her legs pressed close together and smoothed her coat down over her knees, fearful that the driver might glance back and see up her legs to her unprotected *bijou*. Pierre simply smiled and patted her hand.

'The first step is hard,' he said, 'after that – you will see.'

'But where are we going?'

'I promised you a stroll by the Seine. That's where we're going.'

Nicole stared out of the window in blind disbelief as the

taxi turned onto the Boulevard de Sébastopol with its brightly lit shops and cafes. They crossed the rue de Rivoli and drove over the bridge to the Île de la Cité. She recognised with feelings of despair the Palais de Justice to their right and the Prefecture de Police to their left. Automatically she crossed herself quickly, praying silently that she would not be required to attend at either building as a result of this insane escapade of Pierre's – for she was sure that it must be in some way illegal to drive about the streets of Paris in only a coat and with no knickers. They crossed the bridge on the far side of the Cité and the taxi stopped in the Place Saint Michel . . .

'Here we are,' said Pierre cheerfully.

'No, please take me back at once,' she begged, 'I can't get out of the taxi.'

'But certainly you can,' he insisted, his hand under her elbow – and she found herself standing on the pavement while Pierre paid off the driver.

'We'll go this way,' he said, taking her by the arm.

This was total madness, she told herself as she allowed him to lead her along. How had it come about that she, Nicole Brissard, had put herself in this position – naked but for stockings and shoes under her fur coat and walking in public with this strange man? He was taking her along the Quai St Michel, the river to their left. Already it was nearly dark and the book shops along the Quai had their lights on to attract passers-by.

Against her bare skin the silk lining of her coat felt unfamiliar and yet comforting. In some indefinable way, she realised, it had the touch of a lover almost. The movement of her walking caused the silk to caress softly her naked breasts and to brush lightly against her thighs and the cheeks of her bottom. She thought that she would feel cold, but she did not. The truth was that the unaccustomed touch of the coat-lining on her body and the incredible fact of walking about in a state of concealed nakedness – and with a man who knew – these conspired to arouse her eroticism and to make her flushed and warm.

Nicole was aghast when she identified her own emotions. She was also an honest person.

'This it not so intolerable as I thought it would be,' she said.

'As I told you, only the first step is difficult. I am teaching you to enjoy freedom.'

'From what?'

'You are learning to cast off the fetters that exist in your mind – the fetters imposed upon you by your staid upbringing and conventional marriage.'

'How absurd! You are attempting to make me a libertine like yourself.'

'I am no libertine – I am a free spirit. You are here of your own free will. Be truthful now – the reason you are here is that you want to discover what it is that I have to teach you.'

'I fear that you can teach me nothing except infidelity, Pierre.'

'That is not true – not in the least true. I can show you how to find your innermost self.'

'How – by making love to me?'

They had reached the Petit Pont that runs across the river to the Place du Parvis in front of the grandiose facade of Notre-Dame cathedral. Pierre glanced quickly about to make sure that no one was approaching them. He turned Nicole to face him and put his hand inside her coat to fondle her bare belly. He was not wearing gloves and his touch was cold on her skin. She gasped once in shock, then gasped again differently, for the cold fingers were suddenly very exciting.

'You do not understand yourself at all,' he said, 'you defer to the opinions of others and the wishes of your husband. When will you awake to your own needs and desires?'

His hand slid down to the mound between her thighs, squeezed it gently and was withdrawn from her coat. They strolled on, side by side but not touching, past the bridge and along the Quai de Montebello. To their left, across the river, the huge bulk of Notre-Dame reared up against the dark sky.

Nicole said nothing for a while, engrossed in her own thoughts. What he had said was ridiculous, of course, yet perhaps there was a small element of truth in it. Could it possibly be that she was too much concerned with her family duties and gave little thought to herself as a separate person, she asked herself. That she should even think in this way showed that she was already half-seduced by the memory of Pierre's cold fingers stroking her belly.

'You are silent,' he said eventually, 'is your mind troubled by what I said – it was no more than the truth.'

The light rub of the silk lining of her coat against the pink rose-buds of her breasts was really quite delicious, Nicole was thinking. If more women knew about it, Paris would surely be full of women in furs wearing nothing underneath – for she was sure that the sensation would, if she permitted it and walked far enough, lead to a crisis of delight!

So occupied was she with her own sensations that she paid no attention to what Pierre was saying. Needless to say, it was some nonsense about his extraordinary views of life – nothing which a sensible person could take seriously. More important to Nicole was the question of when he would decide that their strange promenade had lasted long enough and find a taxi to take them back to his apartment, where he could appease the desire he had aroused in her. The sooner the better, she thought.

Something he said caught her attention.

'What?' she said, not sure that she had heard him correctly, 'you want to go down onto the towpath?'

'*Sous les ponts de Paris*,' he half-sang, the words of the old song about the lovers of Paris and where they met.

'Out of the question!' Nicole said firmly, 'what am I – a girl picked up in a cheap cafe and taken under the bridge to be mauled?'

'No, you are not that,' he replied quickly, 'let us walk back to the Place St-Michel – we can get a taxi there.'

At last, she thought, as they turned around and headed back in the direction they had come. In spite of the early hour it was almost completely dark. There was not much traffic on this side of the river and few pedestrians, though the time for home-going was close for those who were compelled by their circumstances to work for their living. Pierre guided her across the road and they were soon not far from the old Tour d'Argent restaurant. From there to the Place St-Michel would take not more than a few minutes.

The best intentions go most often wrong, as Nicole was to discover. Her state of mind was no secret – Pierre understood well enough that her eroticism had been savagely awakened by her uncommon circumstances and he was content to stroll along by her side, sure in his mind that he would have his way. Once the volcano of sensuality comes to life and announces its powers by little shakes of the ground, nature will take its course. As well try to bottle up Vesuvius as to check the rising pressure in a human being at this stage. The eruption is inevitable – the onlooker has only to wait.

They were perhaps halfway along the Quai St Michel when Nicole halted, her knees trembling so violently that Pierre had to put an arm around her and support her. Her open mouth and staring eyes told him all that he needed to know – she was almost in a state of ecstasy from the touch of her coat on her bare body and the wild imaginings brought on by her nakedness.

A few steps ahead of them a narrow street – no more than an alley – led off the Quai. He led her round the corner and twenty steps or so into the semi-darkness of the deserted little street. She was without strength to protest as he placed her with her back to the ancient building behind her and stood close, his feet between hers.

'Not here!' she pleaded as he opened her coat to give himself access to her body.

Even in speaking the words she knew that they were futile. What choice had she? Her excitement was at fever-pitch and there was no possible way of avoiding the critical moment she knew to be fast approaching. Perhaps it was better if Pierre brought it on swiftly and so ended her marvellous torment.

160

He opened his expensive camel-hair overcoat, then his jacket, and finally his trousers. Nicole sighed and shook in a mixture of pleasure and apprehension as she felt the blunt head of his stiff projection touch the soft lips between her thighs and then push slowly upwards into her. To do it here on the street, like dogs coupling – it was monstrous, shameful, she thought – yet she was powerless to prevent it. More than that, unless it happened speedily she felt that she would explode. Pierre's hands were busy with her firm-pointed breasts for a while, rolling and squeezing them. The touch sent waves of unbearable pleasure through her, for his hands were like cold fire on her skin. Then his hands slid round her sides and downwards as his thrusting became more insistent, to grasp the cheeks of her bottom and hold her steady.

To preserve the last shred of decency Nicole held the sides of her coat as far round his body as they would go, as if to enclose him in it with her. She knew that it would be only moments before her climax of passion arrived – already she was experiencing in her breasts and belly the tingling which was the prelude to the act of high drama itself. She hoped fervently that Pierre would be equally quick, so that they could abandon this dangerously compromising encounter in a public place.

There were footsteps from her right. She stared wide-eyed over Pierre's shoulder as a man approached in the gloom. He walked straight past without even a glance, for in Paris no one pays any attention to lovers huddled together in a dark corner.

Pierre was strong and forceful, as he had been the first time with her in the rear seat of his automobile. She had been too nervous then to respond but now, in infinitely more risky circumstances, she was responding all too well! With joy – and it must be added, with relief – Nicole abandoned herself to the tremendous upsurge of sensation in her body. She moaned in her ecstasy and clung tightly to Pierre to squeeze her belly tight against him and drive him deeper into her.

He too was only a heart-beat or two away from his

zenith. His hands unclenched themselves from her bottom and moved outwards to force her arms away from him, until he held her by the wrists. He pinned her arms to the wall at shoulder level, so that she felt almost as if she was being crucified against it! He leaned backward away from her until only their loins touched, her fur coat fell open and her entire body was revealed in its nakedness, round breasts, smooth belly, and parted thighs! He stared down at all this tender white skin gleaming in the darkness of the alley, his mouth drawn back to show his teeth in a grimace. The effect was more that of a wolf's snarl than a human expression of tenderness at this most intimate of moments.

Nicole groaned aloud in horror at being so exposed. She fought against his grip in an attempt to free her arms and push him away from her. Let him fountain his passion against the wall – she wanted no more of him. But her struggles were of no avail. He held her easily, his natural strength reinforced threefold by his raging emotions. Fortunately for Nicole, her mental anguish was brief – a few more fast lunges against her set off Pierre's rapturous spasms and she felt the evidence of his release flood hotly into her most secret place. Seven times she counted his urgent convulsion within her, then he relaxed his hold on her wrists, sighed deeply in satisfaction and smiled in the darkness, a real smile this time, not a grimace. The instant he took a step away from her, Nicole wrapped her coat tightly round her and pressed it against her still trembling body with her arms, seeking its protection.

In retrospect, the episode had been exciting, she decided later on, however distasteful it had seemed at the time. Pierre de Barbin had twice treated her as casually as if she were a street-walker, pulling her into the back of his car, standing her up against a wall – all for his very curious pleasure. He was, without doubt, a most unusual person. Who else, in his right mind, would strip a beautiful woman, walk her about the streets and make love to her in such limiting and uncomfortable circumstances? It must be admitted that no woman would find a liaison with him boring – quite the opposite! Yet, to be frank, such encounters were necessarily somewhat less than satisfactory – at least to Nicole. She prefered the comfort and privacy of a proper bedroom, and enough time to savour love's pleasures to the full – not these snatched moments of raging passion in unsuitable places.

Obviously Pierre thought that far too conventional to be of interest to a person of his liberated tendencies. That is all very well, Nicole decided, but as far as I am concerned he is an unsatisfactory lover. Unless he can be made to understand my point of view, I shall stop seeing him. He shall have one more opportunity to understand me, an undertaking which will require great effort on my part – and on his!

For almost a week she refused his invitations to meet him while she gave serious thought to the best way of bringing him to her point of view. When she was ready, she met him for lunch one day – not in any of the fashionable restaurants where she might be recognised, but in a small and charming place on the Left Bank. He was already installed at a discreet table when she arrived, he rose to bow and kiss her hand and she behaved towards him in her most pleasant manner. Over an aperitif and the ordering of their meal Pierre talked easily and without stopping, telling her how much he had missed her, how beautiful she was, how chic her hat was – the usual thousand little things men say on these occasions. Halfway through the meal, as they were enjoying their steak *au poivre* with a salad of chicory and endives, Nicole set in motion the plan she had formulated. Under the table, hidden from all eyes, she slipped off one of her elegant shoes and stretched out her leg towards Pierre. He paused in mid-sentence, his loaded fork halfway to his mouth, and a thoughful expression appeared on his face as a silk-stockinged little foot inserted itself between his thighs, under the linen table-napkin spread over his lap.

'Go on with what you were saying,' Nicole encouraged him.

'Yes . . . where was I?'

'You were speaking of the importance of disseminating your ideals of true personal freedom. I find the subject of great interest.'

The proximity of her foot to his treasured part was very pleasant and Pierre expounded his thesis of liberty, equality and fraternity cheerfully. Meanwhile Nicole was probing delicately with her toes. She located a soft bulge within his trousers, alongside his left thigh, and pressed it with the ball of her foot until she felt it harden.

Pierre interrupted his discourse once more to say softly.

'Chérie – what you are doing is delightful. But the time and place are not appropriate. Later, yes?'

Nicole arched her plucked eyebrows in surprise.

'Why inappropriate?' she asked. 'You spoke a moment ago of total liberty to express our feelings.'

'I was making a general point, you must see that.'

'I understand perfectly. But there is something I would like to have explained to me. It is this – in your ideal republic of complete freedom from restraint, do you envisage women as equal citizens with men? Or will it be complete freedom for men and subjection for women?'

'I see women as equal citizens, of course!' he protested. 'How could you think otherwise?'

'Your protest at my freedom of expression made me suspect that you were not entirely serious.'

'But surely you see that I was speaking of different circumstances,' he said, glancing around the restaurant with a worried expression.

'Are you certain that you are not being hypocritical?' Nicole asked.

He was, it may well be imagined, in some discomfort, both physical and mental, at that moment. The physical discomfort he resolved by setting down his knife and fork and reaching under his table napkin to free his standing part from the pressure of his trouser-leg, so that it could assume a more natural position upright against his belly. The mental discomfort was not so easily dealt with.

'Nicole – we are in a restaurant, surrounded by people,' he said urgently.

'Did you think that I hadn't noticed?' she asked pleasantly. 'The last time we met we walked along the Quais – you fully dressed and I naked except for my fur coat and stockings. That too was a public place – there were passers-by. Yet you took it into your head to arouse me. More than that, you opened my coat and made love to me against a crumbling wall.'

'Ah, it was magnificent!' said Pierre. 'The setting was so exciting – for you as well as for me. You cannot deny that it was pleasant – you gave me proof of your pleasure long before I gave you proof of mine.'

Nicole's little foot had crept forward between his thighs, her heel on the chair cushion, until the sole rested against the swelling inside his trousers.

'I admit it,' she said, smiling at him, 'the experience was bizarre and yet very enjoyable. In the same way, do you not find it enjoyable to be aroused by me now?'

Her foot was pressing rhythmically against its trapped quarry. Her question posed a dilemma for the preacher of liberty from restraint.

'As to that,' he answered slowly, his face pink, 'it is impossible to deny that I enjoy what you are doing.'

'Exactly – the signs are unmistakable. How hard and strong you are, even through your clothes.'

'But that is the point – the signs of a man's excitement are very obvious. When we walked along the Quai, no one could observe that you were aroused.'

'But you knew,' Nicole countered, 'and I certainly knew. So why is it any different now?'

Pierre's face was flushed under the stress of the emotions stirred in him by the gentle but insistent massage of her foot against his most sensitive part.

'Nicole – I beg you to stop,' he said breathlessly.

'Give me your reasons.'

'Because this is too much . . . I must leave the table until I am calm again.'

'If you must – but dare you stand up in your present condition, Pierre? Dare you walk across the restaurant like that? In my opinion the friction of your clothes will produce an interesting crisis before you are across the room.'

'My God, it's true!' he murmured, 'I cannot risk moving from this chair.'

'Then you must sit and listen to me for once.'

'Stop what you are doing, I implore you!'

Her foot ceased its movement and rested lightly against him.

'The theories you explained to me during our walk,' said Nicole, 'I have thought about them and I find them without value. They are no more than a thin disguise for your desire to subjugate women to your will.'

'That is a monstrous thing to say!'

Her foot resumed its exciting but embarrassing motion against him.

'Do not interrupt,' she said, 'or it will be the worse for you. How will you leave the restaurant if I keep you in your present state?'

'I won't say another word,' he assured her quickly.

The erotic pressure stopped.

'If you really believed in your own theories,' Nicole continued, 'then you would not be in the least perturbed when someone else pursued the same logic. You would accept that as a tribute to the validity of your ideas. In short, my friend, you would not at this moment be in the least embarrassed because I have touched you with my foot and caused you to become stiff.'

Pierre opened his mouth to say something, but a warning pressure between his legs silenced him.

'Suppose we follow this thought to its conclusion,' said Nicole, 'we reach an interesting prospect, I believe. If you were sincere in your beliefs, then that sincerity would demand that instead of objecting to my initiative, you would happily co-operate with it. Is that not so?'

'Co-operate?' he gasped, his face a bright red.

Pierre's circumstances were peculiar indeed at that moment. Her foot was still, and for that he was grateful. Nevertheless, its earlier caressing had stirred his passions to an almost intolerable extent. Not just the physical dress, for as all lovers know well, in these matters the physical aspect provides perhaps a third of the excitement and the mind provides the other two-thirds. The thought itself of Nicole's foot caressing his upstanding part in so public a place – the incredible prospect of what it might make happen if she continued – his imagination had seized on these considerations and aroused him to an incredible extent.

'Do you need to ask how?' she said. 'Obviously, you could undo your trouser buttons at once.'

'To let your foot enter?' he gasped.

'More than that.'

'What?'

'Undo your trouser buttons for me, Pierre, pull up your shirt and let your big strong stem out so that I can rub it with my foot. Surely that does not shock a person of your advanced opinions?'

'Oh . . .' Pierre sighed.

'Imagine how very pleasant it will be – the thrilling touch of my silk stocking against the tender head,' she whispered across the table.

Pierre stared down into his lap. Her words had captured his imagination completely. In his mind's eye he envisaged his stiff pink part poking out of his open trousers, its head purple with passion. Nicole's foot pressed firmly against him and he uttered a tiny half-stifled moan of pleasure.

From the other side of the table Nicole gazed humorously at his flushed face and into his eyes – half-open but seeing nothing, blinded by the turmoil of his emotions. She rocked her foot backwards and forwards on her heel as fast as she could, confident now that he was unable to resist any longer. He was entirely in her power, as she had been in his on the Quai St-Michel.

'Ah . . .' he sighed.

Her foot rocked – only a few moments of this treatment were required to push him beyond the limit of endurance. He jerked upright in his chair, one hand flew to his mouth and he bit his knuckle to prevent himself from crying out

167

aloud as the torrent of his passion was suddenly unleashed. Against the sole of her foot Nichole could feel the vibration of his straining part as it discharged itself inside his shirt. She smiled as he shuddered and fought to control himself through his climactic pleasure.

She withdrew her foot and slipped it back into her shoe as a waiter approached the table. He enquired everything was to their satisfaction, a small gesture of his hand indicating the unfinished meal.

'Yes,' said Nicole, smiling brightly at him, 'Everything is to our satisfaction. The food is delicious but we became so engrossed in conversation that we both forgot to eat.'

She took up her knife and fork and resumed her meal. Pierre, his face averted, did the same.

'Thank you, Madame,' said the waiter, topping up their wine glasses.

He departed, convinced that they were so deeply in love that nothing else was of importance to them – a circumstance he had encountered often enough. Such couples annoyed the chef de cuisine, as one would expect, but in the waiter's experience a liberal tip was usually forthcoming when they left.

'Have you recovered?' Nicole asked sweetly.

'My God – what have you done!'

'Surely you have more reason than I to know that.'

'But if someone had seen! The waiter seemed suspicious.'

'Calm yourself. He knows nothing and suspects nothing. Finish your lunch.'

'I cannot eat now. We must leave at once.'

'Where are we going?'

Pierre surreptitiously groped inside his jacket to pull his wet shirt away from his skin.

'To my apartment – I must change out of these clothes.'

'And then?'

'What do you mean?'

'When I accepted your invitation to lunch it was because

168

thought that you had planned some new and outrageous
way of enlightening me further in the ways of freedom,'
said Nicole, 'don't tell me that you have lost interest,
Pierre?'

THE SOLICITUDE OF PAULINE DEVREUX

Taking Gisèle home by taxi, Roger put his arms about her without hesitation and kissed her. She returned his kiss warmly, for at eighteen the whole of life was waiting for the two of them to explore and enjoy. The kiss lasted a long time and during the course of it Roger's hand moved up the girl's side until it touched, then gently clasped, a small and soft breast through the thin material of her frock. Gisèle sighed into his open mouth and the tip of her tongue touched the tip of his tongue. This was not, to be sure, the first time Roger had ever kissed her, nor the first time he had fondled her prettly little breasts. He was encouraged by her sigh and took it to signify that his attentions might proceed further without the hindrance of maidenly reticence on her part.

Could it even be, he asked himself as the kiss continued and his hand stroked her breast until he felt the tiny nipple grow firm through her frock – could it be that Gisèle was not a virgin? His experience, brief though it was, told him that well-brought-up girls of her age quite often were virgins still, and always claimed that they were. This, naturally, was a matter of considerable annoyance to a young man whose blood was hot from kissing and touching, only to be halted in his tracks by a querulous or timid 'No, you mustn't do that!' Ah, those terrible experiences of youth, when nature made it imperative to leave a reluctant young virgin and make one's way – in great discomfort from the pressure of a bulge in the trousers, to the house on the Boulevard des Italiens and there to pay a woman of the house for the privilege of using her warm body to satisfy the raging desires aroused by some eighteen year old girl who refused to spread her legs!

But with Gisèle he felt that matters might turn out differently. Her mouth was hot upon his and her body was responding to his caresses. He gasped as her hand found

170

s way into his lap and tested the extent of his arousal.
Her mouth pulled away from his at last, she giggled and
swung her legs up so that they lay over his thighs. Could
there be a more open invitation to proceed? Roger's hand
abandoned her breasts and slid under her frock and up her
leg until he touched the smooth flesh above her
stocking-top. At that very moment he fell in love with her
for the generosity of her response to him. He knew with
complete certainty that she would deny him nothing that
evening.

The practical question of where the final act in this
drama of the passions could take place was almost driven
from his mind by the surge of emotion let loose in him by
the satin skin of her thigh under his hand. Not in the back
of a taxi trundling through the streets of Paris! Yet as his
trembling fingers eased forward inside her underwear to
encounter the silky floss covering her warm and secret
treasure, Roger was so transported by desire that he
would have been capable of making love to her right there
in the taxi, even under the sardonic eye of the driver, if
need be. But good sense prevailed and with her warm
prize firmly in his grasp he whispered,

'We'll go to a small hotel I know behind the Opera.
When do you have to be home?'

'There's no need for that,' she whispered back, 'there's
no one at home.'

She swung her slim legs off his lap and sat upright a
moment before the taxi stopped and the driver announced
Avenue Montaigne.'

The apartment was dark and silent. Gisèle switched on
no lights but led Roger by the hand along the hall and into
the salon. The long curtains were undrawn and the street-
lamps outside provided the only illumination.

'Is your mother away?' Roger asked as she drew him
down to sit beside her on a long sofa.

'She's out with her friend Larnac.'

'But what if she returns and finds us here together?'

Gisèle giggled.

'She won't be back before two in the morning. She goes

to his apartment with him after dinner and he brings her home when they've finished.'

Further enquiries on his part were made impossible by Gisèle's mouth finding his. In moments they were lying side by side on the sofa and the enchantments of her young body were his to explore and enjoy. In a very short space of time matters had progressed to the point where Gisèle's frock was up round her waist and her underwear discarded. Her left knee was bent and raised to permit free access to her most tender secret and her busy hands bared his quivering appendage to guide it home.

'Ah, chérie . . .' Roger breathed as warm folds accepted him and he eased forward into this delicious haven.

The events of the next few seconds were confused. A scream of rage erupted from somewhere behind Roger, he was seized by the hair and dragged away from Gisèle so violently that he fell off the sofa and landed painfully on the floor. He looked up, bemused by the fall, to see – with what horror can only be imagined – Gisèle's mother standing over him. She was shouting angrily but it took some moments for the import of the scene in which he was an unwilling participant to register fully in his mind. He glanced over his shoulder at Gisèle, just in time to see the pale gleam of her belly and thighs vanish as she pulled down her frock and scrambled off the sofa.

'Go to your room!' her mother shouted, 'I'll deal with you in the morning!'

As Gisèle ran from the room, Madame Devreux switched on a standing lamp beside the sofa.

'As for you,' she raged at Roger, 'my God, Roger Tanguy – it's you!'

'Madame Devreux,' he said hurriedly, 'please, I implore you, do not leap to conclusions.'

'Conclusions!' she retorted, 'I find my daughter lying here with her clothes round her neck and you beside her in *that* condition. What conclusions should I reach then?'

Roger looked down at where her accusing finger was pointing and became aware that his trousers were wide

172

pen and his male part thrusting stiffly out, fully exposed
Madame Devreux's angry stare.

'Excuse me,' he murmured in embarrassment while he
astily concealed the offending member.

'Get off the floor and sit properly,' she ordered, 'there
re things which must be said before you leave.'

Roger seated himself on the sofa and Madame Devreux
at at the other end of it, as far from him as its length
llowed. She was wearing a long saffron nightdress over
which she had thrown, evidently in a hurry, a white
egligée and she was barefoot. Obviously she had been in
ed when Roger and Gisèle arrived at the apartment.
Could it be, Roger wondered, that she had brought her
over back with her and that even now he was in Ma-
ame's bedroom? If so, that would make the predicament
lightly easier to get out of, if he used his wits.

'I hardly know where to begin,' said Madame Devreux
n an icy voice, 'to find my daughter in the very act with
he son of a close friend . . .'

'But surely that is preferable to finding her with a
omplete stranger?' said Roger.

'Is that meant to be funny?'

'Why no, not at all. What I meant was that it is better
or Gisèle to have a dear friend who is someone you know
nd whose family you know than for her to form a
riendship with a person of uncertain origin.'

'You are suggesting that my daughter is in the habit of
asual fornication?'

'Certainly not! Gisèle is a beautiful girl and I am a man.
What more natural than that we should be drawn to each
other in mutual esteem, however deplorable you as a
mother may find it.'

'You have a slippery tongue. Do you love my daughter
or do you merely wish to sleep with her?'

'I adore her!'

'Do you wish to marry her?'

'Marry?' said Roger in dismay. 'Why Madame, surely
she and I are far too young to contemplate so important a
step.'

'Too young to marry but not too young to enjoy th pleasures of the honeymoon – is that it?'.

'As to that . . .' and Roger's mind began to work faste as little incidents from the past presented themselves fror the depths of his memory, 'surely it is you, Madam Devreux, who would be pleased to see me marry Gisèle. think that you have wanted that for some time.'

'Why do you say that?' she asked, her tone softening.

'The way in which she and I have so often met eac other by chance – or so it seemed then – here or at m home and at other places. It was your doing – confess it you have been pushing us towards each other for a lon time.'

'You exaggerate. Of course, I am not saying that would be unhappy if you and Gisèle wished to marry eacl other.'

'Because my father is a Senator?'

'No, no! Because your mother is a close friend an because you are a most handsome and acceptable youn man.'

'But too young to marry for some years yet, I mus remind you. My father would never agree.'

'I don't mean this year, Roger – perhaps not for severa years. But it would please me to think that the possibilit existed.'

'I thought you had a greater regard for my cousir Gérard – and he is some years older than me,' Roge teased her.

'Oh without doubt Gérard is a fine young man and the Brissards are a family of note and distinction. But I've always preferred you to him. Now, tell me frankly, Roger how long has this *affaire* been going on between you and Gisèle?'

'To be truthful, tonight was the first occasion on which I . . .' he broke off and shrugged.

'I see. So tonight my little girl has become a woman.'

'As to that, I can make no comment, Madame.'

'What are you saying? That she has been with someone else?'

174

'I have nothing to say on that, but I remind you that Gisèle is a beautiful young woman and must have had admirers before me. How could she not be beautiful, being the daughter of so elegant and attractive a mother?'

'Flatterer!' said Madame Devreux, passing one hand lightly over her hair, 'Yet it is true, Gisèle has her looks from me, everyone says that. Of course, she insists on pursuing this ridiculous modern fashion of looking like a bean-pole. She starves herself to skin and bone and hides her figure to make herself resemble a boy. Twenty years ago it was very different when I was her age. We young girls then were proud of having figures like an hour-glass. The ideal was to have a full bosom and rounded hips.'

'I have not the least doubt that you were the ideal of every man who saw you, Madame Devreux. You have preserved your voluptuous figure in spite of the dictates of dressmakers.'

'Ah, you understand me,' she sighed, 'yet to you I must seem terribly old.'

'Not at all,' said Roger gallantly, confident of himself now that the point of the conversation had shifted away from himself and his frustrated little adventure with Gisèle, 'vogues come and go according to the whims of expensive couturiers, but the fundamental beauty of woman remains and is unaffected. The Venus de Milo in the Louvre has not ceased to be the ideal of feminine beauty simply because some idiot has decreed that women should flatten their breasts and disguise their hips. On the contrary, we men cherish the ideal in our hearts and wait patiently for the day when women will again display their true and natural charms.'

'To find such good sense in one so young!' said Madame Devreux. 'How refreshing – even, I may say – how encouraging!'

Although Roger was aware of no change of position on her part, the fact was that she was no longer at the other end of the long sofa. Indeed, she was quite close to him, close enough for him to detect the musky fragrance of the perfume she wore.

'You credit me with good sense,' he said, 'but I pride
myself on my good taste. It is apparent to me, as to any
man of discernment, that your breasts are most beautifully
shaped.'

Her response to his boldness was not unexpected.

'Do you think so, Roger?' and her hand smoothed her
bosom gently upwards.

'Without question. As you have said yourself, the
young women of today have no breasts. In some manner I
cannot understand they have transformed nature so as to
deprive themselves of what should be a woman's most
enchanting attributes. It is sad – tragic almost.'

'Quite beyond belief,' Madame Devreux agreed, her
hand still gently smoothing her own bosom through her
negligée.

'Dare I say it?' he exclaimed. 'Yes, your understanding
has given me the courage to say what otherwise I would
never dare – I would consider myself the most fortunate
man in Paris if you were so gracious as to permit me one
glimpse of these delights. There, it is said!'

'I can scarcely believe what I am hearing! A young man
half my age asking me to reveal my bosom!'

'Not asking, Madame, pleading for an opportunity to be
made aware of the glories of one who has the courage and
strength of will to ignore the fleeting silliness of the crowd
and remain staunchly loyal to herself.'

'How can I refuse so enchanting a plea?' she sighed.

She slipped negligée and nightgown off her shoulders
and exposed to him a pair of full round breasts.

'Magnificent!' Roger exclaimed, 'I can never thank you
enough for this rare privilege.'

'You are not disappointed then?'

'You do yourself an injustice to ask that question. Your
breasts are incomparable.'

'Then you do not find them large and inelegant?'

'A thousand times no! They are sensuous in the extreme. May I dare to hope that you will allow me to signify
my admiration by saluting them with a respectful kiss?'

'Roger! How can such a thought enter your head? Not a

quarter of an hour ago you were lying here with my daughter.'

'I can assure you that the incident has been utterly wiped from my memory by the splendours you have been so good as to reveal to me.'

With great tenderness he imprinted kisses on each of her soft breasts. They were warm to his lips, the skin delicate of texture, creamy-white with tiny and delicious blue veins faintly visible through the translucence of the skin. Her nipples were already firm in the centre of red-brown discs almost the size of the palm of his hand.

'You go too far,' she murmured coquettishly as his wet tongue flicked at them.

'Such opulence of warm and tender flesh,' he replied, 'Ah, the foolishness of women who crush such delights brutally inside tight clothes – and the total foolishness of men who admire women with chests like boys! You have given me a glimpse of a world I never knew existed, Madame, and I shall be eternally grateful to you.'

Roger was certain now that Larnac was not in the bedroom. Evidently he and Madame Devreux had parted early for some reason. There was something else of which he was sure – Madame Devreux had been emotionally stirred by the unexpected sight of her daughter and a man in the act of love. She had displayed her emotion in the form of outraged anger, that being what morality required – to say nothing of a mother's instinct to protect her child, even against the child's own wishes if need be. But in truth, as the events of the last few minutes had proved, the anger was only a disguise for a more profound emotion – one which had embarrassed her in the presence of her daughter. Now that Gisèle was no longer in the room, there was no need for disguise – or only such flimsy disguise as would conform to polite convention. The emotion burning fiercely within Madame Devreux's heart was desire. Larnac had been remiss in his duty as a lover, Roger thought to himself as he continued to play with her breasts.

'This gratitude you spoke of,' she said, her voice trembling.

'You may rely upon it.'

'Then you may demonstrate it by resolving a question that troubles me.'

'What is it you wish to know?'

'It is difficult for me to explain without seeming to . . . what I mean is . . .'

'Please speak freely, I beg you, Madame.'

'When I came into the room, half asleep and half awake, to find you and Gisèle lying on the sofa together, I naturally pulled you away from her.'

'Very forcefully,' Roger agreed.

'I was upset, you must understand.'

'I understand perfectly.'

'Well, when you fell to the floor I could not help noticing . . . your trousers were undone, you see.'

'You noticed a certain part of me, you mean?'

'Yes . . . only very briefly, of course.'

'Of course.'

'What I am trying to put into words – the question which troubles me – is this. Had you actually reached the point with Gisèle at which you . . . no, I cannot say it.'

'I understand,' Roger assured her in his most soothing tone, 'do not distress yourself. You put an end to the tender passage between Gisèle and myself some seconds before either of us had reached that point. There, does that relieve your distress?'

His hands on her breasts were doing quite as much to relieve any distress she might feel as any words he could utter.

'Not entirely,' she murmured, 'my mind is still uneasy on another matter.'

'Then allow me to calm it. Tell me the cause of your anxiety.'

'That certain part of you which I happened to see quite by accident – well, Gisèle is very young and very slender. What I saw seemed out of proportion – I fear that you must have hurt her.'

'She gave no evidence of discomfort, Madame, only of pleasure.'

'I find that impossible to believe, Roger. I must ask you to show me plainly what I only glimpsed before so that I can judge for myself what condition she may be in. After all, medical attention may be necessary.'

'Really, Madame Devreux, what you are suggesting is most improper,' said Roger, smiling broadly.

'Not in the least. I am Gisèle's mother. I have a right to know to what she has been subjected. You cannot deny that.'

'You make it sound as if I raped her. I can assure you that she participated willingly.'

'How could she know what was involved, she is only a child.'

'She is eighteen.'

'A mere child. Good heavens, to what has she submitted in her youthful innocence!'

Without further permission, Madame Devreux began to unfasten Roger's trousers. He allowed her to proceed. For one thing, fondling her plump breasts had spread a diffused sensation of pleasure through him which was now beginning to concentrate itself in the part of his body she wished to examine. And for another, the interruption of his love-making with Gisèle only seconds from its culmination had left his nerves outraged to the point where, unless something else happened, it would be necessary for him to seek the solace of a professional woman in the house on the Boulevard des Italiens before going home to bed. And also, though he was not consciously aware of it, he was undoubtedly flattered by the degree of interest in the source of his masculine pride that so elegant a person as Madame Devreux was displaying.

'Very well,' he said, 'it shall be as you wish. I will conceal nothing from you, Madame.'

By then her busy fingers had laid him bare and she was staring round-eyed at his taut stem.

'Heavens!' she said faintly, 'it is not possible.'

'What is not possible?'

'That this huge and distended organ could have been lodged in the tender body of my poor daughter.'

179

'But she is fully grown in every respect. We encountered no problems.'

'No, it is impossible. Why, the circumference is such that I can only just get my hand round it.'

She suited the action to her words and clasped it warmly

'Yet I give you my word, Madame, that there were no difficulties of the type you are suggesting.'

'She must have suffered, my poor daughter. Why, the length is monstrous – there is no way in which it could have been accommodated.'

Roger encountered no resistance as he gently urged Madame Devreux to lie full-length on the sofa with her head on his lap. Indeed if the truth were told, she displayed a certain enthusiasm in approaching her face so nearly to the object of her interest, in order to examine it more closely. Her enthusiasm was, of course, tempered with dismay at the size of what she beheld, though Roger knew beyond a doubt that in this respect he was averagely endowed and that her expressions of dismay were wholly false. He continued to stroke her exposed breasts during the lengthy time when she was eyeing his equipment.

'Your touch is very exciting,' she breathed, her face pink with emotion.

'To caress *you* is very exciting,' he responded, 'it appears to me that you and I have progressed to a level of communication when words would be only a barrier to the exchange of understanding between us.'

'Yes, what you say is unquestionably true.'

Roger's hand moved slowly down under her nightgown to her belly and he stroked it in a gentle circular motion.

'Do you not find me too plump for your modern taste?' she asked, 'I'm not a skinny creature like . . .'

'Like your daughter, you mean, Madame?'

'Please . . . you must call me Pauline. Formality is ridiculous now that we have revealed everything to each other.'

'Not quite everything, Pauline,' and his hand slid further down her warm belly until his finger-tips touched her hidden patch of crinkly hair.

'Ah no – that is presumptuous of you!' she exclaimed and her hand grasped his wrist to prevent his exploring further.

'But why?'

'What sort of person are you, Roger? I discover you with your *hand* between my daughter's legs and immediately you attempt to thrust it between mine.'

'But with good reason,' he answered, 'between hers I encountered the charms of a young girl. Between your thighs I am certain that I shall discover the warm and generous delights of a fully grown woman of the world. Do you blame me for this?'

'Such a comparison can never be permitted! It would be unnatural,' she protested as his finger-tips gained another centimetre or two against the restraint of her hand encircling his wrist. He touched the top join of the fleshy lips under a covering of hair.

'How can that be?' Roger asked, 'I am a man of good appetite. The hors-d'oeuvre was snatched away before I had finished it. Is the main course to be removed before I even begin? If so, I shall leave with my hunger totally unsatisfied.'

'You beast!' she moaned, 'to compare Gisèle and me to the courses of a meal – it is abominable!'

Perhaps she believed her own words, perhaps they were merely a token protest. What is sure is that her grasp loosened on his wrist and his fingers found the vantage point they had been seeking. Madame Devreux gasped loudly as he pried apart those soft folds of flesh and penetrated her citadel.

In all this, Roger's intention was to arouse and please her to the point where she would offer no further resistance, then hoist up her long nightgown and board her as she lay on the convenient sofa. But her degree of arousal was greater than he had realised and he had utterly forgotten the proximity of her face to his free-standing part. Scarcely had he begun to caress her moist bud than she rolled her head in his lap and took his full-stretched device into her hot and wet mouth.

181

'Take care!' he said jerkily, made suddenly aware of how excited he had himself become during the process of playing with her big breasts.

His warning went unheard and unheeded. Madame Devreux moaned in her throat as she pressed home her assault on his most sensitive part. Her back lifted off the sofa and she thrust herself hard against his rubbing fingers. In one moment more Roger was overwhelmed by sensation and his essence was sucked from him. Through his delirious pleasure he was vaguely aware of his companion's legs and bottom thrashing against the sofa cushions as she too underwent her climactic experience.

When she had recovered herself a little, Madame Devreux sat up and put her feet on the floor. She moved away from him, pulled her nightgown up and slid the straps over her shoulders, then closed and tied her negligée.

'Thank God I was able to prevent the final infamy,' she announced.

'What do you mean? There can be no infamy in love between a man and a woman.'

'Between you and me it would have been infamous.'

'But why?'

'You know perfectly well why. Half an hour ago you made love to my daughter. And then you attempt to do it to me. This is infamous, to employ the same organ on a mother and her daughter.'

'I have only the one,' Roger pointed out reasonably.

'This is not a subject for mockery.'

'My profound apologies.'

'You must leave now, Roger, and never come back. You are not to see my daughter again. Is that understood?'

'Do not distress yourself, Madame. I shall take my leave.'

He rose and bowed politely, only then remembering to tuck away his *infamous* organ and to fasten his trousers. To his surprise Madame Devreux also rose to see him to the door, her arms folded firmly across her bosom as if to protect herself from an attack.

'Try to understand my feelings, Roger,' she said to him in

182

the entrance hall. 'It is my duty to protect Gisèle from the consequences of her folly until she finds a husband.'

'I do understand,' he replied, giving her his most charming smile, 'a mother's duty is sacred. May I kiss your hand in farewell?'

She stretched out her hand and he kissed the back of it lightly but with feeling.

'Ah, if only . . .' he sighed.

'If only what, Roger?'

'If only I had dared to direct my attentions towards you rather than towards Gisèle . . . what pleasures you and I might have enjoyed together. But it was quite unthinkable for me to raise my eyes in the direction of so exalted a person as yourself, whatever the urging of my heart.'

'You are an impudent young man,' Madame Devreux said softly, 'I am twenty years older than you. My daughter is your contemporary.'

'Yet what are a few years difference between lovers when their deepest sentiments are engaged. I should have been bolder.'

Her hand was on the door knob, yet she paused at his words.

'Since it is goodbye,' said Roger, 'permit me to kiss you respectfully on the cheek as a sign of peace between us.'

'Do it and go.'

Roger put his hands lightly on her shoulders and kissed her cheek, then the other cheek – and then her mouth, his arms about her to press her body close to him. For a moment she resisted, then as the tip of his tongue insinuated itself between her lips, she relaxed and enjoyed the embrace. After all, it was only a kiss – nothing more would happen.

What did happen was that Roger's hands slid down her back, smoothing her thin nightgown and negligée against her skin, until he could grasp and hold the fleshy cheeks of her bottom.

'No!' she exclaimed, breaking off the kiss, 'you must not do that!'

With half a step Roger turned her so that her back was

183

against the door and his foot between hers. Short of screaming for help, she could do little to prevent him from proceeding further, if that was his intention. As indeed it was, for with one hand he hitched up her loose clothes at the back and with the other he parted the cheeks of her bottom and probed with his fingers until he was touching her furry mound. Madame Devreux attempted to get her hands between their bodies in order to push him away, but he was pressed too close for that.

'Stop it at once!' she commanded nervously.

His finger-tip was within the warm and secret place he had previously stimulated when they were together on the sofa. Madame Devreux's resistance was not long sustained after that. What woman of her age could reject the attentions of a handsome young man once his skilful fingers had penetrated the citadel of her passions? Only the most determined, and in the circumstances in which she found herself, Madame Devreux was not excessively determined. Deep sighs of pleasure squeezed her full breasts against Roger's chest, stimulating her even more. Her hands descended to his narrow hips and held him, perhaps even pulled their bodies closer together, if that was possible.

'I surrender,' she murmured, hardly aware of her own words.

Thus encouraged, Roger hauled her night clothes up around her waist.

'Raise your left leg,' he instructed her, even as he dealt one-handed with his trouser buttons.

'My God, not here! Surely you do not intend . . .'

He cut off her feeble outcry by pressing his mouth to hers in a long kiss. Her foot left the floor, her knee bent upwards and outwards. Roger steadied her against the door while he positioned his firm part at the entrance to her secret spot, then bent his knees a little and pushed slowly and yet inexorably upwards until he was fully embedded. With one arm around her waist and the other supporting her raised leg, he had her fully under control.

The unfamiliarity of the position – or perhaps the

strangeness of her plight – affected Madame Devreux deeply. Her whole experience of the delights of love until that moment had been limited to lying comfortably on her back on a bed, with a partner lying on her. For her, the bizarre nature of what was taking place had a distinctly aphrodisiac quality. Tremors ran through her body, from the centre of her joy up to her breasts and down her legs. But for the support afforded her by Roger she would surely have fallen to the floor. The door against which she was pressed rattled as if sharing in her delight, until Roger shuffled a foot forward against it, without missing a single thrust, to silence this inanimate witness to Madame Devreux's pleasure.

'I'm there!' she exclaimed, her belly shaking against his, 'oh God!'

But Roger was not. Only a very short time had elapsed since their curious passage on the sitting-room sofa and though he enjoyed the recuperative powers of youth, he required a little longer to scale the heights a second time.

Madame Devreux's dark head lolled back against the door, her face flushed and yet content. Her body was limp as Roger drove on towards his goal. She still held him by the hips, no longer pulling him towards her but in submission to what he was doing to her.

Had Roger not been at that moment utterly enrapt by the tremendous sensations coursing through his body, he might even have discerned a certain affection and pride in his prowess in the manner in which she held him while she waited for him to run the last lap of the course she had already completed.

The critical moments, when they arrived, were formidable. Roger panted and jolted and stabbed furiously into her submissive body, beside himself in the sharp joy of the male's conquest. Or seeming conquest – for who is the victor and who is the victim in the encounters of love? He was still trembling and breathing heavily in the afterglow of passion when Madame Devreux reached up to smooth back the lock of hair that had fallen across his perspiring forehead.

He eased himself away from her with care and courtesy, her long night clothes descended to her ankles, concealing all.

'I don't know what to say,' she murmured while he was adjusting his own clothes.

'What should you say, Pauline? Together we have enjoyed a momentous experience and it is for me to express my fervent gratitude to you for making it possible.'

'But I didn't want it to happen, you know that!'

'That is all in the past. There is no reason for regret, only for joy that so enchanting an encounter could be shared by you and me.'

'Perhaps you are right,' she said, smiling at him, 'regret is absurd. Goodnight, then, Roger.'

'I hope that you think better of me now than earlier this evening.'

'I hardly know what to think of you – or of myself. But one thing is for sure – every time I pass through this door in future I shall be reminded of what happened to me against it.'

On the next day Roger met Gisèle by arrangement at Fouquets in the Champs Élysées. His thoughts became more and more complicated as he sat waiting for her at a table on the terrace, but the moment he caught sight of her walking towards him, his spirits lifted. She looked extremely pretty and very young in a sleeveless frock of bright pink with a long yellow scarf tied under the collar and floating with her movements. The late spring sunshine made her light brown hair gleam, so that she was altogether enchanting.

Roger stood to greet her with a kiss on the cheek and she gave him a radiant smile.

'Whatever did you say to Mama last night?' she asked the instant she was seated.

'Why, how was she this morning?'

'Not one angry word – can you believe it? I expected her to be furious and scream at me all morning. I was dreading it.'

'What *did* she say?'

'She said that finding us like that had shocked her but that on reflection she had come to realise that I was no longer a child. She said that I must be treated like an adult and that I must behave like one. She said much more than that, of course, but that's what it amounted to.'

'Did you find out how she came to be there? You told me she was out.'

'Apparently she had a tremendous quarrel with Larnac in a restaurant and walked out on him. I gather that he won't be calling any more. I felt quite sorry for her – I mean, to lose your lover and find your daughter with a lover all on the same evening, it's too much for any woman. No wonder she was angry and upset. How did you manage to calm her down? Or did she just throw you out?'

'I stayed to talk to her for some time. It was not easy, but I urged reason upon her and eventually she took my point.'

'I think you're brilliant, Roger. If we weren't in a public place I'd hug you.'

'I would enjoy that. After all, we were interrupted last night at an unfortunate moment.'

Gisèle giggled at him.

'It would have been better if we had gone to a hotel as I suggested,' said Roger.

'Yes. My little visitor made his entrance and then ran away before I could make him properly welcome. That was very sad.'

'He was settling in very comforably when events forced him to retreat,' said Roger.

She was delightful, he thought – witty, amusing – and so very pretty with her slightly turned-up nose and shining brown eyes. He felt that he loved her to distraction.

'Are you free this evening?' he asked, touching her hand with a gesture that spoke eloquently of intimacies to be shared.

'No, Mama and I are invited for dinner at the Colombes. It will be boring.'

187

'Then tomorrow? Say yes, or I shall burst with love.'

'Not even tomorrow,' Gisèle answered sadly.

'Why not?'

'I have to vist my cousins in the country.'

'But this is terrible! When will you be back in Paris?'

'We could meet on Sunday.'

'And be together in a hotel?'

Gisèle nodded and smiled.

'Yes, I'd like that, Roger.'

Events were to prove themselves more complicated than Roger imagined. He was, after all, only eighteen years old and for all his assumed *savoir faire* he had everything still to learn about the ways of the world – and especially the ways of women. A pressing invitation from Madame Devreux took him to her home after dinner on Saturday evening.

She opened the door to him herself, from which he deduced that the servants had been given the evening off. On this occasion she was wearing a simple evening frock in silver grey with emerald clips on the neckline about where her collar-bones were. The hem was discreetly below her knees, longer than the styles worn by Gisèle.

'Sit down, Roger,' she said, 'will you take a little glass of something?'

'Cognac, if you please.'

He seated himself on the famous dusty-rose coloured sofa on which his consecutive encounters with Gisèle and her mother had taken place. Madame Devreux poured the cognac, handed one of the glasses to him and sat on a chair out of arm's-reach.

'We must talk very seriously,' she announced, her tone pleasant but firm.

'I am at your service.'

'Where to begin . . .? The truth is that I have been upset and worried since the other evening. You cannot imagine how upset I have been, remembering what occurred. I do not blame you, Roger, for anything. It was I who should have known better than to let myself be swept away by unseemly emotions.'

'My dear Pauline,' said Roger boldly, 'what use is this self-reproach? What happened was the natural outcome of the proximity of a man and a woman in circumstances which were, though unusual, extremely provocative. We both responded to the urgent dictates of our hearts, nothing more.'

'Ah, but you are young – you can dismiss from your mind an event which to me is a heavy burden.'

'A burden of guilt, you mean?' he asked in some surprise.

'Guilt, yes – but worse than that, a burden of jealousy.'

'I find it hard to understand what you mean.'

Madame Devreux's expression was woeful.

'Why should it be so difficult to understand?' she asked, 'Am I so old that I cannot be jealous of my own daughter? Am I not a woman too, with a heart as susceptible as that of a young girl? Did you leave me the other evening with the impression that all passion has withered in me?'

It would have taken a man older and more experienced than Roger to distinguish between the real and the false in Madame Devreux's anguish. If, that is, any man ever could. Like all women, she was sincere and yet at the same time had a concealed purpose. She was capable of honest emotions and deceit at the same time – without herself being able to tell the difference. In short, she was a woman.

Oblivious to this, Roger was on one knee before her, kissing her hand.

'Dear Pauline,' he said, 'how could I imagine that you could be interested in me in that way. I am deeply honoured.'

She stroked his cheek fondly.

'What a tragedy we are involved in,' she said, 'if only I were twenty years younger and you were not in love with my daughter!'

'It is true that I adore Gisèle. But believe me, there is a deep and enduring affection in my heart for you.'

'That may be – but how cruel!'

'Cruel?'

'Affection is not the emotion which you have awakened in me. Your feelings do not match mine, that is evident.'

'But I used the word affection in order not to risk offending you. Since you have shown me the way I will speak more openly – I adore you too. The truth is that you stir my profoundest passions.'

'Roger, take care what you say!'

'I have gone too far now to retreat. To be completely frank with you, once I had experienced the delights of your love I knew that I must find a way to return to you for more.'

'But what about Gisèle?'

'I love her too and I must possess her, as I must you.'

'But this is unnatural!'

'For me it is the most natural thing in the world to want to make love to the two women I adore. If you cannot accept that, you must tell me to leave.'

'My God, what will become of us,' she murmured, leaning forward to kiss his face.

'Only that which we desire for ourselves,' he replied, his hands on her waist.

'How can I tell my confessor that I have erred with my daughter's fiancé?'

'Tell him nothing,' said Roger instantly, 'what he doesn't know won't disturb his sleep.'

'But what of my conscience?'

His hands were on her breasts, moulding them through her frock.

'In matters of the heart there is no place for the quibbles of conscience. That is for priests and old women, not for lovers. I want you now, Pauline.'

'So young and already so forceful,' she sighed, her hands on his, pressing them more tightly over her breasts.

In her bedroom she took off the elegant silver-grey frock and stood revealed in a white lace slip and over it, from just below her bosom to her bottom, a white satin corset laced down the front.

'A sign that my youth is past,' she sighed, observing his interest in this garment, 'does it disgust you?'

'Why no, no such thought entered my head. Rather I was thinking that this is a disguise for the exuberance and bounty of your body. I find it strangely exciting.'

'Do you? You will change your opinion as you grow older.'

'Let me undo it!'

He knelt before her to puzzle out the cross-lacing and to unfasten it. When the corset fell away he ran his palms lovingly over her plump belly through her lace slip, then pressed his cheek against it.

'So warm and soft,' he said, 'how delightful!'

He stood up again, his face flushed red, and gently pulled the slip up over her head and threw it onto the bed. Beneath it she wore a bandeau brassiere of open lace-work to restrain her large breasts. She turned to let him find and undo the hooks and eyes which held it at the back. Once that was removed, he leaned against her back and reached round to fondle her breasts for a long time before pulling down her loose-legged silk knickers and planting kisses on the fleshy cheeks of her bottom.

Madame Devreux sat on the side of the bed to remove her shoes and stockings, while Roger tore off his clothes, scattering them across the carpet, before hurling himself on the bed beside her and clutching her fiercely in his arms.

With all the surging virility of eighteen, he gave a convincing account of himself in every way. As for Madame Devreux, she was delighted to have acquired a lover half the age and with twice the strength of Henri Larnac. That Roger had only a fraction of Larnac's finesse was a small matter that could be put right by a suitable course of education in bed.

After the third passage at arms she lay limp and contented, a faint sheen of perspiration between her breasts and over her broad belly.

'Do you really love me, Roger?'

'Madly,' he replied, 'Can you entertain the slightest doubt after the proof I have just given you?'

'And Gisèle?'

'She has not yet enjoyed the evidence of my love as you have. But she will, and soon.'

'Do not torment me!'

'Do not torment yourself, Pauline. Afterwards I shall return to you, to reassure you of my devotion.'

'What – you intend to pass backwards and forwards between us?'

'Why not?'

'You are proposing a conspiracy between you and me, no less.'

Roger shrugged and smiled, confident of his powers. He leaned over Madame Devreux to imprint gentle kisses on the insides of her thighs, her soft belly and the tips of her breasts.

'You are a cynical young man,' she said, 'and an immoral one too. But I find you irresistible.'

Her hand crept between his thighs to appraise the condition of his appurtenance. She also was confident of her powers. In their separate ways she and Gisèle would be able to shape Roger to the pattern they desired.

'Then it is agreed that I shall have you both?' he asked, smiling down at her.

'Why not?' she replied, using his own words.

Dr Moulin was a man of good sense, who understood that certain matters should be arranged with discretion, particularly if the Brissard family was in any way involved. When he was summoned to the bedside of Guy Verney, a short examination and a few questions were sufficient to inform him of the reasons of Guy's weakened condition and to start in his mind a train of thought that involved the interests of the Brissards. In consequence, Moulin instructed his patient to stay in bed and rest until his return the next day. He told Jeanne Verney that her husband was suffering from the strain of over-work, a diagnosis which surprised her. Then, without her knowledge, the good doctor arranged an urgent appointment with her brother, Maurice Brissard.

Maurice was amused by what the doctor told him in confidence.

'You wish me to believe that my brother-in-law has been indulging himself in masochistic practices?' he asked.

'His body is criss-crossed with the marks of old and new whippings and other abuse, Monsieur. Of the condition of his private parts I will say nothing.'

Maurice, who had no particular affection for Verney, laughed aloud.

'Extraordinary! But after all, it is his right to amuse himself in whatever way he chooses. Why have you come to me?'

'Perhaps you have not fully understood the gravity of the case,' said Moulin, a little shocked by Maurice's unexpected levity, 'Monsieur Verney's health is seriously undermined. If he should continue in these practices, I fear for his life.'

'As bad as that, is it? He must have been very enthusiastic about his pleasures.'

'You should not joke, Monsieur. How am I to tell Madame Verney of these things?'

Maurice's smile faded, for he was devoted to his sister.

'Leave that to me,' he said, 'what course of treatment do you propose for your patient?'

'Complete rest, for a long time, away from Paris. Somewhere quiet in the country perhaps. He will require a trained nurse in attendance.'

'Then, if you will be so good, find a suitable person at once. I will take care of the rest. And thank you for coming to me – your discretion will not go unrewarded.'

While Moulin made enquiries of his colleagues for a suitable person to undertake the task of nursing Guy back to health, Maurice visited his sister at her home in the Avenue Kléber. He explained everything to her with complete candour. Jeanne was not as amused as he had been, but she was practical, like him.

'He must be looked after properly,' she said, 'but we cannot risk any scandalous gossip – imagine what Papa would say if this came to his attention! Moulin has shown himself to be trustworthy and we may rely on him to find a discreet attendant. But what about the . . . partner . . . with whom Guy has played these violent games. Do you know who she is?'

Maurice shrugged in distaste.

'Guy may have been a regular visitor to one of the establishments which specialise in this type of activity,' he said, 'I have heard that there is such a place in the vicinity of the Stock Exchange.'

'You must talk to him and find out, Maurice. A few thousand francs may stop any idle talk.'

Guy turned his head slowly on the pillows when Maurice entered his room. His face was pale and drawn – he looked much older than his fifty years. Maurice put a chair near the bed and sat down.

'My dear Guy,' he began cheerfully, 'I am sorry to find you unwell. It seems that you have overdone your little pleasures.'

194

'That doctor has betrayed me,' Guy exclaimed, somewhat dramatically.

'He has your best interests at heart, I assure you. There are arrangements to be made and you cannot expect Jeanne to make them, in the circumstances. So he took me into his confidence. You have to go away for a long rest, Guy. Moulin suggested the country – what do you think?'

'I should be dead of boredom in a week. I would prefer Deauville.'

'Why not? Good sea air, good food, proper care – you'll be a new man in a month or two.'

'I hope so. I am so weak that I can hardly get out of bed. When do you want me to go?'

'Tomorrow or the next day – it is a question of how quickly Moulin can find a properly trained attendant for you. Out of interest, will you tell me something?'

'What do you want to know – my motives?'

'Of course not! Your motives are self-evident – you enjoyed it, so you did it. Whatever Jeanne might think, as a man I find your motives require no justification. My question is this – there are not, in so far as I know, many establishments *de luxe* where a man can obtain these particular services. Do you mind telling me where you found them – was it at the Chabanais?'

'Why do you want to know?'

'I will be frank with you. There is the question of family honour.'

'The Brissard family honour, of course,' said Guy acidly.

'And that of the Verney family. Your wife, your children – we must think of their interests, Guy. We must also consider your interests – it would be impossible for you to resume a normal life in a few months if there were an atmosphere of ill-natured rumour about you.'

'You may put your mind at rest. I have not frequented any of the special establishments in Paris.'

'Then where?'

Guy explained. On one of his regular business trips to

his factory in Nantes he had made the acquaintance of Madame Yvette Bégard and her friend Mademoiselle Solange. In telling this to Maurice he was intentionally vague about his first encounter with these two, but suffice it to say that he had become aware that Madame Bégard and her friend were enthusiasts of the sexual humiliation of men. After the initial shock, Guy discovered an unsuspected truth about himself – he had a natural aptitude as a victim.

'How long have you been visiting these ladies?' Maurice asked, suppressing a smile at the thought of his brother-in-law in the clutches of two provincial women wreaking their will upon him.

'Nearly two years.'

There was a gleam in Guy's eyes at the memory of his visits to Nantes. He was transported by a surge of enthusiasm and babbled of naked women with tall black hoods over their heads, big soft breasts swaying violently as arms were raised to lash him, strong and cruel female fingers which gripped his excited male part and inflicted delicate tortures on it, shiny black patent leather shoes with high heels which trampled his helpless body. To all this Maurice listened closely. He had heard of such things before, but never from one who had participated in these unusual pleasures.

When Guy's energy ran out, he asked him if he could be sure that his friends in Nantes would be discreet. Guy thought about that for some time.

'I don't know,' he said, 'they are such marvellous and demonic creatures. They seize control of you, body and soul. They do horribly fascinating things to you. You scream in pain and beg for more. I tell you, Maurice, there is no pleasure with any woman that is half as intense as the pleasure they inflict upon you.'

'Calm yourself,' said Maurice, smiling at the new burst of animation with which Guy was speaking, 'what you are saying is that they cannot be relied on to remain silent.'

'I am completely in their power!' Guy exclaimed. 'They control me – they make me experience incredible sensations! They are capable of everything, those beautiful naked she-devils! Perhaps they will seek me out when I do not visit them – seek me out and kill me with ecstasy!'

'Don't trouble yourself about that, Guy. I will arrange matters so that you are not disturbed.'

In this way it came about that two days later Guy found himself installed in a hotel suite in Deauville, under the care of Mademoiselle Ernestine Noiret. She was a woman of about thirty, with a strong and pleasant face and dark brown hair. But she was of the size of a boxer! Out of the short sleeves of her plain grey frock there bulged arms strong enough to lift Guy in and out of bed as if he weighed no more than a small child. The legs she displayed between the hem of her frock and her large-size shoes would not have disgraced a marathon-runner. It was evident that Dr Moulin had selected her as much for her physical strength as for her nursing experience. Yet as Guy was to discover, she had a cheerful temperament and was no fool.

On his second day in the hotel, when he had recovered from the fatigue of the train journey from Paris, Guy had his first taste of Ernestine's methods. At ten in the morning she entered his room and swept the covers to the bottom of his bed with a flick of her muscular wrist. There lay Guy in patterned silk pyjamas – a dome-shaped object, his belly the highest point, curving down to his chest and pallid face on one side and to his chubby legs on the other. She put an arm round his shoulders and lifted him into a sitting position to remove his pyjama jacket before lowering him again. She untied the drawstring of his trousers and pulled them off his legs, so that he was naked.

She eyes him thoughtfully as he lay passive. The hair on his chest was already tinged with grey, his arms were flabby, the expression on his face was apathetic. His belly bulged formidably – the result of too many years of over-eating and over-drinking. The marks of his peculiar interests were apparent to her. There were faint red weals on his fat belly where he had been lashed, even the thin

197

lines of healed wounds. She rolled him over to inspect his back and saw the traces on the wobbly cheeks of his behind of frequent whippings.

Ernestine took note of all this and rolled him onto his back again. Close inspection showed her that his nipples had been stretched beyond the normal size – no doubt by the repeated use of metal clamps. There were curious marks in the soft flesh of his thighs which, she concluded, had been caused by the insertion of steel pins to galvanise his jaded sensations – and yes, the limp penis hanging weakly between his thighs bore the same marks. She took it between two fingers the size of sausages and stretched it a little to see the extent of the marks. Without doubt, she said to herself as she released it, Monsieur Verney had been exceptionally thorough in his pursuit of the dark pleasures.

'Monsieur,' she said, 'it is my function to restore you to health. The matter has been put entirely in my hands by your family and your doctor, so you must accept it. I am very expert and I shall soon have you well again, with your co-operation.'

Guy grunted doubtfully.

'You are too fat,' Ernestine declared, patting his bulging belly with a hand as big as a dinner plate, 'a man must be strong, not thin and feeble, but this – this is ridiculous. This paunch must go. I shall personally supervise your diet. It will be appetising and nourishing, but there will not be an excess of anything, believe me. Starting tomorrow morning, you and I will walk together on the beach for half an hour. As your strength returns, the walk will get longer. There will also be twice daily massage, beginning now.'

Guy groaned inwardly. It had been years since he had walked any greater distance than the width of a pavement into a taxi.

'The day is hot,' said Ernestine, 'you must excuse me if I remove my dress before massaging you.'

Guy became slightly more interested as Ernestine fumbled at the fastenings of her frock with her great capable

ands. He sighed gently to himself as it came over her
ead and she stood revealed in a knee-length white slip.

'You are right,' he said, 'it is remarkably hot for June.
Remove your slip too, if you like – it would be a pity to
poil it.'

'Thank you,' she said, 'I didn't like to suggest it myself.
But do not entertain any little ideas about you-know-
what, Monsieur.'

'How could I?' Guy reassured her, 'You have observed
my condition.'

He watched with interest as Ernestine removed her slip
o display her huge bare breasts, each the size of a water-
melon. Her belly was a wall of muscle in which her navel
was visible only as a tiny closed eye, her thighs were those
of a weight-lifter, clad in plain grey stockings held by
unadorned black garters. Between these two points of
interest she wore close-fitting knickers of dark-blue bom-
bazine. Not only did Guy' eyes gleam – his limp part
witched once, but only once, then subsided in wretched-
ness. Not, of course, without Ernestine noticing.

'Poor Monsieur Guy,' she said, 'of what use are you
now to a woman? That little thing won't stand up – and
even if it did, you haven't got the breath to exert yourself
enough to do anything with it. You have ruined your
health and pleasure is only a memory now.'

'But what memories I have!' said Guy.

'I'm sure you do. But now we will start to repair the
damage.'

She attacked his naked body with tremendous energy.
She pummelled him with her big hands and rolled him
about on the bed as if he weighed no more than a feather-
stuffed pillow! This was not the easy massage that soothes
and relaxes tension – it was a whole course of exercise in
itself. She flexed his arms and legs, bending them up,
round, behind, over, utterly without regard for his gasps
of distress. How she worked, this Ernestine! In a few
minutes the perspiration stood out on her forehead from
her exertions, on her broad chest – it dripped down her
massive breasts and trickled down her belly.

199

What of Guy? Ah, the suffering of that treatment! No
the suffering of distorted pleasure which had reduce
him to this condition, but the suffering of muscles an
sinews long unused to such employment. His belly ache
from the twisting and stretching it received, his bac
ached from being forced to bend – not until his hea
touched his knees, for that was impossible, but some
where towards them. His arms ached, his legs ached
and then ached even more when Ernestine put a stock
inged foot into his groin, took him by each ankle in tur
and hauled until he felt that his knees and hips had bee
totally disjointed.

At last it was over and he lay whimpering softly. But i
was not over! Ernestine took a large sponge from a basi
of water and pressed it to his tortured belly. Guy uttere
a shriek – the water was ice cold! She continued relent
lessly, wetting the sponge and pressing it into his armpits
his nipples and into his groins. Even to the soles of hi
feet! Only when he was numb all over did she take a
towel and rub him dry – and that too was agony, for the
towel was rough and her rubbing was violent.

'There,' she exclaimed, throwing the bed covers ove
him, 'we've made a start. You may sleep now until it i
time for lunch.'

Poor Guy, utterly exhausted, fell asleep instantly.

Two weeks of increasingly long walks in the brisk sea
air, of plain food in small portions, of rigorous daily
massage – the regime had its intended effect. Guy'
paunch was diminishing and a healthier colour was returning to his face. Other changes were also taking place, a
most important one being the strengthening of a bond o
familiarity between Guy and Ernestine. He had resigned
himself totally into her hands, obeyed her every word –
and this was perhaps not surprising. His bizarre experiences with Madame Bégard had taught him the joys of
submission. The strange element which must always have
been present in his character had been exposed and
encouraged until he was obsessed by it. Ernestine – so
big and strong – had in his mind taken the place of

Yvette Bégard, though Ernestine cared for his well-being rather than trying to destroy it.

To Guy himself it was a sign that he was making progress that he enjoyed his daily view of Ernestine's near-naked body when she submitted him to her rigorous massage. Ah, the sight of her meaty breasts swinging and bouncing as she pummelled and rubbed him! Her thighs, emerging from her tight knickers – how muscular and thrilling! There were nights when Guy dreamed of those thighs. Ernestine was conscious of Guy's slowly growing interest in her – and of his dependence on her – yet she remained respectful. She invariably addressed him as Monsieur Guy and called him Monsieur Verney when she had occasion to speak of him to the hotel servants. For Ernestine, this was, after all, the best-paid job she had ever had, and she meant to keep it.

One day, as Guy lay face-down on his bed while she chopped with the sides of her hands at his flabby buttocks, she observed a certain change in his expression – his head being sideways on the pillow – along with a change in the muscle tone of his body. She rolled him over and observed that his male part, for so long limp, had swollen to a noticeable size and was attempting to stand erect.

'Well!' she said, 'there's a little surprise!'

'Things are improving,' said Guy, looking at his own success in surprise.

'And will continue to do so,' Ernestine assured him.

'I hope so – but there's a long way to go yet. I hardly know whether to laugh or to cry – laugh that something important has happened or cry that it is so poor a shadow of what it once was.'

In the friendliest way in the world Ernestine took his half-hard part between her fingers and tugged it gently. The pin-marks had faded but would never entirely vanish.

'To be truthful,' she said, 'it is not very strong yet, Monsieur Guy. But at least we have proof that its strength may return in time. Poor forlorn little creature – how badly you have treated it!'

'But how it responded to that treatment!' said Guy with a smile.

'Tell me, if you regain your strength completely, what then? Will you return to your former pleasures?'

'What else can I do?' Guy said sadly. 'The ordinary pleasure of love is meaningless to me now. But, as you have said, I shall be destroyed by what I most enjoy. Dear Ernestine, what shall I do?'

His misery caused the pink part she held to lose its power and shrink back into lassitude.

'There are many alternatives,' she said sympathetically 'for the present, put all thoughts of pleasure out of your head. Have confidence in me.'

On Guy's fourth week-end at the sea-side Maurice came from Paris to visit him and see how he was getting on. He was impressed by the improvement in Guy's physical condition and assured him that all was well with his business. Not that Guy cared very much – he had lost interest in business matters a long time ago, when the dark delights of Madame Bégard's torture chamber became an obsession. He was content to leave financial affairs in Maurice's hands so long as he could stay in the private world of his hotel suite and be nursed by Ernestine.

Before he departed, Maurice talked to Ernestine alone and congratulated her on Guy's progress.

'His physical condition is satisfactory, Monsieur, for only a month of care, and it will improve further. But his will – that is another matter.'

'His will to live, you mean?' asked Maurice, slightly puzzled.

'There is no question of his will to live. I mean that he has lost the will to lead the life of a normal man.'

'With women, you mean?'

'I fear that Madame Verney will not again enjoy the pleasures of marriage with her husband, Monsieur. But more than that – I doubt if he will ever regain his interest in directing his business and caring for his family, and the other activities of ordinary men.'

That Jeanne would not again share a bed with her husband was no great loss, thought Maurice. She had never found any pleasure in Guy's embraces. She had